The Midnight Spell

A young adult novel by Rhiannon Frater and Kody Boye

Dedicated with love to anyone who has felt like an outsider.

Never give up hope

The Midnight Spell
By Rhiannon Frater and Kody Boye
Copyright 2013. All Rights Reserved.

ISBN10 - 1481938401
ISBN13 - 978-1481938402

Cover art and design by Claudia McKinney
Cover photography by Ginger Lee of GingerLeeOriginals.org
Interior formatting by Kody Boye
Edited by Felicia A. Sullivan
Special Thanks to:
Crestfallen (www.kristadams.com) for Grunge Rock Texture
Erico Lebedenco (www.ericolebedenco.com) for Yellow Magician Font
Macca (www.brusheezy.com) for 1000 stars brush

Introduction

The book you are about to read is about best friends.

It's also written by best friends.

The novel was born out of a brainstorming session one night as I made dinner while Kody chatted with me. Kody loves to challenge himself as a writer and was toying with the idea of writing a YA. We knocked ideas back and forth, building on each other's creativity until the core story of The Midnight Spell took shape along with its primary protagonists, Adam and Christy. At first Kody was going to write the story on his own, but by the time we were done discussing the idea and dinner was ready, we had agreed that we should write the book together.

Throughout my writing career I have been adamantly against collaborating with anyone else. Kody had also had some bad experiences with collaboration with other writers, but we both loved the idea so much we decided to take the plunge. Sitting at my dining room table with our laptops, we dove into the world of Adam and Christy.

When one of us would finish our section, we'd excitedly read over the new material and use it as a leaping off point for our next scene. It was a dynamic and fun way to write. Sometimes we got into heated discussions over a plot point, but we also helped the other person out when they were floundering or had writer's block. Throughout the process, we had fun and often found ourselves laughing out loud.

Just as Adam and Christy trade perspectives throughout the story, Kody and I alternated writing the scenes. Kody wrote for Adam, while I wrote for Christy. As a young gay male writer, Kody was able to bring depth and humor to Adam. As the consummate outsider throughout my schooling experience, I gave Christy the same sort of crush I had for years on a boy I never even spoke to and infused her with the horrible awkwardness that most teenagers suffer. Together, Kody and I constructed a world that we both enjoyed writing about.

We're both immensely satisfied with the final version of The Midnight Spell. We know we broke a lot of YA rules along the way, but that's actually what made it fun. If we share a common trait with Christy and Adam, it's that we have seen each other through the worst of times and the best of times. Writing this novel was probably a little of both, but we made it out still best buddies!

We'd love to write about this duo again. Hopefully the response from our readers and sales will indicate a desire for a second book. We have our fingers crossed!

Eternally,
Rhiannon

Prologue

Christy

It all started with a spell. A spell performed at midnight. Little did we know that our simple little love spell to bring the one true love of my best friend Adam to our little hick town would cause so much trouble.

But I'm getting ahead of myself. I suppose I should explain just a little about me and Adam.

Adam and I were best friends from the minute we met in the corner of the school yard of our elementary in Trinity Springs, Texas. The first day of kindergarten we bonded as our outsider status was firmly established in the minds of our classmates. We were the odd kids and our strangeness tossed us together. I was the weird little girl with roses tucked into her braids dressed all in black and he was the short little boy with red hair, freckles and bad allergies. I remember how small he was compared to me and I wondered if he was a leprechaun.

"Do you have a pot of gold?" I asked.

"No. Are you in the Addams family?" he countered.

"No."

We stared at each other with a mix of disappointment and hope.

"Want to play on the swings?" I suggested.

"Sure."

And that was when we became BFFs. We were always together after that day. We sat next to each other in class and at lunch. We played together on the playground and visited each other's houses after school. Despite the scorn of our classmates, we were relatively happy. Sometimes the taunting words hurt, but we mostly ignored our tormentors. We were okay with our exile to the outer reaches of the playground.

The labels given so long ago stuck with us through the rest of elementary, junior high, and into high school. Even as juniors we heard the same insults that we did that first day of kindergarten.

"Witch!"

"Fag!"

Adam and I always smile when we hear the words that are meant to hurt.

Why?

Because they're true.

Chapter 1

The Spell

Christy

Adam regarded me over the black cauldron I had set in the center of my bedroom with the skepticism I've grown accustomed to over the years. Adam is convinced that I'm performing parlor tricks when I show off my paltry magical powers. I'm still growing into my pointy witch hat and have yet to fully come into my abilities. Now that I'm sixteen I'm due for a big magical growth spurt, or at least that's what my mother tells me.

"Are you sure this is going to work?" he asked again for the millionth time.

"Of course!" I said, tossing my brown hair from my face. Sitting on the floor across from him, I carefully arranged the dove feathers around the red candle I had set in the center of the pot. "I studied the spell very carefully." I didn't add that I was substituting a few ingredients that I didn't possess, but he didn't need to know that.

Rubbing his hand over his red hair, he scowled slightly. "I'm not as hard up as you think."

"Have you ever had a boyfriend?"

"You know I haven't." Adam frowned, averting his eyes.

"See? Hard up. You've never even been kissed!"

"Neither have you!"

"And that's not for want of trying! At least I haven't given up before even starting to try."

Adam rolled his eyes. "I don't know what you see in that big ol' dumb lug other than his hot body."

"Shut up and concentrate on the man of your dreams!"

I didn't want to think about my lifelong crush in that moment. Ian is the star of my day and night dreams. With his rippling muscles and blond hair, he's a god come to earth. Every time I see him at school my heart utterly stops, I cease breathing, and my brain shuts down.

"If you're such a great witch, why don't you just throw a spell on Ian then?" Adam watched me arrange red and white rose petals around the candle, his eyebrows drawn into a v-shape.

"Because that would be totally breaking the rules. I can't make someone love me. That would be some seriously black magic," I informed him.

"But it's okay to summon *my* true love?" Adam's lips twitched into a smile. "Aren't you doing this for selfish reasons? I am your best friend, so you do have a vested interest in all of this."

"I'm doing this because it's the right thing to do," I said defensively. "I mean, seriously. Where are we going to find another gay boy in this stupid hick town? We know everyone who lives here and you're the only one pinging on the gaydar." I sighed dramatically and consulted the thick leather bound book I had set next to me. It is one of the countless books my mother has stored in her spell room, which is beautiful and filled with books and jars with exotic ingredients. My favorite part of the room is the white birch tree growing up through the center of it. She doesn't mind if I borrow her stuff as long as I obey the rules she has ingrained in my head since I was little:

Never spell to benefit myself.

Never spell dark magic.

Never spell to compel someone to do something against their nature.

"Thanks for reminding me," Adam grumbled.

"Don't be difficult," I chided him.

"Have you ever tried to do this kind of spell before?"

"Uh, kinda." I try not to lie if possible, so I avoided eye contact hoping he wouldn't push me to explain further.

"I'm waiting to hear how you *kinda* did this before."

"I cast a love spell for Callie."

"Your *cat*?"

"Uh huh. She was lonely and I was eight."

Adam busted into raucous laughter. "If I did believe in magic that would explain her always being in heat!"

"Shut up!"

Callie yowled at him from my bed, her eyes glinting in the candlelight.

Smiling, Adam reached over to pet her head as she glowered at him.

With a sigh, I double-checked the book. It's written in an ancient language that's never been spoken in this world. Though I told Adam I'm descended from Welsh witches, the reality is that my family are descendants of a witch race from another world that lies in the shadow of this one. I know it sounds crazy, but it's the truth. I have seen the history books my mother's family managed to preserve. They're filled with elegant drawings that move across the page depicting the exodus to this world when our own went cold. A terrible cataclysm occurred that robbed it of all its magic and that is why we had to come here. I haven't told Adam any of this. He has enough trouble believing that I'm a spell-casting witch.

Adam isn't supposed to know my true nature. It's supposed to be all hush-hush, but when he came out of the closet to me when he was twelve, I decided to step out of the broom closet so he wouldn't feel alone. We both pondered our revelations, then shrugged it off. It wasn't like we didn't already know that we're both different. Something about us set us so far apart from the rest of the kids in our small town that to embrace the labels we had been branded with all the way back in kindergarten wasn't so hard. That we had to keep our

4

true natures a secret to the rest of the world outside our front doors didn't seem so odd either.

Shutting the book, I crossed my legs, my heavy combat boots clunking against the floor. Clad in black jeans and a brown t-shirt under a lightweight green hoodie, I didn't look very impressive. I had considered wearing a long dress or something dramatic, but since Adam was already being such a pain about the entire spell I decided to just wear my regular clothes. As a tribute to my ancestors, I pulled the hood over my hair.

Adam arched an eyebrow.

"What?"

"Your eyes almost look yellow in the candlelight."

"They *are* amber," I pointed out.

He smiled slightly and shrugged. "It looked cool. Kinda witchy."

"Don't make fun of me, jerk. I'm doing this for you." I felt a little surly. I really did want to bring him someone to love. Adam doesn't admit it, but he is lonely. I guess I am, too, but at least I can stare at Ian all day and dream. Adam can't stare at any boy at school without being called a fag.

Looking properly contrite, Adam nodded. "I know. I know. Sorry. Let's do it."

"Got your list?"

"Yeah." Adam yanked a piece of notebook paper out of his jeans and unfolded it. "What do I do?"

"It's super simple, so don't worry about messing it up," I assured him. "When I point at you, just light it on fire and let it burn over the red candle. Hold it as long as you can without burning yourself, then drop it into the cauldron. Okay?"

"Sounds easy."

I took several deep breaths and held up a piece of white chalk I had liberated from my mom's stuff. With a deft movement, I closed the circle we were sitting in. I am always disappointed when nothing dramatic happens when I do magic. No clap of thunder. No shimmer of power. Nothing. Yet, I know that the circle around us is a powerful deflector of negative energy.

"Ready?"

Adam glanced at his cellphone to check the time, then nodded. "Yeah. I don't have much time before I have to be home."

"It won't take long, I promise."

I held my hands over the pot and closed my eyes. I visualized the beauty of the universe unfolding around us and reached out to the Creator of All. Slowly, carefully, I spoke the ancient words, calling forth the power of the universe to fulfill the desire of my friend's lonely heart. I wish I could say that I felt connected to everything around me and that the ancient power of creation flowed through me, but instead I was just keenly aware of my leg going to sleep. Finishing the words, I pointed at Adam.

Obediently, he held the piece of paper to the candle and watched the edge blacken, then burst into flame. The fire twisted and danced as it licked up the slip of paper, eating away the words Adam had scrawled on it in boring blue ink. We both watched it turn to ash while Adam held onto the very edge so it was nearly consumed by the time he let it fall into the pot. It landed in the small lake of red wax pooling at the top of the thick candle and slowly turned black.

We both sat in silence, watching the last of the embers die away.

"Well, that's it, huh?" Adam sounded amused, but disappointed all at the same time.

Callie yowled from the bed, then yawned.

"Yeah," I said, trying to sound peppy and encouraging. I was a little disappointed by the lack of fireworks, but I'm still growing into my power. Maybe when I'm older my spells will have a little more *oomph*.

Adam nodded solemnly. "Well, I gotta head home."

"It'll work, Adam," I said quickly, reaching out to touch his arm. "Honestly. It will! The book says it is a sure-fire spell."

"Thanks, Christy," he answered, giving me a slight smile. "It means a lot to me that you care, but we both know the chance of me meeting someone in this town is pretty small."

"He's going to come now," I insisted. I felt a small twinge of doubt, but pushed it away.

"I'll see you tomorrow at school," Adam said, standing.

I stood, too, towering over him. I'm three inches taller than he is. Smudging the edge of the circle with my toe, I opened it back up. Again, I was sorely disappointed with the lack of any sort of magical popping noise.

As I watched Adam trudge out of my room, I clenched my hands at my side. "It'll work!"

Callie meowed loudly behind me.

"Even my cat agrees!"

Adam waved and was gone.

Pouting, I stared down into the cauldron. "C'mon, spell. Work."

Adam

I thought my best friend was crazy.

Well, I take that back. I *knew* she was crazy. Ever since Christy and I have been friends, she's been known to attempt the impossible and even the downright-insane. From trying the 'love spell' on her cat, to attempting little 'tricks and charms' for other things, to this mad idea of finding me a boyfriend with a flame and a piece of paper, there's never been a shortage of crazy ideas that's sprung from her mind and into the open. Most people would find it annoying. I find it endearing. I mean, regardless of whether or not the witch thing is true (or even just a little crazy,) I couldn't slight her for trying. If there's anything Christy is, she's a friend who would do anything to help me... even if it meant casting a spell that probably wouldn't work. At least she'd tried.

"It's not like it's going to work," I mumbled, jabbing my hands into my pockets.

It was difficult to admit to myself that I *did* want it to work.

6

After deciding it would be best not to dwell on what had happened earlier tonight in fear of somehow building up my hopes, I focused on going home. To distract myself, I stared at the sidewalk drenched in the dark shadows of the trees that loomed over the neighbors' yards.

Christy and I live three blocks away from each other. It's always been a sort of ritual for the two of us to walk to each other's houses when we want to meet up. As children we used to meet each other halfway and then go one way or the other, to her house or mine, when the streets were clearer and the neighborhood safer to live in. Now Christy usually drives us, since she has a car and I don't. Tonight, I wanted the time alone.

I sniffled slightly. My allergies have a bad habit of kicking up if I'm outside for too long, especially without an allergy pill. But tonight, the weather wasn't even bad, despite my overcast mood.

My thoughts kept returning to what had happened at Christy's house, to the flame and the piece of paper on which I had written my dreams. Regardless of how many times I kept pushing it away, it kept coming back. I eventually decided that if it worked, it worked. If it didn't, there was always the future. There was a vast world beyond Trinity Springs just waiting to be explored.

When the wind came in from the north, I pulled my jacket tighter around me. Rain was a definite possibility. It felt like the calm before the storm.

When I reached my front porch, the entryway's side light was flickering, battered by moths.

I pawed at my pockets and realized I'd forgotten my keys. I prepared to knock, but the door opened to reveal my little sister Amelia who, with her still-babyish looks and ringlets of muddy-red hair, appears to be perpetually mad.

"Mom!" she called.

"What is it, honey?" my mother called back.

"Adam's home late again!"

"Yeah, like you're not up way past your bedtime, Am," my mom answered with her usual sarcasm.

"Busted," I said, ruffling my sister's hair, much to her disdain, before pushing my way through the front door and into the kitchen.

My mother raised her eyes from her laptop, where she was most likely shopping online, and offered a wide smile. "So," she said. "What did ya do at Christy's?"

"We played cards," I said, not in the least bit willing to detail the night's exploits.

"Cards?" my mother asked. "What kind of fun is that? You should've been planning sweet seventeen! Woohoo! Party!" She waved her arms in the air while dancing around the counter to offer me a kiss on the cheek.

"That's sixteen, Mom. Sweet *sixteen,* not seventeen."

"Whatever! I still think you should've been planning your party!"

"With who? Me, my two friends and a cat?"

"Callie? Sure! Why not? She's a party animal from what you told me."

"I said she was a slut, Mom. She's always in heat."

"Scandalous!"

Ah, Mom...she's pretty crazy. How she manages without Dad when he's away on the oil rigs is something I just don't get. There has to be a reason for her perky and near-constant happiness. Maybe that just so happened to be us—me, her social outcast gay kid with the witch for a friend, and her daughter Amelia, who, at the tender age of ten, is just as sassy as our mother. Or maybe it was the espresso. That was a distinct possibility, especially since I almost always caught her adding an extra shot in the morning.

"I made dinner if you're hungry. Though now it's more of a midnight snack," my mother said, making her way toward the staircase and snatching her most recent bookstore conquest from the bookshelf.

"I ate at Christy's," I lied. I doubted I even had the stomach to eat.

"All right! Amelia, go back to bed you little sneak! Goodnight, Adam! Make sure to brush your teeth! And if you do decide to get anything out of the fridge, don't spill it on my laptop!"

"I won't!" I answered.

Amelia was quick to shoot me a dirty look the moment our mother's bedroom door shut behind her.

"What?" I asked, more than a little unnerved by her stare.

"What were you *really* doing?" she countered, narrowing her eyes to fine, dagger-like slits.

"I already said, playing cards."

"No you weren't."

"Yes we were."

"No you—"

"Yes, we were," I said, ruffling her hair.

"Hey! Don't touch!"

"I'm going to bed," I replied, giving her a few taps on the head to spite her before I made my way to the staircase. "Don't stay up too late. You have school tomorrow."

"But you—"

I turned, smiled, then gave her a slight wink, which shut her up almost immediately.

Little sisters. You could live without them just fine, but living with them? That was another story entirely.

I took the stairs and made my way away to my room. Slipping inside, I immediately freed my feet of my shoes and pulled my jacket off before entering my bathroom.

Inside the white-tiled, almost painfully-bright room, I looked at myself in the mirror, noting that I looked a bit pale under my dusting of freckles. The heavy bags under my eyes looked absolutely atrocious.

"Crap," I whispered, rubbing a hand over my auburn hair. "Is that really me?"

I tried my hardest not to stare at the puffy bruised-looking skin around my blue eyes. I looked depressed. I tried to change my pressed expression, but my reflection would not comply. Who could blame me though? I was the only gay boy in my whole town, and my best friend was casting spells to make my life better.

I brushed my teeth, washed my face, then stripped down to my undershirt and underwear before making my way into my bedroom. The moon shining through the window was enough to light my way to my bed. Once there, I collapsed atop it.

Almost immediately, I was asleep.

The metamorphosis of light and colors inside my head overwhelmed me.

It took me a moment to realize what I was seeing.

I dreamed of him.

He was perfect: calm gray eyes, fine straight brows, a proud but not overly-large nose and a pair of exquisite lips, a slight smattering of stubble, and high cheekbones. He reminded me of a piece of art to admire but never to touch.

He smiled and then reached toward me. When I tried to take his hand, I found myself stopped by an invisible force. It was clear then what this dream was actually about. He was perfectly unobtainable. I was alone.

I was torn from the fantasy and placed back into my room.

I rolled onto my side.

Someday.

But when would that *'someday'* come?

Chapter 2

The New Kid at School

Christy

"My life is a tragedy," I declared as I flung the kitchen door open the next morning. Sulking, I trudged to the island in the center of the kitchen and stared into a pot of warm oatmeal. "And getting more tragic as it goes."

"What terrible thing could have possibly happened before seven o'clock on a Monday?" my mom asked, arching her eyebrows. She was seated at the table in the breakfast nook working on her latest jewelry creation. Her oatmeal sat at her elbow, congealed and gross-looking in a bowl she had made herself. My mother is immensely crafty.

"I can't find my black hoodie." I took my usual sugar rush breakfast cereal out of the pantry and snatched up the bowl and spoon she had laid out for me. Slumping into a chair, I pouted. "I like that hoodie."

Outside, the world was still gray and a light mist floated over my mom's garden. Callie was prowling through the foliage probably hunting lizards. I wanted to go back up to bed and forget about the day already.

"I have it with my mending pile. It has a huge tear in the side, Christy."

"I like that tear. It gives it character." I poured a generous helping of colorful, sugary cereal into the bowl and doused it with milk.

Tossing back her thick tawny hair, my mom grinned at me. "Since when do big huge holes in your clothes create a fashion statement?"

"Since my favorite hoodie got one." I shoveled cereal into my mouth, crunching it loudly.

My mother shook her head and continued threading colorful beads on fine silver wire.

Grumbling under his breath, my father entered the kitchen scratching his side. He's a big round man with a full white beard and lots of wavy white hair that he ties back in a ponytail. He looks like Santa Claus, which I love to tease him about. He claims that if he was Saint Nick I would always be on the bad list.

"Hey, Dad. You look like crap," I said as he leaned over to kiss my forehead, then kiss my mom.

"I was up all night." He wandered over to the stove looking bleary-eyed, but strangely happy. He heaped oatmeal from the steaming pan on the stove into a huge bowl and added a ton of brown sugar and milk. "Some idiot on the internet wanted to argue about the founding fathers and the constitution."

My dad is a historian, not only of the witch world, but also the human world. He loves to argue, which may be from where I inherited that particular trait.

"Oh my," Mom said, smirking. "How terrible."

I'm pretty sure I get my sarcasm from Mom, and therefore cannot be held responsible for genetically-inherited snark.

"Of course, I couldn't tell the idiot that I knew the founding fathers, but I managed to make my points and very clearly. I can assure you that I won that argument. They even locked the thread after my last post." With a satisfied grin, my dad sat at the breakfast table and yawned.

"Why can't you be like other dads and just watch porn all night?" I groused.

"Seen it all, done it all," my dad answered.

"Eww."

"Richard, don't traumatize our daughter," my mom said, winking.

"Old people are gross," I muttered.

My parents are horribly mismatched. Dad looks like Santa Claus and mom perfectly fits the stereotypical artist with long flowing hair and eccentric clothes. They look twenty years apart: Dad in his sixties, Mom in her forties. It scandalizes everyone in our small town. In actuality they are separated by almost two hundred years in age. So few of our people escaped into this world that their union is considered quite rare and sacred.

They'd been married for fifty years when they decided to settle down, take on permanent human personas, and start a family. Four years later, they had me. I'll age like a human until my twenties, then I'll have to start glamouring myself to give the impression of normal aging. I sometimes console myself with the idea of making myself look like a supermodel, but my parents claim that is breaking the magical rules.

Anyway, I personally think they're both incredibly embarrassing. They make out like teenagers. Well, teenagers that are not outcasts like me, and quite often.

"Mary Louise, I don't think I could traumatize her any more than she already is after discovering her hoodie is missing." Dad made a show of throwing the back of his hand across his forehead and theatrically looking horrified.

"I am not *that* dramatic!"

My parents burst out laughing.

Scowling, I shoveled the last of my cereal into my mouth. "I'm outta here!" Grabbing my bag, I trudged out of the kitchen. "I'd rather go to school than hang out here with you two."

"We love you, too!" Mom waved, smiling.

"Have a good one, kiddo!"

Stomping out of the house, I wondered why I can't have normal parents who fight all the time and threaten to divorce.

 12

Once behind the wheel of my ancient Volkswagen Bug, I blasted music all the way to school. The sun was taking its sweet time appearing this morning and the headlights from the other cars sliced through the gray murk when they passed me. A light mist floated along the ground and clung to the base of the pine trees that line the school property as I turned onto the lane leading up to the old fashioned brick building that is Trinity Springs High school. Parking in the student lot, I lamented being at school so early. I usually fight the clock, but this morning I had left home earlier than usual to avoid my annoying parents. I had not picked up Adam since his mom likes to drive him to school at least a few days out of the week, so I was even earlier than expected.

Slamming my car door shut, I trudged across the parking lot, already dreading the day. I knew I was in a bad mood because of the spell. I was certain it would work the night before, but doubt was beginning to seep into my mind. I think it's the lack of fireworks that always makes me feel so unsure about my magic. I've seen my mom do magic spells that light up the house like fireworks, but my magic doesn't even have a tiny bit of spark. Though I didn't want the spell to fail because I love Adam like a brother, I also didn't want it to fail and prove I suck as a witch. I hated to admit it, but my ego was definitely on the line.

I was almost to the side door to the school when a girl I had never seen before suddenly bounced off a bench.

"Hi," she said in a perky voice that immediately annoyed me.

"Hi," I mumbled, trying to dart around her.

She was quicker and positioned herself right in front of me. Without a doubt she was definitely not a local. Her blond curls had pink highlights and her makeup was pinup perfect. Dressed in rockabilly-style clothing, complete with saddle shoes, she looked like a sexy, yet cute doll. I'm always trying to lose the fifteen pounds that clings to my lower stomach and upper thighs, but her extra weight looked good on her. She was all curves and cuteness.

I wanted to hate her.

"So, you're totally the outcast chick, aren't you?" she said, grinning as she sucked on a bright green lollipop.

"Why do you say that?" I glowered at her.

She swept her hands dramatically at me as though she were unveiling a masterpiece. "Behold, the surly girl in combat boots, beat-up jeans and a vintage Blondie t-shirt. Add in the hoodie, lack of makeup and the long, slightly ragged hair, and you get... "

"The outcast," I said.

"Yep."

"Why do you care?"

"I like outcasts. They have flavor and this town *so* lacks that. Wait, I take it back. The town has flavor, but it's very vanilla. Not even Mexican vanilla. We're talking boring old vanilla vanilla."

"And I'm not vanilla."

"You're like... espresso."

"And you?"

"Definitely peppermint."

Despite myself, I smiled.

"I'm Olivia, the new girl."

"Christy, the outcast," I said. "You know you're going to be the center of attention today. Hope you're ready for it. We never have new kids enroll."

"That's weird. Because there was a really cute guy in the registration office this morning, filling out the same papers I was."

If lightning had struck me right then, I wouldn't have noticed. I was already thunderstruck. "Are you freaking kidding me?"

Olivia seemed to ponder this, then said, "Pretty sure I'm not."

"Awesome!" I grinned, fairly certain that this was a sign my spell had worked. I had hooked a cute gay boy with my awesome magic skills and now he was at the school. It could not be a coincidence.

It was only five minutes to the bell and the crowd of students grew outside the doors to the school. I kept craning my head, trying to spot the new guy or Adam. Olivia rambled on beside me about being a transplant from Dallas because her mom had gotten some sweet job at the local hospital as an administrator. I halfway listened, but mostly kept looking around for my best friend and his potential boyfriend.

At last the bell rang and we joined the stampede inside. I was maneuvering through the crowd when I saw Adam. His bright red hair tends to stand out in a crowd. I managed to snag his arm and yell at him, "It totally worked!" before having to hurry to my class.

His befuddled expression was priceless and I couldn't wait to see him later to talk about the new boy in school that could possibly be the man of his dreams.

Adam

I rose and began my normal routine before dressing and making my way downstairs, mussing my hands through my hair to free any remaining water droplets. In the kitchen, my mother paced back and forth, talking on the phone in her usual perky voice. My little sister sat at the counter eating her cereal. She shot me a triumphant look almost instantly.

Great. What could she have told mom?

"I have to go," my mother said to whomever she was talking to. "Yeah. Adam just came down. No! *No!* We're going shopping for sure. I just have to drop the kids off at school. Okay. See you later. Bye!" She hung the phone up and offered me a shining grin. "Hey, honey."

"Hey, Mom" I said, making my way around the counter to the toaster. I shoved two pieces of bread inside before turning and looking at my mother. "Shopping, huh?"

"Yup. Going with Cynthia today."

"For what?"

"Shoes!"

"I should've known," I said, rolling my eyes. My little sister continued to leer at me from the counter, but I merely shook it off and smiled. "So what does your addiction demand now? New heels? Boots?"

"Whatever I can find! You know me! A deal's a deal! There's a buy three-get-one-*free sale!*" She extended the last word with more enthusiasm than she should have had at this hour of the morning. I guess that's what espresso does for you.

My toast popped up, jarring my attention.

"Oh, Adam!" my mother said as I lifted the pieces of toast and pulled a butter knife out of the drawer. "I wish you would eat more than just toast!"

"It has peanut butter on it, Mom."

"Still..." She turned her attention on my little sister. "Almost ready, Am?"

"Almost," my little sister grumbled. She never looks forward to school. I tolerate it, but mostly because I have two good friends and enjoy most of my classes.

I slathered the two pieces of toast with a thin sheen of peanut butter and ate them on the way out to the driveway. Once seated in our usual places, Mom started the car and headed off.

Much of the way to Amelia's grade school was spent with my mother rattling on about the places she and her friend Cynthia were going to shop. Her addiction to stiletto heels is almost unfathomable. It makes no sense considering she's a stay-at-home mom. She does, however, tend to wear them to the grocery store. Maybe it was her own personal sign of glory, like Dorothy's ruby red shoes or Cinderella's glass slippers. Queen of the grocery store—that was Mom all right.

Shortly after our mother bid Amelia goodbye after dropping her off at the grade school, she turned her eyes on me and offered me one of her often-used hawk-like looks.

"Mom?" I asked warily.

"Your test is today, right?"

"Uh huh."

She pulled out of the parking lot and started to make her way to the high school.

"You studied?"

"I did. Don't worry, Mom."

"I have to worry. It's a mom thing. You know I have to worry about if you're eating a decent breakfast, if you're studying, if you're doing well in school. All that shit. Plus, I sometimes wish you could find a nice boy to date, though that is probably asking too much of this bum-fuck town."

"Nice language, Mom."

"Well, it's true! Sometimes I wish we lived somewhere with a bit more flair, but—"

"You wouldn't be able to rule the PTA and Methodist Ladies League with an iron fist?"

"Exactly!" she grinned at me. "You know me so well."

"I've known you my whole life."

"You poor kid."

"It's a rough job," I said with a fake, weary sigh, "but someone's got to do it."

"Well, yeah. Since your dad is away on the oil rigs all the damn time, I have to double worry. Not that I'm complaining. When he's home he leaves wet towels all over the floor. I hate that!"

"Life is rough," I said sympathetically.

"Yeah, so then you go buy shoes!" My mom pulled into the high school parking lot and braked. "C'mere!"

Forced into a tight hug, I endured the kiss on my cheek just before I opened the passenger door. "See you later, Mom."

"Knock 'em dead, kiddo! Love you!"

After slamming the passenger door shut, I made my escape.

I settled into my seat in Mrs. Berry's eleventh grade English class, praying that I would pass the test. I had studied, but I always got nervous before exams. Given that I was the first student to take my seat, I had to endure the mental agony and psychological torture that occurs when watching a teacher planning a test for the day. Mrs. Berry cleared her throat and began to hum some horrible old tune as she scrawled the ever-ominous words *Test Today* across the lower half of the boards, complete with three bold underlines. My thoughts shifted to Christy. I couldn't help but think about what had happened the previous night, and the few short words she'd called to me before I had entered the classroom.

It totally worked!

Until that moment, I had completely forgotten the midnight spell.

It'll work! she'd called out as I walked out her bedroom door the night before. *Even my cat thinks it will!*

Callie's lucky. She's a cat with nine lives. I only have one. I got the short end of the stick there.

My cell vibrated in my pocket.

After taking a quick look at the front of the class to make sure Mrs. Berry and none of the other students filing in were paying attention, I slid the phone out of my pocket and flipped it open.

Adam! You're gonna freak! There's a new guy in school and word is he's totally freaking hot!

My phone vibrated a second time, nearly sending it out of my hands and onto the floor before the throng of incoming students.

Meet me at the regular place at lunch and we'll totally stalk him!

Christy had pursued her own crush for years, to the point where she'd made a fool of herself time and time again. But, then again, what was the harm in looking? That was probably all I was going to end up doing anyway. Trinity Springs was boringly straight. I'd resigned myself to that fact years ago. I could name one gay person off the top of my head: me.

From the side of the room the door opened, instantaneously drawing almost everyone's eyes to the newcomer.

My mouth dropped open.

The new arrival reached back to push his hair behind the nape of his neck and scanned the room with his magnetic gaze.

No. It couldn't be.

There's no such thing as magic, yet the guy from my dream the night before stood in the doorway. His face was exactly the same. His strong nose, his exquisite lips, his straight-edged brows that appeared harsh, yet empathetic. Even his eyes were the same color I'd seen in my dream, steel-gray and the shade of clouds filled with the most welcome of rains.

To my surprise, he glanced toward me and his finely-shaped lips curled into a smile. I could have sworn that my heart stopped beating. I had to force myself to breathe.

"Mr. Black," Mrs. Berry said, instantly knocking me out of my reverie as she turned her attention to the newcomer. "A pleasure to see you. Did you find your way here all right?"

"Yes ma'am," the guy named Black said. "I got lost, but I found the room finally."

"You'll sit there, next to Adam." She pointed.

He started toward the desk beside me as the bell rang.

"But first, Mr. Black," Mrs. Berry continued, "why don't you introduce yourself? I'm sure everyone here would like to know who you are. Wouldn't you, class?"

A resounding chorus of grunts and 'sures' followed. I was only able to nod.

The new guy straightened his posture, offered a slight smile, then cleared his throat, almost as if he were nervous to be in such a large group. "Uh... hi," he said, his voice deep. "My name's Mark Black. I'm from Houston. I moved back here with my mom and dad because my parents were originally from Trinity Springs."

"Oh! A native!" Mrs. Berry clapped so enthusiastically I thought for a moment her French tips would fly straight off. "Splendid! Absolutely remarkable, Mr. Black. Please, take a seat."

"Thank you," Mark said, bowing his head.

When he settled into his seat, he turned and smiled at me before directing his attention to the front of the room.

This couldn't be happening. I had to be dreaming.

I pinched myself and was surprised to feel pain.

Nope. I was definitely *not* dreaming.

My cellphone vibrated a third, then a fourth and fifth time. I still couldn't understand how Christy was able to get away with texting in class so often. It was a miracle she hadn't had her phone taken away yet.

Just as I was about to reach down and turn my phone off, Mrs. Berry began to walk the rows of desks to pass the tests out. "You have the whole period," she said.

I accepted my copy of the test, passed my row's set of papers back, then pulled my pencil from the edge of my desk and went to work.

Much of the period was spent working on the abysmally long but not overly difficult test. Having anticipated it being much harder, I found it refreshingly easy. While filling the bubbles *not* like the Christmas tree pattern I'd expected to use, I occasionally glanced over at Mark. Each time I looked, his gray eyes met mine.

I was unsettled, but reveled in the small sparks of pleasure I felt each time our eyes met. I'd never felt like this before. My gaze was repeatedly drawn to him, like two polar edges of magnets fighting to come together. Mark just smiled. It was almost like he could sense whenever I looked at him. My heart beat faster with the knowledge that he was at least all right with my attention. Considering the way most of the guys in the school treated me, Mark was a saint—an angel with grand sparkling wings that gleamed gold beneath the school's fluorescent lighting.

I managed to tear my eyes away from Mark and looked up at the clock. I took note of the amount of time I had left and returned to my work. It was almost impossible to concentrate with Mark's presence beside me. It seemed to pulse with the continuous beat of my heart. Somehow I managed to push through the test.

By the time I finished, the bell rang and the students began to rise from their seats.

"Turn your papers in here," Mrs. Berry said, patting the tray on her desk.

I rose, along with Mark, and dropped off my paper in before heading toward the door.

Once more I caught his eyes with mine and offered a slight, unsure smile. He returned it with a short nod and a grin, then was gone.

I felt breathless in his wake.

The remaining periods were spent mostly in apprehension. I wished desperately that Mark would walk in and take his place in each class. Despite my hopes and prayers, that didn't happen. Throughout History, Math and French, I replayed our interaction over and over. I wondered if I had read more into his smiles than what was actually there. Despite my cynicism, I couldn't help but wonder if somehow he was the manifestation of my dreams. The result of the midnight spell.

The lunch bell rang. I filed out of the classroom, drew my phone from my pocket and discovered that I had twelve new text messages.

"Christy," I mumbled, then began to click through the top few.

Adam! Why aren't you answering me?

Can you see him?

What's he look like?

Where's he sitting? By you?

I chuckled and typed a short return message: *I saw him. On my way.*

I slid through the throng of students loitering in the hall, stepped into the cafeteria, and got my lunch before making my way toward the back of the room. Seated at one of the long, painfully gray tables was Christy, along with a new girl I'd never seen who had blonde hair with pink highlights.

"Adam! Adam! *ADAM!*" Christy said, anxiously waving me over, the tone in her voice rising the closer I got to the table.

"I'm coming!" I laughed.

"Well, hurry up! You're taking too freakin' long!"

"Hold your horses!"

"Horses?" the new girl asked, narrowing her eyes as she sucked on a lime-green lollipop. "Wow. Now I *know* you guys live in the middle of nowhere."

18

"South of the Middle of Nowhere, actually." I wiped the sweat off my hand on my jeans before extending it toward her. "I'm Adam."

The girl plopped the lollipop out of her mouth. "Olivia. From Dallas. Nice to meet you." The girl returned the lollipop to her mouth and grinned around it.

"So," Christy said, leaning over the table almost to the point where our noses could touch, "dish."

"He sat next to me."

She gave a squeal of delight. "Details!"

"Uh... tall, sorta. At least four inches taller than me. Dark hair. Gray eyes. *Really* gray eyes. Like..." I paused, then tapped the table. "Like this."

"Oooh. *So* not a good description," Olivia remarked.

"You didn't answer my question!" Christy said, settling in her seat.

"What question?"

"Did he *talk* to you?"

"You never asked that," I said, playing coy to annoy her. "And no, he didn't."

Christy frowned. "Darn," she pouted.

"At least he seemed fine with me looking," I said, throwing her a bone. "He even smiled each time I did."

"That's so awesome!" Christy crossed her fingers. "Maybe he's gay!"

Olivia snorted. "The dude's a big walking blimp on the gaydar. I tagged him as soon as I saw him."

"Who's a blimp?" a voice asked.

I raised my head to find Drifter, the youngest and possibly most social of our miss-matched group of outcasts, standing beside me, hands braced on the table and eyes drifting between Christy, Olivia and me.

"Hey, Drifter," I said.

"Hey," he replied. "So who's gay?"

"The new kid," Christy said.

"I like your name, Drifter," Olivia said in a perky tone.

"It's a nickname," Drifter replied with a smile. "Raymond Garcia at your service."

"Why do they call you Drifter?"

"Because he never stays in one place for more than five minutes," Christy explained.

Drifter's hazel brown eyes scanned the table and his brows furrowed in what looked like confusion before he settled on the seat beside me. "So—who's the new kid everyone's talking about?"

"That's not me," Olivia amended.

"Mark Black," I said.

"Sexy name," Olivia said. "And so gay."

"I haven't seen him," Drifter said. "When did he get here?"

"Supposedly today," I shrugged.

"He's gotta be gay," Christy insisted, once more locking her eyes on me. "So, Adam..."

"What, Christy?" I slightly rolled my eyes as I looked at her.

"Do ya like him?"

"I don't even know if he's gay," I said, which prompted frowns all around the table. "What?"

"Don't start doing that," Christy warned.

"What?"

"Getting down on yourself," Drifter said, setting an arm across my shoulders. "You tend to expect the worst."

"Not the worst. Just realistic."

"This guy is *totally* gay," Olivia said. "I saw him. He might as well have been an extra in *Queer as Folk*. You know, an extra behind the scenes, in the back of a club with his eyes on the—"

"Before we go into *that*," Christy said, straightening her posture and offering the biggest smile she could possibly give, "let's just make Adam aware that he totally has a chance with this guy."

"I hope so," I said.

"Don't hope," Drifter said. "No use in hoping if you don't try and make something happen first."

Christy

I tried not to badger Adam about the new guy at school, but I couldn't help myself. The second I got home that night I tried to call him. Adam texted back that he had to have family time with his mom and little sister, so I spent the next two hours sulking in my bedroom. Sprawled across my bed, I worked on my homework for a little while before completely losing my train of thought and picking up my cellphone again. Scrolling through my contacts, I called the only person I totally trust other than Adam.

"What's up?" Drifter asked, picking up after the first ring.

"I need the lowdown on the new guy. Did you manage to meet him?"

Drifter laughed and I could imagine his hazel eyes sparking with amusement. "You're so impatient."

"Adam is my best friend," I muttered. "C'mon. I didn't see the new guy all day at school and I was looking."

"Fine. Fine. I managed to talk to him for all of one second. He just said hi and kept walking. And I don't have gaydar, so don't even ask me if I think he's playing on the same team as Adam."

Flipping onto my back, I stared up at the ceiling. My mom painted the constellations of our old world on it against a dark blue background when we first moved into the house. I always find the painted sky comforting, but not today. Doubt was beginning to eat at me. What if the spell hadn't worked and I had raised Adam's hopes needlessly? What if I had built all this up only to crush him?

"Christy?"

"Meet me tomorrow before school. Okay?"

"Sure." Drifter hesitated, then said, "Christy, you have to remember that Adam is a big boy and you can't always protect him or make things good for him."

"Yes, I can," I answered, then hung up.

Adam didn't call for another hour.

"Hey, Christy, what's up?" he said when I hastily answered.

"About the new guy—"

"C'mon, Christy. Don't give me grief about him again. I'm keeping an open mind, okay? But I'm not getting my hopes up either."

"He was totally hot, wasn't he?" I bit my bottom lip as I stared at a picture of me and Adam when we were in the fifth grade that I have on my bed stand.

"Will it make you happy if I say he was totally dreamy?"

"Yes!" I smiled, despite my growing worry. "Yeah, it makes me happy. Maybe my spell worked."

"Well, I wouldn't go that far."

"Oh, screw you," I retorted.

Adam laughed, which lifted my spirits. "Can I go do my homework now? I have to pass English."

"Yeah. And tomorrow at lunch I want a full report on the new hunk."

"You got it."

I climbed off my bed after we hung up. Slipping onto the window seat, I peered through the glass at the rising moon. I believe in magic and I believe in wishes, so I wished with all my heart that everything would work out the next day.

Chapter 3

Love Notes

Christy

Drifter was waiting for me in the parking lot the next morning. The air was a little cool, but the gloomy weather from the day before was gone. The sun was peeking out over the pine trees and the sky was pink and pale blue. I was over my panic attack from the night before and determined to uncover all I could about the new guy today. My mom had sewn up my black hoodie and I wore it over a red t-shirt. Still in my combat boots, I was actually wearing a short skirt over leggings today. I even matched colors.

"So are you still on the warpath?" Drifter asked. His dark hair was wet from his morning shower and he was eating a Pop Tart.

"Yeah. Totally. You know Adam. He'll blow off everything and be all shy." I heaved my messenger bag over my shoulder and headed toward the school.

"You can't blame him. Everyone tends to give him hell." Drifter munched on his breakfast as he walked along beside me.

"Yeah, but he has us. And we're going to look out for him."

"So what's the plan?"

"I know you work as an office aide during third period. Do you think you can get any info on the mysterious Mark Black?"

"So we're stalking him?"

"Totally."

Drifter pondered this, then shrugged. "I can see what I can find out, but you know they keep a lot of that information confidential. Plus, his file isn't going to say anything about him being gay or not."

"I know that, but I think the more we know, the better. Right?"

"Hey, Christy!"

My heart skipped several beats. I knew that voice oh-too-well. Turning around, I felt a big goofy smile spread across my face. "Hi, Ian!"

The tall, insanely cute boy with the close-cropped blond hair and soul-melting blue eyes flashed a huge grin and I felt my knees start to tremble. Locking my legs into a wide stance, I tried to keep upright as he approached.

"I was wondering if you could help me out with my history and English homework again. You know, books just confuse me. All those words," he said as he drew close enough to peer down at me. "You're pretty smart, so maybe you could help me out, huh?"

I'm always fascinated by how gold his eyelashes are. I was only dimly aware of Drifter at my side and Ian's football buddies lingering behind him. Ian smelled wonderful and I tried not to visibly take a big whiff.

"Uh, yeah, sure. Totally. When?" I could feel my hand trembling as I gripped the strap of my bag tighter.

Ian was so close to me I was drowning in his shadow.

"I'm thinking your place. Tonight. Around six?"

"You know where I live?"

Ian laughed like I had just cracked a joke. I wasn't sure how to take it and sort of just stared at him, unsure if I should laugh along, or not.

"That's funny, Christy. I'll see you later then," he said, brushing past me, his friends following in his wake.

"It's a date then," I called after him. "I mean, not a date, but a homework date, I mean... "

"Just be quiet and play it cool," Drifter whispered.

I shut my mouth as I watched Ian saunter away, laughing and joking with his friends.

"I'm a total moron," I finally said.

"You could have played it cooler," Olivia said, joining us. Today her lollipop was red.

"You saw that?" I winced.

"It was slightly painful, but could have been a lot worse."

Drifter shook his head, his hazel eyes looking more green than brown today. "Christy completely loses her brain whenever Ian is around. It's been like that for years."

"I didn't throw up Kool-Aid and cookies on him this time," I said defensively.

"Were you in like kindergarten or something?" Olivia asked.

"No, it was last year at the Christmas party," I confessed.

Drifter chuckled and I smacked him.

"It was pretty epic, Christy," Drifter insisted.

"I thought I would die." I'd been pretty sure that my life was over before it had begun. Adam had run up and pulled me away before I could burst into tears. "Enough about me. We have a mission to perform."

"Is this about the new gay guy?" Olivia asked.

"Of course," I answered.

"I'm in!" Olivia sucked away on her lollipop, waiting for me to continue.

"First step, we find out his schedule."

"I'm on it," Drifter said and headed off toward the school.

"And what do we do?" Olivia asked.

"Find out everything we can about him," I answered, grinning.

Olivia and I cornered Adam at his locker. From the look on his face, which I will define as loving amusement and not irritation, he was ready for whatever we were about to unleash on him.

"Why do I have a feeling I'm screwed right now?" he asked warily.

"Okay, this is the deal-io. You must report in as soon as first period is over. You must dish everything. Every look. Every word. Everything." I informed him.

"Oh-kay. Why?"

"Because she's trying to figure out if this guy is the one for you," Olivia piped up.

Adam rolled his eyes. "C'mon, Christy. We just exchanged a few looks yesterday. He's totally hot, I will admit to that, but I'm playing this very cool. He may not be gay."

"Oh, no. He's gay. Pinging on the radar like crazy," Olivia assured Adam. "Plus, he's so clean. No straight guy is that clean. I will admit that you are surprisingly boy-normal grungy, but that guy... too clean."

Frowning at this assessment of his personal hygiene, Adam shook his head. "You're both crazy."

"No, I'm trying to keep tabs on what is going on with my best friend. If that makes me crazy, I can deal with that," I declared.

"I hardly know you. I'm just along for the ride," Olivia said honestly.

"You're wickedly truthful," I said with admiration to her.

"I know. It's a gift." Olivia grinned.

"Well, you two just give me some space and let me find out things on my own. No secret maneuverings behind the scenes and all that." Adam gave me his best imposing stare.

"Would I do that?" I asked defensively.

Adam sighed with exasperation. "Okay, what's going on?"

"Drifter is going to try to get the lowdown while working as an office assistant today," Olivia answered him.

"You can dial down the honest button now," I told her, slightly peeved that she told.

"He could get in trouble," Adam protested.

"He's smart. C'mon. He's Drifter. He's like the single most beloved human being in the entire school. He can hang out with the jocks *and* the chess club," I said.

"And once you have this information, then what?" Adam sighed again, shaking his head.

"I haven't gotten to that part yet." I shrugged.

"I gotta get to class," Adam said, giving me that cute quirky smile that tells me he adores me, but wouldn't mind tripping me down a flight of stairs.

I waved my cellphone at him. "Remember to report in! Text me when I text you!"

Adam gave me a half-hearted wave as he walked away.

"He's not going text me back, is he?" I said, disappointed.

"Nope. Not at all," Olivia agreed.

Adam

The looks between Mark and me continued throughout first period even though Mrs. Berry commanded attention with her voice alone. I always met Mark's quick glances with shy ones. Every time he threw one my way I felt all giddy yet completely unsure. Here he was, the new guy in school—tall, good-looking, possibly gay—looking *and* smiling in my direction. For a guy like me, it seemed like a dream come true, and I felt stupidly flattered and nervous.

By the time first period ended and I made my way out into the hall, I was about ready to have a heart attack.

As the other students stampeded out of Mrs. Berry's classroom, I scooted over and made way for those with lockers near the room. I was almost about to walk off when someone bumped into me.

When I looked up, I was staring into the calm gray eyes of none other than Mark Black.

"Hey," I somehow managed.

"Hey," he replied, offering a slight nod before disappearing up the hall.

That one word was enough to make my skin tingle with pleasure. I couldn't believe he'd actually bumped into me, much less *talked* to me.

Before I could get too overwhelmed with what had just happened, I brushed the feelings aside and made my way down the hall to Mr. Barker's history class.

After seating myself in my usual spot, I took a deep breath.

My phone continued to vibrate in my pocket. A quick check to see that Mr. Barker was not yet in the classroom was enough to inspire me to pull my phone out of my pocket.

ADAM! the message said. *WHY AREN'T YOU TEXTING ME?*

Because I'm in class, I replied, then clicked send before sliding the phone back into my pocket.

Something falling on top of my desk caught my attention.

I looked up, saw a note, then looked around curiously.

Mark Black was making his way toward the empty seat two rows over.

Unsure if it had truly been him who had dropped the note, I snatched up the paper, hid it under the desk, then unfolded it.

Hey, the note began, in neat but blockish handwriting. *Sorry I bumped into you. My name's Mark. I just transferred into this class. You're Adam, right?*

Was I supposed to respond to this? I'd never had this kind of attention before, much less passed notes to a guy I might like.

Picking up my pen, I stared at Mark's square, blocky handwriting, then scrawled, *Yeah, I'm Adam* on the line beneath his note before folding it and gesturing to the girl next to me to pass the note to Mark.

Several moments were spent in cruel anticipation. I bit my lip, fidgeted with my fingertips and popped my knuckles, all in an attempt to distract myself from how much time it was taking for him to respond.

Just when I thought I'd have a brain aneurism, the note was tossed back onto my desk. I immediately opened it.

Nice to meet you, Adam.

Though the words were short and sweet, they did a little to build up my confidence.

You moved from Houston? I wrote back.

Two or three minutes later, the note was returned to me with the words, *Yeah, I did* on it, followed by, *Are you from here?*

We continued sending notes back and forth, using the poor girl between us as our personal messenger. He asked how old I was. I replied sixteen, almost seventeen. I asked the same in kind, to which he replied that he, too, was seventeen. I then asked if there was a specific reason why he moved back down here beside the fact that his parents were originally from Trinity Springs. While he was extremely vague, I was fine with that. I didn't expect him to tell me his life history, especially not through notes going back and forth in a public place.

I was just about ready to send another reply when Mr. Barker walked in with a pull-away projector. He shoved it next to our courier's desk, immediately severing the line of communication.

Biting my lip, I held the note steady in my hands and continued to watch Mr. Barker tinker with the bulky contraption. My eyes went from him, to Mark, then back to the girl between us before finally falling to the note in my hand.

Was it worth the risk of getting in trouble and having to read the note in front of the class?

After a quick and sad thought, I decided it wasn't. It could wait until later.

I folded the note to hide it in my pocket. Regardless of how much I wanted to send a reply to him, it wasn't worth getting in trouble, especially if it meant possibly outing me and Mark in front of everyone.

The moment before I could slide the note into my pocket, I caught sight of Mark's sad eyes watching me.

Would he be hurt if I didn't at least attempt to try?

With heat in my chest and panic in my heart, I scrawled the only few words I could think of onto the piece of paper: *Do you want to meet for lunch?*

I glanced at Mr. Barker, then to the girl between me and Mark before extending the note toward her.

"I'm done," she whispered.

I shot her my nastiest look. It seemed to work, because she accepted the note and passed it over to Mark.

Mr. Barker raised his head. "Mr. Black?" he asked.

"Yes sir?" Mark replied.

"What do you have there?"

"Oh, this?" Mark smiled. "I'm just doodling."

"Just make sure not to do it during class."

Mr. Barker resumed messing with the projector.

The note was returned soon after. I scrambled to open it and ended up tearing the corner of the page.

The words on the paper nearly broke my heart.

I go off-campus for lunch.

I couldn't help but sigh.

With a nod, I turned my attention toward Mark and offered him a brief smile. I directed my eyes to the front of the class just as the projector burst to life and displayed a slide of the United States during the American Revolution.

I still had three classes to go before lunch.

I resigned myself not to defeat, but to uneven odds as I settled down at the table across from Christy and the new girl, Olivia. With a sigh, I reached up, ran my hands through my hair, and looked across the table at my friends, both of whom had perplexed looks on their faces.

"What's wrong?" Christy asked. Her face paled soon after. "Oh God. He didn't—"

"No. It's not that." They both waited. "He just goes off-campus for lunch."

"Oh...well it's not like he doesn't like you then."

"Or that he isn't gay," Olivia added. "Remember, he's—"

"A big blip on the radar," I said. "I know."

Olivia shrugged and sucked on her lollipop, this one pink, and scanned the room, as if searching for the one person who was obviously not going to be there.

At first I'd been bummed after finding out Mark went off-campus for lunch, but after thinking about it, it wasn't really that big a deal. I supposed I could always catch him later. Who knew? Maybe I could even meet with him after school. That, or we could end up in the same classes together. He was already in English and History. There was always the possibility that he could transfer into my others.

"So what happened in class?" Christy asked.

"What do you mean?"

"Did you talk to him? Get his number and text him?"

"We passed notes," I smiled. "As lame as that sounds."

"Totally not lame!" Olivia declared. "Well... if you didn't get caught, anyway."

"Which we almost did."

"You or him?" Olivia eyed me thoughtfully. "You don't seem like the sneaky type."

"Him. And he's way more sly than me. He said he was 'doodling' when Mr. Barker noticed him writing back to me."

"Mr. Barker?" Christy snorted. "He's so lame. I told you not to take his class."

"It's not that horrible. You just... can't pass notes there."

"He was a total jerk to me that time I was passing notes for one of the stupid football players. Which I was only doing to score points with Ian," Christy groused.

"You're such a criminal," I teased.

"Enough of the history lesson," Olivia said, then paused shortly thereafter. "No pun intended."

"Obviously," I chuckled.

"What all happened?" Olivia waved her lollipop at me.

"Yeah, dish!" Christy urged.

"I sat down, checked my cell after my nosey BFF sent a message, and had something dropped on my desk."

"From him!" Christy said triumphantly. She was obviously taking full credit for the latest development.

"Yeah. So... I took a moment to try and *not* panic, then opened the note."

"Which said?"

I reached into my pocket. After a few desperate moments of searching for it and thinking that I may have lost it, I pulled out the wrinkled piece of paper and passed it across the table. Christy and Olivia immediately began to pore over it as if it were the greatest thing to ever be discovered by two teenaged girls.

"What's this?" Olivia asked, fingering the scratched-out line.

"The part where I was trying to figure out what to say."

"That's when you got up the nerve to ask him to meet you for lunch," Christy nodded, tapping the spot.

"Which didn't happen," I sighed.

"Don't get down on yourself," Christy smiled, reaching across the table to take my hand. "Give it some time, Adam. I *know* my spell worked."

"Magic?" Olivia snorted. "Pfft."

At that moment, I could do nothing but agree with Olivia.

Had Christy's spell worked, or was this whole thing just one big coincidence?

Christy

I kicked my dirty clothes under my bed and pulled the comforter over my rumpled sheets. Snagging the few stuffed animals I've been keeping out of nostalgia, I tossed them into the closet and closed the door. Callie yowled from inside. I cracked the closet door open and she walked out, snapping her tail at me indignantly.

"Sorry, Callie," I muttered and kicked a few shoes under the bed.

My room is on the third floor of my parents' Victorian. It's an awesome room with high windows and a great view of the street below through the branches of the pine and oak trees lining our property. I swept everything on my desk, except for my laptop, into a laundry basket and shoved that in the closet, too.

"Cleaning your room?" My mom leaned against the doorjamb staring at me curiously. She held an ancient broom in one hand and I could smell the magic pouring off of her. Magic smells a lot like chocolate chip cookies, in case you want to know.

"Ian, the man of my eternal dreams, is coming over so I can tutor him." I hated how high and excited my voice sounded.

"So that's the reason you're wearing a dress and cleaning your room?"

I looked down at the simple spring dress my mom had bought me for Easter. It had a kind of vintage look to it, with tiny sprigs of bluebonnets scattered all over a white background. I'd tossed on a blue hoodie that matched and was wearing ballet flats. Self-consciously, I ran my hands lightly over the skirt. "Too much?"

My mom grinned, shaking her head. "No. You look adorable. But there is no way in this world or any other that you can have a boy in your room."

My shoulders slumped as I crossed my arms over my breasts. "Moooooooooooom."

"No whining. You know the rules."

"Dad is totally going to embarrass me if we're downstairs."

"He will not," my mother answered.

"You know he will! I've never had a boy I like over here before and Dad can't resist embarrassing me in front of new people."

"Christy, he's just being friendly," my mom said with a sigh.

"*Embarrassingly* friendly," I grumbled.

"You and your friend can study in the kitchen. I have to start dinner anyway. We're having tacos!"

I scrunched my face up. Mom's idea of tacos bears no resemblance to anything ever created in Mexico. It only qualifies as a taco because the special spinach tortillas she concocts look a little like taco shells.

"Why don't you come downstairs and help me chop up veggies until your boyfriend gets here?"

"See! That is the type of comment that will totally humiliate me!"

"Touchy, touchy." My mom grinned and walked away, dragging her broom behind her. Little wisps of light lingered in the air in the wake of the bristles.

Snatching up my messenger bag, I trudged down the stairs behind her. The broom continued to leave magical traces as my mom descended past the second floor where my parents sleep, have their sitting room, and library.

"Time for you to go to sleep," my mom told the broom and tossed it into the air.

It zoomed over my head, forcing me to duck, covering me in sparkles of light. It tore around a corner and disappeared from sight. I strongly suspect that the broom is out to get me. Seriously, it's always showing up in my room at weird hours of the night, it likes to appear at random spots in the house like it's spying on me, and it always likes to cut it a little too close whenever Mom lets it fly around on its own.

"That broom is a brat," I mumbled.

"A little like someone I know," Mom teased.

"It hates me."

"It does not. It's just playful."

"Yeah, and Chucky is just a doll."

We reached the bottom floor and headed past the living room where my dad was howling with laughter at some C-Span show. Dad has a weird sense of humor.

"Christy has a new friend coming over. Don't embarrass her," Mom called out as we passed.

"Boy or girl?" Dad asked.

30

"A boy!"

I frowned as I heard my father say with a little too much enthusiasm, "Oh, this will be fun."

Once in the kitchen, I tossed my bag onto a chair and helped my mom gather the ingredients for what she calls tacos. Flicking her tail, Callie slid through the kitchen and out the cat door into the garden. I suddenly wanted to escape with her.

My earlier excitement at the prospect of hanging out with Ian was quickly evaporating as I considered the real possibility that things could go terribly wrong. I love my parents, but they're legitimately *old* school. And not even from this world.

I had just finished chopping up a mango (yes, a mango) when Ian was ushered into the kitchen by my father. From the look on Ian's face, I suspected Dad had trapped him out on the porch for a few minutes. Dad's hand was resting on Ian's broad shoulder when they entered.

Ian swept his eyes over our kitchen, taking in the high cabinets with the frosted glass insets, the high pressed-tin ceiling, cast iron stove (that's custom made and is actually very modern), and my mom's wild curls and bright grin as she rushed around the island to greet him.

"Oh, you must be Ian! We're so thrilled to meet you!" Mom said, shaking his hand. "We've heard so much about you."

I considered ramming the butcher knife into my chest and taking the easy way out.

"Yeah, uhm, cool." Ian nodded his head. "I'm pretty popular at school. The whole football thing."

Lowering my head so I could hide behind my bangs, I darted over to Ian and took hold of his arm. He seemed startled but came with me willingly. I pushed him toward a chair at the breakfast table and slid into the one next to him.

"We have a lot of studying to do," I said briskly.

My parents can't get a clue. They both followed, hovering over us.

"So what are you studying?" my father asked, peering down at the book Ian had shoved onto the table.

The book was fairly battered and sheets of frayed notebook paper were crammed into the center of it. Ian pointed at the title. "English."

"They're a very morbid lot," my father said. "I prefer the Irish."

"Dad!" I pointed at the hallway.

Dad pretended to be frightened of me, jumping and hiding behind my mom. "She's getting that look."

Ian stared at my parents with a lopsided smile on his face. It was pretty apparent that he had no clue how to take them. Heck, even I don't know how to deal with them most of the time. How was he supposed to deal with parental weirdness overload?

"Richard, we probably should leave them to their homework," my mom decided with a sigh.

"I have to work out anyway." My dad patted his stomach.

"That's cool. I work out a lot too," Ian said, giving me an odd expression.

I shrugged and gave him an apologetic look.

"In my younger days, I had rippling muscles, not rippling fat. Enjoy it while you have it." Dad winked.

I gave my dad my fiercest look.

Dad grinned, kissed my mom, waved to us, and sauntered out of the kitchen looking far too satisfied. My mom smiled and returned to fixing dinner.

"Your parents are... different," Ian whispered to me, his blue eyes melting away my brain.

I stared at him for a few seconds too long before recovering. "Oh, yeah. They're total freaks." I popped my English book open and turned to our assignment. "Just ignore them and they might leave us alone."

Ian laughed. It made my toes curl with delight. Leaning toward me, he opened his book, and pulled out his half-finished homework. I could smell his cologne and toothpaste he was so close to me. It took all my willpower not to stare into his gorgeous face. I thought I was doing a great job of hiding my nerves until I picked up a pen. My hand was shaking so violently the ballpoint beat a staccato rhythm on the table. I dropped it immediately and blushed. I could feel the heat in my face.

Ian's grin just widened even more.

How I survived the next forty minutes I will never know. I managed not to make a total fool of myself and my parents actually left us alone. I wished I could say I stopped feeling like a total spazz, but my stomach wouldn't stop doing flips. Ian didn't seem to notice as we worked together and I was glad he kept me focused on the homework. Otherwise, I would have just stared at him dumbly.

Callie slipped through the cat door and hopped onto the chair across from us. Her golden eyes regarded us thoughtfully over the edge of the table. Only her ears and eyes were visible. Ian slowly became aware of her.

"Your cat?"

"Yeah. That's Callie."

My cat directed her gaze solely at him.

"She's cute."

"She's a bitch."

Callie's ear twitched.

Ian laughed. "I think she understood."

"Probably. She's too smart sometimes. She can even open doors."

"That's cool. Is she your only cat?" Ian reached slowly across the wood surface of the table toward Callie.

Callie's eyes narrowed.

"Yeah, she's it."

He lightly touched her head and she sniffed his fingers. She gingerly moved out of his reach, repositioned herself on the chair, and stared at him again.

"I thought you'd have a black cat," Ian remarked, laughing at Callie's prima donna attitude.

"Why would you think that?" I asked. A second later, understanding washed over me. I immediately bristled and was glad our homework was done. I shut my book a little too hard.

Ian didn't notice.

I could feel my mother's gaze on me, but she didn't say anything.

"I guess I should get going," Ian said, still not noticing my hurt feelings.

"You could always stay for dinner," my mom suggested.

I shot her a fierce look.

"Nah. Tonight's family night at my house. I gotta get going. Thanks for the invite though." He folded his homework and shoved it into the book as he stood.

Callie and I exchanged looks and I felt like I wanted to cry. I was so sick of this stupid town. Maybe I am a witch, but when kids call me that I know they mean it as an insult. I was so absorbed in my dark thoughts I didn't realize at first Ian was waiting for me.

"Christy, why don't you see Ian out?"

I looked up at my mom and saw the compassion in her eyes. I nodded, stood, and brushed past Ian. I briskly walked down the long hallway to our front door. Ian trailed behind me. I sensed his curiosity about the house and my family and it hurt. It wasn't because he liked me. It was because he believed the rumors.

"Your house is awesome," he said as we passed under the big chandelier in our front hall. "It looks bigger inside than outside."

I flinched. The house *is* bigger inside than outside. Mom keeps adding rooms that only exist inside the house. "Oh, it's just the layout."

We passed the living room where my dad was huffing and puffing with his Wii. He was playing tennis dressed all in white. If I hadn't been so mad, I would have died of embarrassment.

"It's really pretty. Lots of art and antiques." Ian stared at a painting that's actually of my great-grandmother. With a human in the house, the painting was still. It usually repeats the same movements over and over again. It's like a painted videotape of my ancestor drinking tea and smiling. It's pretty cool.

"My parents traveled a lot before they had me. They collected stuff from all over the world."

"That's awesome." Ian turned slowly toward me and gave me a rakish grin that almost compelled me to forgive him.

I thrust open the front door and stepped out onto the porch.

"I knew all those rumors about you weren't true," he said.

Lifting my eyes, I saw him staring down at me with a sheepish look. "Huh?"

"The witch thing. Your house is awesome. Your parents are kinda weird, but cool. I mean you're kinda an alternative chick, but it works for you."

My lips slowly turned up at the corners and my fingers nervously played with my skirt. "Oh, thanks."

"Hey, I'm having a party Saturday. Why don't you come?"

I lost my voice. My stupid lips wouldn't even form words. I turned to stone.

"I mean... if you want to." He was obviously mystified by my sudden frozen state.

I managed to squeak out, "No, no!"

He looked surprised. "You don't want to go?"

I cleared my throat. "I totally want to go! I mean, sure, that sounds cool."

Ian nodded his head. "Awesome. So I'll see you there."

"Uh, can I bring friends?"

"Like that new cute chick at school?"

"Yeah. Olivia. Maybe Adam?"

Ian hesitated, then nodded again. "Sure. Sure."

"Cool. We'll totally be there."

"See you around."

I watched him walk away, my heart beating so hard in my chest I was sure it was going to bust out and splatter on the porch. With one last wave, he got into his truck and drove off.

Pulling my phone out of my hoodie pocket, I hit Adam's name. "You will so not believe what just happened to me! I think the spell might be working for me, too!"

Adam

"The spell might be working for you too?" I whispered, pressing the phone closer to my ear as Christy continued to ramble on. "Christy, what're you talking about?"

"I said—"

"I *know* what you said, but I thought the spell—" I caught sight of Amelia darting into the room. "I gotta go," I said, then hung up before Christy could continue.

Amelia raised her head over the back of the couch.

"Am," I said, voice rising as my little sister rounded the sofa. "I thought you were helping Mom?"

"Who were you talking to?" my little sister asked.

"Christy," I replied.

"What were you talking about?"

"School."

"I heard you say *'spell.'*"

Of anything Amelia could've heard, she had to hear *that*.

"Uh... yeah," I said. "Spell."

"What kind of—"

"She wanted to know how to spell a word."

"No she didn't," Amelia said, matter-of-factly and with a heightened, I'm-ten-and-I-know-everything voice. "You were talking about something else, something like—"

"What're you kids talking about?" Mom said, craning her head around the threshold into the living room.

"Adam was talking about magic!" Amelia cried.

"I was not," I replied.

"Magic only works if you're wearing the right pair of shoes," my mother replied. "Like Cinderella, or Judy Garland."

"Who?" Amelia asked.

34

"The girl who played Dorothy," I said. "You know... the *Wizard of Oz*?"

"Oh! Okay. But wait... does that mean Christy has a pair of magic shoes?" Amelia put her hands on her hips and glowered at me.

"Sign me up for that," Mom said, "especially if they do things like clean... and cook... and buy even more shoes for me!"

My phone chirped.

"Is she doing magic through the phone?" Amelia asked, mystified as I raised my cell and looked at its touch screen.

"She's not doing magic," I said. "We weren't even talking about magic."

"But I thought—"

"Amelia," our mother said. "Go upstairs and brush your teeth. It's almost bedtime."

"But I don't—"

"Go, little missy. Now!"

My little sister skittered up the stairs.

I used the moment to my advantage and slid out the door to the backyard patio. I pushed my hands into my pockets and took a slow breath. I didn't need my little sister ragging on me on top of all the other stuff going on. The spell had me jumpier than I realized.

"Thank you for being so nice to your sister," my mother said, letting herself out through the sliding glass doors. "I swear," she continued, tilting her head up to look at the pecan tree. One thick branch has grown out over the patio and my bedroom. It's the bane of my mother's existence. "Every time I ask your dad to get that taken care of he says, *I'll do it later*. Well, Mr. Adrian Hunter, that *later* might be *get it out of Adam's bedroom* later."

"You can't blame him," I shrugged. "He's only home for so long."

"Yeah. I know." She took a cigarette out of the pack she was holding in her hand and lit it with the old Zippo. Afterward, she took a long, deep drag, then exhaled. "Hey, Adam?"

"Yeah, Mom?"

"Is everything okay?"

"Everything's fine. Why?"

"You seem a bit... off."

"I do?"

"Yeah. Did something happen at school today?"

"No."

"You're sure?"

"I'm sure Mom," I replied. "Besides, the last time something really bad happened was in sixth grade."

"Which I'm still mad as hell about," she said. "That damn boy. What was his name? Stephen? Steffan?"

"It was Skylar, Mom."

"That asshole. He nearly sent you to the hospital."

"But Christy and Drifter showed up."

"Thank God for them." She exhaled another mouthful of smoke. "It could've been so much worse. At least it wasn't anything like Jasper, Texas."

"No kidding," I said, settling back against the wall.

The wind skirting along the side of the property kicked up Mom's hair and blew her smoke to our left. Mom took another moment to compose herself before turning her head and asking, "So everything's been okay?"

"Everything's been fine, Mom."

"You're sure?"

"I'm sure." My hand sunk deeper into my pocket. The piece of paper Mark and I had written notes on crinkled beneath my fingertips. "There's a new boy at school and I think he might be gay."

"Really?" Mom asked, eyes glimmering with interest.

"I'm not getting my hopes up, but he seems maybe interested in me."

She shrieked and pulled me into a one-armed hug. "That's great, Adam," she said, planting a kiss on my cheek. "What's he like? Have you talked to him?"

"We passed notes," I shrugged, "and I bumped into him in the hallway a few times."

"What's he look like?"

I recounted what I had told Christy, right down to Mark's gray eyes. Mom let out another slight shriek and pulled me into another hug. "You like 'em tall like I do!"

"Uh... Mom... it's kind of hard *not* to be taller than me."

"Oh stop it. You're not that short. You're taller than me!"

I tilted my head downward to look Mom directly in the eyes. "Mom, you're five feet tall."

In response, she chuckled and slapped my shoulder. "Ok," she said, "remind me that I belong in the Lollipop Guild. Whatever. But the question is...do you like him? What's he like?"

"I'm not too sure. He's... quiet."

"Quiet?"

"Like I said, I haven't talked to him too much."

"But you *have* talked to him?"

I pulled the note out of my pocket and passed it to her. "Sort of," I laughed.

It took Mom less than a minute to read the paper. Once finished, she folded, returned it to me, and bumped me with her elbow. "Oh, Adam," she said. "I'm so happy for you."

"I'm not getting my hopes up yet. I'm not even sure if he's gay."

"Maybe not... but maybe you'll get a friend out of this. That's something, isn't it?"

"Yeah," I said. "I guess it is."

Chapter 4

Making Progress

Christy

"You have A Look," Drifter said warily the next morning as Adam and I climbed out of my car.

Adam looked at me curiously.

I scowled at both of them.

"Hrmm. She does! I think she was hiding it on the way over here by talking about Ian," Adam confided to Drifter.

They stood side by side, arms crossed, looking at me as though I had sprung two heads and dragon wings.

"Ian," Drifter said shaking his head. "The never-ending crush."

"Her version of boy crack." Adam snorted in playful contempt.

"Shut up, both of you. I got us invited to his party, so you can both shove it."

"I was already invited," Drifter said.

"I don't want to go," Adam added.

"I hate both of you." I hoisted my messenger bag over my shoulder and trudged toward the school.

"She smells better than usual today," Adam remarked to Drifter. "Which I think is highly suspect."

"Her clothes match, too. She's obviously trying to impress more than usual."

I gave them both a dark look. I had decided to put a little more effort into my clothes for the day. My blue jeans and red hoodie were new and I had pulled on my red Converse to match. My shirt was a vintage Madonna. I was rocking it.

"Our little girl is all grown up," Adam said, lightly mocking.

"Seriously, both of you, shut up. I'm in a very good mood today and you're not going to ruin it."

"Who's ruining what and why?" Olivia popped out from behind her SUV. Today her lollipop was blue. Her saddle shoes, rolled up jeans, and red checkered shirt were a little too retro for my taste, but she wore it well.

"We're invited to Ian's party on Saturday," I informed her.

"Big hunky blond guy with no brains?" she asked.

Rolling my eyes, I nodded.

She pondered this new information as she crunched on the edge of her lollipop. "I'm okay with crashing the popular boys' party, but being invited just takes the fun out of it."

"C'mon, you guys! We have an invitation! That's never happened to us before, Adam! Can't you be excited?"

"Oh, yeah. I'm thrilled to be hanging out with the guys who called me a fag all through junior high. We can hold hands and sing songs." Adam shook his head, his expression a mixture of amusement and annoyance.

"He doesn't do that now! He's nicer to us now!" I protested.

"This means something to Christy. We should be supportive. We should all go together." Drifter gave me a reassuring smile.

Adam shrugged. "Fine. But I'm not going to have a fun time."

"Yeah, cause going to a party to have fun is so lame," Olivia said, jabbing him with her finger. "Maybe the cute gay boy will be there."

"What is going on with that anyway?" Drifter asked.

"Nothing, okay? C'mon you guys, give me a break. We just barely started talking yesterday," Adam said, holding up his hands defensively.

"Your waging of this crusade has much to be desired," Olivia decided.

Adam sighed, but he was also slightly smiling. "I'm just nervous. Okay? Maybe he's not... maybe... "

"Maybe zombies will rise and eat all of us," I said sarcastically. "C'mon, Adam, you were writing notes back and forth. If you were a girl, you'd totally be scrawling 'Adam loves Mark' all over your notebooks."

Olivia held up her notebook to reveal bright pink hearts around black sharpie letters that spelled out *'Olivia loves Ethan.'* "I present Exhibit A."

Drifter shook his head, but he was smirking. "Dude, I got to agree. Passing notes back and forth is a good beginning."

"Maybe it was a buddy thing," Adam said. "A totally, 'hey, dude, what's up?' kinda of thing going down."

"How often have you and I passed notes?" Drifter lifted both of his eyebrows.

"Uh, never," Adam admitted.

"Ha!" I exclaimed triumphantly.

"*Ha*! yourself, woman!" Adam grinned and turned a cute shade of red.

"Ah, look! He's blushing!" Olivia tweaked his cheek.

Adam fought her off good-naturedly. "Ugh! I'm not!"

I joined in the fun of trying to pinch his reddened cheeks and Adam ducked away laughing.

Drifter stepped between us. "Leave him alone. He's trying to play it cool."

"More like trying to avoid playing," I said, sticking out my tongue.

"Ask him to lunch," Olivia suggested. "Again."

"I'll send him a note," Adam said, shrugging. He was obviously trying to get us to lay off him.

"Pffft, notes." Olivia crunched on her lollipop.

"Well, I'm stuck in note writing mode because he's not around during lunch. How else can I break the ice?"

"Talking to him?" Olivia suggested.

"Maybe he'll go to the party," Drifter added.

I just smiled.

"She's got that shifty look again," Drifter noted warily.

"Definitely up to something," Adam agreed. Slowly, it dawned on him what I may just be up to. "Oh, no, Christy. Don't you dare talk to him!"

"Would I do that?" I smiled sweetly.

"Yeah, you totally would. Christy, if you love me you won't do anything to embarrass me."

I studied my nails, which were painted a vibrant blue.

"Christy?" Adam said in a cajoling voice. "Promise me no rash moves."

"I hear your voice, but I just can't make out the words."

"Christy, c'mon." Adam took a hold of my shoulders. "If you love me, you'll not do anything to embarrass me, right?"

"I would never do anything to embarrass you," I agreed. "Unless it was for your own good."

"You're so screwed," Drifter said, laughing.

"I have to get to class!" I turned on my heel and walked away on my personal mission to unite Mark and Adam in boyfriend-dom. I could hear Olivia hurrying behind me.

"We're totally going to stalk Mark, aren't we?"

I grinned at her. "Oh, yeah."

"Any idea where we are going?"

I tugged a piece of paper out of my jean pocket. "I have his locker number."

"Ohhhhh!"

"Drifter got it for me. So we just need to casually hang near Mark's locker and spring on him the second we see him."

Olivia grinned, her teeth a pale blue from her sucker. "I really like the way you think."

"If I don't do something, Adam is totally going to blow this." I was pretty sure about that fact. Adam is too cautious, too skeptical, and too shy for his own good.

I led Olivia around to the entrance near the library, the shortest way to where Mark's locker was located. The sun rose over the tree line that edges the school property. Already the cool air was starting to dissipate. I flexed my shoulders, the skin between my shoulder blades prickling as the sun's rays struck my back.

"He does seem really shy and sweet. It must suck being the only gay boy in town." Olivia cocked her hip and scrutinized the groups of kids descending on the various entrances to the school. We weren't allowed inside the building until the bell rang for first period.

"There used to be a lesbian named Madison, but she moved away. She was pretty cool. She only lived here for a year though."

Girls that I didn't want to deal with were headed our way in a tight little clique of expensive clothes, perfectly coiffed hair, and clear complexions. Courtney and Britney were the leaders of the group. The Barbies weren't top tier popular girls in the school because they were juniors. They'd reign in our senior year, but all through my school years they had been the bane of my existence.

There is a zero-tolerance rule in our school district when it comes to physical bullying, but the administration tends to look the other way when it comes to the verbal stuff. The only physical altercation that Adam and I were ever in was with a kid named Skylar who ended up moving away when his dad went to prison. Skylar was pretty messed up to begin with, but while he was wailing on Adam, Courtney and Britney had been cheering him on. I'll never forgive either one.

Britney is the perfect blond pixie and Courtney's her dark-haired opposite. Trailing behind them were Maribel and Jennifer. Maribel is a tiny little Latina girl with the biggest, darkest eyes I've ever seen and sleek dark hair. Jennifer is a sun-worshipper and her skin is super-dark and her hair super-bleached.

"Bitch patrol," Olivia decided as the group neared us.

"You called it."

"They have that totally too-sweet thing going down." Olivia flashed them a sickly sweet version of their smiles.

Courtney narrowed her eyes suspiciously.

I pretended not to see them, letting my bangs hang in my eyes.

The scent of their mingled perfumes was pretty rank when they stopped behind us. I couldn't make out their words, but I could hear their voices whispering and the snickers. I went through a chubby phase in junior high and it took a long time to lose the weight. I still need to lose fifteen more pounds to be in the healthy weight range for my height, but they make me feel like a walking blimp with their snide comments and disdainful looks.

Olivia regarded them openly, appraising them with barely-concealed disdain.

"Ignore them," I said under my breath.

Olivia slowly rotated around to face the door. "They're so obvious."

"Uh huh." I could feel those four sets of dark fringed eyes glowering at my back. Sometimes I wish I could have super-witch powers and turn them into toads. But I'm pretty sure that qualifies in the black magic category. Still, it's fun to imagine.

The bell rang and I shoved the door open. Olivia scooted in behind me and we rushed toward our destination. Our shoes squeaked against the highly polished floor as we edged out other students hurrying toward their lockers. The hallway was quickly filling up and we dodged around clusters of kids. I mentally counted off the numbers on the lockers as we headed toward Mark's.

"Hot gay guy at two o'clock," Olivia hissed.

I caught sight of the very tall, very good-looking boy heading toward the locker. It pained me to admit he was even hotter than Ian. His gray eyes flicked toward us as we reached his locker scant seconds before him. Peering up at him, I suddenly lost my voice. He really was quite mesmerizing with his perfectly sculpted face and dark silky hair hanging rakishly over his forehead. He raised his eyebrows, waiting.

"Uh... " I stammered.

"So, I'm Olivia," my friend said, rescuing me. She thrust her hand out toward Mark.

40

He gingerly shook her hand, a confused, but amused expression on his face. "Nice to meet you. You're new, too, right?"

"Yep. From Dallas."

"I'm from Houston."

"Big city slickers in podunk high, huh?" Olivia grinned around her lollipop.

"Hey! Podunk chick standing here," I protested.

Mark and Olivia exchanged knowing smiles.

Frowning slightly, I held out my hand. "I'm Christy."

"Hi, Christy. I'm, Mark."

The press of his hand was very light. His skin was like silk. I wondered what hand lotion he used. My hands are like sandpaper.

"I... uh... was wondering if you'd like to have lunch with me, Olivia, Drifter, and Adam. Hang out. Get to know each other," I blurted out.

Mark tilted his head, his beautiful eyes flicking between me and Olivia. "Drifter and Adam? Friends of yours?"

I bristled slightly. "Adam is my *best* friend. Short, cute, redhead. Kinda quiet."

Mark's perfectly shaped lips smirked slightly. "Yeah, I have him for some classes. I recognize the name now."

"So, anyway, want to join us?" I had to admit he had this edgy mysterious thing down pat.

Nodding, he slipped past us to his locker. "Sure. Sounds good. I'm up for meeting new people."

"Awesome. See you there," I said triumphantly. Grabbing Olivia's arm, we scooted away from him.

"Well played!" Olivia said high-fiving me.

We almost walked into the Barbies. The four of them regarded us with utter disdain.

"As if you have a chance," Courtney said, her voice dripping with sarcasm.

Olivia giggled and said, "Ping, ping, ping," eliciting confused looks from the four of them.

"As if *you* have a chance," I said scathingly.

Olivia and I pushed past the Barbies, grinning.

Adam

I arrived at Mrs. Berry's class to find that I was alone. I placed my stuff on my desk and started toward the back of the room to grab our morning free-write papers. I was almost there when I caught a glimpse of someone out of the corner of my eye, and turned to see who it was.

Mark Black stood at the desk beside mine, watching me.

"Hey," I said, trying to not be a chickenshit like Christy accused me of being.

"Hey," he replied, then smiled. "You usually here this early?"

I shrugged. "I try not to be."

"I don't blame you." He gave me a wry smile.

I made my way to the back counter and Mark's footsteps followed.

Nervously, I decided to bite the bullet and start up a conversation. "How's it going?"

"It's going all right," Mark replied.

I couldn't figure what to say next.

Mark gingerly fingered through the free-write papers beneath his hand. "Do all the English teachers do this, or just Mrs. Berry?"

"I think it's just Mrs. Berry," I shrugged, turning and keeping pace with him as we returned to our desks. "You don't like to free-write?"

"Oh no, I do. Honestly, it's my favorite thing about English, even if that does make me sound like a nerd."

"Nothing wrong with that," I smiled. "I kinda like it myself."

Back at my desk, I wrote my name and the day's date at the top of my paper before returning my attention to Mark. "How do you like Trinity Springs?" I decided to try to keep the conversation going even if my stomach was in knots.

"Small towns are cool," he said, with a slight shrug. "A lot different from Houston."

"I can only imagine. I've lived here my whole life," I said.

Mark just grinned, his gray eyes twinkling. "Trapped, huh?"

"Yeah. But I'm going to UT when I graduate. I can't wait to move to Austin."

"Austin's cool."

"You've been there?"

"A few times. It's a chill place. People are pretty decent."

There was a lapse in the conversation. I tried to figure out what to say next while not trying to stare into those beautiful eyes. "You know anybody here yet?"

"So far, no."

"It's never fun to start at a new school," I commiserated.

"It depends on if you make friends or not."

"Yeah, I guess so."

"Like with that new girl? She's been doing okay. What's her name? The one who started when I did?" Mark arched an eyebrow in thought.

"You mean Olivia? The one with the pink in her hair?"

"Yeah. Her."

"She's actually been hanging out with us."

"I noticed," Mark said, a slight smile crossing his face.

He had noticed me and my friends! I had to take that as a good sign. But when? It was possible that he had seen her hanging around with me and Christy before school.

"So Christy is your best friend, huh?" Mark continued.

"How'd you-oh, wait!" I put two and two together and felt like strangling Christy. "They talked to you?"

"I ran into them earlier, yeah."

"I hope they didn't pester you. They can be annoying."

"Nah, they were cool. They were just trying to help me out."

I had a slight heart attack at his words. Had they talked about me? Of course they had-why else would they have stalked Mark before class? Christy was on a mission to try and get me a boyfriend. She'd stop at nothing to get what she was after.

"That's good," I said.

"They told me I should meet up with all of you for lunch."

"Oh," I said. I was definitely going to strangle Christy.

"They said it would help me meet people."

"That's true."

"I'm always willing to meet more people," Mark said, offering a smile that gave me a shiver.

Mrs. Berry shuffled into the classroom and made her way toward her desk.

"So... you'll come?" I asked, leaning forward so our conversation wouldn't be overhead.

"Sure. Why not? How am I going to get to know anyone otherwise?"

I smiled.

The students began to file into the room.

I was victorious.

Just as I was beginning to revel in my victory, Mark was nowhere to be seen.

Where could he have gone?

We'd gotten separated in the shuffle at the end of Mrs. Berry's English class. Mark had simply disappeared into the crowd. Sitting in Mr. Barker's History class, watching the door like a hawk as the clock above ticked down the last few minutes of the first period break, I wondered if he had ducked out of school. Had he fed me a line to get me to back off? A meteor could've fallen through the ceiling and I wouldn't have noticed it, all because my thoughts were set on one thing: Mark Black.

As Mr. Barker rose at the front of the class to begin what would be the opening lecture, the bell rang and knocked my attention back to the present.

"Hello class," Mr. Barker said.

"Hello Mr. Barker," everyone said.

"Now, as we've been discussing the past few days, we're going to be talking about the American Revolution and its effect on the thirteen colonies. As you all should probably know, New Hampshire, New York, Pennsylvania, Massachusetts, Rhode Island, Connecticut..."

The rest of Mr. Barker's words were lost as I stared at the door.

What had happened to Mark?

The sound of my name drew my attention to the front of the class.

"Mr. Hunter," Mr. Barker said, clearing the fog from my eyes and the wax from my ears. "Are you with us?"

"Yes sir," I said. "Sorry. Spaced out for a minute there."

"Make sure you don't do it again."

The door opened.

My attention shot to the side.

A girl who'd managed to miss the first bell entered the class and scurried over to her desk.

I sighed.

Mr. Barker continued to mark names down on the attendance sheet.

Where could Mark have gone? He was supposed to be here too. It made no sense for him *not* to be here, unless something more important had come up.

A family emergency, maybe? Could he have gotten sick?

Knowing that my plans were foiled and my attempts once again shot, I sighed and decided to play it as cool as humanly possible.

There was still a chance Mark could walk into the room.

All I had to do was wait.

Christy

The lunchroom was sheer chaos as usual. There was a mad scramble to line up against one long wall to suffer the cafeteria food. The snack bar line was just as long. The rest of us losers with lunches from home claimed our tables as fast as we could. There are primo spots in the cafeteria and there is always a lot of jockeying to get them. The students are not allowed outside to eat anymore since a few seniors took a joy ride through town and crashed a few years back. I hate it when everyone gets punished because of a few morons.

Olivia and I occupied a round table in the far corner of the cafeteria. There's a large poster on the wall with the school mascot snarling down at us. It's supposed to be a hog, but it looks more like a deranged, mangy dog. Whoever decided to paint the lunchroom a burnt yellow must really hate kids. But the table in the corner was the best one as far as I was concerned. I slid into the chair with my back to the corner so I could watch the room.

Slamming her Betty Boop lunchbox down on the table, Olivia surveyed the room with eagle eyes. "Hrmm, no sign of Mark."

"He better show up." If Mark stood us up, I would track him down and give him an earful. I don't care how good-looking a guy is, he does *not* ignore my best friend.

Drifter wandered over to the table with a tray of hot cafeteria food. The entrée resembled enchiladas. I sometimes think Drifter is like this perfect person sprung to life to make us all look bad. He actually had salad as a side dish and an apple for dessert.

"So did you talk to him?" Drifter took a seat. He'd actually bought milk and water as his drinks for his meal. Yep, perfect.

"We're that obvious, huh?" I asked him. I took out my bag of potato chips and slapped it between my palms, popping it open.

Drifter snorted. "Well, yeah."

"Have you talked to him yet?" Olivia asked. She nibbled on a chicken salad and whole wheat sandwich.

Blech. Everyone was being healthy. I popped my can of soda in defiance.

With a nod, Drifter opened his bottle of water. "Yeah. A few times. Mark seems cool. Kinda quiet. I figured he was trying to sort out who everyone is." He gestured to the clusters of kids forming at each table.

He had a point. You could tell exactly where the popular kids were sitting, the jocks, the drama kids, the band kids, the goths, the kickers, and the other kids who just floated in the middle of it all were, of course, the outsiders. Except for Drifter. He can sit at any of those tables and they love him.

Crunching on my potato chips, I scanned the room and the heavily jammed doorways. The second bell began to ring and kids scooted inside the doors before they were shut by the teachers. I spotted Adam near the front of the line at the snack bar. He was probably buying Frito pie or something else horribly unhealthy.

"I wonder where he is?" I muttered, prying open a package of Lunchables.

"Adam is in line," Drifter said, pointing.

"No, Mark," Olivia corrected him. She had carrot sticks instead of chips.

It was like a conspiracy.

"Oh, I saw him talking with Courtney before I came in here." Drifter occupied his mouth by shoving a bunch of iceberg lettuce into it.

I narrowed my eyes. "Why is he talking to *her*?"

Drifter shrugged, conveniently chewing.

I looked at Olivia pointedly.

"Totally pinging," Olivia assured me. "She's probably just trying to put moves on him."

Adam appeared at my side with a tray. He set it down and I hit him.

"What?" he asked, surprised.

"Salad? Since when do you eat salad?" I popped a cheesy pizza into my mouth, chewing angrily.

"I was in the mood for a salad," he protested.

Taking a long swing of my soda, I glowered at him.

Olivia pinched my leg. "Look!"

Courtney strode into the cafeteria looking quite pleased with herself. Mark was in her wake. Every eye in the cafeteria was on them as they made their way across the room. They arrived at the center table where the popular kids were clustered. I watched with an ever growing sense of unease as Mark was introduced around the table by Courtney.

Adam glanced over his shoulder, sighed, and tucked into his salad, ignoring the whole fiasco.

"He said he would eat with us," I protested.

Adam shrugged. "I guess not."

Drifter regarded the scene with some interest, then shrugged. "You had to expect one of the Barbies to make a move on him."

"Total bitches," Olivia growled.

Sighing, I watched with a sinking heart as Mark chatted with the popular kids. The girls were especially perky about his presence at their table, but I noticed Ian watching him thoughtfully. I shoved my mini-pizzas in my mouth, not really tasting them as I chewed. Maybe Olivia was wrong. Or maybe Mark was in the closet. Or maybe he was bisexual and going to play both fields. It killed me to see Adam eating in silence, his eyes fastened on his meal.

Maybe I had built all this up just for him to be crushed.

Then, it was like the heavens parted, as Mark waved goodbye to Courtney and her minions and headed toward our table. I loved the way her mouth dropped open as the other Barbies leaned toward her, chattering excitedly. I grinned as Mark slid into the chair next to Adam.

"Got delayed," Mark explained.

Adam shot me a quick look that I couldn't quite decipher, then nodded to Mark. "No problem. Courtney has a way of getting her way."

Mark glanced back at the Barbies and their table. "Yeah, I can see that." He laughed lightly as he folded his arms on the table, leaning forward. "Girls like that are always bad news."

Drifter shrugged. "She's kinda spoiled. I get along with her fine."

"You get along with everyone," I pointed out. I was grinning like a maniacal bitch at Courtney.

"Aren't you going to eat?" Olivia asked Mark.

He shook his head. "I already ate. I'm diabetic, so I have to make sure to take my insulin. I headed home early to eat and take my shot."

"Oh, so that's why you don't eat in the cafeteria," Adam said, his face lighting up.

"Yeah. It's a pain. It came on all at once when I was younger. I can control it, but it can be inconvenient." As he spoke, his eyes flicked toward Adam. I swore I saw a spark between them.

"That sucks," Drifter sympathized.

"We didn't mean for you to skip class to join us," Olivia said apologetically.

"Nah, don't worry about it. I'm still trying to find my way in this school. There's a lot fewer kids here than my school in Houston. Makes it a little more... uh... "

"Complicated?" Drifter offered.

"Yeah. You can't just fade into the background if you want to. I'm used to hanging on the fringes."

I kept willing Mark to look at Adam more, but he was adept at keeping his attention on all of us equally.

"Adam and me are totally fringe people," I said quickly, sounding like an idiot.

"What's with you, Olivia? You could totally be hanging out with them," Mark said. "You're cute, you're wearing expensive clothes, you've got that popular girl vibe."

"Pffft. Popularity is overrated," Olivia said dismissively. "I like hanging with the people who are actually *real.*"

"I hang out with everyone," Drifter said around a mouthful of enchiladas. "People like me."

Mark glanced at Adam curiously. "So is it the red hair? Is that why you're on the fringes?"

Adam looked like a deer in headlights. He sputtered slightly, then took a swig of his diet Coke. His eyes flicked to me as he drank, obviously looking for a lifeline.

"Oh, he's gay," I said quickly.

Everyone at the table froze.

"Nice save," Adam muttered.

I smiled weakly. "Oops."

Mark just shrugged. "I am of the live and let live philosophy."

"I like that philosophy!" Olivia said perkily.

I gave her a pointed look, arching an eyebrow.

"Ping," she answered me.

"So I hear there is some big party at Ian's on Saturday. Are all of you crashing it?" Mark asked.

"Actually, Christy got us an invite," Adam said. "She has a thing for Ian."

"Touché," I grumbled.

"A bad crush. She's had it for like... oh... since we were in kindergarten," Adam continued, obviously enjoying humiliating me.

"He's hot," I said in my defense.

Mark laughed out loud, his gray eyes crinkling with delight. "I didn't notice."

"Well, he is," I said moodily.

"She's like a moth to his flame," Drifter said, shaking his head.

"Well, don't keep that up, or you'll get burned," Mark advised.

"Thank you for agreeing with me." Adam, the traitor, smiled at Mark. "She needs to hear it from someone else other than her gay boyfriend."

I rolled my eyes dramatically, shoving potato chips in my mouth.

Leaning forward, Mark lightly touched my hand, pulling my attention to his lovely, dreamy eyes. Why do the boys get the gorgeous velvety lashes and I get scrubby, short bristles? The universe is so unfair.

"Christy, we don't know each other well, but want to go to the party with me?" Mark asked.

Adam almost dropped his drink. Drifter's fork stopped midway to his mouth. Olivia almost choked on her carrot.

"Huh?" I squinted at him in confusion.

"Sometimes guys step up when there is a little competition," he said, his eyes darting toward Ian.

I followed his gaze, then looked back at Mark's fingers lightly resting on my hand. "Oh."

"So, how about it?"

Giving Adam a snarky smile, I said, "Sure. I'd love to go with you."

And just like that, I had a date with my gay best friend's crush.

Adam

"Oh my God," Christy said on the other side of the phone call. "Oh my God. Oh my God. *Oh my God!* I am *so* sorry Adam. I shouldn't have said yes, but at the moment I was totally feeling a bitch vibe because of you picking on me and you *know* I wouldn't—" Her voice was desperate over the phone.

"I know," I said, then sighed. "Really, Christy, it's okay. Don't worry about it."

"I cannot be held responsible for the date. Yes, I said *yes*, but that was just because I was feeling surly. It shouldn't have happened. I should never be put in a position like that because I'll just do something crazy! I just don't understand how that could've happened. I mean, I wasn't *hitting* on him or anything," she said, her voice finally cracking. "But on the bright side we'll all be hanging out together at the party and—"

"Christy. Calm down. Really, don't—"

"But I betrayed you!" she shrieked.

"I think you're overreacting *just* a little bit."

"She totally is! He totally pings!" Olivia's voice said from the other end of the call. "It's totally a ploy on Mark's part."

Mom poked her head out from around the corner. *Who're you talking to?* she mouthed.

Christy, I mouthed back, then readjusted my phone along my jawline. "Well... think of it this way: you out me to a *really* hot guy to try and get him to ask *me* out, then he turns it around and asks *you*. You have to love the way that turned out."

"No one ever asks me out! Especially a hot guy like Mark! What was I supposed to do? I freaked!"

"Maybe this is what you get for stalking hot guys," I teased. "Maybe it's your punishment. Karma beating you in the—"

"Adam!"

"Calm down, Christy. I was kidding."

"But you—"

I lowered the volume on my phone as Amelia came barreling down the stairs. "Really," I said, then winked at Mom, who offered a confused look before returning to the kitchen. "It's okay. Like I said before-if he isn't gay, oh well."

"Oh well? *Oh well!* Are you out of your freakin' *mind?* Me and Olivia have been scheming for the past—"

"Is this a confession?"

Christy offered no reply.

"Pinging!" Olivia's voice said in the background.

"Really," I continued, "don't worry about it. You stalked, you tried, then you got the hot guy. All in a day's work, right?"

"This isn't helping," Christy grumbled.

"Like I said, don't worry about it."

"But what about the party?"

"No point in going now."

"But we can all hang out!"

"I'm not wanted there anyway, especially not by Ian." The moment of silence that followed seemed to prove my point. "Really, Christy, it's fine. Don't worry about it. I gotta go, but like I said, *don't worry.* We tried. That's all we could've done, right?"

"I guess," Christy sighed. "Bye, Adam."

"Bye, Christy. Bye, Olivia!"

"Pinging!" Olivia called out.

The moment I ended the call, Mom walked back into the room. "Everything okay?" she asked.

"Depends on how you look at it," I shrugged.

"Uh oh. What happened?"

48

"You know the hot guy at school? The one we thought was gay?"

"Yeah."

"Christy got him to come to lunch with us."

"Oh Adam, that's—"

"But then he asked Christy out to Ian's party."

Mom's face instantly fell. "Oh."

"Yeah," I replied. "I'm trying to figure out whether to be happy for Christy or sad for myself."

"Oh honey," she said, crossing the few feet between us and wrapping her arms around me. "I'm so sorry. I know how much you were hoping."

"It's okay, Mom. I'm all right."

"I know you are, but still-it hurts. I know it does."

"At least you and Dad were popular and had a good high school experience," I said, patting her back a few times before drawing away.

"Just because we were popular doesn't mean we didn't have our share of hurdles. Trust me. Hell, us just getting together was a big drama."

"How did you guys end up hooking up?"

"He had just gotten on the football team the first time I asked him out."

"And?"

"He said no."

"Why?"

"Because he was with some other blonde bimbo bitch," she said, then covered her mouth with her hand. "Sorry."

"I've heard it before."

"Anyhow," she continued, "he was with this blonde... *girl*... named Heather, and you know all about Heathers, right? Anyway, *Heather* was also part of the cheerleading team... but he didn't like her too much after a while. She was always hanging around moaning that she wanted to *'go somewhere else'* or that she thought something was *'too stupid to be here for it.'*"

"So how did you end up dating?"

"He dumped her and then she went freaking crazy."

"Wait... what?"

"I told her to stop moping about it one day during cheerleading practice and she called me a slut. *Apparently* she thought I had stolen your father from her."

"And she—"

"Yanked my hair. Let's just say it didn't end well for her."

For being only five-foot-or-other, I did not doubt my mom's story. Dad swore she had a mean right hook.

"Heather didn't bother us anymore after that," Mom said, then offered a fine, sun-shiny smile.

"At least you and Dad ended up together."

"That's not the point though, honey. The point is, sometimes things happen for a reason. Maybe this guy really isn't straight. Maybe he's just using Christy to get closer to you."

"To get closer to me? Why would he do that?"

Mom shrugged. "Boys are weird," she offered, "and you don't get better with age, if you want to know the truth."

"Thanks Mom."

"No problem. But hey-I gotta jam. Cake in the oven, yannow?"

"I know," I smiled.

Before she could dart into the kitchen, Mom leaned around the corner. "What about that party you were talking about?" she asked. "Isn't it this Saturday?"

"I'm not going."

"You totally should, hon. Like I said, you don't know why this might be happening."

With that, Mom disappeared into the kitchen, leaving me to my own devices.

She could be right. Maybe there was a reason for Mark suddenly becoming interested in Christy.

"Hey, Mom!"

"Yeah?"

"I'm going to that party this Saturday," I said, reaching into my pocket to grab my phone.

She offered a cheer from the depths of the kitchen.

I grinned.

Hey Christy, I typed. *Pick me up this Saturday. I'm going to Ian's party with you.*

Chapter 5

Unexpected Events

Christy

The girl in the mirror definitely didn't look like me. I stared at my reflection in awe.

"This so isn't me."

"Nope. Not at all. But that was the point, wasn't it? What you wanted?"

Olivia was sitting on my bed petting Callie. I was surprised that my usually very judgmental cat liked her already. Olivia's pink-streaked blond hair was carefully coiffed into a retro style complete with a big gardenia in her hair. She also wore a pale blue dress that looked like something an old movie star would wear. Instead of looking dorky, she looked awesome.

Meanwhile, I looked totally... different.

Placing my hands on my hips, I watched the girl in the red dress and bright red lipstick in the mirror mimic me. Olivia and I had left early that morning on a road trip to the nearest big town with outlet stores. We had hit Ross and Marshalls, scouring the racks for a dress that would actually make me look like a real girl. By the time we settled down for lunch at Cheddar's, we had found the red dress and black strappy heels I was now wearing. Before heading home to Trinity Springs, we had stopped by Sephora and bought a matching lipstick.

"Do I look slutty?" I said worriedly.

"I would say we avoided slutty by flirting outrageously with sexy," Olivia assured me.

The dress skimmed over my body and ended just below my knees. It had a mandarin collar that my parents wouldn't have a fit over, but it made me look a bit busty. Olivia had fussed with my super-fine hair until it was up in a cute bun with wisps falling around my face. It had taken tons of hairspray and gel to get my long bangs out of my eyes. I trusted Olivia to do my makeup and I now had just a bit of black eyeliner to give me slight cat eyes, mascara, and bright red lips.

"This stupid slimmer slip thing is so tight," I groused.

"You're the one who wanted to buy it," Olivia said with a giggle.

I tugged on the dress, feeling the snap of spandex in the garment beneath it. "At least I can breathe. Barely." The tight little flesh-colored slip of death did make me look slimmer, so I would endure it.

"Wow."

I turned to see my mom in my doorway. Her mouth was open and her eyes were filled with tears.

"Mom?"

"Oh, my!" She smiled and rushed over to crush me in her arms. "You look so grown up!"

"It's the dress and the lipstick."

"And the heels," Olivia added helpfully.

"Can you walk in those?" Mom stared at shoes worriedly.

"Because of the platform sole, it's really only the equivalent of a two inch heel," Olivia pointed out. "She hasn't fallen to her death. Yet."

My mom held my hands as she studied my outfit. "Well, it's very pretty. Maybe a little old for you, but not a bad first try at being a young lady."

"I feel like a fraud," I admitted.

"Well, you look lovely. All the boys will be staring at you. Maybe not the boy downstairs right now talking to your father though." My mom's brow furrowed. "Why are you dating a gay boy?"

"Told you he totally pings on the gaydar," Olivia said with a grin.

"Totally," my mom agreed with her.

Callie, the little traitor, was on Olivia's lap purring loudly.

"It's not a real date. It's to make Ian notice me."

"And that makes sense how?" Mom's eyebrows lifted with curiosity.

"By making her seem desirable by being unattainable. Ian will totally notice she's a girl now." Olivia's chirpy voice and big smile made me giggle.

"It's been so long since I dated I guess I just don't remember all the rules." Smoothing my bangs to one side, my mom smiled at me lovingly. "You really are pretty, Christy. It doesn't take a nice dress and makeup to show it. Just remember that."

Olivia kissed Callie's head before sliding off the bed and setting Callie on my pillow. Brushing the cat fur off her skirt, she sauntered over to us. "I guess we should get going since Mark is here."

"This party has chaperones, right?" my mom asked worriedly. She led us out of my room and down the stairs.

"Mom, c'mon," I said, rolling my eyes.

She sighed. "Okay, but I trust you to not get into trouble."

"Mom, this is my first party. I'll be lucky if I don't throw up from nerves."

"We'll all be hanging out together," Olivia assured her. "I'm sure we'll be fine."

"It's just that some of those kids used to be so *mean*. Remember that Skylar incident?"

"Skylar moved away. And we defended ourselves pretty well."

The house was on its best behavior since we had humans in it. It was under strict orders and so far nothing seemed unusual. After Ian's observation about the inside of the house, Mom had the house contract just a bit tonight. The ceilings weren't as high or the rooms quite as big. I caught a slight movement out of the corner of my eye as we passed the second floor. I glanced back and saw the broom duck out of view.

That stupid broom is such a sneak.

Callie scurried down the stairs in front of us and scampered into the entry hall as my dad and Mark's voices reached our ears. Dad was explaining the wonders of the Wii to him, much to my embarrassment.

"It's a bit like magic, I think," my dad was saying. "I get a great tennis workout, but in my living room. You should come over and play sometime."

"Sounds cool," Mark answered.

I gave him massive points for that.

Entering the living room, my mom stepped aside and swept her hands toward me with great flourish. "Ta da!"

"Wow! Is that my little sugarplum?" my dad asked, grinning.

"You look great," Mark said, approvingly.

To my surprise he walked over and kissed my cheek.

"Uh, thanks," I said awkwardly.

"There's definitely a pretty girl hiding under that hoodie," my mom said with a smile, her eyes watching Mark curiously.

"Pffft, I always knew that." Olivia gingerly unwrapped a pale blue lollipop, her eyes flicking toward Mark.

"You'll make a great entrance at the party," Mark assured me. "The dress was a great idea."

I was surprised to feel my face flushing. I couldn't play it cool when my hopes were so high. Ian was finally paying attention to me and I desperately wanted for him to finally notice I was a girl. It's embarrassing how many grandiose fantasies I've had about him being my boyfriend, but those dreams never felt close to reality until now.

"Okay, gather close! Taking pictures!" My dad was holding up his phone.

I wanted to run for the door, but Mark slid his arm around my waist and leaned into me. Olivia struck a perfect pose next to me and we endured my dad taking a few shots.

Afterward, we had to suffer admonishments to be careful as Mark promised my parents that I would come home safe and sound. Olivia looked amused by the gauntlet we had to run past my parents to make it out onto the front porch. We finally made it to Mark's sleek black sedan and climbed inside as my dad took pictures with his phone and my mom waved.

"Your parents are pretty nice," Mark said as he started the car.

"They're embarrassing," I complained.

Mark shook his head, his dark hair falling rakishly over one eye. I could totally see why most of the girls in school and Adam were crushing so hard on him. He was totally dreamy. "They just care about you. You should enjoy it."

"My parents totally embarrass the crap out of me. It's like a rule with parents," Olivia said, sitting in the backseat and sucking on her lollipop.

Slowly pulling his car away from the front of my house, Mark glanced at her in the rear view mirror. "At least your parents care enough to embarrass you."

"I take it your parental controls are on the suck side of the scale?" Olivia asked.

"Yeah. They had me because they had to." Mark shrugged. "Then when I didn't live up to their expectations they pretty much ignored me."

I felt bad for Mark in that moment. The tension in his face and the sadness in his voice spoke volumes about his home life. I wondered if his parents were harsh on him because of him being gay. I lightly touched his shoulder.

"Sorry to hear it," I said. "I complain about my parents, but I know I'm lucky."

"You really are," Mark assured me. Then he flashed a bright smile my way, and the sadness was swept from his face. "So we have to get Adam, right?"

"Yeah, he decided to tag along," I said, relief in my voice. I was determined to make it up to Adam for stealing his potential boyfriend for the night.

"That's good. He'll have fun."

"His house is right—"

To my surprise, Mark drove straight to Adam's house.

"—here." I looked at Mark suspiciously.

He didn't appear to notice as he honked the horn twice.

I glanced into the backseat at Olivia and she gave me the thumbs up.

Adam hurried out of his house, his cute little mom following close behind him. His bratty sister lingered in the doorway. Mark rolled down his window as Adam slid into the backseat beside Olivia. Adam's flustered face said it all. He was just as excited and nervous as I was.

"Hi! I'm Ashley, Adam's mom," his mother said, holding her hand out to Mark.

He lightly pressed it and smiled at her. "I'm Mark Black."

"It's supercool to meet you! Adam has told me all about you."

I flicked my eyes toward Adam to see him covering his face with embarrassment.

"Good stuff, right?" Mark said in a playful tone.

"Oh, yeah! Totally! Hey, are you Olivia?" Ashley waved at her.

"Nice to meet you," Olivia said with a sweet smile.

"I'm just glad they have new friends to hang out with. After all that bullying shit a few years ago—"

"Mom," Adam said, his voice pleading.

"Right! You kids have fun! I'm so excited that you're going to a par-*tay*! Woo!" Ashley hopped back from the car, her hands over her head as though she was cheering a touchdown.

Mark waved goodbye, raised the window, and we made our escape.

"Your mom is sooo a cheerleader," Olivia observed.

"Head cheerleader," Adam confessed.

"I think she's cute." Mark was grinning, clearly amused.

"Oh, she's a bundle of cute," Adam agreed. "She's just excited we're all hanging out. Thanks for picking us up, by the way."

"No prob. I'm looking forward to tonight."

I saw Mark's eyes glance toward the rearview mirror. I smiled happily, glad that things seemed to be back on track.

Ian's house is on the opposite side of town where the more modern homes are located. His dad works for the oil industry, but he's not a foreman like Adam's dad. He's actually a high level executive, so their house is huge, surrounded by a lot of acres, a pool, and even a horse stable. Ian's parents often travel, so his house was pretty much party central. It's just outside of city limits, so the parties usually don't end up being busted by the local police.

Mark seemed to know exactly where to go and we ended up in a small parade of cars heading out of town. I nervously kept fussing with my skirt and Olivia flicked her fingers at my shoulder to get me to stop. The latest underground band to hit it big was pumping out of the car speakers and the conversation was light and fun. A pickup careened past us, the truck bed crammed with football players. They were hollering and whooping it up as they turned sharply onto the long drive up to Ian's house.

Mark shook his head at the idiocy. "Surprised none of them fell out."

"Bunch of losers," Olivia agreed.

"A little brain damage might actually help them." Adam winked at me.

Mark's car followed the pickup up to the big ranch-style house. Apparently, Ian's mother has a thing for outdoor decorations from Mexico, and three mariachis made out of metal stood next to the front door. The drive was packed with cars and a few parked on the wild grass next to the manicured lawn. Music thumped out of the house and the outdoors lights flicked on as the sun set in the distance.

Killing the engine, Mark swung around in his seat. "Ready to have fun?"

Adam rubbed his hands nervously on his jeans and shrugged. "Why not? What can they do to us?"

"Lynch mob?" Olivia suggested.

Mark shook his head, laughing. "Nah. More like be stunned and amazed at the sexy girls and hot guys invading their party. Right, Adam?"

"Yeah," Adam answered, just a shade too shyly.

Bravely, we climbed out of the car and headed into the party.

All my bravado died the second I was in Ian's house. Suddenly, I felt like a moron in my red dress and high heels. I wanted to run to the bathroom and wipe off all the makeup and take down my hair. When I stepped into the tiled entry hall I felt like a huge lumbering oaf as the slim, petite frames of the Barbies came into the view.

All four sets of perfectly made up eyes settled on me.

I resisted the urge to tug on my dress, hide behind my side-swept bangs, or cross my arms protectively over my breasts.

They didn't say a word.

They broke into peals of laughter.

Lowering my head, I tried to hide my sudden tears.

Mark's arm wrapped around my shoulders and he leaned into me, whispering, "Ignore them." Raising his head, he proudly escorted me past the Barbies as they lapsed into stunned silence.

Adam and Olivia linked arms and followed us into the huge living room and adjoining dining room. The furniture was pushed up against the walls and kids were everywhere. Drifter had come early to set up his DJ equipment and he was tucked into a corner bobbing his head to the music. Everyone was clutching bright red plastic cups and I was suddenly parched.

Mark took my hand and guided me through the throng of kids. Seeing just who all was at the party made me feel like an even bigger loser. From the chess club to the goths, the entire school population seemed to be crammed into Ian's house. I glanced back at Adam and he gave me a sweet, encouraging smile. Mark guided us through the party to the kitchen that was bigger than most houses in our town. I couldn't believe how big it was. There was even a fireplace that was large enough to barbecue an entire cow in. Ian was perched on a counter next to several kegs chatting with his buddies. The mere sight of him made me want to run away. I forgot all about Mark, Olivia and Adam. My heart stuttered in my chest and I felt sick to my stomach.

"Here," Mark said, thrusting a red cup into my hand.

There was sweet smelling punch in it and I gulped it as Mark tackled the spread of food laid out on a long kitchen table.

"Don't panic. Keep cool," Adam whispered. He kissed my cheek sweetly and scooted past me to follow Mark to the food.

We had lost Olivia somewhere in the crowd. Alone, staring at Ian like an idiot, I downed the rest of my punch and tossed the plastic cup into a large garbage can that was already filling up. Ian was laughing, his eyes sparkling. His blond hair glinted like gold as he tilted his head while listening to his friend spinning a joke. The blue shirt he was wearing hugged his muscled chest and showed off his powerful arms.

"Here you go," Mark said, handing me a plate.

I looked at him in surprise.

"Trying to be a good date," he said with a wink.

The red plastic plate was loaded down with a small pulled pork sandwich, chips, salsa, flautas, and a few chocolate chip cookies. I was suddenly starved and started in on the chips. Seeing that I was missing a drink, Mark walked over to the punch bowl that was set up near the kegs.

I couldn't hear what he said to Ian, but I saw Ian's eyes fix on me as Mark spoke. He smiled and waved at me. I almost upended my whole plate trying to wave back, but Adam steadied my wrist in time to keep me from making a fool of myself.

Walking back, Mark handed Adam and me each a cup of the punch. There was a bit of a smug look on his face and I nudged him with my elbow.

"What did you say?"

Mark grinned as he leaned against the wall next to me. "I told him that he had a great party going on and that the girls were pretty hot, especially my date."

"You did *not*!" I almost hit him, but Adam was still holding my arm.

"Okay, you cannot be allowed to hold a plate," Adam decided. He rescued it from me.

I felt flushed and overwhelmed. I could see Ian's eyes straying toward me now that he knew I was in the room. I upended my cup and swallowed the punch.

"Whoa!" Mark exclaimed, pulling the drink from my hand.

"What?" I asked him, then humiliated myself by burping.

"There's liquor in there," Mark said.

"Uh..." I stared at him, realizing that I was feeling a bit peculiar.

"Eat more food," Adam urged me.

"Uh…" I said again, flushing. I sat down hard on a stool shoved up against the kitchen cabinets. "Whoops."

Olivia finally appeared, two boys from the drama club on her heels. She was giggling, flattered by their attention. She saw Adam and Mark hovering over me and ditched her entourage.

"What's the drama?" she asked worriedly.

"She drank two of these," Adam said, holding up the evidence.

"In the span of five minutes," Mark added.

"Oh, crap!" Olivia pointed at the plate of food. "Eat! We haven't eaten since lunch. You drank liquor on an empty stomach!"

I snagged the sandwich and started to eat it. I was feeling woozier by the moment and stupider every second. I had barely arrived and already I had blown it. My parents allow me sips of wine and champagne at special events, but I'd never had liquor. My head started to swim and my face felt fire-hot.

"How could you let her drink so much?" Olivia chastised Mark.

"I didn't realize," Mark protested.

"Seriously, we turned our backs and she gulped them down," Adam said, coming to Mark's defense.

"I'm not drunk, am I?" I asked, my words slurring. I giggled. "Oops."

"Eat!" Olivia ordered. "Mark, get her water."

Obeying, Mark waded back into the throng of people near the food and drink.

Snickering at the foolishness of it all, I shoved some chips in my mouth. Olivia grabbed a napkin and blotted my mouth, trying to shield me from prying eyes.

"What's up?" Drifter asked, joining us.

Olivia quickly explained.

"You okay?" Drifter asked, concerned.

I giggled in response.

"We're screwed," Drifter decided.

My head was swimming and suddenly I couldn't remember why I had been so nervous. The world felt magical and wonderful. I felt bold and beautiful. I couldn't stop smiling and giggling.

Adam nudged me to keep eating and I pushed the plate away. Sliding off the stool, I stood on wobbly feet and pondered kicking off my high heels. Drifter took hold of my arm and I pulled away.

"C'mon, I'm fine," I assured them.

The room swirled around me, then settled back down again. Licking my lips, I saw Ian staring at me curiously. Mark rejoined us, holding out a cup of water.

"Drink this," Olivia ordered, snatching it from him and pushing it to my lips.

I swept her hand away and was dimly aware of Adam being drenched. I pushed between Olivia and Drifter and darted away from their grasping hands, laughing. The world felt so alive and vibrant. How had I ever been afraid of being here? I was beautiful and I could have Ian if I wanted him.

Avoiding their clutching hands, I wove through the crowd of people toward the place where Ian was perched chatting with his guests. He saw me coming and gave me a quizzical look. Someone caught my elbow, but I jerked my arm away. I sidestepped around one of the big hulking football players and found myself directly in front of Ian.

His golden hair was a halo around his head. He was an angel.

"Hi!" I said loudly.

"Christy? You okay?"

"I'm pretty!"

"Yeah," Ian agreed, looking confused and slightly concerned.

I burst into tears at his words. "I am?"

Then the floor tilted upward and dumped me into his arms. I noted how good he smelled, then felt myself falling down the rabbit hole, like Alice in Wonderland.

Adam

Mark and I stood next to the swimming pool listening to the sounds of the party. We had slipped outside in the aftermath of the chaos surrounding Christy collapsing. Mark had been willing to drive her home, but Drifter had insisted that he be the one to return her safely. Ian had carried Christy out to Drifter's truck, with Olivia and Drifter following.

Dripping all over the kitchen floor, I had ducked outside to try to dry off. To my surprise, Mark followed.

"Sorry you got drenched," Mark said, offering me a towel he had swiped from a stack near the pool.

"Don't worry about it," I replied. "It's no big deal." I patted at my shirt with the towel and tried not to worry about Christy. I couldn't imagine how she must be feeling, especially considering how much alcohol she drank in such a short amount of time. "Poor Christy."

"I'm sure she'll be fine. Olivia will take care of her," Mark assured me.

"Her parents are pretty cool. They should understand," I said. "Why does everything involving Christy and Ian have to end badly? First it was the Christmas party, now this."

"Ian actually feels responsible." Mark smirked.

"He should!" I laughed. "He's the one who didn't tell us there was liquor in the punch."

"True," Mark said.

"Oh well," I sighed, tossing the towel onto one of the lawn chairs. "Not much we can do about it anyway."

"Not really."

"At least someone's taking care of her."

"That's all we could ask for."

"Hey, Mark," I said, drawing my eyes away from the house so I could look him straight in the face. "You mind if I ask you something?"

"Shoot."

"Why did you—"

The door burst open and the Barbies and their cronies spilled out, laughing loudly. Music pumped out of the house, breaking our quiet moment.

"She's such a joke," Courtney said in a loud voice. "She gets a date with a hot guy and immediately blows it. What a moron!"

I scowled at the Barbies and at the intrusion.

"Adam, let's get away from the house. I can hardly hear what you're saying over all that noise."

Mark looked significantly at the busily gossiping girls. Courtney cast a curious look in our direction, but Mark ignored her as she waved. He led me away from the pool and toward the copse of trees that lined the side of the property. Here, away from the house and all the activity, the sound was duller, and the glow from the outdoor lamps cast just enough light for us to see one another.

"What did you want to ask me?" Mark asked, turning to look at me just as we stepped into the thicket of trees.

"I wanted to ask," I said, "why'd you bring Christy to the party?"

"What do you mean?"

"I saw you hanging out with the popular kids the day you came to lunch with us. You could've easily just stayed with them and left us alone. You could have just come here on your own."

"I could've, yeah, but that would've been pretty dickish. Besides, I came out here for two reasons," Mark said with a shrug. "One, to make Ian jealous for Christy. And two, to spend time with you."

What?

Had I heard him correctly?

No. It couldn't be. I had to have been hearing things. There was no way he could have just said-

"Adam?" Mark asked, waving a hand before my eyes.

"Sorry?" I asked, I said blinking.

"Did you hear what I said?"

"I... I heard the first part, but I don't think I heard the—"

"I said I came out here to spend time with you."

So I *had* heard him correctly.

"You did?" I asked. "Really?"

"Yeah," Mark said, taking a step forward. "I did."

Unsure what to do and petrified that the alcohol was starting to take its effect on me, I merely stood there dumbstruck.

I begged to question whether or not this was actually happening, especially to me. It didn't seem possible that the newest guy to enroll in school would end up being gay, much less interested in me. Forget the love spell—this was fantasy territory already.

"Mark," I said, clearing my throat in the hopes that I wouldn't betray my emotions.

"Yeah?"

"Why have you put so much effort into trying to get close to me?"

"What do you mean?"

"Why didn't you just come up and ask me out at school?"

"I didn't come up to you at school because I know you're not out," Mark said, kicking a pinecone away from his foot. "I've heard the things people say about you, so I didn't want to add fuel to the fire. No point in making your life more miserable."

"But that still doesn't explain why... " I faltered, my nerves getting the best of me.

"Why I like you?" Mark asked, raising an eyebrow and looking amused.

"Uh, you do like me?"

"I said I liked you," Mark replied.

And of all the stupid things I could've said, it had to have been, "Why?"

"Why?" Mark laughed, as though he'd just heard something he couldn't believe. It took a moment his chuckling to die down, but when it did, his eyes softened and his lips curled down into a frown. "Why wouldn't I like you?"

"It's just surprising," I answered, fingering the back of my neck.

"I take it you've never had a guy say he likes you, huh?"

"No. Sometimes I wonder if there's anything *to* like."

"You think there's nothing to like?" Mark asked. "You mean... like your blue eyes? Or your smile, your laugh? Even your hair?"

"My hair's horrible," I laughed.

"Just because it's red? It's the color of passion, Adam, of *flame*. You burn even when people try to blow you out. Doesn't that say something about who you are? What you're like?"

If pigs couldn't fly before, they could now. I don't think they'd make it too far though, especially since all oxygen within the air had ceased to exist. I dropped my gaze to the ground.

"Maybe I've had the fantasy of a guy liking me for so long that when one finally does, I don't know how to handle it."

A pressure weighed down on my upper back. It took the press of Mark's fingers along my ribcage to make me realize he'd actually touched me.

"Adam," he said, nodding when I looked up at him. "It isn't a fantasy. Just because you're stuck in some hick town with a bunch of assholes doesn't mean—"

A bark of laughter echoing from the pool stabbed through the silence of the night.

Mark's arm slid off of my back. "Trouble?" he asked.

I nodded.

The three guys who were strolling across the yard had served as my ultimate tormentors over the years, though they were nothing compared to Skyler. All big and broad-shouldered, they ruled the halls with a vengeance only an iron fist could provide. All were mean, but the biggest and baddest of them all was Jayden. At six-foot-three, he towered over the rest of Trinity Springs High's football team and dominated the field as a linebacker. He was infamous for hurting people during games, but even though they were claimed as accidents, people knew better. Jayden was a ticking time bomb waiting to go off. Alex and Brian, his left- and right-hand men, had nothing on him.

"Football players," I replied. "We should go. Now."

"Why?"

"The big one, Jayden—he's got beef with me."

"Then we better go back into the house," Mark said leading me out of the tree line.

"Yeah, they're probably coming out here to smoke up anyway," I agreed.

When we made it within three feet of Jayden and his crew without any issue, I thought the worst of our troubles were over.

"What's up, fag?" Jayden said, then slammed his elbow into my back as he passed by.

Next thing I knew, I was on my knees on the ground.

"You offering?" Brian said mockingly, grabbing his junk as he sauntered by.

Leaping to my feet, I answered, "You flirting with me?"

"Stupid faggot," Jayden sneered. "You wish. My man meat would break you."

The jocks laughed and made their way toward the wooded area.

Mark watched them depart with stormy eyes, then turned to me. "You okay?"

"Yeah," I said. "I'm fine. I'm used to their crap."

"Come on. Ignore the jerks." He stuck out a hand. "Let's go have some fun."

Hours passed by in a blur. The music, the atmosphere, the thrill of adrenaline coursing through my veins, I danced in the living room with the other kids without a care in the world and eventually began to lose track of time. Though I vaguely remember pulling out my phone to check the time, I couldn't actually read it through my blurred vision. When the party began to die down and Mark was pulling me out of the crowd, I was overcome by all that had occurred.

"Come on," he said, taking me by the shoulder and leading me out of the house. "I should probably take you home."

Though I did my best to act as calm and collected as possible, I'm fairly sure I had an extra beat to my step.

In his car, and out on the main road that led back to Trinity Springs, I leaned back in my seat and watched the countryside, the hills rolling by and the line of trees waving in tune with the wind.

"So," Mark asked, speaking for the first time since we'd gotten into the car and left Ian's house. "You have fun tonight? Despite Jayden?"

"You don't know the half of it," I laughed.

The smile I caught from Mark out of the corner of my eye only continued to prove my point.

"Well," he continued, "I'm glad you had fun."

"Did you?"

"I did," Mark nodded, shifting his hold on the wheel. "It was nice to see you relaxed and having fun."

"What do you mean?"

"It's not like you're *completely* awkward-because you can talk to people who are your friends or who you're comfortable around-but it seems like when you're in a group of people you ... well... 'freeze up,' I guess you could say."

61

"I'm used to people judging me."

"I know how that is, but I feel for you. At least in Houston there are *some* gay kids. Here it's just... well.... you and me."

"Yeah."

"It just sucks to know that you've been here all alone for so long."

"No kidding," I mumbled.

"But you know what, Adam?"

"What?"

"As long as I'm around, you won't be alone."

"I..." I started, then stopped, the butterflies swimming in my stomach and lifting up into my chest. "I..."

"It's all right. You don't need to say anything."

I smiled.

The rest of the drive back from Ian's house was spent in silence. Mark made no move to make small chat, and even though there were more than a few opportunities to say something, he chose not to. Instead, he allowed us to revel in the moment, as if it were something precious for us to both hold and nurture.

By the time we got to my house, it was one-thirty in the morning and the porch light was flickering on and off.

"Don't let your mom know you drank at the party," Mark said, pulling up alongside the sidewalk.

"I won't," I said, reaching down to unlock the door.

"Hey, Adam?"

"Yeah?"

"I had a really great time tonight. It was nice... talking to you without having to worry about what someone else thought."

I fingered the seatbelt for several moments before sliding it into place. "Tonight meant a lot to me," I said. "Thank you."

"No, Adam, thank *you*." Leaning forward, Mark closed the distance between us, took my face in his hands, and pressed his lips to mine.

Time seemed to lose all meaning. In what was only a few seconds, hours seemed to pass by, trapped in bliss that could never be broken.

As he pulled away, a smile on his face and a glimmer in his eyes, my heart drummed within my chest. "Have a good night," he said.

"You too," I replied, then slipped out of the car

He waited until I unlocked the front door before driving off.

I let myself into the house, and heard the sound of someone moving in the kitchen. Having not expected anyone to be up, I pulled a piece of gum out of my pocket and slid it into my mouth to cover the smell of alcohol on my breath.

"Hey, honey," Mom said, stepping out of the kitchen.

"Hi," I replied, blinking in the luminescence as she flipped on the light.

"Is everything all right?"

"It's bright in here," I laughed. "Sorry, we've been in the dark for the past hour."

"No,no, it's fine." She paused. A smile crossed her lips. "How was the party?"

"The party was fine," I said, continuing to chew my gum as she led me into the kitchen. I walked to the fridge, pulled out a soda, then spit my gum in the trash before taking a swig off of it. It tasted awful after the spearmint. "Christy got sick, so Drifter and Olivia took her home."

"Uh oh. What'd Mark think of that?"

"He was okay." I paused. "Hey, you remember what I said about Mark asking Christy out?"

"Yeah."

"He told me that he only took Christy to the party to make Ian jealous," I said. "Then after I got water spilled over me and we went outside, we started talking and he told me he was gay."

My mother squealed. "Oh my God!" she said. *"See? I told you going to this party would was a good idea."*

"Something like that," I smiled.

"So who brought you home?"

"Mark did." I gave her a sheepish smile.

"So it was... just the two of you?" she asked, narrowing her eyes and giving me an unsure look.

I laughed. "Mom," I said, "it's fine. Really. Besides, it's not like you can just put two gay people together and they'll... well... *do* something."

"I know, but I'm just making sure."

"He did kiss me though," I said, blushing.

"Oh," she said, her tone flat. "He did?"

I wasn't sure what to say. "Yeah," I said. "He did."

"Don't you think that's moving just a little bit too fast?"

"I—"

"I don't know how these gay city slicker boys from Houston act, but in Trinity Springs we don't—"

"Really, Mom, it's cool."

"Adam," she sighed, shaking her head. "Don't think I'm overreacting, please. I just want to make sure you're safe."

"I know."

"Still... you barely know this guy, and you were alone with him for how long?"

"Uh..."

"But hey, I'm not saying *not* to have fun. I'm just saying to be safe."

"I know." I sighed.

She pulled me into another hug and pressed a kiss to my cheek. "Well, I'm glad you had fun. You should be getting off to bed though. You know what tomorrow is."

"Church. I know."

She pressed another kiss to my cheek. "Goodnight, Adam."

"Night, Mom."

I turned and started for the stairs.

When I finished cleaning up before bed, I collapsed onto the covers, spread out, and smiled.

Mark was gay.

And he liked me.

Chapter 6

Secrets

Christy

I woke up feeling like someone had used my head to ring the bells of Notre Dame. Rolling onto my side, I groaned. Callie was lying on my bed next to me and she regarded me with her big golden eyes.

"Kill me," I urged her.

Callie yawned.

"She's alive," Olivia's voice said.

Drifter and Olivia stepped into view. Olivia had her hair in pigtails and was dressed in jeans and a cute white top. Drifter was dressed in his usual uniform of jeans, a t-shirt, and a shirt with the sleeves rolled up. They both peered down at me curiously.

"Did I die?" I asked.

"Nah. You passed out drunk," Drifter said, slightly smiling.

Memories flooded back. "Oh, crap. I passed out on Ian, didn't I?"

"That's the bad news," Olivia said.

"What's the good news?" I dared to ask.

"He carried you out of the party!" She held out her phone. A picture of me in Ian's arms glowed on the screen. My head was on his shoulder and he looked like a hero rescuing the stupid drunk girl.

"I suck," I decided, but smiled.

"We brought you home," Drifter explained. "Your mom and dad were pretty upset at Mark, but we explained what happened."

"Did they yell at him?"

"Nah, he stayed at the party with Adam. Me and Drifter brought you home." Olivia sat at the end of my bed and Callie crawled onto her lap.

I glanced toward my windows. The sun was filtering through the pale blue curtains and it looked like maybe it was early afternoon. I fumbled with my clock, turning it to face me. It was 2 o'clock.

"We came over to see how you were doing and your mom let us come up to wait in your game room until you woke up." Olivia petted Callie while Drifter flopped into the big chair I use for reading.

"We've been playing your Xbox. You have some cool games," Drifter said, grinning. "You're more bloodthirsty than I realized."

"I'm a bloodthirsty total loser," I grunted.

"Nah," Drifter assured me. "You made a mistake."

"At least you didn't throw up on Ian this time," Olivia pointed out.

Groaning, I covered my eyes. "Am I grounded?"

Shaking her head, Olivia said, "Nope. We explained it was an innocent mistake. You weren't even there forty minutes."

"Ian must think I'm an idiot." I threw my blanket over my head.

"I think the whole school thinks you're an idiot," Drifter amended.

"Not helping!" Olivia chastised him.

"Just kill me now," I said, staring through the intricate weave of cloth.

Olivia peeled back the comforter and looked at me. "Nah."

"Yeah."

Drifter tossed a stuffed animal at me. "C'mon, Christy. You'll survive this."

"I'm the world's stupidest girl."

"You're not. And wallowing in self-pity isn't doing you any favors." Drifter sounded like my mother.

Sitting up, I stared at my friends. "I like self-pity. Because obviously, I'm not getting any pity from my friends."

Olivia held Callie before her mouth and said in a high-pitched voice, "My human owner is being a dork. She's totally not cool like me, Callie-the-awesome."

Callie's narrowed expression seemed to echo Olivia's sentiments.

My beautiful red dress was hanging on the back of my closet door and I was in an oversized t-shirt. My mom had obviously taken care of me. I felt bad. She had trusted me to not get into trouble and I had done just that.

"Any word from Adam?" It felt weird to not have him here. For so long it had just been me and Adam and occasionally Drifter. Our little world seemed so much bigger now that Olivia and Mark were part of it.

Drifter tossed me my phone. I activated the screen and saw twenty messages from Adam. Scrolling through them, I slowly started to smile. He had kept me updated throughout the rest of the party and had left three messages since noon.

"Adam had a good time with Mark last night," I said, grinning.

"Oh, deets!" Olivia scooted closer to me.

"Uhm, apparently, Mark came out to him," I said, looking at the messages.

"Yes!" Drifter applauded.

"They kissed!" I continued dramatically.

"Those whores! I love it!" Olivia laughed.

"Adam had fun at the party, believe it or not. He even danced!"

Drifter and Olivia high-fived.

"And Mark took him home afterward and wants to see him again" I giggled with delight, clutching my phone to my chest. "At least one of us had a good time."

"It's all going to work out. We just need to chill," Drifter decided, nodding with satisfaction.

"Well, at least it's working out for him," I said, feeling a little bit better.

"Want to go to the movies with me and Drifter?" Olivia asked. "It starts in forty minutes."

Plucking at my bottom lip, I shook my head. "I want to mope more. Mentally prepare for tomorrow."

"It's the latest superhero movie." Drifter stood up and pretended to flex rippling muscles. "It'll be a blast."

"It has that chick that kicks major ass," Olivia added.

Flopping over onto my side on my bed, I shook my head. It made me feel a little sick. "My head is all swimmy. With my luck, I'll go to the movies and Ian will be sitting in front of me and all that action will make me throw up all over him."

"She has a point," Olivia said, glancing toward Drifter.

"Are you sure, Christy?" Drifter nudged me with the nose of a stuffed animal. "It'll be fun. I'll buy the tickets and the snacks."

I playfully shoved the pink bunny away. It had been a gift from Adam when I was eight and it was looking a little ragged, but I loved it. "I want to wallow in misery."

"I give you twenty-four hours to be miserable, then it's off the menu," Olivia warned me.

"I'm with Olivia on this," Drifter agreed.

I stuck my tongue out at them.

"Okay, loser, we're out of here." Olivia leaned over and gave me a hug. She smelled like flowers.

Drifter ruffled my hair, his hazel eyes warm and kind. Drifter is definitely one of the coolest guys around. "See you tomorrow."

I waved as my friends slipped out my door. Callie trailed behind them, giving me one last thoughtful look before vanishing out the doorway with the flick of her tail. I flopped back onto the bed, making my head throb.

Glancing over toward my closet, I saw the old broom peeking out at me.

"Ugh! Spy!"

It zoomed out of my room, a trail of magic blooming behind it.

Stupid broom. Even it has more spectacular magic than I do.

Not wanting to let a perfectly good Sunday go to waste, I rolled out of bed and dragged myself to the bathroom. After a long bath soaking in sea salts and lavender bubble bath, I yanked on jeans, a tank top and a short-sleeved hoodie that has a goth fairy on the back, and headed downstairs.

As I passed my dad's study I heard him typing furiously on his keyboard. Probably in yet another argument on the internet. The broom skipped ahead of me, almost tripping me on the stairs, and I grunted angrily at it. Reaching the foyer, I looked around for my mom. The house always feels empty when I don't see her right away. The broom slid past me, Callie riding on its bristles, and I frowned at both of them. Callie licked a paw as the broom slid around me and down the short hall that leads to the spell room. I followed.

The door to the spell room is hidden. It blends perfectly into the wall and only when it opens do you realize it was ever there to begin with. It swung open to let the broom and Callie in and I ran to catch up. I can't enter unless aided. My magic is too weak to unlock the spell that holds the room secret. I scooted in right before the door shut.

The spell room is circular, bookshelves packed along the curved wall, with a small desk and a long spell table set in the center next to the trunk of the white birch tree that stretches up out of sight. A tiny bit of the witch world's magic resides here and if you stare long enough up at the top of the tree you catch glimpses of sky and clouds.

Callie leaped off the broom and settled on the desk while the broom whooshed upwards into the tree. The bookshelves rise as high as the tree. They're crammed not only with books, but bits and pieces of treasures of the old world.

"Mom?" I called out.

"On my way down," her voice floated downward from above.

I slumped into a chair and stared at the collection of herbs she had laid out on her spell table.

Hair billowing in an unseen wind, her long skirts ruffled by her descent, my mom rode the broom down to the floor, standing on the gnarled handle. She clutched a big jar of brightly colored toadstools.

"Show off," I grumbled.

Stepping off the broom, she leaned over and kissed my cheek. "One day you will come into your power."

"Can it be before tomorrow? Before I have to face all the kids at school?"

My mom ruffled my hair and hugged me. "Everyone makes mistakes."

"Not like I do. I'm epically good at it." I sighed, rubbing my palm over the satiny surface of the old wood. The desk is ancient. My great-great-grandfather made it.

"I know it's hard for you, Christy. Living between two worlds and trying to make it in a world that doesn't understand you. Your father and I understand. You're judged a lot more harshly than the other kids in this town because you're an outsider."

"And fat."

"Stop that," Mom chastised me.

I sighed.

"Christy, I know things went very badly for you last night. You're a little naive about the way the world works. But you're still growing up and messing up is part of the maturing process." Mom arranged the toadstools in a circle on the table and began weaving various dried flowers around them.

"Tomorrow is going to be bad at school," I said moodily.

"But you won't die, will you?"

"No. But I'll want to."

"It'll pass, Christy. I promise you." She finished her task, waved a hand, and bright sparkles of light filled the room for a second. Where the makings of her spell had rested was now a small pot of thick, black earth.

"Can you just skip me through time to around a week from now?"

Handing me the pot, my mom shook her head. "You'll get through it and be stronger for it. If things get out of hand, tell me and your father and we'll talk to the administration. Hopefully, everyone will have forgotten that you got so drunk."

"That's it! Forgetting powder! Give me that!"

"Christy," my mother said, smiling softly. "That's an abuse of magic."

"Fine! I'll endure it." I held up the pot. "What's this?"

"The pecan tree out back has an illness. Go sprinkle that around the roots."

I slid to my feet and headed toward the door. My mom flicked her hand and it opened.

"Mom, I just wish I wasn't such a loser."

"You're not, Christy. You're much more than anyone realizes."

"Yeah. A failed witch." I slipped out of the room before she could correct me.

I exited the house through the laundry room, snagging one of the picnic blankets folded by the back door, and trudged past the small greenhouse, the lush garden, and the small pond to the pecan tree. Trying not to feel annoyed, I slowly dumped out the rich magical dirt around the tree in a circle. Tiny flecks of light shimmered in the air then faded away. If only my magic would do even that, I'd feel a little better about my witch status. Then maybe I wouldn't feel like such a loser at school.

As soon as I finished my task, the pot vanished from my fingers.

I sighed.

A failure at life and a failure at magic.

I trudged back into the garden and found my favorite spot beside a small fountain of stone fairies pouring water into a basin. I spread out the picnic blanket and sprawled on it. Staring up through the boughs of the trees, I watched the fluffy clouds languidly passing overhead. Callie walked over my stomach and nudged one of my hands. I let her nose my palm, then scratched her behind the ears.

Was it really so wrong to want a life that wasn't so horrible?

With a sigh, Adam laid down next to me. I hadn't even heard him approach. Tucking his hands behind his head, I saw his blue eyes regard me as I stared at him out of the corner of my eye.

"We're moping, huh?"

"Yep."

"Gotcha." Adam crossed his ankles and turned his gaze upward.

I followed suit. We laid there for a few minutes before I said, "When Debbie moved away to Dallas over the summer, I thought that maybe Ian might notice me since he was finally single."

Adam didn't say anything. I was grateful. Every girl in high school had probably thought the same thing. Debbie and Ian had been a thing throughout junior high and most of high school until she broke it off when she found out her family was moving.

"Did he say anything after I left?"

"Ian doesn't talk to me," Adam reminded me. "But I think he looked concerned when it happened. He didn't look pissed off. He didn't joke about it."

"That's good, I guess." I brushed my palm over the freshly cut grass beside the blanket. "Congrats on the kiss, by the way."

"Thanks!" Adam grinned.

"What was it like?"

"Nice. Kinda hard to remember, since I didn't expect it. But it was nice."

"I hate you." I frowned. "I'm kissless."

"Nah, you love me. I'm your best friend in the whole world."

I scooted closer to him and rested my head against his shoulder. "I'm such a failure, Adam."

"No, you're not."

"I'm going to get so much grief tomorrow."

"I won't let anyone hurt you. I promise." Adam wrapped his arm around me so I could snuggle against him. "Mark, Drifter, Olivia, and I will be there for you."

Closing my eyes, I knew he was right. I had friends who cared for me, but it didn't stop me from being anxious. I hated feeling like the school's loser at love. Even kids in chess club had boyfriends and girlfriends. My only date so far in my measly life was with Adam's potential boyfriend.

"Hey, kids! Want to go get ice cream?"

I sat up to see my dad standing on the back porch. He was dressed in long shorts and a Polo shirt. He looked like a gnome on vacation.

"You game, Adam?" I asked.

"Do you have to ask?" Grinning, he helped me gather up the picnic blanket and we followed after my dad.

As we neared the door, Adam slung his arm around my shoulders. "I'm glad you're my best friend."

I nudged him with my elbow. "You're not too bad yourself."

Adam

The Barbies were at it again.

Great.

Mark and I were heading down the hall to class when we saw the commotion near Christy's locker. Cornered against her locker by Courtney, Britney and Maribel, Christy had her head down, hiding under her bangs as the Barbies went in for the kill. One of the Barbies, Jennifer, was mysteriously missing from the pack.

"You think *you're* special?" Courtney asked, flipping her dark hair over her shoulders.

"You're pathetic," Britney said. "Absolutely pathetic."

"Hey, Christy!" Maribel called. "You're nothing but a dirty little cu—"

"Shut up!" Christy shoved her way through the Barbies and made a beeline toward the opposite side of the hallway. Near tears, she paced along the side of the wall in a meager attempt to get away from them. All three followed.

"Ok," I said, taking a long, deep breath and balling my hands into fists. "I have to do something about this."

"I'm right behind you," Mark said, following as I strode across the hall.

Just before the Barbies could corner Christy up against the wall, I stepped forward and in between them. "Hey," I said. "Knock it off."

"Get out of here," Courtney said. "Our issue isn't with you."

"Figures," Britney added, giving me the meanest, coldest stare she could muster. "Like a fly to honey. A fag defending his hag."

"Look," Maribel groaned, holding her fists up in a mock representation of how my balled hands looked at my side. "Poor little Christy has to have the *shrimp* come to her protection. Hey, Adam-wanna fight me? Huh? Huh?"

"Leave her alone," I growled.

Maribel took a threatening step forward. "Why don't you—"

"That's enough," Mark said, stepping around me and positioning himself before Christy. He reached out and dragged me away from the three girls. "Beat it, you guys."

"You're with *them?*" Courtney asked, narrowing her blue eyes at me and Christy.

I saw Christy look up and give the Barbies a victorious smile. "Yeah, he's with us."

Courtney bit her lip. "Really?" She gave Mark a significant look, twirling a lock of her hair with her fingers.

Mark stared directly into her eyes and nodded. "Yeah. I am."

Courtney smirked.

A crowd had started to develop around us. People were already starting to point and whisper amongst themselves as we, the outcasts, and Mark, our newly-knighted hero, stood face-to-face with the most popular girls in school.

Mark narrowed his eyes.

The sound of a teacher ordering everyone to class instantly made the crowd disperse.

"Don't think this is over," Courtney said, ignoring Mark, directing her words at Christy. She flipped her hair and walked off calmly.

"Bye, Mark. Bye fag-boy. Bye hag-pig," Britney said, grinning as she waved good-bye and followed her leader.

Maribel merely laughed and took off with the other Barbies.

"Are you okay?" I asked, taking hold of Christy's shoulders.

"I... I'm fine," Christy said.

I could feel her trembling. "No you're not. I *know* you're not."

"Just when I was hoping they'd leave me alone this year, this had to happen." She lifted her head. Just as I'd suspected, she was crying, but she reached up and feverishly brushed her tears away.

I stepped forward and gave her a hug.

Mark reached out and pressed a hand to her shoulder. "Don't let them get to you, Christy."

"I know," Christy replied, pushing me away. "Still... I'm so sick of it."

Breathless, Olivia stopped right beside us and looked directly into Christy's face. "I heard something went down with Christy and the Barbies! You okay?"

"The Barbies are bitches," I said.

Christy was hiding behind her bangs again, wiping her eyes.

Olivia pushed herself between the two of us and gripped Christy's upper arms. "Come on," she said. "Let's get you cleaned up."

"Okay," Christy whispered.

"Call me if they show up again," I said to Olivia.

Olivia gave a slight nod before she led Christy down the wall.

"I can't believe them," I said, shaking my head and trying my hardest to not lose my temper.

"They're idiots," Mark said. "Don't let them bother you."

"How *can't* I when they're harassing my best friend?"

"Hey, what happened?" Drifter asked, coming up from behind us. He reached up to pull his office aide name tag off his shirt as his eyes darted between me and Mark.

"The Barbies let into Christy," I grumbled.

"No. They didn't! I thought they were leaving her alone this year!"

"Nope," Mark said. "They cornered her at her locker."

Drifter's eyes narrowed. "Not cool," he said. "Not cool at all."

"Olivia's taking care of her," I sighed, leaning up against the lockers.

"She'll be all right. She always is," Drifter decided. "Not cool that they're harping on her though."

"We can't let them get away with this," I muttered.

"There's nothing we can do about it except keep Christy away from them," Drifter said.

"But it's *Christy!*"

"Getting revenge on the most popular girls in school isn't going to earn you any favors," Mark said. "Besides, if anything, it might even make it worse for Christy."

"She's already got it bad," I said.

"No need to make it worse." Drifter patted me on the shoulder. "You're a good friend, Adam, but you gotta lay low. Hopefully, this will blow over."

I scrubbed my hand over my hair, then nodded. "Yeah. You're right."

"I'm off to class. Catch you at lunch." Drifter headed off down the hall into the thinning crowd.

Mark and I watched him disappear before I sighed, and said, "Drifter's right."

"He's got it pretty bad for her," Mark said.

"Huh? I don't think he's even Christy's type."

"What's not to like about him? He's cool, he's popular, he's fit. He's even on the track team, so that technically makes him a jock."

"She likes Ian," I said. "That's that."

Mark shrugged. He reached into his pocket, pulled out his cell to check the time, then sighed before returning his eyes to me. "We should probably get going," he said. "Mrs. Berry's class starts in a few minutes and we're clear on the other side of the school."

"Yeah," I said. I started forward, Mark at my side, but stopped short. "Go ahead without me."

"What're you going to do?"

I pulled my cell out and lifted it so Mark could see Christy's picture. "Gonna send her a text," I said. "Or a few of them. Whatever works best."

"You sure?"

"I'll be there. Don't worry."

With a short nod, Mark shrugged his binder up his arm and began to make his way down the hall.

Hey, I said, typing the message as quickly as I could on my touch screen. *I have to go to class, but text me. Let me know you're okay. Okay?*

With that, I glanced down the hall, waiting for her to answer. If she wanted to ditch class, I would go with her.

Those bitches suck. But I'll be okay. Ditching with Olivia. Back at lunch.

I quickly asked her if she wanted my company.

Go to class. It was cool seeing you with Mark. See you later.

With a sigh, I texted back that I loved her, then rushed to class.

Christy

It was a good thing I rarely wore makeup, or it would have been smeared all over my face. Olivia and I ditched all our morning classes and only came back to school at lunch time. We hid out at her house. It was one of the newer houses on the edge of town and we played with her cute little Chihuahua while watching all the weird morning talk shows. We learned way too much about celebrities and cooking.

Though the students aren't allowed to leave campus for lunch, I knew which side door was left unlocked to allow the teachers outside to smoke. We dodged through it before the regular smokers finished eating. Clutching our lunches, we headed down the hallway to the cafeteria.

We were almost there, safe and clear, without detection, when Ian stepped out of the boy's restroom and cut us off.

I gasped, clutching my lunch against my chest. Olivia almost slid into him. "Oops!"

I stared through my bangs in terror at Ian. He had barely avoided us slamming into him, and he looked at us in surprise. Slowly, he grinned.

"Hey, Christy, howya doing?"

I gulped. "Uh, okay."

"You kinda scared me the other night. For a second I thought you were going to barf on me again," Ian said, his bright blue eyes looking more amused than annoyed.

"I didn't barf," I said defensively. I looked at Olivia in alarm. "I didn't, right?"

"Only on the side of the road on the way home," Olivia said helpfully. "You were totally spared, dude." She popped her pink lollipop back in her mouth and grinned around it.

"Sorry about that. Most of the kids know the punch is spiked, but I guess you'd never been to one of my parties before."

"Uh. No." I winced. I sounded like a moron.

"Yeah, the whole Adam thing holds you back a little, huh?" Ian said sympathetically.

"Hey, he's my best friend and don't you dare talk shit about him!" I blurted out the words before my internal censor could kick in.

"Whoa, I didn't mean... " Ian held up his hands as if to ward me off.

"What *did* you mean?" Olivia demanded.

Ian shifted on his feet uncomfortably. "I will admit that I don't know how a dude can look at another guy and you know... "

I narrowed my eyes.

"... but that's his thing. As long as he doesn't look at me that way, I'm good." Ian smiled broadly. "My dad is way conservative about that stuff, but I'm open-minded."

"Yeah, sure you are," Olivia said darkly.

I felt close to tears again. I thought that Ian had stopped being a jerk about Adam when he stopped paying attention to him, but maybe I was wrong.

"Adam would never be interested in you," I said finally. "You're not his type."

Ian blinked, surprised. "I didn't mean... "

"Yeah, you don't mean a lot of stuff," I said, close to tears again.

Lapsing into silence, Ian stared at me thoughtfully. "You're mad at me."

"Yeah," I said, admitting it and inwardly laughing at the absurdity of it all. Ian was finally talking to me and all I felt was anger. "You know, just because someone is gay it doesn't mean they want to screw every guy around. They're just like us, you know. Looking for someone who will love and respect them. He'd never fall for someone like you."

Olivia put a supporting—or was it a warning?—hand on my arm.

"You only love yourself," I finished, my voice dropping.

Ian's beautiful blue eyes widened, anger filling them.

"I wish I had seen that before," I muttered, darting around him.

Olivia followed in my wake.

"That's not fair!" Ian shouted after me.

I kept my head down as I slipped into the cafeteria, Olivia on my heels. We made it to the corner table and found Mark and Adam sitting there. Drifter was eating with the drama club today. I fell into a chair and wiped away angry tears.

"What did they do *now*?" Adam demanded, starting to stand up.

Mark put his hand on his arm. "Don't upset her more."

"She kinda told off Ian," Olivia explained. "He made a stupid speech about tolerating gays as long as they don't hit on him."

I wiped my eyes with my fingers. "I'm just tired of people saying stupid stuff when it comes to you, Adam."

Mark reached out and took my hand. "You're a good friend, Christy."

Adam scooted around the table to hug me. The way he smells makes me think of good things. I clung to him for a second and he kissed my cheek.

"You didn't have to blow it with Ian for me, Christy," he said at last.

"As if I ever even had a chance," I said with a sigh.

Maybe it was seeing Mark sitting with Adam, or the light in Adam's eyes since Mark had kissed him, but I was finally seeing that I was making myself miserable over a boy who probably wasn't worth it. I clutched Adam's hand and smiled at him.

"Besides, who needs stupid boys when I have you?" I continued.

Mark's expression was quite somber as he watched us. I could see he was worried in some way. Adam gave him a slight smile and it touched me to see Mark return it with a warm one of his own.

"Who needs rotten guys when you got killer friends?" Olivia asked, grinning.

I smiled, thankful for all of them. "Exactly."

Embarrassed at my outburst, I pulled my hand away from Adam and tugged open my lunch. "I'm starved. Let's eat."

Adam

The only coffee café in Trinity Springs was virtually empty.

"So," Mark said, settling down directly across from me with his cup of steaming-hot coffee in hand. "Got any ideas for Mrs. Berry's poetry assignment?"

"Not particularly," I replied, ignoring the hot chocolate that simmered before me. "I just wish it was something simpler though, like writing a poem or something."

"You write poems?"

"Uh... sorta," I confessed, grinning when Mark offered me an easy smile. "What's that look for?"

"I'm a bit of a poetry aficionado myself, if you want to know the truth."

"Know any offhand?"

"Have you ever heard *For Annie?*"

"Who's it by?"

"Edgar Allan Poe."

I frowned. "I never even considered him," I shrugged.

Mark took a sip of his coffee, cleared his throat, and recited, as if he knew it by the back of his hand:

Thank Heaven! The crisis-
The danger is past,
And the lingering illness
Is over at last.

"It's a beautiful poem," he continued, taking another sip of his coffee while trying his hardest not to laugh. "What're you smiling at?"

"You," I said.

"That reminds me," Mark said. "About us." He placed his cup of coffee on the table, wrapped both hands around it, then sighed, the sound long, drawn out, and resembling something like the beginning of a long speech. When he didn't continue any further, I frowned and lifted my cup of hot chocolate, using it more to hide my expression than to actually take a drink off it.

What could Mark have on his mind that would have changed his mood all of a sudden?

Just when I thought I should ask, Mark cleared his throat again, lifted his eyes, then said, "I think we should come out."

"What?" I wasn't sure if I had heard him right.

"Come out," he continued. "You know... of the closet."

"Shh!" I hissed, jabbing a finger to my lips, my eyes flicking to the baristas cleaning the espresso machine and the few occupied tables around us. "They might hear you."

"Who?"

"We're in a small town, remember? *Trinity Springs?* Everyone knows everyone here."

"Oh," he frowned. "Right."

"Besides," I said, lowering my hand and my voice when I thought it was safe enough to continue. "Why would we do that?"

"To let people know about us."

Us? What was he talking about?

"I'm... not sure what you mean," I continued, leaning forward so I could hear whatever he had to say better.

"You know... *us.*"

"I'm... uh... not sure what you're talking about."

"Our relationship, Adam."

"What relationship?" I asked, more than a bit unnerved at the fact that people around us might possibly be listening. "We've only known each other for... what? Less than a week?"

Mark's eyes darkened a shade and a slight frown curled one side of his lip down.

Had I struck a nerve?

"I think it might be better... if we make it known," he continued, now obviously struggling with his words, "that we might be together."

"Why?"

"Well, for one, it'll get the Barbies off Christy's back. And two—"

The sound of a barista approaching cut him off. "Can I get you gentlemen anything?" she asked.

"More sugar," I said. She gave me an odd look before turning and scampering off. "I don't know if you're aware of this," I said, leaning forward once again, "but Trinity Springs isn't exactly the safest place to be gay."

"What do you mean?"

"I got the shit beat out of me in sixth grade by this guy named Skyler just because he thought I'd *looked* at him funny. That was in *sixth grade,* when *we were twelve.* I'm not saying it would happen again, but honestly, I don't want to take any chances."

"I can understand that," Mark said, though the tone in his voice had changed quite drastically since we'd begun our conversation. His eyes fell to his drink.

I nudged the toe of his boot with my foot. "Hey," I said. "Look at me."

It took him a moment to raise his eyes, but when I did, I smiled and tapped his boot again. "I think you're a cool guy," I said, "and there's nothing I'll ever be able to do to repay you for helping my friends out, especially Christy. I just don't want to take any chances on either of us getting hurt."

"I understand." Mark straightened his posture and gave me the biggest smile he could offer. "Sorry for pushing you. It wasn't my intention."

76

"It's okay," I said.

Mark tapped my shoe with the toe of his boot.

I smiled.

"Looks like someone has an English assignment," Mom commented as she stepped up behind me and peered over my shoulder.

"Yeah," I said, lifting my head. "I do."

"How'd your date with Mark go?"

I nearly spit out the water I was drinking. "Mom!"

"Well, *it* was a coffee *date*."

I did my best to swallow what was in my mouth as Mom laughed and made her way around the counter. "It was homework at the coffee café," I shrugged.

She paused, turned, then raised an eyebrow before laughing as Amelia darted to the room. "Hey sugarplum," she said. "How was school today?"

"It was fine," Amelia grumbled, hopping up into the stool next to me. She made sure to offer me a leery, all-knowing look. "What're *you* doing?"

"Homework," I said.

I still wasn't sure whether or not Amelia knew about what was going on between me and Mark. So far, Mom hadn't said anything to her, at least not to my knowledge, but even then I had to wonder. Amelia seemed to know *everything* that was going on. Nothing missed her eyes, or ears for that matter.

"Mom?" Amelia said, turning her head to look at our mother across the island.

"Yes, honey?"

"Does Adam have a boyfriend?"

This time, I couldn't stop myself from spitting water out of my mouth. "Amelia!"

"Adam!" Mom cried. "The mess you made!"

"Well, does he?" Amelia asked, indifferent to the reaction she'd just caused. "I heard him talking on his phone several times with *Mark*."

"No," I said, snagging a wad of paper towels from the rack. "I don't."

"So, who's Mark?" Her glare was accusing.

"None of your business, twerp."

Amelia took extra care in sticking her tongue out at me before darting out of the room.

"You can't be mad at her," Mom offered as I stooped to clean up the floor. "She's only ten."

"I'm not mad at her," I replied. "At least she's okay with me being gay,"

"It's all she's ever known, Adam."

"Still... I'm thankful more than anything."

"Well... I'm glad." She waited for me to stand up before giving me an eye. "So... how *was* your date with Mark?"

"It was fine," I said. "We talked."

"About?"

"The poetry assignment. Our friendship. What happened to Christy today at school."

"Wait. What?"

"The Barbies attacked."

"Them bitches," she said.

"They called Christy a," I hesitated and started to spell out the insult. "C-U—"

"I know how to spell!" Amelia called out cutting me off.

"We know you can honey!" Mom called back. "Really?" she then asked me. "And nobody heard this?"

"That's when I stepped in."

"Oh no. You didn't do anything too drastic, did you?"

"No. I just got between them and Christy."

"And?"

"Mark helped defend her and told them to back off."

"He did?" she asked, impressed.

"He did," I nodded.

"Good," she said. "I like that he stood up for Christy. Those girls deserve to be put in their place."

"I just wish they'd leave Christy alone," I sighed. I looked down at the textbook, closed it, then picked it up and started for the threshold leading out into the living room. "I think I'm gonna get online and do this. At least then I can find what I'm looking for."

"Good luck!" she said.

Despite all the weirdness of the day, I was actually starting to feel like I was having good luck.

Chapter 7

Confrontation

Christy

Today Olivia's lollipop was yellow. She sucked on it noisily as we wandered behind the cluster of the students on the field trip to the local history museum. I trudged along beside her, clutching the strap of my messenger bag. The bus ride over to the museum had been awkward. I had to sit near Ian and the Barbies. Drifter was in the back of the bus with the football players, so I had ended up alone, just staring out the window, ignoring the chatter around me. Olivia had ended up in the second bus with Adam and Mark. It was not a good omen for the rest of the day.

Our history teacher, Mrs. Guerra, is a hands-on type of teacher and decided it was best for us all to go to the local museum to learn about the history of Trinity Springs. The entire junior class was excused from classes for the day to go on the field trip.

It was a unique form of hell.

Once out of the bus, Olivia had caught up with me and we exchanged conspiratorial smiles as we glanced back at Mark and Adam trailing behind us. It made me happy to see them together even if no one else outside our little group realized what was happening between them.

In the last few weeks, the weather had grown cooler, the days had grown shorter, and the usual round of illnesses at the school started. It seems every year there is one terrible bug everyone ends up with. This year's big illness was pretty scandalous. It started with Jennifer, but quickly spread. Mononucleosis is called the "kissing disease," so immediately everyone began to speculate about who had been doing what with whom when it began to spread. Since Jennifer was patient zero, it was all the more scandalous. Jayden, the big ugly lout she often dated during the summer, started a bunch of horrible rumors about her, but the teachers held an assembly and blamed the outbreak on the water fountains.

Jennifer was back with the Barbies, but she had lost her tan during her illness and looked unusually pale. She followed in Courtney's wake, her head down, her eyes hidden behind big sunglasses.

"She looks bad," Olivia said as we trudged along the sidewalk toward the building that had once been the county courthouse. It had been replaced by a more modern building in the 70's and had fallen into disrepair before it had been converted into a museum in the 90's. It's massive, with three floors, lots of fancy windows, towering pillars, and pressed-tin ceilings.

Mrs. Guerra and the other history teachers herded us all toward the front of the building where the statue of the city's founder stood proudly. Jiri Skala's visage was emblazoned impressively in bronze. The town had been settled by Czech immigrants and a lot of the old traditions are a part of the town's culture. Well, at least as far as the festivals are concerned that drag tourists' dollars into the tills of local merchants.

Mrs. Guerra stepped into the shadow of the Jiri Skala's statue and began a long, very drawn out explanation about how the Czech leader had brought his people to Texas.

Adam and Mark scooted through the gathering of students to our side. Mark was looking pretty hot in a gray t-shirt that matched his eyes. He winked at me, jerking his head toward Ian. I barely caught Ian looking away from me.

I shrugged.

Ever since I had told off Ian, he appeared to actually notice me, therefore, I made a point of turning away if he caught my eye and heading in the other direction.

I tried to pay attention to what Mrs. Guerra was saying, but having lived here all my life it was hard to be impressed anymore by the Disney version of the immigration of poor farmers. I stifled a yawn and glanced over at Olivia.

Soooo boring, she mouthed.

Mrs. Guerra wrapped up her speech and we finally walked toward the air conditioned sanctum of the museum.

"I can't believe we had to have permission slips for this," Adam said wryly.

Mark laughed. "Yeah. It's not like a statue is going to come to life and eat us."

"That would make this trip interesting. Especially if it ate one of the Barbies," Olivia giggled, nudging me with her elbow.

To add insult to injury, we had to pay the two dollar "donation" fee to get into the museum. Like little kids, we had turned in our money and our permission slips to Mrs. Guerra. We lined up, and the museum curator counted off heads as we passed through the security checkpoint.

"Really? Security? In Trinity Springs?" Olivia narrowed her eyes and swung her purse onto the conveyor belt to be scanned.

The guard ushering us through the metal detector gave her a cold look. "Terrorists could attack anywhere."

"Uh huh," she said skeptically.

I stifled a laugh and chucked my bag onto the belt. The boys easily got through security since they weren't carrying anything with them. Olivia and I collected our things and joined the rest of the students in the foyer of the building. The rotunda above our heads was pretty impressive with its murals of the immigration.

"She keeps saying Czech Republic," Mark said, shaking his head.

"So?"

"They emigrated from Bohemia. The Czech Republic is a new country," Mark responded.

"Oh, a history nerd? Who would have thunk it?" Adam teased.

"My parents are from here," Mark reminded him. "I know all about this stuff."

"My parents are from here and I try not to know any of this," Adam answered.

"Let's see what kind of grade you end up with," Mark said, flashing his insanely charming grin.

The blush on Adam's cheeks was cute.

"May I please have your attention?" Mrs. Guerra called out.

We reluctantly obeyed as she handed out maps of the museum and our assignment.

"You need to answer all the questions and turn these to me by the end of the day. You can work in groups. List the names of everyone you worked with on this project on the back page. Cheating is not allowed. You must work together."

"And this gets even more boring," Olivia sighed.

I snatched my map and worksheet from Mrs. Guerra with a tight little smile. She hates me. I tend to fall asleep in her class.

"I expect you to work on this, Christy. Don't let Adam do all the work."

"Oh, I'll make sure she pulls her weight," Adam assured her, a very solemn look on his face.

Mrs. Guerra gave him an appraising look, her dark eyes scanning his face. "Make sure you do that." She walked on, passing out the stapled packets of paper.

Olivia, Adam, and I handed Mark our papers at the same time.

"Have fun with that," I told him.

"Don't get any answers wrong," Olivia added.

"Since you know all this stuff," Adam finished.

The three of us scampered off laughing.

"Hey!" Mark called after us, then followed.

After several hours of staring at maps, old photographs, and bits and pieces of a bygone era, my eyes were beginning to cross. The founding fathers of Trinity Springs had kept just about everything. They were real pack rats. We were still on the bottom floor and had yet to go up to the second floor where the time period from 1900 to present day was covered in great detail.

Standing behind the velvet rope that kept us from a recreation of a small family shack, I stared at the mannequin that was supposed to be a girl my age writing in a diary.

"I wonder what she's writing?" I said aloud.

"Dear Diary, living in this museum sucks." Olivia unwrapped another lollipop.

"She's probably very unhappy because her family is going to marry her off to the neighbor's son," Mark said somberly. He was scribbling away on his worksheet.

"Why would you say that?" I asked.

81

"Back then, girls your age were married and with kids already. Boys my age would be husbands. We'd be working our own land." Mark glanced at me with his keen gray eyes. "It wasn't as easy then to be a teenager as it is now."

"Especially for people like me," Adam scowled. "Ugh. I would have been forced to marry a *girl*."

I tickled Adam. "And ended up with girl cooties!"

"Also known as babies," Olivia said, making a face.

Adam fought me off and grabbed my hands. "I would have married you though."

"Yeah? Really?"

"Oh, yeah. Cause you'd let me have illicit affairs behind your back," Adam answered, trying to tickle me.

"I'd want details afterward!"

"That's 'cause you're a perv," Adam remarked. He wrapped his arms around my chest and lifted me off the ground, swinging me around.

I laughed, enjoying the moment.

"Stop that," Mark's voice said sharply, cutting through our roughhousing. A second later, he pushed us apart.

"Hey," Adam protested.

Mark's handsome face was twisted into a scowl. "We'll get in trouble."

Olivia widened her eyes, then slowly rolled them. "Whatevs."

"Mr. Black," Mrs. Guerra called out from nearby. "Nurse Schulz is here for you."

"What's up?" Adam asked, his brow furrowing.

"I have to go get my insulin shot," Mark answered with a sigh. "I'll be back after lunch. See you then."

Mark gave us back our handouts, then walked briskly toward Mrs. Guerra and the school nurse.

"He was a little testy," Olivia noted.

Adam slightly lifted his shoulders. "I think he's just wanting a good grade."

"Or moody that you won't commit," I suggested.

Adam rubbed his hair with his hand, mussing it up, but it looked cute. "Well, yeah. But I believe in taking it slow. I mean, he's like the first guy who's ever liked me."

"And he's unbelievably hot. I totally see why you're not going for it." I poked him in the chest. "Wimp."

"Hey! I'm a cautious kinda guy. I just want to make sure that it's the real thing and not rush into anything."

"My spell totally worked and you know it," I said, continuing to poke him.

Adam laughed, fighting me off.

"Spells, pffft," Olivia intoned.

I've let Olivia believe I'm a wanna be witch and I'm fine with that. She's cool with most things about me, so her dismissal of my potential magic powers is something I can overlook. Especially because I have yet to have the big magical growth spurt my parents keep promising. I'm such a broken witch.

The students picnicked outside on food brought in from a local sandwich shop. Drifter was part of a different group of students, but came over to say hello for a few minutes while we waited in line. Afterward, we found some shade under a tree and sat down to munch on our sandwiches and chips.

Though sometimes I hate our small town, today it was really pretty with some of the trees starting to turn color. Brightly colored leaves danced over the grass while we ate and the breeze was fresh and relaxing.

"I so want a nap after this," Olivia moaned.

"I know. It's such a great day to be anywhere but here," I lamented.

"Eh, it could be worse," Adam said, loudly crunching a chip. "We could be trapped in a classroom right now."

Adam is good at making valid points.

All the water I had been drinking from the water fountains finally decided it wanted out. I finished off my sandwich and excused myself. When I left my two friends, they were both lying under the tree chatting, looking like they were about to nod off. I slipped through the back door of the museum, entering the cool gloom of the building. The restrooms were located in a narrow hall near the only elevator in the building. I hurried toward the door, hoping I was ahead of the line of girls that would eventually end up forming. There are never enough bathrooms for women in these facilities. I was just pushing the door open when I heard low voices speaking nearby.

The only reason I decided to spy is because one of the voices sounded scarily familiar and I heard Adam's name said very clearly.

It was Jayden and his cronies.

On tiptoes, I moved closer to the men's bathroom, straining to hear. I couldn't make out the words that were being uttered because whoever was inside the restroom was speaking in low tones. Every few seconds Jayden's voice would answer, louder, harsher, angrier. Again I heard Adam's name. Chills slid down my spine. If someone was planning to hurt Adam, I would do something terrible to them. I didn't know what, but I would!

What happened next is difficult to explain. I'm not even sure how it all went down, to tell the truth. I heard the quick approach of footsteps from inside the men's bathroom and tried to back away to the refuge of the women's as fast as I could while not making a sound. But as the door yawned open and a boy began to emerge from the restroom, I knew I would never make it. I was suddenly very afraid to be discovered and threw up my hands.

I felt something inside of me physically pop. It was a swift pain, then my body slid back against the wall and pressed against it. It was as if I were pinned there by a great hand.

Mark stepped out of the restroom and looked around curiously, his gray eyes sweeping up and down the length of the hall. I know his eyes settled on me more than once, but he never saw me. I could see the intensity in his gray eyes as he looked around and the tension in his neck and shoulders when he stepped into the center of the corridor, looking back and forth. At last, he seemed satisfied and walked toward the exit briskly.

I let out a breath I didn't even realize I was holding and the invisible hand that had held me in place vanished. I scrambled into the ladies' room and was just closing the door when I saw Jayden step out of the bathroom rubbing the back of his neck and looking confused and maybe a little mad.

My nerves and my bladder got the best of me, and I scurried into a stall to hide and take care of my business all at the same time. As I sat with my feet propped up on the back of the stall door, I worried that Jayden would slip into the restroom to find out who had been spying on him. With trembling fingers, I pulled my phone out of my hoodie and started to text Adam. I was only a few letters in when a messaged popped up from him.

Mark is back. Hurry up.

I stared at the screen, trying to make sense of what had just occurred. I had heard Mark in the restroom talking to Jayden, but what did that mean? Was Jayden harassing Mark? Did he think Mark was gay? But Mark had been odd when he had stepped out of the restroom. He hadn't looked upset. He had appeared maybe a little anxious over the possibility of being overheard.

And then, somehow, I had gone invisible or something, because Mark had not seen me.

So what did it all mean?

Did it even mean anything?

I hesitated, then finally texted that I would be out soon.

I finished in the restroom and was just drying my hands when a throng of girls arrived. It had to be the Barbies, of course. I shoved past them and out into the hallway. Tucking my hands into my pockets, I walked with my shoulders hunched up and my head down. I wanted to get outside to my friends and put the weird episode behind me.

My thoughts were a whirlwind within my mind. I obviously had overreacted and somehow made myself disappear. Was that horrible popping sensation inside me my power finally awakening? I was so over the fieldtrip now, but had no choice but to slog through the rest of the day.

Of course, I had to make things even worse by not watching where I was going. I yanked the door open, stepped forward, and slammed into Ian's chest so hard I bit the inside of my cheek, smacked my nose against his hard pecs, and sent myself ricocheting to the floor.

"Christy!" Ian quickly leaned over to help me up, his hands trying to tuck under my arms.

I flailed at him, trying to get him to let go. I was suddenly terrified I would be too heavy for him to pick up. Surprising me, he got a good grip and heaved me off the floor.

"Are you okay?"

Tears were tracing down my cheeks and my nose throbbed. I raised my hand to my lips as I tasted blood. "I'm fine," I mumbled, trying to get around him.

"Christy, I wanted to say—"

I held up one hand, warding him off, and fled out the door.

When I reached my group of friends, I was still dabbing blood from my lips with the corner of my hoodie. Adam immediately rushed to my aid while Olivia thrust some napkins at me. I felt stupid and paranoid about the entire episode until I saw Mark's gray eyes watching me.

They were still beautiful, but they were hard as slate, thoughtful, and somehow frightening.

Adam

I stayed behind in the school library to copy some notes I wasn't able to take for French class due to the field trip. At least twenty minutes after the bell had rung, I left the original notes off at my French teacher's room and hurried out of the nearly empty school. I had missed not only my opportunity to catch a ride home with Christy, but also to take the bus. At least the day wasn't too warm for a long walk home.

I shifted my books higher up my arm and continued along the field that led off the school property. I was just about to step onto the sidewalk when I heard someone call out.

"Hey, Adam," the voice said. "Stay behind to play with dresses in drama class?"

"I don't play with dresses," I said, turning to face the owner of the voice. "They're all in your size anyway."

Jayden Croft, captain of the football team and the bane of my existence, stood no more than ten feet away, blowing smoke out of his mouth and readjusting his hold on his cigarette. Buzzed military cut gleaming in the light of the midafternoon sun, scarred lip turned down into a scowl, he flicked the butt of his cigarette out of his hand just as his buddies came up. Flanked by Brian and Alex, they began to clear the distance between us at a pace that scared the living hell out of me.

Great. Jayden Croft and his meathead jock friends were going to beat the shit out of me. My day couldn't have gotten any better.

"Stupid faggot. I'm not a sissy boy like you," Jayden continued, flexing his fingers and popping his knuckles. "I'm glad to find you here though. I've been looking for you."

"Why?" I asked warily.

"Because word is you've been spreading some pretty nasty rumors about me."

Rumors? What was he talking about?

"What?" I asked, trying to remember whether or not I'd publicly said something about Jayden in the past few days.

"Don't *what* me, faggot. You know what you said."

"I don't have any idea what you're talking about, *meathead*. Leave me alone."

"Get 'em, guys."

Brian and Alex burst forward.

It took me less than half a second to run. I pumped my legs as hard as I could in a desperate attempt to clear the property line just as a pair of arms grabbed me from behind and pulled me backward.

A short moment later, I felt the flat of a palm slap across my face.

I blinked, stunned.

The sun shifted behind a cloud.

Jayden stood directly before me, fist up and no more than an inch away from my face. "Feel that?" he asked, slapping the right side of my face with his other hand another time. "Feel that, faggot? Huh? Feel that?"

"Leave me alone," I somehow managed, kicking at the shins of the person holding me.

"Oh no. You're not getting off that easy. Not this time."

"That was your fault," I said, grimacing as the bully slapped my face the third and hardest time. "You're the one who threw the rock."

The last major incident I had with Jayden was when Christy's car had sustained damage when Jayden had thrown a fist-sized rock at it. Because of the zero-tolerance rule about fighting and bullying, he'd been expelled for two weeks.

"You shouldn't have been causing shit then, huh? And now you're causing shit again! Narcing on me throwing the rock is one thing, but spreading rumors that *I* tried to come on to *you?* That's another story."

He reared his hand back.

I spit in his face.

He slammed his fist into my gut and sent me to my knees.

"Now listen here, fag," Jayden said, tilting my head up so he could look me straight in the eyes. "I'm going to teach you a lesson you're *never* going to forget, and I promise it's going to hurt like hell. And if you narc on me again, I'll make sure you never talk again. Pick him up, guys."

Brian and Alex lifted me to my feet and locked my arms behind my back.

"Get him," Alex said. "Teach him never to mess with you."

"Oh, don't worry," Jayden said. "I will."

I closed my eyes, anticipating the first blow.

The sound of squealing tires rang through my ears and opened my eyes.

Mark's car rested no more than a few feet away. Mark rounded the front of the vehicle in a few short steps. "Hey!" he called. "Why don't you pick on someone your own size?"

"Gladly," Jayden said, charging him.

Brian and Alex released their grip on me. I fell forward, but managed to catch myself on my hands and knees before I landed on my face.

I lifted my head.

Jayden threw the first punch. Mark dodged out of the way and ran straight for me.

Brian and Alex sprinted forward.

Mark moved fast, easily evading Brian. He had just reached me when Alex tackled him to the ground.

"Mark!" I cried out.

Mark managed to get his foot up, planted it into Alex's gut, and used the momentum to send him flying over his head. His leg then lashed out, hooked the back of Brian's heels just as the jock was about to kick him, and yanked him off his feet.

Mark rose swiftly.

Jayden ran forward.

Mark grabbed the meathead by the arms and threw him to the ground as if he were nothing. Jayden's chin impacted with the asphalt with a resounding crack.

"Leave him alone!" Mark shouted.

"Sticking up for the fag?" Jayden said, spitting out blood.

"Yeah," Mark replied. "Because he's *my* fag."

Reaching down, Mark took hold of my arm, helped me to my feet, and guided me toward the car.

"Come on," he said.

"You'll be sorry you ever messed with me!" Jayden cried out. "You'll be sorry, Mark Black!"

Mark helped me into the car, then stalked back to where the three boys were getting back on their feet.

"Mark!" I screamed. "No!"

Fear filled me as I watched the big, hulking football players descending on Mark. When Alex dove for Mark, I scrambled to get out of the car to stop them. My stomach throbbing in pain, I stumbled onto the asphalt and could only watch as the bullies attacked.

A fist flew into Mark's face.

I cried out.

Blood sprayed.

I was afraid that it was Mark's blood flying through the air. A second later, Alex was hurled aside, his face slick with the blood gushing from his nose.

"You like that?" Mark roared, grabbing the back of Alex's shirt and dragging him on the ground. *"YOU LIKE THAT?"*

Alex grunted and struggled to rise. Mark dropped him to the ground and pressed his foot into the jock's back, pinning him.

Mark was so consumed by rage that he didn't even see Brian coming up from behind him.

"Look out!" I cried.

Before the bully could strike, Mark turned and backhanded Brian across the face. One more punch to the side of the head was enough to render him useless on the ground.

Jayden stumbled to his feet. He turned, spat out a mouthful of blood, then growled and charged forward.

Mark grabbed Jayden and tossed him.

The jock landed with enough force to knock the breath out of his lungs.

"Don't worry," Mark said, reaching up to wipe the blood from his face as he began to stalk toward Jayden. "There's more where that came from."

"No!" I called. "No Mark! Stop! *They're not worth it!*"

"You're worth it," Mark growled.

I ran forward, snatching at Mark's arm. *"They're* not! Let's go!"

The muscles in his arm tensed, then loosened when he looked into my face. The anger burned in his beautiful gray eyes and his lips slightly trembled rage. With a short nod, he let me pull him toward the car.

Sliding into the driver's seat, Mark buckled his seatbelt, sighed, then shifted the car into drive, and accelerated away from the three boys pulling themselves off the ground.

It wasn't until several minutes later, when we were a fair distance away from the school and on our way to my house that he pulled over. He killed the engine. His eyes were livid with anger.

"Mark," I said. "Are you—"

He slammed his fists into the steering wheel.

The horn went off.

I jumped in my seat.

Mark threw the door open and made a move to get out.

"Mark," I said, reaching forward to grab him. "Please, don't—"

"They hurt you," he growled, a bead of blood sliding down his bloodied hairline and over one eyebrow. "They deserved it."

Mark stepped out of the car.

After untangling myself from my own seatbelt, I slid to the driver's side and gripped the tail of Mark's shirt before he could stalk off.

"It's okay," I said, the muscles in my arm tensing as Mark tried to pull away. "It's okay Mark. It's over."

"It's not over!" he shouted, twisting out of my grasp. "They hurt you, Adam! *They hurt you!"*

"But it's over," I said. *"Please,* Mark. Just calm down and listen to me for a second."

The fire in his eyes was unlike anything I had ever seen: mouth curled into a snarl, fists clenching and joints popping-even his skin had an abnormally red glow. His rage burned strong, and for a moment I wasn't sure just what I was going to do. It seemed nothing I could do would ever stop him.

"Mark," I said. "It's over. Please. Stop."

He raised his fist, slammed it down on the roof of the car, then growled, reminding me of a lion moving in for the kill.

Defeated, I collapsed into the driver's seat.

A sob escaped my chest.

All tension in the air ceased to exist almost instantaneously.

"Adam?" Mark asked, stepping closer. "Adam... Adam? Are you all right?"

"No I'm not all right!" I cried. "I just nearly gotten the shit beat out of me and then you went berserk!"

"I'm... I'm sorry," he said, reaching forward to take my hand.

"There's blood all over your face," I said. "God, Mark-it looks like you killed someone."

"Are you hurt?"

"No."

"Your face."

"What?"

Mark reached up and brushed the back of his hand along the right side of my face. "Look in the mirror," he said.

I glanced in the rearview mirror. I was surprised to see what looked like the beginnings of a bruise beginning to flower across my cheekbone. "It doesn't hurt," I said, then grimaced as his hand pressed against my skin. "Okay. Yeah. That hurts."

88

He gestured for me to move over. I climbed into the passenger seat and Mark slid back behind the wheel. He took several deep breaths, steadying himself.

"What were you doing at school so late anyway?"

"Taking notes." I paused. "What were *you* doing?"

"Trying to find a book in the library," Mark said. "Any idea why they followed you?"

"Something about me spreading a rumor that Jayden 'came on to me' or something like that." I sighed and bowed my head. Though I told myself I wouldn't cry, the tears came anyway, hard and fast, burning from my eyes and scalding my cheeks. "Dammit, Mark. Just... *dammit!*"

"Hey, hey," Mark said, taking hold of my shoulders. "Adam, listen to me. Everything's fine. You're safe now."

"They could've hurt me a lot worse than they did," I said, unable to restrain the sob that followed. "It could've just been just like in sixth grade and Skylar... he..." I trembled in the moments I couldn't finish.

"What'd he do to you?"

"He almost sent me to the hospital. That's how bad he beat me up."

"But I was there this time," Mark said.

"Yeah, but just because you saved me once doesn't mean you're going to be able to do it every time."

Mark gave no reply. Instead, I bowed my face into my hands and sobbed.

An arm slid around my shoulder. I melted into the touch, then the embrace that followed.

"Shh," Mark said, bowing our heads together. "It's okay, Adam. Don't cry."

Regardless, I did, though at that moment I could've cared less.

It took me at least ten minutes to calm down. By the time the tears and sobs stopped coming, I felt so drained that I just wanted to sleep.

"Adam," Mark said.

"Yeah?" I asked.

"I want to be there for you," he said.

"What?"

"When things get bad. When you're sad. When you're angry. When you're by yourself and you think you're all alone in the world. I... I want you to know that you have someone standing by your side."

I raised my eyes.

When our gazes fell upon one another's, I felt a deep, longing pain in my heart for an answer to a question that I'd asked my entire life.

Was I alone?

I shook my head.

"Yeah," I said, leaning my head against his shoulder.

"Yeah what?"

"I want to be with you."

Mark pressed his lips to the side of my temple.

I sighed.

In that moment, things seemed more peaceful than I could have ever possibly imagined.

"Make sure you let your mom know what happened," Mark said, taking hold of my shoulders as we stood on my front porch. "Let her know that I didn't hit them for any reason but self-defense."

"I know," I said, reaching up to press my smaller hand atop one of his.

"And if the cops come by, just tell them the truth: *you* didn't do anything. I was the one who fought."

"Don't worry. I will."

He waited a moment to see if I would respond any further, then bowed his head against mine for a brief moment. Then he turned and walked back to the car, my gaze following him the whole way there.

As the car disappeared around the corner, I reached up, gingerly applied some pressure to the side of my face, and took a deep breath. My mom was going to freak out.

I opened the door and stepped inside.

"Adam?" my mother's voice called out from deep in the house. "I was getting worried. I was just about to call when—" She rushed toward me then saw my wounds. "What the *hell* happened to your face?"

"Long story," I said.

"Who did this to you?" She came to me, her hand reaching to lift my chin so she could see the damage.

She led me down the hall to the bathroom and sat me down on the closed lid of the toilet as I explained what had happened. Throughout my story, Mom took meticulous care in cleaning my face with a warm washcloth which, when pulled away from my face, was spotted with blood.

"I can't believe this," Mom said, continuing to pat my face. "This is absolutely ridiculous."

"I didn't say those things about Jayden, Mom."

"I know you didn't, honey. Why would anyone spread those rumors to begin with?" She fussed with my face, her brow furrowed with concern. "You and Jayden?" She shivered.

"Mom, that's just... ugh. Gross, really."

"I can agree with that sentiment. That boy did inherit his father's looks."

Amelia peeked into the bathroom. Unlike usual, she made no snide remark, and she didn't make any attempts to try to steal the attention from me. "Mom?" she asked.

"Yes honey?"

"Can I have a soda?"

"Go ahead, hon."

Amelia disappeared down the hall to grab her drink and return to her cartoons in the family room.

"She must've noticed my face," I said.

"She cares, she just doesn't know what to say," Mom assured me. "Your dad will be furious. He'll want me to call the police and report this." She began to dab my face with Bactine, making me wince.

"Mom, you can't."

"Why not? Look what they did to you!"

"Mark saved me."

Mom paused in treating my wounds. "He did?"

"Yeah, he did. And he beat them up really good. If you report it to the police, I don't want him to get in trouble."

Understanding bloomed in her eyes, and she nodded. "God," she said, drawing me into her arms. "I think he's my new hero."

"And he asked me to be his boyfriend."

"What?"

I pulled away from her embrace and looked into her eyes. "He told me he wanted to be there for me," he said. "And protect me."

"You know he can't protect you from everyone, Adam."

"I know, but... he cares about me, Mom."

"He must if he's willing to put himself in the line of fire." Mom looked at the clump of bloodied cotton balls, sighed, then tossed them into the trash before returning her attention to me. "I guess we have a guest of honor for your seventeenth birthday. You know, other than you."

I grinned, nodded, and winced as she continued to bandage my face.

"Maybe if you're lucky, you'll be healed up for your party."

"Mom, I'm always pretty," I teased her.

"Yes, you are!" She grinned at me. "You take after me after all!"

Christy

My hand was trembling when I hung up the phone with Adam. I couldn't believe the story he had just told me. I was so scared and angry, I felt like throwing up yet again. Jayden had *hurt* my best friend. I clenched my hands tightly at my side as dark thoughts filled my mind. Curling up on my bed, I pressed the heels of my hands against my eyes, trying not to give in to the terrible desire to rush downstairs and find a spell that would make Jayden regret ever touching Adam.

I was grateful that Mark had saved Adam, but it killed me to think of Adam being hurt even a little bit. Tears slid down my nose and created a puddle on my pillow. Anger gave way to guilt. I should have waited for Adam to finish at the school instead of rushing off. I was annoyed by Ian staring at me on the bus back to the school and had bailed as soon as we arrived in the parking lot. If I had just stuck around, Adam never would have been pummeled by Jayden and his crew.

At least Mark had been there...

I sat up sharply and stared at Callie with widened eyes. She was in the middle of cleaning her front paw and paused to regard me curiously.

"Mark and Jayden were talking today," I said to her.

She slowly dragged her tongue over her paw, her expression contemplative.

My thoughts were a whirlwind. What did that mean? Did it mean anything? Was it just a coincidence?

I scooted off the bed and hit the floor running, skidded around the edge of my bedroom doorway and nearly ran into the broom.

91

"Ugh! You're such a sneak!"

It swept around me, then flew down the stairs.

Bounding after it, I could feel my heart thundering in my chest. I wiped away my tears as I jumped down the last few steps.

"Mom!"

"In the kitchen!"

Callie raced into the kitchen ahead of me, leaped onto the island countertop, and yowled at my mom.

"What do you mean?" Mom stared at Callie.

Callie cast a look in my direction.

"Well, Christy? Is this true? Are you upset over something that happened to Adam?" she asked, carefully shaping oatmeal and raisin cookies on a baking sheet with a spoon.

I frowned and slumped against the counter, reaching for one of the freshly baked cookies. "Yeah, it's true."

Callie brushed up under my chin with her head, her tail wrapping around my neck, before she settled beside the fruit bowl near my elbow.

"The broom is spying on me again," I groused.

Mom sighed. "I'll talk with it."

"It's creepy."

"It's just curious about you, that's all." Mom turned and shoved the baking sheet into the oven. "Now, what's this about something happening to Adam and you being upset with Mark?"

I nibbled on the edge of the cookie, hiding behind my bangs. "I'm probably overreacting."

Mom's crazy curls were tucked up in a ponytail and she was wearing a long flowing red dress with a peacock shawl wrapped around her waist. "Talk to me."

"Okay, I overhead Jayden and Mark talking in the boy's restroom today."

"And this is unusual why?"

"Jayden hates gay guys."

"Does he know Mark is gay?"

"He does now. Mark beat up Jayden for hurting Adam."

Mom arched her brows. "Okay, I'm missing something..."

I quickly explained the field trip, Adam being attacked, and Mark rescuing him. I left out my possible magic disappearing trick though. It sounds lame, but the thought of telling my mom made me feel like I was telling her about my first period. Pure awkwardness. Plus, Adam was more important.

"Ah, I get it now." She took a cookie and leaned against the counter, a thoughtful look on her face, chewing slowly.

"It's just kinda weird that Mark was talking to the guy who beat up Adam."

"What if Mark was telling Jayden to leave Adam alone?"

"The really weird thing, Mom, was that Jayden told Adam that he heard that Adam was claiming Jayden hit on him. Adam would *never* say that. Even as a joke. We're snarky, but that sort of thing can get us beat up. Well, it did." I felt like crying again at the thought of anyone hurting Adam.

Mom and I munched on our cookies, pondering the situation.

"You don't think Mark told Jayden that Adam said that, do you?"

I shook my head, reconsidered, then shrugged. "I don't know."

"So what is Mark like usually? I only met him the one time he was pretending to be your date."

"Sweet, cute, nice, funny, kind of quiet at times." I reached for another cookie. "Plus, he really is into Adam. You can see it so clearly. How he looks at Adam is really... annoying."

Mom laughed and opened the refrigerator to retrieve the milk jug. She poured three glasses out. I was about to correct her when dad entered the kitchen.

"What's up? I got your summons." He pulled a stool out and plopped into it. He was in jeans and a t-shirt that read 'You're wrong.'

Mom set a glass in front of him, obviously expecting me to answer him.

"Uh..." I managed.

"Is this dinner?" He eyeballed the plate of cookies.

"Sure," my mom answered.

"Awesome! I love cookie dinner night!" He took four and began to munch on them. "So, someone talk."

With a sigh, I told him the story.

"Well, it does seem fishy, squirt."

"Don't call me squirt."

"Princess, I have to say it does seem a little on the odd side. But how would it benefit Mark to have his potential boyfriend beat up?"

"How does it benefit him to save his boyfriend from being beat up?" Mom countered.

I winced. "Ugh! No! He wouldn't!"

"What do we know about this Mark?" Dad tilted his head toward me.

I shrugged. "He's new in town."

"A knight in shining armor is always appealing," Dad said. He was obviously pondering the whole scenario. "I remember the time that Luna demon was after your mom and I saved her. That's how we ended up with you, kiddo."

"Eww. Way too much information!" I plugged my ears.

Mom pulled my fingers out. "Do you think Mark might do that? Set up Adam?"

"That's the thing, I have no clue! I really don't know him like Adam does."

My dad shrugged. "He seemed nice enough when he was here."

Frowning, my mom sipped her milk.

"Should I tell Adam?" I asked cautiously.

"Tell him what? That his new guy might have set him up?" Shaking his head, my dad touched my arm. "You have zero proof. Just suspicions."

"Can we cast a truth spell?" I asked hopefully.

"Selfish gain," my mom said automatically.

"It would be for Adam!" I protested.

"But you're doing it so *you* feel better," Dad pointed out.

"Mark seemed like a nice boy when he was here." Mom ate another cookie and washed it down with more milk.

Callie started drinking my milk and I let her. I didn't feel much like eating anymore. I laid my head on my folded arms. "It's not fair!"

Rubbing my shoulder, my dad said, "That's life, kiddo. You really shouldn't say anything until you know for sure. For all you know Mark and Jayden were talking about the weather."

"It's always just been you and Adam and now things are changing. You may be feeling threatened by Mark," my mom said tactfully.

I glanced up at my mom. I felt a smidge guilty over her comment. I did feel a little threatened by Mark. Adam was spending a lot more time with him. Of course, I was hanging out with Olivia a lot, but it was not the same thing. "Think I'm jealous?"

Mom shrugged. "Maybe. But there could be something to all of this. I wouldn't talk to Adam about it though."

"Talk to Mark," my dad suggested.

I scrunched my face up in disapproval.

"If you're really concerned, talk to Mark. Find out the truth, kiddo."

I flicked my eyes back and forth, studying my parents. They're big dorks, but they're smart. "Fine. When I get a chance."

"It may be nothing," my dad continued. "And talking to Mark may smooth out any misunderstandings."

I nodded, resting my chin on my hands. "I hate my life."

"No, you don't." Mom patted my head.

"It's just puberty. Soon you'll get the big ol' magic whoosh and feel even more crazy. Teenage angst and magic puberty. Oh, joy! Can't wait!" Dad grinned at me playfully.

"About that... " I said.

Both my parents leaned toward me.

I told them about going invisible.

They broke out laughing.

I hate my life.

Chapter 8

Good Times

Adam

"You know how nervous I get when my mom throws one of these things," I said, adjusting my cell phone against my ear so I could rummage through my closet. I had yet to find what I was going to wear to what my mom was calling my 'birthday slash new boyfriend' party.

"You'll be just fine," Christy said. "Besides, I don't get what you're so nervous about. It's just a party."

"About me, and most importantly: about me and Mark."

"Don't worry. It's no big deal."

"You'd get after me if I said anything remotely like this if it was your party."

"I would not!"

"Oh. That's right. You'd probably just throw up all over everyone."

"Bite me, Adam."

"Gladly." I held the phone before my mouth and clicked my teeth. "When're you going to be here anyway?"

"I'm waiting on Olivia," Christy replied. "Anyway, we'll be there soon. And remember-don't be nervous. Your mom is awesome! And she will embarrass the crap out of you, so just prepare for it."

"Yeah. I guess you're right."

"Bye, bye, birthday-boy."

"Bye."

I hung up the phone and turned to view the scene before me. My bed was almost entirely covered with the shirts I'd found too boring or plain. At this rate it didn't seem like I'd find anything that would impress Mark. Then again, when I thought about it, would he even care?

"Adam!" my mother called.

"Yeah!" I called back.

"Someone's here to see you!" she returned in a sing-song voice.

Crap.

I stripped out of the undershirt I was wearing, tossed it into my dirty clothes hamper, then randomly dug through my pile of shirts. I only realized the shirt was a pale salmon color after I put it on.

Oh well. I couldn't do anything about it now.

After taking a moment to examine myself in the mirror, I smoothed my hair, then ran out of my bedroom and barreled down the stairs.

I could faintly hear the sound of two people talking coming from the kitchen.

"It's so nice to finally meet you," my mother said. "Really, Mark, I can't say it enough. What you did for Adam the other day was just awesome!"

"Hey," I said, stepping into the kitchen.

"Hey," Mark replied.

He stood in the front entrance with an arm braced on the doorjamb and the other pressed against his side. In a dark v-neck that showed off his muscular upper body, a pair of blue jeans and his usual black boots, he looked the image of perfection-much more than I did, considering it was my own birthday party.

"What're you doing here so early?" I asked.

"I thought I'd surprise you," he replied. I couldn't help but blush.

"Aww. How sweet," my mom replied.

Mark smiled, though he made no move to step forward. Instead, he readjusted his place in the doorway and continued to watch me with his calm gray eyes.

What was taking him so long to come in? I briefly considered the idea that he could be nervous because he was meeting my mother for the first time, but Mark didn't seem like the nervous type. He exuded confidence. He shouldn't have been nervous at all.

"Well," Mom said, beckoning him in, "don't just stand there! Come in, come in!"

"Thanks, Mrs. Hunter," Mark replied.

I was caught off-guard when he came up, leaned forward and placed a soft kiss on my lips. The sound and flash of a picture being taken lit up the room. "Mom!" I cried.

"Your first!" she gushed, artfully darting away as I made a playful move to grab the camera.

"Mom!"

"Ha! Gotcha!"

Mark slid an arm around my shoulders and drew me against his side. "To answer your question," he said, "I wanted to beat the crowd."

"Why?"

"Because I wanted to meet your mom before everyone arrived."

The sound of another picture being taken drew both of our attention. "Mom," I groaned.

"That was the last one," she blatantly lied.

Smiling, I looked into the living room just in time to see Amelia step into view, dressed in a casual pink-and-white-flowered dress.

"Aww!" Mom cried. "Am! You look so adorable!" She took a picture.

"You must be Mark," Amelia said, completely disregarding our mother as she narrowed her eyes at my boyfriend.

Oh no. What was Amelia up to now?

"Hi," Mark said, crouching down and extending his hand. "You must be Amelia."

"Yeah," she said. "I am."

She gingerly reached out, touched Mark's palm, then pulled her hand away before looking over at our mother. "When're we eating?" she asked.

"As soon as everyone arrives," Mom said. She took another quick picture of Amelia, much to my sister's displeasure, then looked at us. "Why don't you boys sit here in the kitchen while I step out for a smoke?"

"All right," I said, acknowledging the all-knowing eye she offered before she stepped out on the back porch.

Mark did a visual sweep of the house. "Wow," he said. "This is nice."

The kitchen was fairly impressive. Dressed in fine white paints, intricate wood cabinets and a sweeping, checkered linoleum floor, it resembled something classic while still sticking to its more modern roots. Add in the entire line of stainless-steel appliances and you have the Hunter family kitchen.

"It's nice," I shrugged, seating myself on one of the island's stools. "At least, I think it is."

"It is," Mark agreed. He scanned the kitchen a second time, taking in the 'Happy Birthday Adam' sign hanging above the kitchen/living-room threshold, then returned his attention to me. "How many people are going to be here?"

"You, Christy, Olivia, Drifter..."

"Anyone else?"

"Nope, just us." I shrugged.

It was hard to believe that no more than three or four days ago Mark had almost beat to a pulp the three biggest and toughest jocks in school. Here, dressed in nice clothes and with a smile on his face, he looked nothing like my furious defender, my knight in shining armor. I was surprised to notice that his hands were now fully healed. After the fight, his knuckles had been busted pretty badly.

"Mark?" I asked, leaning forward in the hopes that Amelia wouldn't hear.

"Yeah?" he asked.

I touched one of his long, elegant hands. "Your hands are already healed?"

Mark blinked. His beautiful gray eyes darkened to the point where they almost turned black. "Oh, yeah. Neosporin is great stuff." He grinned at me, his mood brightening. "I'm fine, Adam. You don't have to worry about me."

"It's just... it hurts to think you got injured protecting me. You were so angry at them. I don't even know how to describe it."

"Hard to believe?" He waited for my nod before continuing. "Yeah. I guess you can say I have a split personality when it comes to that sort of thing. I will always defend you."

"I know you will," I said, reaching down to take his hand. "You proved it to me that day."

97

Mark leaned in, wrapped his free arm around me, holding me in a tight embrace before pulling away.

The door opened.

Mom sauntered in, closely followed by Christy.

"Happy birthday!" Christy cried, setting what looked to be a tub of punch on the floor before throwing her arms around me. "I can't believe you're already seventeen!"

"Thanks, Christy," I said, looking up at both Olivia and Drifter as they filed in behind her. "Hey guys."

"Hey," they both said.

Christy held on to me for another short moment, then reached down before liftingd the tub of punch and saying, "Hi, Mrs. Hunter."

"Hi, Christy," my mom said, hugging her after she set the punch on the counter. She spotted Olivia and made a beeline toward her. "We met only briefly, but I just want to welcome you to our home!"

Olivia's regular lollipop was green today, which stained her teeth a pale shade of lime when she opened her mouth and smiled. "It's very nice to meet you! Adam and Christy told me all about you."

Mom fastened a sparkling eye on me. "Oh, really?"

Olivia nodded.

Waving her hands, my mother laughed. "Oh, it's all true! All of it! Especially the shoe fetish!" She extended her small foot so everyone could see her sparkling high-heeled shoe that looked like something Lady Gaga would wear. "I'm a shoe whore!"

Mom took her time gushing over the group and then led us into the living room. The couches had been rearranged to face the TV so we could watch movies later on.

"Oooh, let's get this party started!" Mom said.

"Thanks for coming, guys," I said, offering each of them the warmest smile I could.

"It's your birthday," Christy said. "We wouldn't miss it for the world! Would we?"

"Nope," Drifter said. "We wouldn't."

"Besides," Olivia added. "There's cake!"

"The cake!" Mom scampered into the kitchen, quickly pursued by Amelia.

My small group of friends settled into their seats-Christy, Olivia and Drifter on one couch, me and Mark on the other.

"Your mom is so tiny and cute!" Olivia said in a hushed voice.

"She's like a crazy munchkin," Drifter agreed. "She's pretty awesome."

"She's a hyper-active pixie," Christy added.

"Totally overloading on pixie dust," I finished, laughing.

"She's very different from my mother," Mark said, slightly frowning.

"How so?"

"My mother isn't so lively," Mark answered, then flashed his swoon-worthy grin.

"Cake!" my mom announced.

I looked up to find Mom carrying the colossal cake into the living room. The vanilla frosting with what looked to be a series of blueberries on top looked absolutely delicious.

"Wow," Mark said, admiring the creation as Mom set it on the coffee table.

"And it was made with you in mind," my mother said to Mark, winking. "I bought a diabetic cookbook just so you wouldn't have problems eating it! Am I great or what?"

"Thank you Mrs. Hunter," Mark shifted uncomfortably on his chair, "but I don't think I'll be eating any cake tonight."

"Oh?" Mom pouted.

"I've felt sick the whole week." Mark patted his stomach. "I'm avoiding solids right now."

The look of disappointment in Mom's eyes was so obvious it almost hurt. "Well," Mom said, looking down at the cake, "that's all right. I'm glad to see you're here though. And more for Amelia to eat! She likes cake."

"I love cake!" Christy said, leaning forward. "It looks so good!"

Amelia leered at Mark from behind my mother. All I needed was for her to not to like Mark and make our lives miserable.

Mark leaned forward to admire the cake. He looked hungry, but it was obvious from his words that his stomach wouldn't have it.

I wondered what he could be sick with. I'd heard mono was going around, but if that were the case and he had it, wouldn't I have already gotten it too? It wasn't called the kissing disease for nothing.

I briefly considered the idea that he might not like cake before he squeezed and patted my shoulder. "Your mom is pretty awesome for making a cake I can eat."

"She's really great," I agreed.

Mom disappeared into the other room.

"It looks great," Mark said with a light smile, raising his eyes to scan the room "I don't mean to hurt your mom's feelings. I just don't feel too hot. Probably something I ate."

"I get that. I'm sure she does, too." I caught movement out of the corner of my eye.

Mom reappeared, gifts in her arms, all wrapped in fine, decorative paper. "Present time!"

What would've taken a few short minutes was prolonged into a half-hour festivity as Mom demanded I hold up what she had purchased for pictures. I got mostly clothes, some books, a few pieces of jewelry, including a stud for the piercing in my left ear. Christy, Drifter and Olivia each offered up gifts of movies, music, and gift cards. I even, surprisingly, got a card from my dad, though where he'd got it from I wasn't sure. Inside was fifty dollars, along with the words *I love you* written in his short, scratchy handwriting.

Mark glanced at it, impressed. "Your father approves of you, huh?"

I nodded. "He's pretty cool."

"His dad is like this massive giant of hugs," Christy offered.

Mark smiled sadly in a way that made me want to hold him close. "That's really cool. I wish mine approved of me."

"My Adam is the most amazing kid ever! Other than the rest of you sitting here and Am!" my mom grinned, snorting slightly as she laughed.

By the time it was all over, punch was being passed around and cake was being served.

"Oh," Mark said, standing. "I almost forgot."

He reached into his jeans, fumbled around in his pocket, then withdrew a small, ivory-colored box imprinted with what looked like an elephant decal on top. He offered it with little more than a smile and nod.

"You didn't have to do that," I said, reaching forward to take the box.

"I wouldn't be a very good boyfriend if I didn't get you a gift, now would I?"

"True," I laughed.

I looked at the box in my hand, smiled, then lifted the cover off.

I pulled the cloth wrapping out of the box, unwrapped it, and looked down.

It was a heart, plum-colored and the size of a quarter. With an intricate series of golden wires that wrapped around its surface and made waves like constellations around its figure, it couldn't have been any more beautiful. At first I was awestruck, but it took less than a second to find the snap along its right-hand side. Inside there was a phrase, embossed in the metal itself. It said: For all of time. Forevermore.

"It's... Poe," I said, raising my eyes to look at Mark.

"Sort of," he said, crouching down beside me to look at his gift. "It's a play on his words, anyhow."

"This had to be expensive," I said, running my thumb along one of the wires.

"It doesn't matter." Mark's gaze melted my heart.

"Mark, you didn't need to do this."

"If it's any consolation, it was much cheaper than it looks."

"Thank you," I said, taking extra care to set the plum-colored heart on the coffee table before wrapping my arms around him.

I held him for several long moments, lost in his touch and even more stranded in his compassion. Around us the room was silent, as if the people within it were waiting for our moment to end.

When I pulled away, I laughed and kissed his cheek. "Thank you," I said.

He kissed my other cheek and pulled away.

My mother broke the moment. "Come on! Let's party!" Mom crossed the room in a few short steps and started the music. A sappy love song sounded from the speakers. "Oops!" she cried. "My fault! Sorry!"

She switched it over to the local radio station and music flooded the room.

Christy

Talk about awkward.

Though Adam looked pretty happy with Mark at his side while his mom zigzagged around the room like Tinkerbelle on Adderall, Olivia, Drifter, and I sat on the sidelines like some really big freakin' extra wheels. To make it

100

worse, Adam's little sister, who's always a grumpy little bitch, seemed to be taking it to the next level.

I shoveled cake into my mouth with gusto, surprised that it tasted so good, watching Mark and Adam wrapped up in their own little bubble of happiness. The quick, intimate touches were gag worthy. The sweet smiles they kept giving each other were even worse.

Drifter caught my eye and raised an eyebrow.

Olivia rolled her eyes.

I know I should've been happy for Adam, but it felt all wrong somehow. Even Adam's mom, who is always over-enthusiastic about everything, appeared to be forcing herself to be extra perky. I knew what was bugging me, but I wasn't sure why everyone else seemed so *off*.

I had yet to talk to Mark about what I overhead that day at his museum. Trying to find a moment alone with Mark was almost impossible because he and Adam were now always together.

The flash from Adam's mom snapping my picture yet again blinded me. I already had spots floating on top of the spots already obscuring my vision. Olivia giggled as I rapidly blinked my eyes, trying to focus.

"Oh, so cute!" The camera flashed again at Mark and Adam. "I can't wait to upload these to Facebook!"

Adam grinned at his mom dancing around to some horrible pop song, her brown hair flipping around her face. She's pretty young for having a teenage kid and it shows. Adam is seventeen and his mom had him when she was seventeen. She looks even younger than her age, which makes most of the women in town hate her. I usually think she's adorable, but tonight she was annoying me.

I glanced over at Amelia. She was shoveling cake into her mouth while glaring at Mark. It was pretty clear she didn't like him. Which is weird. Everyone likes Mark. I like him. I think. Well, I do like him. I just don't want there to be any dark secrets that he's hiding from Adam.

Mark caught me staring at him and gave me his slow, dashing smile. I hate how it makes me tingly. Not that I'm attracted to him *that* way, but he has this aura about him. It's magnetic. Even now that he is out of the closet at school, girls still flirt with him and most of the guys seem to like him. It's made life for Adam easier now that Mark is openly out and his boyfriend.

I returned the smile and occupied my mouth by forking the rest of the piece of cake into my mouth.

"The cute is enough to kill," Olivia whispered to me, giggling.

Adam picked up the gift Mark had given him for the hundredth time, turning it around, grinning. It felt wonderful to see him so happy, but I couldn't feel *happy* for him. I needed a break, so I picked up all the plates to take into the kitchen.

"Oh, thanks, Christy! You're a doll!" Adam's mom called out.

I hang out in their house a lot, so I know where everything is located. I piled the plates and forks in the sink, got the scrub brush, and opened up the cabinet under the sink to pull out the dish soap. I stood up and gasped.

Mark stood right next to me holding out some glasses. "I thought I would help."

101

"Oh, thanks. Great."

I took the glasses from him and set them in the sink. Turning on the hot water, I started to scrub furiously. Now that I was actually alone with him, I didn't want to be. I was nervous about broaching the subject with him.

Mark leaned his hip against the counter, arms folded over his very nice chest, and smiled at me slightly. "Are you okay?"

"Me? Okay? Great!" It was a lie. It sounded like a lie. I wasn't okay. I was all sorts of wrong. I wanted Mark to be Mr. Wonderful and I was utterly terrified he wasn't. I was really starting to regret my stupid spell.

Glancing toward the living room, Mark slightly inclined his head toward me. "No one is listening, but me. C'mon. What's wrong, Christy? You were giving me some weird looks tonight."

I attacked the cake crumbs like they were evil demons, trying not to say something incredibly stupid.

"I overhead you talking to Jayden the day he beat up Adam!"

And failed.

Mark lightly shrugged. "I talk to a lot of people."

His manner was so disarming, I just gaped at him.

"Is that really what was bothering you?" He grinned at me playfully.

I set the scrub brush down, but kept the water on to hide our conversation. It took me a few seconds to process my thoughts and fashion them into words. "Maybe I'm stupid... or... just... you know... paranoid, but... you talked to the jerk who beat up my gay boyfriend on the day it happened."

Mark's smile diminished.

"And... it just seems weird." I went back to washing the dishes, trying to avoid his gaze.

"Why weird?" His voice was quieter.

I rinsed off a few plates, then turned back around. "Okay, what would you think if your gay boyfriend—"

"He *is* my gay boyfriend," Mark said. His friendliness was gone. His voice had become gray like his eyes, neutral, colorless.

"Hey, I *jokingly* call him that," I said, slightly defensive. Okay, a lot defensive.

"But he's my boyfriend. Not yours. He's your best friend. I get that. I also get that maybe you're jealous and blowing this all out of proportion in your mind."

I frowned at Mark. "I don't have some weird crush on Adam. He's like my brother. I love him like a brother. We even did the whole blood thing, cutting our fingers, and pressing them together, doing that promise, all that. Just tell me what you talked to Jayden about."

"I asked him for paper towels. I threw up after lunch." Mark shrugged.

"Huh?"

"I got back from lunch, threw up, and realized the stall I was in didn't have toilet paper. Jayden was in there and I asked him for paper towels. Then he asked me why I was throwing up. I guess because of the whole mono scare." Mark pinned me with those intense gray eyes of his like I was an ant under a magnifying glass.

"Oh."

"Look, Christy, I know things are hard for you ever since the whole thing with Ian went down. I know you're feeling sad about that and now that Adam has a boyfriend, that has to be awkward for you." Mark reached out and lightly brushed my hair back from my face.

I'm not sure how to describe what I felt because it was like nothing I had ever experienced before in my life. When he touched me, it felt as though his fingers had rays of cold energy pulsing out of them. The coldness pressed into my mind feeling like a rush of ice water. I gasped, swaying. It almost felt like he was holding my brain in his hand, searching for some secret spot.

I raised my hand, pushing him away. I felt dizzy and a little sick to my stomach. Looking up, I was surprised that he looked shocked.

"What was that?" I gasped.

Mark squinted at me. "I touched your hair. That's all."

"No, I felt... " I faltered. What had I felt? Maybe it was a magic puberty thing that had to do with *me*, not him at all. "Sorry. I think I'm coming down with something."

Mark slid his arm around my shoulders and tilted his head down toward me. "It's okay, Christy. I do get it. Like I was saying. I know this is tough for you. I want you to know that I do care about Adam with all my heart. I'm not trying to take him from you. I would never do anything to hurt him."

Shivering, I nodded. I was feeling all sorts of wrong now. Cold and a little weak. I wanted to pull away from Mark and gather my thoughts, but I didn't want to be rude either. Mom and Dad warned me that as my magic awakened I may have physical symptoms. I wondered if that was what I was experiencing.

I felt Mark brushing my bangs back from my face, the cold wave thrusting into my head again. I shoved him away, gasping.

"Christy?" He frowned. "What is it?"

I fled to the downstairs bathroom and threw up.

The drama that followed was embarrassing. Adam's mom rushed into the bathroom to help me clean up and to see if I was okay. Amelia saw the mess I made and promptly threw up all over the hallway. Adam was forced to clean that up with Drifter's help, but Olivia ran to the upstairs bathroom to throw up when she saw Amelia's vomit.

Yeah, I totally ruined Adam's party.

"Oh, God! I hope it wasn't the cake!" Adam's mom wailed as the chaos started to die down.

Olivia came back downstairs looking less green. She had a false alarm. Adam's mom meanwhile gave me and Amelia something that tasted horrible to settle our stomachs. Adam and Drifter hovered around me like worried hens and I had to push them away. I felt like crap, my head throbbing, and my stomach churning.

Finally, realizing I was not going to feel better, Drifter and Olivia took me home while Adam's mother carried Amelia upstairs to bed.

As I sat in the backseat waving sorrowfully to Adam, Mark stood behind him. He didn't wave. He didn't smile.

He just stared at me.

Adam

"If I didn't know any better," I said as I continued to pick wrapping paper and streamers off the floor, "I would say this was the most awful night of my life."

"I'm sure you've had worse," Mark offered.

That sentiment did little to calm my nerves.

"Guess that didn't help much," Mark said, "huh?"

"Not really," I replied.

"Sorry."

"No need to be sorry," I sighed, leaning forward to pick up a plastic fork from the table.

Mark caught my hand, thumb stroking my wrist. "Let me," he said.

I didn't bother to argue. "Thanks. I hate cleaning up."

"You're the birthday boy. I'll clean up and you chill."

We exchanged smiles and the tension in my chest alleviated somewhat. I was worried about Christy, but also felt bad that my mom's carefully laid plans for an awesome birthday party had gone down the toilet—literally—several times over, and in a very dramatic fashion.

After making sure we had disposed of all the trash and cleaned up the remnants from the party, I stood near the door, ready to see Mark out. When he slid his jacket onto his shoulders and reached down to check for his keys, he turned to look at me and asked, "Can we talk for a minute? Alone? Outside?"

I grinned, thinking of a possible kiss. "Yeah, sure."

A minute later, we stood on the porch, looking at the neighboring houses across the street and his car in the driveway.

"I wanted to apologize," Mark said. "None of this would've happened if I wasn't diabetic."

"It's not your fault," I said. I didn't bother to add that my mom's idea of baking a cake is from a box.

"Still... " he sighed, then shook his head. "I guess that's not what's really bothering me, though."

"Is something wrong?"

"I wanted to talk to you first, just in case the story got twisted from what really happened."

"Huh?" I frowned.

"Tonight, when Christy took the plates into the kitchen to do the dishes, I offered to help. While we were cleaning up, she asked about why I had been talking to Jayden at the museum a few days ago."

A chill crept over my spine. Though the shiver could've easily been masked by the wind that came up, Mark's wavering eye seemed to catch hint of the gesture. "Why were you talking to Jayden?" I asked.

"That's what Christy was wondering. That's why I wanted to get to you before anyone could put any doubts in your mind. Look, Adam... " Mark sighed and pressed his palms onto the wooden railing.

"What were you and Jayden talking about, Mark?"

"I got sick. I asked him for a wad of paper towels. That's it."

"But if that's it, why would she twist the story?"

"Honestly," Mark shrugged, "I think she might be a bit jealous."

Jealous?

Why would Christy have any reason to be jealous of Mark?

"I'm not sure what you're saying," I said. "I guess I just don't understand what you're talking about."

"Think about it, Adam. We've been spending more time together. We talk on the phone. We hang out after school. We share something special, something Christy *can't* have with you. It's bound to make her feel left out. Look, I know you've been friends for a long time, but I just want you to be careful, okay? Sometimes when people think they're threatened, they'll lash out."

"Christy would have no reason to attack our relationship."

"Can you be so sure?"

The air took on an ominous chill.

Brushing my arms, I turned my eyes away from Mark to look out into the shadows. Why would he even insinuate that Christy, my best friend in the whole world, would try to force us apart? I was happy. She *was* happy for *me*. I mean, there was reason for her to be cautious, especially since I'd been attacked right after she heard Mark talking to Jayden, but that didn't mean her concern was jealousy, did it?

My reverie was lost when I felt him draw up behind me and drape an arm around my waist.

"Please don't think I'm being harsh," he whispered, his lips so close I could feel his breath against my ear. "I just care about us and don't want anything to happen to you."

"I know," I sighed. I pressed my hand over his, gazing into his eyes. "You should probably go. Mom's going to be wondering why I've been out here so long."

"All right." He freed his arm from my waist and started for the stairs. "Adam?"

"Yeah?"

He pressed a kiss to my cheek.

When he pulled away, the beams of light streaming from the porch reflected off a cross dangling from his chest—one with three beams, the bottom one crooked.

"I've never seen that before," I said, mystified by its old, burnt-looking texture. "Is it a cross?"

"Of Saint Andrew," Mark nodded, reaching up to finger the support beam. "It's an old heirloom that's been passed down in my family for generations. I'm surprised it's the first time you've mentioned it. I wear it all the time."

"I think it's been under your shirt," I mused.

"Oh. That." Mark's slight smile faded as he looked down at the cross dangling from his neck. "You know how it is. Not many people look kindly on something that looks so... different."

"Are you religious?"

Mark stepped forward and pressed a hand to my cheek. "I believe things happen for a reason."

"Yeah," I whispered. "I do too."

Mark pressed his lips to mine and held them there for a long moment. When he pulled away, he said, "Happy birthday, Adam. Goodnight."

"Goodnight," I replied.

I watched him from the moment he stepped off the porch until the time he drove away.

When I walked back into the house, I decided that this hadn't been such a bad birthday after all.

Christy

When I shuffled onto the front porch of my house, I wasn't surprised when my dad opened the door. He always has an uncanny sense about when someone approaches the house. My mom says it's from his days as a warrior. It's hard to imagine my dad being a fearsome slayer of monsters when he opened the door wearing his flannel pajamas and wearing fluffy bunny slippers. He claims the slippers are comfortable. Insert massive eye roll here.

"Home so soon? What's up, pumpkin? Drunk again?"

"Ha, ha," I responded, shoving past him and into the foyer. "No, I'm not."

"Oh, my! Vomit breath!" He waved his hand before his face. "Are you sure you're not drunk?"

"I did throw up, but not because of liquor. Trust me. I can wait until my twenty-first birthday to get trashed again." Rubbing my head, I still felt a bit queasy.

Callie sashayed down the stairs and wrapped herself around my ankles, purring loudly. The motion was strangely comforting.

Dad rested his hand on my forehead. "You don't feel warm. Are you coming down with something? There's that kissing bug going around town. Who've you been kissing?"

"Just Callie, Dad." Picking up Callie, I nuzzled her and kissed her head. She sniffed at my mouth, intrigued. Cats are weird. "Actually, Dad, I think I need to talk to you and Mom about something."

"Oh, dear. That was a serious voice. I get nervous with your serious voice."

I couldn't tell if he was joking or not. Wrapping an arm around my shoulders, he guided me into the living room where I crashed onto a sofa, still clutching Callie. Dad offered me a peppermint from a candy dish and I obligingly took it. Popping it into my mouth, I sucked on it while we waited for my mother to appear. I knew the second I told Dad I needed to talk to them that he had silently summoned her. They have this amazing bond where they

106

can touch each other's minds and speak over distances. Dad jokes that it saves on the cellphone bill.

Dad was just propping his bunny slippers onto the coffee table when Mom appeared in the doorway. Her crazy tawny curls were standing up all over the place and she was dressed in a white caftan with ornate silver embroidery on the sleeves. Tiny flecks of magic twinkled around her as she moved and she smelled delicious. She had obviously been in the spell room.

"What's up, Christy?" Mom asked, plopping down beside Dad and sitting cross-legged.

Sinking into the deep, soft, pale blue cushions of the overstuffed sofa, I tried to gather my thoughts into a coherent story. I still felt really weird after my experience with Mark and I sighed with irritation.

"Just start at the beginning," Dad advised, noting my discomfort.

"Okay. I'll try." Tucking the peppermint under my tongue, I took a deep breath and started. I gave them a quick rundown of the night until the moment when Mark had followed me into the kitchen. "The whole night was really weird. Just forced. I thought maybe I was imagining it because of what happened at the museum and that I was still weirded out. But when Mark came into the kitchen it got weirder." I crunched on the peppermint then swallowed the remaining shards of candy.

"Go on," my mother urged me.

"Yeah, get to the good parts," my dad added.

Rubbing Callie's ears, I gazed down at my mom's familiar, wishing with all my heart I could just forget what I experienced and what it might mean. "Mark and I talked about the whole thing with Jayden. He said he was just asking Jayden for paper towels. When we were talking, he touched my hair and I felt like this cold wave of power wash over me. It made me feel really sick. It happened twice when we were talking, but Mark didn't seem to notice. He was really intent on making it very clear that Adam is his boyfriend and that I'm just the best friend." The bitterness in my voice surprised me, but then again I was feeling pretty surly.

Mom and Dad exchanged looks and my mother leaned forward, her elbows on her knees. "Describe exactly what you felt."

"Well, it was like ice water being poured over my brain or something. It made me sick and that's why I threw up."

"Good to know we're not raising a drunkard," Dad said with a wink. He was obviously trying to alleviate the mood, but failing.

Mom looked a lot more serious about what had happened, but that's how they roll. "Richard, stop joking. This is actually pretty serious."

"Okay. I have my serious face on," Dad said, but he looked more like a pouty Santa Claus than a dour father.

"Christy, when you felt that energy, was it coming from Mark?"

"I don't know. It first happened when he touched my hair, but it happened again when he wasn't doing that."

"And you said everyone was off during the party?" Mom was obviously taking mental notes on what had occurred.

"Yeah, it was totally like everyone was playing a role in a school play and very, very badly and with way too much enthusiasm. Well, everyone but Adam and Mark." I rolled my eyes. "They were totally too cute in an in love way. Totally gross."

"Those disgustingly in love people. How do we endure them?" Dad's hand sneaked over to my mom's knee and settled on it.

My upper lip twitched in one corner. My dad calls it my snarl-face.

"Richard... " Mom squeezed his hand tightly and gave him an admonishing look. "This is really serious. It's just not teenage angst. I've been sensing something the last few weeks and it's growing stronger."

"Something bad?" I felt a chill slide down my neck.

Mom nodded.

"Mary Louise, why didn't you say something sooner?"

"I wasn't sure at first. Changes in the season can stir things up in the spiritual realm. Plus, Christy is going through witch puberty. There have been a lot of fluxes in power simply because of her."

"I haven't done much though! I can't even make things happen unless I'm upset," I protested.

"You're affecting more than you realize, Christy. You're this beautiful flower of energy that is slowly unfurling and it affects all the energies around you. Very soon you will manifest your full abilities." Mom leaned forward, her eyes sparkling like diamonds. "There is a dark power uncoiling in the town. It feels old and like it has roots here. I suspect it's been here a very long time waiting to reawaken. Your puberty may be the thing that is stirring it to life."

"I don't like the sound of this," Dad said grumpily. "Makes me want to go grab my sword."

"I don't like it much either," I agreed. "Why would it be after me?"

"I'm not sure it is *after* you, but it may have been *awakened* by you. It sounds like it may have been affecting the party and Mark. Even you. Perhaps that power is behind Jayden attacking Adam." Mom ran her hands through her long hair, then clutched fistfuls of it. "I need to do some serious scrying and try to locate it."

"So some big bad monster is waking up in the town and is going to do what?" I frowned. "And why do I suddenly sound like Buffy?"

Mom shot me an amused smile. "Willow, dear. You sound like Willow."

"I'd rather be kung-fuing the bad guys," I groused.

"If there is an awakening power in the town, your mom will figure out what it is and we'll deal with it, not you." Dad set his feet on the floor and leaned across the coffee table to take my hand. "We will deal with, Christy. I don't want you to worry. Your dad is a big bad warrior. I have taken the head of more than one bad monster. Buffy doesn't have anything on me."

It was the first time I had ever seen the warrior inside my dad and felt his strength in his hand. I always think of him as a big cuddly oaf, but in that moment I saw the man my mom had fallen in love with. "I trust you, Dad."

"Good girl."

Callie placed her paws on my shoulder and hopped onto the back of the sofa. She sat right behind me, her tail wrapped around my neck. It felt a little like a hug, but also like a protective gesture.

My mom scooted around the coffee table to sit next to me. Taking one of my hands, she closed her eyes and I felt the petal-soft tendrils of her magic flow over me. The unease I had been feeling since my interaction with Mark dissipated.

"There we go. Getting rid of the last of that icky power." Mom lifted a hand to press her palm against my forehead.

Again, I felt her soothing power chase away the vestiges of that cold magic that had assaulted me. "Thanks, Mom."

Opening her eyes, she pressed a kiss to my cheek. "All gone."

"What was it?" my dad asked, looking concerned.

"I'm not sure. It was very cold. A taste of death was in it. We may be dealing with a specter." Mom combed her fingers through my hair and it felt wonderful. I could feel her magic pouring into me.

"Ugh. Ghosts. Hard to hit a ghost with a sword," my dad complained.

"But if it's coming after me shouldn't I fight it?" Even though I felt warm and tingly now that my mother had banished the icky magic completely, I bristled at the thought of just sitting by. "Shouldn't you give me a spell or a talisman or something like that?"

"We're not sure what we're facing right now, so I can't weave a specific protection spell for you," my mom admitted. She clutched my hands tightly, trying to reassure me. "But the house is warded. Nothing can come in that we don't invite. You're safe here."

"But what about out there? What if this thing starts messing with my friends even more? What if it's affecting Mark? Or Adam?"

"There isn't a one spell-fits-all remedy, Christy. You have to trust me that I will do my best to figure out what this is and take care of it."

"Your Mom is right. You need to keep living your life, but let us know if anything else weird happens to you or your friends. We'll sort this out," my dad assured me. "You just need to keep being a kid and enjoying your life."

I stared at them incredulously. "You don't trust me to help?"

"No, honey, that's not it—" my mom started to say.

"No, that *is* it. Yeah, my magic is all wonky right now, but you can't just keep me out of this. I'm in it. That bad magic glommed onto me and almost ruined Adam's birthday! It made me barf, which made Am barf, and then Olivia almost barfed—"

"Oh, my!" My mom's eyes widened.

"Well, that explains the vomit breath."

"Dad!"

"Richard, you're not helping. Christy, I understand that you want to help. I know you're unsettled. But the good news is that it couldn't get a hold of you. It just made you a little sick. What you describe sounds like an attempted possession. It's obviously not strong enough yet."

"Yet! You said yet! It's not strong enough—YET!"

My mom exchanged looks with my dad and I just knew they were secretly talking.

"It's not fair that you're keeping me out of this when it's affecting me!" I stood up and Callie yowled at me. "Don't you start, too, Callie!"

"Christy, calm down," my dad ordered.

"No, I won't! It's not fair. Not only do I have to deal with my best friend's new boyfriend telling me that I'm now second-fiddle, I have my parents telling

109

me the same thing about magic. I'm the one that *thing* attacked tonight. I think you should teach me to fight it!"

"I can't teach you to fight something when I don't even know what it is yet!" Mom stood up and set her hands on her hips.

"Will you teach me once you know?"

Again, my parents exchanged looks.

"I knew it!" I brushed past my mom, heading toward the foyer.

"Christy!"

"It's not fair! I'm a witch with wonky powers, Adam's new boyfriend may totally not like me after tonight, Adam is probably mad at me for barfing all over the place, I'm fat, and Ian is a jerk! My life is ruined!" I turned to make a dramatic exit and tripped over the broom. I managed to keep my balance and the broom skipped away. "And this broom is totally out to get me!"

Without waiting for them to answer, I fled up the stairs. I heard my mom call after me and my dad telling her to let me be. When I reached my bedroom, I found Callie sitting in the center of my bed waiting for me. I didn't see her come up the stairs in front of me or even leave the living room. She has an uncanny way of just appearing sometimes, though she's good at getting locked in closets. I flopped onto the bed and she immediately nestled into my side. Yanking out my cellphone, I started to text Adam an apology, then thought better of it. It would probably be better if we just talked on the way to school.

Covering my face with my hands, I muttered, "My life sucks."

Callie bopped my hands with her head, then pushed her way under them. It's hard to be totally mad when a cat is giving you kitty kisses. I snuggled her up and resigned myself to moping until I fell asleep.

$\mathcal{C}$hapter 9

Trouble in Paradise

Adam

The morning after what could only be described as the worst birthday party of my life, Christy wouldn't stop apologizing.

"I'm so sorry, Adam," she said, weaving the car through the early morning traffic as we made our way to school. "I am *so, so, SO* sorry about last night. I didn't... I mean, it wasn't—"

"You couldn't help it," I replied. "Don't worry about it."

Amelia and Olivia getting sick was all on account of Christy-that much was obvious. I still didn't understand why Christy had gotten sick. While my mom had lamented that the cake might have been the reason why, I knew for a fact that Christy didn't have a problem with eating blueberries, so there was no reason why a blueberry, or a blueberry-filled cake, would've bothered her.

"Seriously," I said, pulling my gaze from the window to look at her. "Don't worry about it."

"I'm *so* embarrassed."

"Christy, it's okay. Let it go. For me. Now, okay?"

"Okay, okay." Christy came to a stop at a stoplight and took a deep breath. "So, what happened after we all left last night? I mean, after World War Barf?"

"Me and Mark watched a movie. Amelia was still sick and Mom was ready to lose it."

"I still feel bad about that. I hope she doesn't think it was because of the cake."

"Nah. I ate the cake and I was fine."

"I don't think that's what made me sick anyway." Christy made a big show of studying the road, seeming to avoid something that was on her mind.

"Then what did?" I asked suspiciously.

"I don't know." She shrugged in a way that made me wonder if she was lying.

"You sure?"

"Yeah. It was just embarrassing." She gave me a sheepish smile.

I smiled back. "Okay then. Just wondering."

Christy pulled up next to the school and began the task of trying to maneuver through the throng of cars occupying the parking lot. Even though it was early in the morning there were already a lot of people here—so many that Christy actually had to circle the parking lot several times in an attempt to find a parking spot. By the time we neared the door for our fourth time, she sighed and pulled over.

"Get out," she said. "I'll go find a spot."

"Catch you later."

I got out, closed the door, and made my way toward the school.

I caught a flicker of movement out of the corner of my eye, and just as Christy's car was disappearing into the depths of the parking lot, the Barbies descended upon me.

"Hey, *Adam,*" Courtney said, flipping her hair over her shoulder as she, Britney, Jennifer and Maribel came forward. "How's it going, short stuff?"

"Leave me alone, Courtney," I replied, attempting to make my way around them.

Britney and Maribel stepped forward, instantaneously blocking my path.

"We have something we need to... *talk* to you about," Courtney said, drumming my shoulder with her long, carefully-manicured fingers. "Something that we think you should *know* about."

"Yeah," Britney said, her green eyes narrowing in on me. "We do."

While waiting for one of the three to continue, I shrugged my backpack further up my shoulder and eyed each of them cautiously. "What do you want?" I finally asked.

"We just want to make something clear," Jennifer said, coming up from around me before stepping behind Courtney. Her lack of a tan made her seem even more ghastly than before.

"Okay. What is it?"

"Do you think," Maribel continued, "that you're *special* just because he hangs around with you?"

"He hangs around with me more than he does you," I replied. "He *is* my boyfriend, after all."

"You think *that* makes you special?" Britney asked.

I once again tried to make my way around them. They made a wall with their bodies and trapped me. "Leave me alone," I said. "I'm tired of dealing with you."

"We know something you don't," Maribel said. "Something that would *crush* you."

"I don't care what you think you know."

"Mark isn't who you think he is," Courtney said. "And he especially isn't what *you* think *he* is to *you.*"

"What the hell is that supposed to mean?" I narrowed my eyes.

Courtney's bright teeth flashed from between her thin pink lips. "It means," she said, "that you better prepare to be disappointed, because Mark isn't as interested in you as you think he is. What we know will *destroy* you."

"Watch your back," Maribel said. "You're about to be stabbed in it." She raised her fist and made a downward-thrusting gesture.

The Barbies turned and flounced into the school as a throng of students from a school bus streamed around me.

I frowned.

What could they have been talking about?

"Adam!" Christy called, running up from behind me. "Finally found a spot that is almost in Siberia."

I stared after the Barbies, confused, angry, and a little scared.

Christy saw my expression and said, "Adam, what's wrong?"

"Nothing," I answered, dismissing the whole episode, or at least trying to.

"What did the Barbies want?" Christy eyed them suspiciously.

"Something about Mark."

"What? "Her voice sounded odd somehow.

"Honestly, they didn't say anything outright. I think they're just trying to cause trouble."

"Ugh," Christy said. "Seriously? I thought they were over this?"

"Apparently not," I sighed.

"Don't listen to anything they say to you, Adam. They're trying to mess with your head."

"I know." I looked over at the school. My hopes that this would be a good day were already dashed.

We entered the school and stepped through a series of black and orange streamers that dangled from the ceiling. Around us the school was abound with Halloween cheer. The office to our right was decorated with hanging spider webs, the bulletin board was covered with stickers of cats, crows and pumpkins, and each of the teachers' individual doors were covered with their own unique decoration for the holiday. We maneuvered through crowd of students until we made our way to our lockers, where we both dropped off our bags and gathered our books for the day.

Christy glowered at a really gross rendition of a witch. "Stereotypes."

"You mean you aren't going to turn green and warty?"

"Shut up!"

One of the warning bells rang as soon as my books were in my arms.

"See you later?" Christy asked.

"See you later," I said with a reassuring grin

We split apart and made our way for each of our individual classes.

Hopefully what had happened earlier wouldn't foreshadow the rest of the day.

Christy

I love and hate Halloween. On one hand, it's a pretty magical time of the year. My mother always throws herself wholeheartedly into the holiday. She decorates the whole house, fills a cauldron with candy and sits on our front porch dressed like Endora from *Bewitched* in a long flowing purple witch dress. Dad just thinks the whole thing is a blast and eats way too many of the treats Mom bakes. When the trick-or-treaters come around, my parents go out of their way to put on a great spooky show. The kids love it.

I mostly love the holiday except for when I'm at school. The local fundamentalist churches always launch an anti-Halloween campaign and the kids from those churches hand out pamphlets with warty witches on the covers. Maybe I'm just sensitive, but I really hate all the green-skinned depictions of witches. It makes me think of how kids have always called me a witch all my life. People wonder why I feel ugly. Sheesh. If they got compared to an old crone with bad teeth, a hooked nose, and a nasty complexion, they would probably not feel all that gorgeous either.

To make matters worse, the Barbies go on the warpath during the holiday, hosting a big party that's very exclusive, strictly invite only. They dress like trashy versions of the Disney Princesses and make sure to make fun of anyone who dares to wear a homemade costume to school. Of course, Adam and I are always in homemade costumes, since those are actually the best.

Already the school was gearing up for the holiday and the Barbies were ratcheting up the nastiness. I hated that they were trying to cause trouble with Adam already. I thought maybe because Mark is pretty popular they'd leave Adam alone. Of course, I was wrong. I should have known better. Those nasty girls love to hurt people. I briefly wondered if my mother's mysterious big bad monster was behind some of it, but dismissed the idea. The Barbies don't need to be possessed to be total bitches.

I knew I wouldn't see Adam again until lunch, so I tried to text him. He sent me back a quick answer that everything appeared fine with Mark. That was a relief, but I still didn't like the idea of the Barbies hounding Adam. They rarely give up once they've selected their latest target.

I was still feeling down from the night before. I didn't like that something evil was in town and appeared to be targeting me and possibly my friends. It sucks to feel helpless in the face of possible danger. Now that I was aware that for sure that something was amiss, I could see now how things had been odd in school for a while. The mono outbreak was weird enough, but there was just a strange new vibe in the air now. The world felt out of balance and I couldn't blame it on my woes with Ian, Adam's love life, or my magic puberty. The world felt a bit drearier in general.

During third period I ended up volunteering to decorate the bulletin board outside my History class. Mr. Novak had already asked me before class if I'd be willing to do it for him, so after attendance I walked up to the front of the class. He gleefully handed over several large envelopes filled with laminated posters and a bag full of orange and black streamers. He's a stickler for the real origins of Halloween, so his decorations tell the story behind the myths. It's the only reason I volunteered, other than getting out of class. No warty green witches on this display. I was actually going to get a grade for the bulletin board. Only the top two scorers on the last test had the option to volunteer.

"And your helper is Ian," Mr. Novak said with a wider smile.

I wanted to bop him upside his bald head.

"Your tutoring really helped him," Mr. Novak said. His conspiratorial air was sweet, since he obviously thought I still had a crush on Ian, aka the big stupid lug. My sour look made his smile diminish slightly as curiosity bloomed in his eyes.

I heard the squeak of Ian's sneakers behind me and I hugged the decorations close as I stormed out of the room. My classmates made catcalls as we exited, only making things worse.

The door clicked shut behind us. Ian and I stood alone in the cold, empty sprawl of the hallway.

I could see him out of the corner of my eye, handsome and awkward, staring at me.

"So, uh, Christy... "

I dropped the decorations on the floor. For pieces of colored laminated paper, they made quite a nice racket. Of course, the scissors, staplers and tape tucked inside one bag helped. A door opened down the hall and a teacher shushed us.

"Sorry," I said.

She gave us a harsh look before returning to her classroom and shutting the door with a loud click.

"Christy, I... uh... "

"We need butcher paper," I said, still not looking directly at him and stormed down the hall. My boots clunked against the floor. I flipped up my hoodie and thrust my hands into my pockets.

Ian's squeaking sneakers followed.

The workroom off the teacher's lounge was empty. The rolls of colored butcher paper were tucked into a long dispenser along one wall. Most of the orange and black was already gone. I clutched the ragged end of the yellow roll.

"Christy, huh... "

I ignored Ian, pulling on the paper, unwinding it as I tried to coerce it into a manageable roll. With an exasperated sigh, Ian took the bunched up paper from me. I made a sound of protest, but relented when he did a much better job of rolling up the yellow paper into a tube.

While he did that, I stood staring at the toes of my boots. I was wearing black leggings under an army green mini-skirt and a worn brown hoodie. I was nowhere near the polished perfection of the Barbies, so I couldn't figure out why he kept looking at me.

"What?" I finally said, unable to stand the tension in the air.

"What did I do to make you hate me?" he asked, actually sounding hurt.

I turned toward him, hiding my gaze under my long bangs. His blue eyes actually looked sad, kind of puppy-doggish.

"You're stupid," I blurted out.

He winced, hurt springing into his features. "Gee, thanks."

"Not like stupid in school. You obviously did okay in history class," I relented, slightly softening my angry tone.

"I just used the study techniques you taught me," he confessed.

"But you're really stupid when it comes to Adam," I continued, my anger rising again.

Ian paused as he reached for the scissors on the shelf above the butcher paper. The yellow paper was in a nice roll and all he had to do was cut it free. "Adam? You're mad about Adam?"

"Well, yeah! All that stupid stuff you said about him!"

Ian squinted at me. "I don't hate Adam. I think he's okay. I told you that as long as he doesn't hit on me, I'm cool with the whole gay thing."

"That's so lame!"

"Well, if it helps, I don't like girls hitting on me either!" His blue eyes flashed. "I hate it when people treat me like I'm just some object to win and hold up like a trophy!"

I put my hands on my hips and glared. "Oh, yeah? Then why do you flirt with all the girls in school all the time?"

"I'm just being nice! Not flirting!"

"You weren't like that when Debbie was around!"

"Because she got jealous!"

I don't know why I was so angry. Maybe part of it was because Ian had sounded so ridiculously cliché in his attitude toward Adam, or maybe it was because it took me completely ignoring him to get him to even want to talk to me. I was so furious in that moment, I couldn't think straight.

"Well, you suck!" I flicked my hands toward him dramatically.

The yellow paper he had clutched in his hand suddenly unfurled like a huge bat wing, exploding across the room. We both gasped and jumped back. My hands came down and the roll of butcher paper suddenly spun on the rack, jerking the length we had unwound, zipping around until it was rolled up around the spindle.

Ian and I both stared at the yellow roll of paper in surprise, then at each other.

"You did that!" Ian gasped.

"Did not!"

"You so did! You did this," he demonstrated how I had moved my hands, "and it did that!"

"That's so... retarded!"

Ian studied me, fear and awe mixing in the depths of his blue eyes. He looked at the roll of paper, then at me. "Do it again."

"I didn't do it!"

"I saw it!"

I tried to dart around him, but he yanked my wrist, jerking me close. I was suddenly pressed up against him, my eyes staring into his. I had never been so close to any boy in my life other than Adam. I felt as if all the air left my lungs and I couldn't breathe. I felt the strength of his body pressed up against mine. It sent shivers of pulsing silver energy through me. I felt as though sparks were about to erupt from my skin and shower the room in rainbow colors.

"Your eyes are so blue," was the stupid thing I said.

"Huh?"

I twisted my wrist free and fled down the hallway. His sneakers squeaking along the highly polished floor alerted me to his pursuit. I whipped around a corner and headed toward the double doors that led to the outside.

"Christy," he hissed.

The energy of my anger, desire, and desperation was crawling up my throat from my stomach. I felt like I wasn't just going to throw up breakfast, but a whole lot of magic. On impulse, I flung my hands outward.

The double doors slammed open in front of me.

I ran through them and twisted around to see Ian almost to the doorway.

I raised my hands again and flung them toward the doors. They banged shut, blocking Ian from escaping the school. Through the window inset in the door, I saw his surprised and frightened face staring at me.

The doors rattled as he tried to open them, but I kept my hands up. I could feel the power slipping through my palms and pressing against the door. I could barely breathe as I stood in the cool fall air feeling the surge of magic flooding out of me.

"Lock," I whispered.

The loud clicking of the tumblers sliding into place startled both me and Ian. He shook the doors, trying to open them as I cautiously lowered my hands. The locked doors held.

"Christy," he called out. "I want to talk to you!"

Shaking my head, I dashed down the sidewalk. I had to escape. To hide.

Olivia found me sitting in my car almost an hour later. "What's up?"

I looked up at her, wiped a tear away, and said, "I hate puberty."

"Eh, it'll be over soon," she said with a shrug. She reached into her purse and offered me a red lollipop.

Taking it, I sniffled loudly.

"Ian was looking for you. He asked me for your phone number," she continued.

"I hate Ian, too." I unwrapped the lollipop and shoved it into my mouth.

Olivia arched an eyebrow. "You had a fight with him?"

"He's stupid," I grumbled.

"You know, ignoring him like this is only making him more interested in you."

"I'm not playing hard to get," I said defensively. "He said stupid stuff about Adam."

"Yeah, but he was also showing interest in you. Or at least he wasn't showing complete disinterest in you. Then you got mad at him. Don't you think maybe you were being defensive because it was easier to crush on him when he ignored you? Than to maybe actually get to know him? Find out if he likes you?"

"He's almost the most popular boy in school. Next year he *will be* the most popular boy in school because Jeremy Ross graduates this year. I'm the outcast that is fifteen pounds overweight and gets zits." I held up my bangs so Olivia could see the whopper in the middle of my forehead. "He thinks I'm a witch and that's why he has any interest in me at all!"

"A witch, huh?" Olivia leaned against the door and pondered this.

"All of them have called me a witch ever since I was a kid. They're all jerks. Ian is a jerk. I hate him."

"So not giving him your phone number was the right choice, huh?"

"You didn't give it to him?" I was upset by the pang of disappointment that I felt. I inwardly chided myself for being so dumb. Ian was a jerk. I had to remember *that* and *not* the way I felt when his body had been so close to mine.

Olivia shook her head. "I told him I wouldn't betray you that way. So that was the correct move, right?"

I nodded my head vehemently. "Yes, absolutely." I fought the urge to look toward my cellphone. Last year I had almost worked up the nerve to call Ian when I had moved hell and heaven to discover his phone number. I had chickened out. I still had it programed in my phone. What would I have done if his name had appeared on my screen? Now, I realized, I would never know.

"So, ready for lunch?" Olivia tilted her head, staring at me curiously.

"Yeah. Totally." I slid out of my car and shut the door. I had no idea what I was going to tell Mr. Novak. I had totally ditched his class.

Together, Olivia and I wound our way across the parking lot and through one of the side entrances of the school. I should have known he would be waiting for me, but my jaw dropped just a little when I saw Ian leaning against the wall. His usual entourage was missing and he quickly moved to intercept us.

"Hey, back off," Olivia said sharply to him.

He ignored her. "Christy, I told Mr. Novak you got sick and he totally understood. He said we can finish the bulletin board tomorrow."

I brushed past Ian, trying very hard not to look into his desperate blue eyes.

He fell into step beside me. "I'm sorry about what I said earlier."

"Dude, seriously. Don't you know when to back off?" Olivia glared at him.

"I'm just trying to say I'm sorry," Ian said defensively.

"Why do you even care what I think?" I asked, suddenly wanting to cry. "You never paid attention to me before! Only when you needed me to tutor you!"

The boy of my dreams threw up his hands, shaking his head. "Fine, Christy! Fine! I'm sorry I hurt your feelings and I'm sorry I was probably a jerk in the past. But I am a good guy. I'm not stupid. And I'm not a jerk. And I'm not going to tell anyone what you are." With that, he stormed off down the hall.

"Wow," Olivia gasped.

I stared after Ian, not sure how to even interpret his words.

"What did he mean 'what you are'?" Olivia asked. "Did he mean a witch?"

I nodded mutely.

Olivia rolled her eyes. "Pffft, witches."

I was relieved that she dropped the subject of Ian and witches right away. Together, we hurried to the cafeteria to meet up with the rest of the crew.

Adam

"Another day without eating lunch with Mark," I sighed, settling down into our usual spot in the lunchroom. "He's off-campus again."

"Because he's been sick, Adam," Olivia asked, "or because he's diabetic?"

"I don't know. He didn't tell me. All he said was that he wouldn't be here for lunch today."

Drifter shrugged, idly tossing his apple hand to hand before taking a bite out of it. "It's not like you won't see him later."

"Yeah. I know." I didn't want to talk about my earlier conversation with the Barbies. Mark had seemed okay through all our classes, smiling at me and being his normal charming self, but I had noticed the Barbies smirking at me. When he had excused himself for lunch, I hated that I felt awkward. Though I did miss his company, it wasn't uncommon for him to go home for lunch. His mother always fixed him specially prepared meals at home. Mark only spent lunch with me maybe two times a week.

"So, Adam," Christy said, drawing my attention away from my food. She'd been quiet since I arrived at our table. We both seemed a little upset today. I wondered what was going on with her, but thought I'd wait until later to talk to her. "Had any more problems with the Barbies today?"

"The Barbies are at it again?" Drifter asked, eyes shifting from Christy, then to me.

"They were bothering him this morning." Christy shoveled a carrot stick into her mouth.

"About what?" Olivia asked.

"Same old, same old," I said.

I didn't want to stir up any more trouble by relating what had happened earlier. The Barbies, as well as the jocks and other popular kids, always inhabited the space a few tables over from us. Though it was highly unlikely they would hear anything we were saying, I wanted to stay on their good side—or, at the very least, remain neutral, which at this point was all I was trying to do. Without Mark here, there was no form of visible protection. We were simply the loser outcasts.

"Okay then," Drifter said, eyeing me thoughtfully. "So.... about Halloween."

"What're we doing?" Olivia asked. "Haunted house? Matching costumes? Trick-or-treating?"

"Nothing wrong with that," Drifter said. "I like free candy."

"You've got to be kidding me! We can't do that again." Christy pouted. "Aren't we too old?"

"Hey, I like Tootsie Pops. Don't judge," Drifter grinned.

"Oh, now you're in my territory!" Olivia protested.

"It's my favorite. You don't have a corner on lollipops, you know," Drifter kidded her.

"Well then, Mr. Sweet-Tooth," Olivia said, leaning forward so she and Drifter could look each other straight in the eyes. "How many licks does it take to get to the center of a Tootsie Pop?"

"A lot more than you think and it's a bitch counting," he said, which instantly drew giggles from both Olivia and Christy.

"But seriously," Olivia said. "What're we doing?"

"I don't know," I said. "Don't look at me." I held up my hands in surrender. "You guys decide."

"Are there any parties we can go to?" Olivia asked.

"We're so not going to get invited after what happened at the last one," Christy sighed. "We'll probably end up doing what we always do." Christy hung her head.

"And what's that?" Olivia asked.

"Trick-or-treating," Christy and I chorused.

"Cool! Candy! And we have to find a haunted house," Olivia said.

"No haunted houses in Trinity Springs," Drifter said sadly. "The churches don't even like trick-or-treating. They co-host a fall harvest festival out in the town square, but a lot of kids still trick-or-treat."

"The harvest festival is lame. They don't even allow scary costumes," Christy protested.

"It's either that or we hang out at Christy's house," Drifter offered. "Her mom super-decorates the place."

"No!" Christy cried. She blushed when all of us centered our eyes on her. "I mean, no-let's not go to my house. We know how that'll end."

"With your dad exercising on the Wii," Drifter nodded, which drew a frown from Christy. "Well, it's true!"

"He's addicted! It's my family's shame," Christy wailed.

While the conversation was enough to raise my spirits, I still missed Mark. His charming, casual manner always to put me at ease when I was apprehensive. Just what could the Barbies have meant when they said that they knew something about him that would destroy me? Could there have been some deep, dark secret that everyone else knew and I didn't? Was there some backstory that had followed him from Houston? I knew Mark cared about me, and while I couldn't exactly say that he loved me, I knew he wouldn't intentionally do anything to hurt me... would he?

No. He wouldn't. To think that was ridiculous.

"Great," I mumbled, shifting in my seat.

"What's up?" Drifter asked.

"Now I have to pee."

"I call dibs on your apple."

"Go ahead. I wasn't going to eat it anyway."

Drifter immediately snatched my apple.

After rising, I made my toward the set of bathrooms that lay just outside the lunchroom.

Once I finished, I stepped out into the hall just before I saw the janitor's closet open.

My mouth dropped open. My heart stopped beating in my chest. I'm fairly sure my brain even ceased to work.

120

None other than Mark and Jennifer, the fourth and one of the most notorious of the Barbies, had emerged from the closet. Both seemed frazzled with their hair skewed in all directions. Before either of them could see me, I turned and bolted into the bathroom.

No. I had to be seeing things. Mark had gone off-campus for lunch. He wouldn't have lied to me. I *had* to be seeing things.

I peeked out into the hall and I realized I wasn't hallucinating. Jennifer ducked into the girl's bathroom and Mark walked quickly away from the lunchroom area. My heart sinking, I rushed back into the cafeteria.

When I reached our table and settled back down, Christy's eyes immediately fell on me. She instantly saw something was wrong.

"Adam," she said, her voice unsure and much lower than it normally was. "What happened?"

"I just saw Mark come out of the janitor's closet with one of the Barbies."

All my friends could do was stare.

Christy

"So what did he say?" I demanded. I tried to remain calm as I drove, not wanting to do something stupid like crash my car.

Adam shifted in the passenger seat of the car, looking uncomfortable. "I didn't say anything."

"Why not?" I couldn't believe my ears. The day had been full of suckage from the get-go, but what Adam had seen at lunchtime had topped it off.

"He was fine after lunch. Held my hand. Was super-sweet. I wanted to say something, but every time I looked at him he was giving me that look." Adam shrugged.

I knew exactly the look Adam was talking about. Heck, it even melted *my* heart when I saw it. Mark's eyes looked so beautiful and loving when he gazed at Adam, slightly smiling with those gorgeous lips of his. It made me all dewy-eyed to see it.

"Oh," I answered.

"Yeah." Adam rubbed a hand over his hair. "I mean, what if I'm wrong. What if I didn't see him?"

"But you *did* see him. You said so!"

Adam didn't answer. He just stared out the window miserably.

I slapped my hand against the steering wheel. I was so angry, yet I had to keep it together for my best friend. Everything felt so wrong, and I felt helpless. I just couldn't understand how things were going south so fast in Adam's and my world.

"Maybe she was hitting on him and he had to fight her off," Adam said at last. "The Barbies are persistent, you know and everything felt fine between us when I saw him again."

"Maybe," I said grudgingly. It's not that I wanted Mark to be the bad guy. I honestly wanted him to be the best boyfriend in the world for Adam. Yet, after the museum and birthday party incidents, I was having some slight misgivings. Misgivings I was totally willing to ignore until Adam told us about spotting Mark with one of the Barbies.

Adam sighed. "It has to be something simple, right?"

I swallowed my anger, nodding my head. Adam needed me to be supportive, not add fuel to the fire.

"He does like me, right? I'm not imagining the way he looks at me?"

"Absolutely not! He has a total thing for you." I wasn't lying. I knew in my heart that Mark had feelings for Adam. It was pretty clear to see every time I was around them that Mark was completely into Adam. "It's just so weird that he'd be with a Barbie in the janitor's closet. I just don't get it."

"Me neither." Adam sighed. "I guess I'm going to have to talk to him about it whether I want to or not."

Biting my lip, I nodded. Even if Mark was totally into Adam, something was seriously wonky about him being with a Barbie in the janitor's closet. If it had been anyone else I would assume that they were in a heavy duty make out session. I really couldn't figure out what else they would be doing in there.

"Do you think he's bisexual?" I blurted out.

Adam's horrified expression made me feel like a dog turd. "I don't think so," he stuttered. "And even if he is that doesn't give him the right to be making out with a Barbie, *if* that's what he did."

"True, true." I tried to concentrate on the road while I drove, but it was hard when I could literally feel Adam hurting beside me. "I guess you're just going to have to talk to him. I could take you by his house if you want."

Adam fidgeted in his seat, his fingers tugging at the cuffs of his jacket. "Uh, I don't know where he lives."

"Seriously?"

"Nope. I haven't met his family yet either. We usually meet at the coffee shop, take walks around downtown, and hang out at school."

"Dude, that is so suspicious," I said, forgetting to be gentle.

"I don't think he has a good home life, Christy. It's not that suspicious if you think about the things he's said about his folks not really being interested in him."

I was basically driving around in circles, not sure of where we were going. We had agreed to hang out after school, but neither one of us had actually agreed to any particular plan. I wanted to help Adam, but since he didn't know where Mark lived it's not like we could go surprise him at home.

"Do you want to call Mark and go over and see him?" I suggested.

Adam shook his head, his red hair glinting in the fading sunlight. The sun set a lot sooner in the fall in our corner of Texas. School let out at four o'clock, but already the sun was on the horizon.

"I don't think I'm ready to talk to him about what I saw yet." Adam tilted his head to one side, staring out at the sunset. "This is the first guy who I have ever had feelings for and has returned them. I just don't want to blow it."

The idea came to me in a big spurt, like my ideas are prone to do. "A spell!"

"Christy... ." Adam gave me an exasperated look.

122

"Adam, I can totally do a deception spell. I have one in a book in my room. It's not that hard to do at all. And my powers are getting stronger, so I know it will totally work."

Exhaling slowly, Adam shrugged. "Sure. Why not? What will it hurt?"

"Are you patronizing me?"

"Kinda." Adam grinned at me.

I rolled my eyes. "Fine. Be all condescending, but when my spell works you'll owe me a big apology and a double-dip cone at Dairy Queen."

"You got a deal," Adam answered, and though his smile was tinged with sadness, it made me happy to see it nonetheless.

When we reached my house Mom was in the kitchen working on her jewelry and Dad was in his study. Adam and I ducked out to the garden and gathered the items I needed for the spell. It was obvious he thought the whole endeavor was silly, but I felt very confident since my experience with Ian. My powers were growing even though I wasn't in full control of them yet.

Since I couldn't access the spell room yet, I resorted to grabbing a few things from the pantry while Adam distracted my mom with chit chat. I grabbed a few sodas and a bag of chips to cover up what I was doing and Adam and I hurried upstairs.

Adam is the only boy allowed into my room, but I still didn't dare to shut the door all the way. I left it open a sliver and placed the chair from my desk near it so it would slow down any sneaking parent.

Collapsing onto the bed, Adam played with Callie, who had mysteriously appeared out of my closet. I don't get her fascination with it, honestly. She's always getting locked in there. I dug under my bed for my cauldron and the small chest I keep some spell stuff in. Both were gifts from my parents on my sixteenth birthday. It's basically a witch starter kit.

"Okay, I need you to totally pay attention and do what I tell you," I said to Adam.

"Sure thing, Miss Bossypants." Adam scratched Callie behind the ears while she stared at me thoughtfully.

"No snitching," I told her. She hadn't told Mom about the love spell, so I hoped she'd keep silent on this one, too.

Callie narrowed her eyes at me, then yawned.

Out of my bookcase I removed a bright purple book with a cartoon witch on the cover wearing a pointed hat and riding a broom. Happily, the witch is actually cute and looks nothing like the warty-type. Flipping the book open, I looked for the spell.

"You have got to be kidding me, Christy," Adam said, laughing. "You're doing a spell from 'Spells for Starter Witches' for real? I bought you that on your birthday!"

Frowning, I continued to flip through the book. "Just because you bought it at a regular bookstore doesn't mean the spells won't work. Especially if you're a real witch like me."

Hearing the hurt in my voice, Adam stopped laughing. "Okay, okay. True. If you're a real witch, it won't matter."

I gave him the stink-eye, detecting sarcasm.

Sitting next to me, he slung his arm around my shoulders. "Really, Christy, I appreciate this."

"You better," I retorted, but melted into his side. I lay my head on his shoulder, feeling a moment of contentment. Adam always makes me feel safe and yet strong.

"Do the spell. I'll be totally cooperative."

"Good. Now, play with Callie and let me finish setting up."

Even if Callie is a couple of hundred years old and a witch's familiar, she cannot resist a dangling ribbon. Adam played with her while I snipped the heads off of my mother's roses and cut the stems, thorns and all, into equal sizes about three inches long. I poured a bottle of spring water into the cauldron and started lighting my white candles with my Bic lighter. My mom can light a candle with the touch of her finger, but I'm still not able to do that.

I flipped up my throw rug and drew a fresh chalk circle over the old one, careful to leave one spot open. I set all my stuff in the center of the circle and arranged the three candles around the cauldron.

"Okay, ready."

Adam remembered my previous instructions and carefully entered the circle through the opening. Callie followed him, much to my surprise, and took up the spot that formed a triangle within the circle. She sat solemnly staring at me. Taking this as a good sign, I closed the circle by drawing in the final piece.

My ears popped and a flash of light blinded me briefly.

"What was that?" Adam gasped.

Blinking rapidly, I grinned. "The circle closing."

Rubbing his ears, Adam looked at me skeptically. "Maybe it was an energy surge or something."

More confident than ever, I stuck out my tongue at him.

Adam looked at me with uncertainty.

Callie touched the edge of the cauldron with one paw. I got the distinct feeling she was telling me to hurry up.

"Okay, so, I'm going to say the spell and you're going to shake that silver chalice filled with rose stems and ask aloud to know who the deceiver in your life is, then toss it in the cauldron. The stems will spell out a name."

Adam drew in a sharp breath, then nodded. "Okay. I'm ready."

Opening the book to the page marked, I read: "Great wisdom of the universe reveal to me the question I ask of thee with a pure heart and in desperate need." I pointed to Adam.

"Who is my life is lying to me?" Adam covered the silver chalice with his hand, shook it, then tossed the rose stems into the cauldron.

All three of us, Adam, me, and Callie, leaned forward to stare into the water. The stems swirled around in the water, bumping into each other, and sending ripples along the surface. Gradually, the stems stopped bobbing around and settled into a pattern.

"M," Adam whispered.

"A," I added.

Adam visibly gulped. "R."

124

We both leaned closer to the pot watching the stems form the final part of the word.

"E?" we chorused.

Callie looked back and forth between us, then stuck her head deeper into the cauldron.

"K." Adam blinked slowly. "Marek? I don't think your spell can... uh... spell."

"That's totally weird. "I gaped at the word floating in the cauldron. I had fully expected it to say Mark, but instead it read Marek. "Um, that doesn't really make sense does it?"

"Well, it looks like Mark except for the E. Maybe it's backwards? Karem? Do we know a Karem?" Adam looked amused, but also greatly unsettled.

"Karen?"

"Do we know a Karen?"

I shook my head. Callie was still staring into the cauldron thoughtfully.

"So, Christy, what does it mean?" Adam asked.

"I don't know what it means," I confessed. "I mean, it looks like Mark."

"But it's not," Adam pointed out. "What if this Marek person is someone real?"

I grinned slowly. "You believe in the spell?"

"I didn't expect it to say anything, but it actually does," Adam said in a cautious voice. "I'm willing to give it the benefit of a doubt."

Squealing, I clapped my hands.

Adam looked annoyed. "Look, if I believe that the spell worked, then either the powers that be have no idea how to spell or this Marek person is someone I have to worry about. It doesn't say Mark."

"Marek *is* very close," I said and bit my lip.

"But it doesn't say *Mark*."

I wasn't sure if Adam was trying to convince me, or himself. "You have a point."

Adam scrubbed his hands through his hair. "Okay, so... we're still back to square one. I need to talk to Mark. And apparently watch out for a Marek or a Karem."

I hated the edge in his voice. "I'm sorry that it didn't do what we hoped."

"Yeah, me, too. More questions than answers now." Adam looked at the cat. "What do you think Callie?"

Callie's golden eyes peered up at him thoughtfully, then she yowled.

"What did that mean?"

"I don't speak cat. I don't have that power yet," I grumbled.

Climbing onto Adam's lap, Callie rubbed against him as though consoling him.

"Well, I guess I'd better get going and call Mark."

"Okay. Text me and let me know how it goes?"

"I will." His posture was tense and his expression worried.

I scrubbed open the circle. My ears popped again. Adam raised his hand to his head, but said nothing. Together we stood and stared at each other.

"I hope it's all innocent," I said at last.

"Me, too. I hope he has a good explanation and all this can be forgotten." He glanced at the word in the cauldron one last time. "Thanks for the spell."

"Any time," I answered lamely.

Adam strode out of the bedroom, his shoulders drooping under the weight of his emotions. I stared down into the cauldron.

"Marek," I read again. "Who the hell is Marek?"

Adam

Though I tried not to let my nerves get to me, they eventually did. Lying in bed, toying with the drawstring on my hoodie, staring at the ceiling—music played beside me, and while the pops, drawls and twangs of computer-made electronica filled the room, it did little to distract me from the matter at hand.

The longer I put off talking to Mark, the longer I would feel like this way. I mean, if I thought about it, I had a fifty-fifty chance of the situation being nothing more than a misunderstanding. Sighing, I reached for my cell when the almost-inaudible 'pop' notification noise sounded.

New message, it read.

I sat up and rubbed my eyes before clicking it open.

Hey, Mark said. *Wanna hang out?*

It seemed odd that he would message me just when I was at my wits end.

"That doesn't mean anything," I mumbled, clicking the white space beneath his message to write a reply. "You know that."

I closed my eyes, took a deep breath, then began to hold it.

I had to let this go. If I worked myself up before I met up with Mark, there was a very high chance I could let that rule my reaction.

Sure, I typed after a long exhale. *Nona's?*

Nona's, Mark's text replied. I could almost hear him saying the name of the coffee shop right beside me. *Pick you up in 30.*

I brushed my teeth, threw on a fresh set of clothes, then picked up my wallet and house key before heading downstairs.

"Hi honey," Mom said, lifting her eyes from her computer. "Feeling better?"

"Huh?" I frowned.

"You always play music in your room when you're depressed. That's the only time I ever hear it."

"Oh." I paused. "Yeah, I'm okay."

"Want to talk about it?"

"It's nothing, Mom. Don't worry about it."

"I will worry about it and will eventually wrangle the information out of you. You're warned." She shoved her glasses further up her nose and scoffed at the computer screen. "Oh, hell *no* she didn't."

"Are you on Twitter again?"

"Yes! I mean, no! Maybe! I—" She frantically began to type out a reply.

126

Mom's greatest obsession, other than shopping for shoes online, is Twitter. She's a bit obsessed with hashtags, so anytime something comes in about one of her favorite shows and she doesn't agree with it, she has to reply. Today's topic was million-dollar weddings. I think her thrifty nature sometimes gets the best of her.

"Sorry, honey," she said. "This bit—I mean *lady*—said that there's no such thing as a good dress under one-K."

"It's okay," I laughed. "I'll be gone for a little while. I'm going to Nona's with Mark."

"Again?" she asked.

"Again?" I frowned. "It's not like I'm at Nona's all the time."

"Three, four times a week. Friday's game night, so you're here then, or I break your kneecaps, and Sunday you're at church, so I can't really say anything about that." She shook her head and closed laptop, her rhinestone stiletto shoe decal catching the light. "I guess what I'm saying is that you're spending a lot of time with Mark lately. I'm concerned."

"About what?"

"Don't you think you're moving a little too fast?"

How was I supposed to judge what speed I should be moving with Mark? "I don't know," I said, glancing toward the window to check for Mark's car, then back at my mother. "I can stay home more often if you want me to."

"No, no. I'm not saying that at all. I'm glad you're getting out of the house. It really says something when you have a more active schedule than Amelia, and she's *ten*. Those slumber parties, you know?"

"Yeah," I laughed. "Can't forget them."

"I am concerned about one thing though," she said, rounding the island. "And I know you're going to give me hell and say that I'm being embarrassing, but—"

"Oh God," I groaned.

"You *are*... you know... being careful, right?"

"*Mom—*"

"It's just that they never taught the gay kids what it's like. I don't want you to get hurt."

"I know, Mom. Don't worry. I'll be careful." The sound of Mark's car pulling up and then its resounding honk broke my train of concentration. "I gotta go."

"Don't be out too late," Mom said, wrapping me in a hug before I could go out the door. "Text me if you need anything."

"I will. Love you."

"You too."

I couldn't have been more thankful for the sight of someone's car.

The relief over getting away from my house and arriving at Nona's quickly disappeared when the reality of the situation came into play. In our usual spot beside the window, I toyed with the orange juice Mark had bought for me and tried to figure out how to broach the subject.

"Something wrong?" Mark asked, lifting his coffee to his lips. "It looks like something's bothering you."

Leave it to Mark to get straight to the point.

"It's probably nothing," I laughed.

"Want to talk about it?"

After taking another drink, I pressed my cup to the table, wrapped my hands around it, then forced myself to look into my eyes before I began. "Like I said... it's probably just nothing, but I wanted to talk about... well... uh... you."

"Me?" Mark frowned.

"Yeah," I said. "It's not like I'm jealous or anything, but I've noticed lately that you get along with a lot of the girls at school. And considering they're still interested in you even after we've come out, I was just wondering... "

Mark chuckled in the silence I offered to him. "If I was bisexual?" he asked, taking another sip of his coffee. I nodded before he shook his head. "No. I'm not."

"Then I guess that means that you and Jennifer weren't doing anything in the janitor's closet."

Though I applauded myself for being straightforward, Mark's befuddled expression chilled the applause in my head. "You... don't think me and Jennifer were... *doing* anything, were you?"

"That's why I was asking you."

"No. Never. I would *never*, Adam, especially since I'm with you." Mark set his hand over mine. "Look: what you saw was me getting Jennifer off my back. She came on to me outside the bathroom and I thought it would be better if we weren't seen together, so I pulled her into the janitor's closet. Call it a stupid mistake on my part."

"Yeah," I sighed.

"I'm sorry, Adam," Mark replied, lacing our fingers together. "I didn't mean to make you feel this way. I mean... just knowing I hurt you... and knowing how bad I'd feel if it was reversed... it only makes me realize how much I love you."

I blinked. "You... love me?"

"There's been a lot of guys... well, a few—a lot of assholes and a few sweethearts—but I've never felt like this with anyone other than you. You're like this fire that keeps burning. This light I can always walk toward, which means a lot considering how bad things are for me at home."

There. Just like I thought. Spoken from his lips themselves. "That's why you never invite me to your place," I said.

"Because I didn't want my mother to ignore you? Or my dad to call you a fag, say you were worthless, say that you and me will never go anywhere because we were just two fags who'll get AIDs and die? No. I'd never take you there." Mark shook his head. His trembling fingers, quivering lip and downturned eyes were the kingdom that fell before my eyes. "Everyone thinks I've got it so good because I'm some hot-shot city-slicker, because I have nice clothes, because I have a nice *car*. This shirt I'm wearing? I got it from the second-hand store for five bucks. *Clearance* at a *second-hand* store. And my car? That was my dad's throw-away."

"Mark," I whispered.

128

"Everyone thinks that I've got it made, Adam. But you know what? I *don't*. I get up every morning and go to bed every night realizing that I live in my own version of hell. I mean... I know you and Christy have a history, being best friends and all, and I get that, but... it kills me, sometimes, knowing that I can't always be with you, that there are things I won't ever understand."

"You'll understand them someday, Mark."

"No I won't. I've never had a friend like Christy, and seeing you and her together is just... it makes me realize that you have so much more in your life than *me* when the only thing that keeps me going is *you*."

I didn't realize the tear that landed on my hand was my own until I felt moisture running down my face. "I'm sorry," I whispered.

"I'm not," Mark replied, and smiled despite what were most-obviously tears in his own eyes. "You know why? Because I wouldn't have you if it weren't for the hell I live in."

I tightened my hold on his hand.

It was seeing him suffer that made me realize how good my own life was.

Mom, Amelia, Dad—they all loved me.

Mark, though... he only had one person.

Me.

Chapter 10

Halloween

Christy

The Junior Class Halloween party was held in the early afternoon after the Seniors had their party then blew out of school early. Senior privilege and all that crap. The gym decorations were a little ragged after enduring the Freshman and Sophomore class parties in the morning. I bet most of the torn decorations were the doing of the Seniors. They're such jerks about everything since it's their last year in a high school and they believe they rule the school.

I can't wait to be one.

Olivia and I arrived together, Olive dressed as Bettie Boop, complete with a black wig and flapper dress, while I dressed as Alice from the video game *Alice: The Madness Returns*. I really rocked the blue dress and blood-splattered apron. When visiting Austin with my mom, I had bought black and white striped tights and big black boots with shiny buckles at the Secret Oktober store in South Austin. My big fake plastic dagger slathered in fake blood looked awesome, too.

The Barbies were decked out in their traditional trashy Disney princesses outfits and had already taken up position by the fake pumpkin patch where people were posing for photos. The jocks were dressed in their regular game uniforms, but were wearing zombie makeup. I had to give them points for the idea.

Olivia laughed out loud when she saw them. "Maybe the zombie football players will eat the Barbies if we're lucky."

I caught sight of Ian talking to Courtney. She flirted with him outrageously while he fiddled with a piece of fake skin glued to his neck. It looked pretty gruesome, which I had to admire.

"What are we looking at?" Adam asked, joining us. He looked adorable dressed as the White Rabbit from the same video game my Alice costume came from. The top hat had rabbit ears glued to the sides and he wore a dark red coat we had found at a Goodwill store. A big fake pocket watch the size of a dinner plate hung from a chain around his neck. Adam and I always coordinate our costumes.

"The brainless football players dressed up like brainless zombies," Olivia answered.

"If they want brains they're looking in the wrong place," Adam said with a grin.

"I was about to say the same thing," I said, pouting.

"The whole situation just sets up that joke far too perfectly," Olivia decided. She unwrapped a multi-colored lollipop and tucked it between her red bow-shaped lips.

Drifter sauntered over to us dressed in jeans and a black t-shirt. Hair heavily gelled, his tan skin slathered in white makeup and covered in glitter, it wasn't hard to figure out who he was supposed to be. We all burst into laughter.

"That's so wrong!" Olivia exclaimed.

"Dude, where are your fangs?" Adam asked.

"He doesn't have fangs," Drifter answered, striking a pose as I snapped his picture with my phone.

"What kind of lame vampire doesn't have fangs?" Adam protested.

"What kind of lame vampire goes out in sunlight?" Olivia rolled her eyes.

"What kind of lame vampire goes to high school?" I added.

"Maybe he was bored and just wanted to be around people," a voice said from behind us.

We all turned around to see Mark. He hadn't been at school all day, so we were all surprised to see him. Adam said Mark had been under the weather and he did look a little pale, but he was also extremely handsome in a red button down silk shirt, black leather jacket, and black jeans.

"Nice Angel costume," Olivia complimented him.

"Huh?" Mark looked confused.

"Oops." Olivia widened her eyes. "*Buffy* reference. You obviously don't adhere to the Joss Whedon code of life."

Mark scowled slightly, obviously not understanding what she was talking about. Meanwhile, I wanted to get back on topic.

"But if you're a vampire, why would you want to hang out with teenagers? We're all angsty and stuff." I admit I never got on the sparkly-vampire bandwagon. Every good witch knows it's the fairies that sparkle.

"Speak for yourself," Drifter said, elbowing me. "I'm chill."

I playfully stabbed him with my knife. "You're abnormal."

Sliding an arm around Adam's shoulders, Mark leaned slightly into him. "Well, maybe the vampire died when he was a teenager and wants to be around people that were going through the same stuff he was when he was changed."

Adam glowed with happiness and I was relieved that the whole scare with Jennifer had ended up being no big deal. Even though my spell wrote out the word *Marek,* I had to wonder if my own fears made the stems form that name. Maybe I wanted it to say Mark and the spell had been fighting back.

Drifter shrugged. "It's not like vampires are real anyway."

"Vampires, pfft," Olivia said in obvious agreement.

My parents had never clarified whether or not vampires exist, but I like to be cautious. "Well, if they exist I'm sure they're not hanging out in lame

132

Trinity Springs High School. And if they did, they'd probably be over there with the brainless football player zombies and slutty princesses."

Olivia's eyes widened just as the last of the words slipped from my lips. Adam winced and covered his face and Mark slightly smiled.

"Hey, Ian," Drifter said, trying to break the sudden tension.

Slowly swiveling about on the platform heel of my boot, I came face to face with Ian. His face was covered in fake latex bite wounds and the makeup gave him a ghastly dead pallor.

"Hey, Drifter, awesome sparkles. Olivia, you look cute. Mark, neat costume. I'm a big fan of the *Angel* TV show. Adam, I like it. The White Rabbit goes really good with Christy's Alice." Ian was obviously trying to be nice and overlook my big mouth. "Christy, I gotta say you have the best costume. That knife looks wicked."

I had been specifically avoiding Ian since the incident where I outed myself as a witch, so I floundered for something to say. Finally, I held up my fake knife and waved it under his chin. "You try to eat me, or my friends, and I'll slice off your head."

My nerves made me sound like a psychotic bitch. The shuffling of feet around me and the whisper of "harsh" by Drifter let me know I had blown it once again. At that moment I considered throwing up on Ian just to get away.

Ian raised his eyebrows slightly. "Uh, you may have to work really hard at it since that's a plastic knife."

"True," I said, grateful for his save. Embarrassed, I could feel my cheeks flushing.

"But before you decapitate me, I was wondering what you guys are up to tonight?"

"Trick-or treating, the usual," Olivia answered. "We didn't get our invite to the Slut-o-rama ball."

I threw Olivia a bright grin and she winked.

Ian actually laughed at that. "Well, I'm going to go make a quick appearance at Courtney's party, but a bunch of us are heading out to the old bridge to hang out. Remember when Ms. Guerra dragged us to the museum and talked about the old days?"

"Yeah, a total snoozefest," I answered.

"Well, one of the nerds—" Ian hesitated, looking a little stricken.

"We're the outcasts, not the nerds," Adam assured him.

"Well, they uncovered this really cool story about a ghost that appears out on the bridge on Halloween. It used to be a really big deal to go out there on Halloween to try to see him before the churches got a curfew passed to stop it. He hung himself from the bridge railing because some chick broke his heart or something."

"That's gruesome," Olivia said in awe. "I love it!"

"Why does it have to be some girl who broke his heart?" Mark's question was soft, but a little terse.

Again the tension ratcheted up around us. Ian looked at me of all people to save him.

"Well, even if it was a guy he was heartbroken over," I said diplomatically, "they would have covered it up."

133

"Besides, girls are evil," Adam said, winking at me. "Especially ones with bloody knives!"

I waved it at him, giggling. "Watch it, bunny. I may be in the mood for rabbit stew!"

Ian cleared his throat and shifted his stance slightly, his hands on his hips. "Well, anyway, I was wondering if you'd like to tag along, Christy. And your friends, too, of course."

My mouth dropped open and I found I had no voice.

Olivia kicked the back of my shoe.

"Uh... .why?" I stuttered.

Adam audibly moaned.

The pretty blond boy leaned toward me, whispering, "Well, I thought because you're... you know... it might make the ghost want to... you know... come out?"

I narrowed my eyes at Ian.

He looked around nervously, then placed his lips close to my ear. "You're a witch."

"And you're a big dumb jock," I answered, pushing him away, scowling.

He grinned. "So you're coming."

Olivia kicked my boot again.

"Yeah, we're totally coming," Drifter said for all of us.

"I wouldn't miss it," Adam agreed.

"Ghosts plus Halloween equals awesome!" Olivia traitorously added.

"So give me your number so we can coordinate," Ian said pulling out his phone.

In spite of being fiercely angry at him over Adam, and scared that he might out my witch nature to the world, I was overwhelmed that a moment I had daydreamed about for years suddenly was a reality. Ian was asking for my number. I stared at him mutely, my mouth slightly open.

Adam stepped forward and quickly told Ian my digits, his hand resting on my waist, slightly rubbing it. He was obviously being supportive, but my brain was overloaded and on the fritz.

"Okay, cool. I'll call you guys when we're heading out there. Can't wait!" Ian grinned one last time and sauntered away.

Swinging about, I glared at my friends. "You all suck."

"Uh huh, and you kinda have a date with Ian," Olivia said, preening triumphantly.

Adam enfolded me in his arms and I clung to him. "He's a big oaf, but he is trying, Christy. Give it a shot. Isn't that what you told me about Mark?"

"Don't freak, Christy. We're all going to be there. It'll be cool," Drifter gave my shoulder a squeeze.

Looking up, I felt like my face had to be as red as a tomato. "You all still suck."

"We've totally got your back, right, Mark?" Adam said, his arm still around me.

Mark was very still. I realized he hadn't spoken in some time. He looked even more pale than before and maybe a little ill. Finally, he shook his head. "You guys go. I think I'll stay in tonight."

134

"Mark, why?" Adam looked crestfallen and a little concerned.

"I'm just not feeling it and I'm a little under the weather. Besides, I'm the odd one out. You and Christy are all matching costumes and stuff. This is your night."

"We always wear matching costumes," Adam said, looking a little panicked and slightly defensive.

"You two could have totally matched," Olivia said, twirling her lollipop in the air. "Adam would make an adorable Buffy."

"Or an Oz. Then Mark could have been Willow," Drifter suggested.

"Or a gay Angel and gay Oz!" Olivia's eyes gleamed. "That would be so hot."

"I need to bail," Mark said abruptly. "I'll catch you guys later."

"Mark," Adam said, reaching out to grip Mark's hand, but Mark shrugged him off and headed toward the door.

"Party pooper," Olivia muttered.

"I'm going to go check on him," Adam said, hurrying after Mark.

"More trouble in paradise," Olivia noted, her gaze trailing after the two guys.

"Love isn't easy," Drifter sighed.

"Mark is just not feeling well and I think his home life is rough." I also had a feeling that Mark was feeling jealous about Adam and me again.

"Hopefully they can work it out before tonight." Olivia wagged her eyebrows at Drifter and me. "Because tonight we're going to have fun if it kills us and everyone in this town."

Adam

"Mark," I said, pursuing him through the halls. "Come on, talk to me."

He quickened his pace. At first I thought he did so because of me, but when he beelined for the bathroom and threw the door open, I sighed. Though I knew chasing him into the bathroom would look bad, I did so anyway just in time to hear a stall door slam shut and someone fall to the floor.

"Mark?" I asked. "Are you—" The sound of retching cut me off mid-sentence. Great. Sick the night of Halloween, and it wasn't even because of candy.

I took a moment to decide my course of action before shuffling to the mirror spread out along the wall. I leaned forward, took a deep breath, and tried to fight off the stings of worry stabbing at my conscience, which failed to work entirely.

The sound of retching stopped. "Are you okay?" I asked.

The toilet flushed and Mark stepped out. Pale as ever, he stalked to the sinks and washed, then wet his hands before splashing water over his face.

"Did you take your insulin?" I frowned, pressing a hand against the small of his back.

"I'm fine," he gasped, leaning forward when I began to rub his spine.

"You didn't answer my question though."

"I thought it was going to be an easy night," he replied. "A little walking, a little laughing, then us staying inside and watching TV."

"We've been talking about trick-or-treating for weeks," I said. "And walking... it's not that much. It's from the park to the bridge and back, ten minutes tops."

"Try being diabetic. You get to run around acting like a little kid with your friends. I don't."

Stung, I stopped rubbing his back. "This isn't about you being sick, is it?"

The bloodshot eyes that looked back at me in the mirror answered my question. "You don't think it's childish?"

"Spending time with friends?"

"We're almost adults, Adam. One more year and we're out of school. College. The *real world*. You know, where we have to pay bills, file taxes, stuff like that."

"If this is about me going out with them, I'll cancel. I don't want you to feel left out."

"Don't bother. I'll just be a downer anyway." He straightened himself out and turned for the door. "Thanks for helping me. I think I'll just go home."

"Don't drive if you feel sick," I said.

The door closed behind him without a reply.

I sighed.

Here, alone in the boy's bathroom and dressed like a rabbit, it took little to realize the situation.

I'd fallen down my own rabbit hole.

Christy

"Christy's friends are about to arrive so everyone has to be on their best behavior. Understood?" my mom said out loud in the foyer of our house. She was wearing her flowing purple and green Endora costume, a fancy red wig, and had her eyes made up with shimmering makeup to emulate Samantha's mother on the TV show *Bewitched*. The pictures in their frames and the paintings on the walls stilled. The broom zoomed around me in two tight arcs then zoomed up the staircase. The house visibly shuddered as it retracted to match the size it was outside.

"Define best behavior..." My dad was decked out what I can only define has Halloween camouflage. The pants, shirt, and gloves were spattered with fall colors and he had a skeleton mask tucked into his back pocket. He looks like a disembodied head when he lays among the Halloween decorations outside. The plan this year was to lie in a big pile of leaves and sit up and terrify the little kids.

My mom narrowed her eyes. "Oh, no. I'm not falling for that again. If I tell you not to do something, that's exactly what you'll do. Just... .be a good father, okay?"

"Define being a good father," my dad said with a wicked twinkle in his eye.

I pretended to stab him with my fake knife and he made a big show of staggering away in pain. Chuckling, Dad bounded back to my mom's side. "So is this an impromptu party?"

"We're just meeting up here before heading out." I swung my trick or treat bag at my side. I had made it one year with Adam in art class. It's just a simple beige cloth bag that we painted on with fabric paint, but I love it. Adam drew a great cat on it that looks a lot like Callie.

Speaking of my judgmental cat... Callie sat primly on a chair tucked under a window that overlooks the front yard. She was obviously watching the early trick or treaters with keen interest. Her ears flicked forward than back, then she turned and meowed.

"Yay, company!" Dad darted forward to open the door.

Picking up a huge cauldron packed with candy and baked treats tucked into orange cellophane and tied with black ribbon, my mother headed out the front door followed by my father. Drifter, Olivia and Adam were heading up the walk from Olivia's SUV. Still dressed up in their Halloween costumes, they had freshened up their makeup. Adam had added drawn on whiskers and a bunny nose. He looked adorable.

"You look awesome!" My mother clapped her hands. "I love it."

"What's with Glitterman? Dad asked. "Is that a new superhero?"

"I'm Edward," Drifter explained. "The vampire guy that all the girls like."

Dad lifted both eyebrows. "They just don't make vampires like they used to."

"It seems you're missing someone," my mom said. "Where's Mark?"

Adam shuffled his feet and sighed. "He's sick tonight."

"Oh, that's a shame! Have a candy!" Mom held out the cauldron and we all grabbed as much as they could with both hands.

Shoving their treats into their bags, my friends clustered around my parents laughing and chatting. I nervously fingered my cellphone in my pocket, hating how excited I was at the prospect of Ian calling me.

"So what's the big plan tonight?" My Dad fussed with some of the skeletons hanging from the porch roof while he spoke, arranging the cobwebs and plastic spiders artfully.

"Trick-or-treating to start," Adam said. "Ghost hunting later."

"Ghost hunting?" My parents sounded like an echo and both looked at us curiously.

"There's this legend about the old bridge. A bunch of us from school are going to go check it out," Adam answered. "It'll be cool."

"I bet the football players are going to prank all of us," Drifter said, unwrapping a cookie and starting to eat it with gusto.

"They're so going to prank us. It's so obvious," Olivia agreed. As to be expected, she was sorting through the lollipops she had snagged out of the cauldron. She finally settled on a green one.

"Ian asked Christy to go," Adam added, winking at me.

I narrowed my eyes.

"The big dumb jock you helped with his homework?" My dad had a mixture of fear and pride in his expression.

137

"Yeah. But it's totally not like a date," I said quickly. "He's obviously just wanting us to get scared with the rest of the kids going."

"He likes her," Olivia proclaimed. "He's intrigued by her anti-social ways."

"I'm not anti-social. I hang out with you losers," I protested.

Drifter smirked. "The hard to get thing is working."

"I'm not playing hard to get. There is no getting of the me. He's a stupid dumb guy!"

"She doth protest too much," my dad decided.

My mom was staring at me as though I had grown horns and wings, or something along those lines. "Don't pick on her, Richard. If she's not into the boy, don't push it."

"Oh, she's totally into him." Olivia gave me a wide grin around her lollipop.

"You all suck." I declared.

"So you keep saying. Maybe we should have dressed like vampires," Adam teased, tickling my side.

"Just remember your curfew," my mom admonished. "I don't want you out too late. I know tomorrow isn't a school day, but still."

"I know. Midnight. I'll be home," I promised.

Leaving my folks to terrorize the neighborhood kids, the four of us started off down the street to collect as much candy as humanly possible. Though we are often teased for our age, the people in our neighborhood always hand over the candy. They love seeing our costumes and we play it up for the elderly people who remember us from when we were very little.

We briefly ran into Adam's mom. She was dressed up like Glinda the Good Witch and Amelia made a really cute Dorothy, if Dorothy was an anti-social brat who scowls all the time that is.

"So cute! I love it!" Adam's mom exclaimed, hugging me. She's so cute and adorable. She's like a little pixie. "Pictures for Facebook time!"

Even though the sun was almost down on the horizon, we clustered around Amelia, who hadn't stopped scowling, for several photos. Finally, we escaped Adam's mom and headed back toward my house. There was still no call from Ian and I was starting to think it had all been a cruel joke. Maybe he just built me up to crush me as revenge.

We rounded the street corner and Olivia squealed, clapping her hands.

To my shock, and somewhat dismay, Ian's truck was parked behind Olivia's SUV and he was chatting with my folks.

"Kill me. Kill me now." I stopped in mid-stride, horror washing over me.

"It'll be fine," Adam assured me.

"But... but... "

Drifter captured one arm and Adam the other and they shoved me forward with Olivia leading the way.

"... but... but... "

"No, buts! It will be awesome!" Olivia waved her lollipop at me.

Breaking free of Drifter and Adam, I hoisted my trick-or-treat bag onto my shoulder, gripped my fake knife, and stomped toward Ian.

"Hey, Christy!" he called out when he saw me.

I faltered.

"Keep walking," Adam ordered, nudging me on.

 138

I regained my senses and somehow made it to where my parents and Ian stood chatting like old friends. Even with his zombie makeup partially melted on his face, Ian was too dreamy for words. I felt like a fat idiot standing next to him.

"I just love that costume," Ian said to me. "It's killer. I totally thought you'd be dressed like a witch or something."

Mom's eyes slightly widened and Dad scrunched his forehead.

"Why would you think that?" Mom asked in a way too sweet voice.

"So we're totally going to the bridge, right?" I said in a gush of words.

"We should totally go right now!" Olivia said, trying to help rescue Ian.

"Yeah, so we can get good... uh... ." Adam faltered.

"Parking!" Drifter added.

"Yeah, parking!" Adam said with relief. "And good spots on the bridge, too."

"To see the ghost," Olivia said, snagging Ian's arm.

Looking befuddled, but adorable, Ian said, "Okay! Yeah, let's go! Nice seeing you Mr. and Mrs. Wynne!"

My dad waved and my mom lifted an eyebrow. She looked scarily like Endora in that moment.

"Okay, we'll follow you to the parking lot near the bridge," Olivia said to Ian.

"I can take some of you with me," Ian offered.

Adam shoved me forward. "Christy can go with you. Her boots make it a tight fit in Olivia's car."

I slitted my eyes at Adam and he grinned.

"Cool! Awesome! Let's go!" Ian said, his fingers closing around my wrist.

I felt dizzy and a little afraid.

Within seconds, I was alone in the cab of Ian's truck with him starting up the vehicle, chatting away about how boring Courtney's party was. I would like to say that we had an awesome conversation, but the truth is I barely said a word until we reached the park. I mostly sat in terrified silence, sucking in my stomach as hard as I could, nodding to everything Ian was saying.

"I brought this old lantern that my mom says came with my family from Europe. This should totally get the ghost to come out, especially if you hold it," he said with enthusiasm pointing to an object wrapped in a towel on the floor near my feet.

"Uh, okay... " I said, swallowing hard.

Once he parked the truck, I was relieved to jump out and rejoin my friends. Olivia had maneuvered her car into the spot next to Ian's truck and I couldn't skirt around it fast enough to be with Adam and Drifter.

Ian followed in my wake and stood next to me.

Panicked, I looked at Olivia for help. Instead, the bitch snagged Adam and Drifter by the arms and led them toward the bridge. "Let's go find this ghost!"

My knees weakened as Ian slid his arm around my shoulders. "I'm so glad you're here, Christy. With you here the ghost is sure to show up and it's going to be awesome."

Trudging along like Herman Munster on my big boots, I walked with Ian to the bridge.

I wasn't sure what I was more afraid of: the ghost, or that this was actually some weird date.

Chapter 11

The Ghost

Adam

While Mark's absence initially stung, I was able to push the uneasy feelings aside and enjoy what Halloween truly is about: friends, trick-or-treating, and, apparently this year, a haunted bridge.

"I can't believe it," Drifter said through a mouthful of candy. "I mean, *look at it.*"

"Don't eat too fast!" Olivia chastised. "You'll choke yourself."

It didn't take more than a glance to see that Drifter was gorging on Tootsie Rolls.

Walking along the road that led from the park to the bridge in our costumes and carrying our candy, we were pretty spectacular—an insane girl with a knife, a rabbit, a sparkling vampire, a zombie jock and, of course, Bettie Boop—but the real attraction was the crowd walking to the bridge.

Kids from all over town had flocked to this area of Trinity Springs all on account of one little field trip. From ghosts, to werewolves, to damsels in distress and the knights who saved them—you couldn't look anywhere without seeing someone in costume. This area was normally dead. Seeing it like this was unbelievable.

"Keep that up and you'll be a different kind of vampire by the end of the night," I grinned, shooting Drifter a wink as he bit the head off a gargantuan Tootsie Roll.

"Hey!" he cried. "What's that supposed to mean?"

"It means," Olivia giggled, "that'll you'll be a certain vampire who happens to live on his own cereal box."

"Oh," Drifter mumbled. "Count Chocula."

"Bingo!" Olivia smirked.

Though our laughter was a chorus to the night, Christy's occasional mumble was the gift that kept on giving.

"Think she'll turn off her mute button anytime soon?" Olivia whispered, gently elbowing me.

"She hasn't thrown up yet," Drifter mused.

"She'll be fine," I said. "She just has to get over being absolutely terrified of him. Then everything will be okay."

Olivia's trademark grin was followed by the opening of a Tootsie Pop. "Don't get any ideas," Olivia leered, narrowing her eyes at Drifter, who only bared his fangless mouth in response.

"I vant to suck your Tootsie Roll!" Drifter hissed, then faltered. "Man, that sounded..."

"Dirty," Olivia said with delight.

Ahead, Ian continued to prattle about Christy's costume, much to her chagrin.

"... then there was that one part, where you're stuck on this massive chessboard and you have to solve that stupid puzzle. I mean, *really? A puzzle?* I can't even solve crosswords most of the time, and what's worse is that after I solved it, one of those stupid teapots killed me! Talk about embarrassing! That happen to you?"

Christy's short 'uh uh' was only matched in pitch by the gentle clink of the old lantern Ian had loaned her swinging from her hand.

Ian finally stopped boring Christy with details about the game, and said. "We're almost to the bridge. You'll get the ghost to come out, won't you, Christy?"

"Sure," she said in a doubtful voice. "And I'll ride my magic broomstick across the moon while I'm at it."

Ian's eyes lit up immediately.

"Pfft," Olivia said. "Flying witches."

"No ghosts or flying witches," Drifter spoke up, "but here comes something maybe just a *little* bit scarier, and with less clothing."

I turned my head just in time to see none other than two of the slutified Disney Princesses heading right toward us.

"Great," I said. "What would Halloween be without them?"

"I know, right?" Ian asked, waving his hand at the Barbies. "Hey Britney, Maribel! Cool seeing you here."

The princesses paused, staring at the zombie football player, then at my best friend at his side. They exchanged looks, then Maribel broke out laughing.

"You have *got* to be kidding me!" Britney shook her head. "Wow, Ian. You're really slumming it tonight, huh?"

Ian looked startled by the venom in their voices, but Christy and I gave each other knowing looks. The two Barbies were here not for fun, but trouble.

"Christy and her friends are cool," Ian said defensively.

"Too many knocks to the head on the football field, huh?" Maribel asked, her voice filled with poison. "It seems you got a bit of brain damage if you're hanging out with these losers."

Ian's face flushed and he lowered his chin, flustered.

Christy and I rolled our eyes. We were used to this treatment, but Ian definitely was not.

"We're not here for you anyway, Ian. We're here for Adam." Maribel put her hands on her hips and glared at me. The Princess Jasmine costume looked like it would suffer a nip slip at any moment, if not fall off altogether. "It's a good thing you're not down your rabbit hole, because we have something special for you."

Folding my arms across my chest, I presented my most bored expression for their viewing pleasure. "Let's get this over with. What do you want? I mean, other than to make my life a living hell?"

"Why, Adam," Britney smiled. "Why would I want to do that?"

"To kiss Courtney's ass," Olivia said with a smirk. "The queen bitch obviously doesn't like Adam because of his hottie boyfriend, A.K.A Mark."

"Shut up, Slutty Boop," Maribel said, waving her hand dismissively about the air.

"We have a message from Snow White," Britney said, the perfect portrait of Cinderella in her blue and white dress and fake glass slippers.

"Snow White?" I asked. It occurred to me that Courtney had dressed up as that princess at school. "Which is?" I asked.

Britney reached into her bag.

I expected a note.

Instead, I was only just barely able to duck before a rotten apple flew at my head. It soared through the air until landed on the road behind me with a squishy splat.

"Your apple is rotten," Britney said with false sympathy. "Now that you've tasted it, it's only a matter of time before you're in your little glass coffin and Prince Charming won't come and save you."

Britney and Maribel flashed their infamous bitch grins before they turned and flounced back toward the parking lot. They were probably returning to Courtney's party to check in with her.

"Wow," Ian said. "Harsh."

"You have stupid faces and stupid hair and you look like hookers in Disneyland!" Christy shouted after them. "And your stupid plastic shoes look nothing like glass! And you—"

I clutched Christy's arm. "It's okay. They're leaving."

"Well, that was just special, wasn't it?" Olivia said, rolling her eyes. "And way overly dramatic."

"So they're still on Adam's case," Drifter said. "Lame."

"Of course," Olivia said. "They're the freakin' princess mafia of Trinity Springs High."

"Who'll go to any length to break me and Mark up," I said with a shrug. "Don't worry about it. I don't care. It's just them being stupid."

"Total bitches," Christy said.

"Adam," Ian said. "That was uncool. Sorry you have to deal with that."

All I wanted to do was enjoy Halloween with my friends, *without* the Barbies. "Let's just go to the bridge. It's not like anything worse could happen, right?"

Though Christy offered me that all-knowing you-just-jinxed-us-for-good look, I winked and continued up the road, shortly pursued by my friends.

Though the crowd around us had lessened during my confrontation with the Barbies, the number of people was still staggering. From the drama club, to the chess team, to the band and lesser-known groups—even the math club was out tonight, each dressed like the varying numbers of pi. Surprisingly, the jocks were nowhere to be seen, which was a blessing I'd dare not speak of in Ian's presence. I didn't want to ruin Christy's evening.

Soon enough, we were nearing the oldest bridge in Trinity Springs.

It wasn't much of a spectacle. Up close, it looked like any old bridge—old, lonely, with rust slowly crawling across the surface of the metal beams crisscrossing the structure. It looked like something that had come to die here and had never been buried, left alone without a proper funeral. It'd been tethered off for as long as I could remember by a fraying rope that looked like it'd snap off at any moment, and while an old sign dangling from the rope proclaimed 'Danger: Off Limits' in big bold letters, they'd faded over time, much like the bridge's history. It didn't matter anymore, though. The kids did what they wanted. They might as well blame the museum if anyone managed to get hurt here.

"We should totally go out there," Ian said, making his way toward the rope.

"In these shoes?" Olivia asked. "I don't need to go falling to my death, thank you very much, much less a watery grave."

"Come on! Where else are we going to see the ghost?" Ian protested.

"Probably under the bridge," Christy said. "Where... you know... the guy hung himself?"

"How'll we know when it comes?" Ian looked skeptical.

A scream cut through the night.

"When the first person screams," Olivia grinned.

"I saw it!" a girl near the edge of the river said, trembling. "I *saw* it!"

"Saw what?" Batman laughed, taking his Catwoman date into his arms.

"There's nothing out here. You're just worked up, that's all. There's nothing to be afraid of," one of the skeptics from the math club said.

"It was in the trees across the bridge!" the girl wailed. "It had red eyes!"

What had initially been a happy, jovial time was reduced to unease and confusion. The few laughs that echoed across the area were a bit too nervous to be reassuring.

"There's nothing to be worried about," one of the girl's friends said. "It's just a stupid story. Like the Bunnyman."

"The Easter Bunny?" the sobbing girl asked, which instantly drew a bout of laughter along the road.

No one made a move to tell the girl that the Bunnyman was actually a serial killer.

Though the tension had left the air, I continued to stare at the tree line where she said she had seen the ghost.

"Hey, Adam?" Drifter said. "What're you looking at?"

"Nothing," I replied. "Just the trees. Why're you—"

The sensation of a wave of cold air brushing along my arm froze me in place. Then, eerily, I felt someone briefly squeeze my arm. I looked swiftly over my shoulder, but there was no one standing close to me.

"Cat got your tongue?" Drifter laughed, playfully slugging my arm.

"Y-yeah. I guess."

"Are you all right?"

"Was that you who just touched my arm?"

"Yeah. I slugged you."

"No. Before that."

"What're you talking about?" Drifter frowned.

"I think I just got a little spooked," I laughed.

The fog spooling over the river clung to the water's surface like spiders on their webs.

A whisper sounded in my ear.

"What?" I asked.

All sound ceased to exist.

No birds. No crickets. No cars. No wind. Nothing. Nothing at all. Not even the sound of laughter could be heard echoing across the area.

The breath slipped from my lungs. Though I was able to regain it, I couldn't shake the feeling that something bad was about to happen.

The wind, which had been still up until that moment, drew forward.

The clouds shifted, obscuring the moon.

A bird called out.

Adam.

The world snapped into focus. Kids were laughing, making scary Halloween noises, eating candy, and whispering amongst themselves about who would see the ghost first. It seemed like my bad feeling had been nothing more than just a feeling—a thing born of paranoia on Halloween.

"Thank God," I whispered. "Everything's just fine. I didn't hear a ghost call my name."

A pair of red eyes flickered in the trees.

My breath caught in my throat.

The eyes vanished.

I had to be seeing things. This wasn't real. It couldn't be. My head was just playing tricks on me. But then again, it was Halloween, the perfect day to walk around in a grim reaper costume or along the road like a werewolf to scare the living hell out of people. It had to be a prank. It couldn't be anything but.

A scream made me jump. A chorus of screams followed the first, then nervous laughter rippled through the crowd. If I had dressed up as the Cheshire cat for Halloween, I would have said that we were all mad down here.

"Look!" someone screamed.

I looked at the tree line across the river.

A second pair of eyes came into view.

A third came after that.

A fourth followed.

They began to hop across the rocks jutting out of the water sprawling from the far bank to just under the bridge.

Someone screamed. "What's happening? What's going on?"

"Nothing's happening!" her friend cried. "It's just Halloween! Nothing more than—"

A series of figures stepped from the trees to our side.

For a second, everything went quiet, like a gag had just been shoved into the collective mouth of Trinity Springs High. The figures paused, tilted their heads. Then they burst into a run toward us.

145

Panic filled Trinity Springs' only recreational area. Screams tore across the night. They cut through the air like daggers and drew sweat on a cold night. People ran. They fell. They rolled into the ditch that ran alongside the road and blubbered incoherently as a night of fun was reduced to nothing more than horror.

They sounded mad. *Barking* mad if anyone had a word for it, running around and screaming as though they were being chased by the devil themselves. It was almost as if we'd stepped into a world tumbling on the brink of oblivion, with the globe tilting to one side and everyone slowly falling over.

"Oh God," Drifter said. "Oh God oh God oh—"

"It's a prank," Olivia said, calmly digging through her bag for another lollipop.

"How can you be sure?" Drifter asked, not looking convinced.

"There's only one ghost, Drifter!" Olivia stood her ground, not moving despite the people panicking around her. "I can't believe people are so stupid. It's a trick. It's *Halloween!* It's supposed to happen. People see a few red eyes and everyone panics like it's the freaking zombie apocalypse! I mean, what is this? *Paranormal Activity?* I don't see any ghosts dragging anyone off."

Soon only my small group of friends remained beside the misty waters of the river. In the distance came the sound of slamming car doors, engines revving and wheels squealing as the teens fled.

"It's happening," Ian said with awe, watching the robed figures like a kid at the video game store. "You did it Christy! You brought the ghost!"

"I didn't light the lantern yet!" Christy protested. "And I'm not a witch!"

A hand touched my shoulder.

I spun.

A figure with glowing blood-red eyes stood before me. "Hey, Adam," it said, its voice distorted. "Are you scared yet?"

I tightened my hold on my candy bag, ready to strike.

"Back off!" I ordered.

The figure didn't respond.

It stepped forward.

I raised my candy bag.

Christy leapt in front of me, waving the lantern and fake knife. "Back off!" she screamed.

She swung the lantern.

It slammed into its chest and instantly elicited an '*ow.*'

I snatched her around the waist and yanked her back. "Be careful, Christy," I said.

"Scared, fag?" The creature grunted, shuffling forward.

"Not really," I replied. "You're wearing glasses with fake glowing eyes and a Walmart costume. Plus, I recognize your voice, Jayden."

"You were scared," Jayden answered, yanking off his hood. "Admit it. We scared the ever-living hell out of you *and* your friends."

"More like everyone else, *but* us," Drifter corrected.

I resisted the urge to hit Jayden in the face with my candy bag, certain a few candied apples would leave a nice bruise.

The shrouded figures pulled their hoods from their heads to reveal their true, football-team identity.

"Ha ha," Olivia said. "Very funny, guys. Very funny."

Ian looked vastly uncomfortable. "Uh... guys," he said. "This was incredibly lame and stupid."

"Why?" Jayden asked. "*His* boyfriend isn't here."

The football players snorted.

"Yeah, but I'm here," Ian said, his tone firm yet menacing.

I continued to glare at Jayden, refusing to be afraid of him, but also surprised Ian had my back.

"Well, you got what you came for," Olivia said, gesturing to the bridge and surrounding areas with her lollipop. "You scared everyone off. I hope you're proud of yourself, guys, because you pulled off one hell of a prank. And the fog machine? *Classic.*"

"What fog machine?" one of the jocks asked.

I turned to see fog spilling from the tree line across the river.

"Don't give me that," Olivia groaned.

"It's not us. Really, it—"

"Did you do it?" I heard Ian whisper to Christy.

Frightened looks and threatening glares were aimed at my best friend. Christy visibly shivered and took a step back. "I'm not a witch," she whispered, panic in her voice.

I moved to defend her, but Olivia was ahead of me. She took one quick step in front of Christy, blocking her from the view of the pranksters. "Her? A witch? Pfft." Olivia took her lollipop from her mouth and stepped forward. "Funny thing," she said in a rather ominous voice, "all this time you've been thinking that Christy was a witch. But honestly, *I'm* the witch."

"Oh God," I groaned. What did she think she was going to do?

Olivia dramatically raised her hands and closed her eyes. "I call upon the powers that be," she said, waving her lollipop in her hand, "to summon the water, the air, the creepy things that drift through the night."

The football players looked worried, a few taking steps back from Olivia. Drifter snickered, Christy cowered, and Ian looked confused.

The fog began to drift over the bridge and slither toward us.

"Bend to my will and do my bidding." Olivia flung her hands forward, and to my surprise, a small strand of fog crept up the bank and toward the jocks. "Consume their souls, forces of darkness!"

I would have never believed sixteen-year-old guys could scream like that. Their frantic yelps were only matched by their footfalls as they high-tailed it away from the bridge.

Olivia dropped her hands, rolled her eyes, and popped her lollipop back into her mouth. "Losers."

"Did you... did... you?" Ian gestured to the mist creeping over the ground.

"Pfft, no. It was just obvious from the breeze which direction the fog would drift, which was toward the idiots." Olivia smirked.

"Well played, Olivia, well played," Drifter said with approval.

I had to admit it had been a blast seeing the bullies run off in terror. The night was once more looking up. "Now that they're gone, let's find us a ghost," I said, beginning my trek toward the bridge.

"You're not serious," Ian replied. "After *that?*"

Olivia thumped Ian on the arm. "It's *fog*. A cold front was supposed to come in tonight. The morons would've known that if they knew how to watch the weather."

"Maybe the fog was the ghost," Ian suggested.

"How can it be?" Olivia asked. "We haven't summoned it yet."

A quick glance at Christy was enough to make me think she was in her own personal version of hell. She obviously did not want to do this. I could see the tension in her face and the uncertainty. How long had she fought against the witch tag? I was out of the closet, but she wasn't out of the broom closet. I may be skeptical about her being a witch, but Christy believes it.

I gestured to our surroundings. We were once more alone in the foggy night. "Now that Olivia's grand counter-troll against the jocks has succeeded, and to perfect effect, where are we supposed to summon the ghost?"

"I... I... " Christy hesitated, her eyes flicking toward Ian.

"C'mon, Christy," Ian pleaded. "It will probably only work if you do it."

"It's all fun and games anyway," Olivia said with a shrug.

"Yeah, this is just for fun. It's not like any of us believes you're really a witch," Drifter added helpfully.

Ian looked at our friends in confusion. "But she is one."

Christy shifted on her big platform boots, her eyes downcast.

I stepped forward and rested my hand on Christy's shoulder. "If you don't want to do it, I'll do it. This is just for fun. We're not taking it seriously, right?" I didn't want to think about the strange cold touches I had experienced, or my name being whispered, certain I had to have imagined it.

Flicking her eyes toward Ian, she sighed. "Fine. It's just for fun and not a confession of any witchy-dom." She pinned a fierce look on Ian.

"Right," he said, winking.

She rolled her eyes. "Down here," she said.

I stepped aside.

Christy led the way to the bridge.

"So," Olivia said. "What do we do now?"

I first crossed my arms over my chest, then slid my hands into my pockets when I realized their trembling might show my nerves. I was still a little rattled from earlier. Before us, Christy hopped over to one of the lone rocks standing in the low water under the bridge, crouched down, and opened the lantern's glass door, a lighter held in hand.

"How will we know when it's here?" Ian asked, reaching into his pocket. "Do I need to use this ghost-tracking app I downloaded? It beeps when the ectoplasmicwhateveryoucallit energy comes close."

"We'll know when it's here," Christy said. "And we won't need an app. Be quiet. We have to let it come to the light."

She struck the lighter and lit the candle. The glorious red flame winked to life.

With a nod, Christy closed the lantern and stepped back. "To the spirit of the young man who hung himself on this bridge," she said, sliding her lighter into her pocket. "We have lit this candle on this sacred night of Halloween to pay our respects to the memory of your life. Please, come to the light. Seek comfort and give us a sign to let us know that you are here."

No one said a word.

The flame flickered, dancing its gracious mantra.

"How long is this going to take?" Olivia asked, sucking on her lollipop.

Drifter was eating yet another Tootsie Roll.

"I don't think long," Christy said, obviously nervous. She kept shifting on her feet and looking at Ian. I was convinced that she was going to fall into the drink if she weren't careful.

The wind began to blow.

"What was that?" Ian asked.

We lifted our heads.

Surreal could not have described the sight.

The last leaves of autumn began to fall.

First the leaves drifted with the wind as if channeled over the river by some cosmic force and began to dance above our heads. Shifting, constantly, they twirled through the air like stars falling to earth in the darkest night. Their presence loomed like a sign of what was to come. Did it want to give us a sign? A message? Maybe it was just the wind and it had nothing to do with the ghost of Trinity Springs. Either way, the world before us was in motion—seemingly, by the will of a ghost.

The cold grappled with me.

I gripped the collar of my jacket and tightened it around my shoulders.

Adam, a voice said.

The leaves parted overhead before cascading to the ground on either side of our group.

What felt like a pair of arms wrapped around my shoulders, then disappeared instantaneously.

In the aftermath, I shivered, unsettled by what had just occurred.

"Was that it?" I asked, looking up at Christy.

"What?" Christy turned her head. She looked confused. "The leaves?"

"No. I thought something touched me," I answered, faltering.

"Seriously?" Christy gaped at me.

"What's that?" Ian exclaimed.

"Now that's just creepy," Olivia decided, hands on hips.

"Wow," Drifter said around a mouthful of candy.

It dangled from the middle railing upon the bridge. Long and frayed, it shifted in the wind not once, but twice before its length settled into place, the noose the halo of one man's suffering.

Hands shaking, Christy stared at the noose. "Okay... it worked."

"Now what?" Ian was obviously awed by the sight.

Clustered together, we stared at the rope, not truly believing what we were seeing.

"Uh, we should send it on its way," Christy muttered. In one swift move, she reached down to lift the lantern from the ground. "We thank you," Christy said, "for letting us know you're here. You're not forgotten." The moment she blew the candle out, the noose disappeared.

What sounded like a long sigh drifted across the wind as the leaves lifted from the ground and blew away over the river.

"Wow, "Ian whispered. "That was amazing."

"Come on," Christy said. "Let's go. We've been here long enough." She appeared unnerved and a little frightened, which is exactly how I felt.

Together, we started down the road in silence. The whole while, I couldn't help but wonder, who was this ghost, and why had he touched me?

Christy

My costume lay on the floor-where I had shrugged it off. Callie pawed at the buckles on my boots while I stared at the hole in my tights with dismay. When had that happened? I had no clue. The whole night was a surreal blot in my memory. To top things off, I felt a little queasy. Though I wanted to blame the enormous amounts of candy I had consumed throughout the night, I knew what my upset stomach was really about.

That dangling noose hanging from the bridge.

Shivering, I ran my comb through my damp hair. A hot shower hadn't removed the chill that had seeped into my bones when I had performed the ritual to call the ghost. Callie brushed past me and into the closet.

What is it with cats and closets?

Another icy wave flowed up my spine and embraced my brain. A headache was stirring. I fumbled the bottle of aspirin out of my bed stand and swallowed a few pills with a chaser of cold water from the cup I leave next to my bed when I sleep.

That poor ghost. I regretted summoning him.

I had tried very hard not to summon anything. With everything within me, I had wished for my powers to remain quiet and not draw a poor ghost out into the world of the living to be gawked at. There was something terribly sad about a young man taking his life. What had driven him to walk down to that horrible bridge with a rope in his hand and hang himself with it? Had it really been a broken heart? Could someone really kill themselves over a lost love?

My cellphone vibrated again. I knew it was Ian. He was so pumped up after the spectral rope had appeared he hadn't shut up the entire way back to my house. I'd had to slam the door on his cute, annoying face to get him to go home. Happily, my parents were too busy watching some horror movie about witches —that had them howling with laughter—they hadn't given me the third degree about our ghost hunting. I had feigned tiredness and escaped upstairs.

My brain was a mess because of the events of the night. A piece of me was elated about Ian hanging with us and even defending Adam against the jocks. Another piece was scared to death that I had betrayed my family by summoning the ghost. Our kind cannot be revealed to humans. That's been drilled into my head since I was a kid. And lastly, I felt sick at the thought of stirring up the spirit of some poor soul who had tried to find relief at the end of a rope.

Again I shivered as I remembered the noose.

Callie emerged from my closet, yawned, and headed toward my bed. I rolled my eyes, wondering which of my hoodies I would find on the floor covered in cat fur. Leaping onto my rumpled comforter, she headed toward my pillow, where I knew she would hunker down, only allowing me a small corner.

Picking up my phone, I read Ian's latest text.

Want to get together tomorrow and talk about the ghost?

Unexpectedly, tears flooded my eyes. Sitting on the edge of my bed, I wiped my wet cheek on my blanket. For so many years I had wanted Ian to notice me and ask me out. Now he was finally interested in me, but it was for the wrong reason. He was thrilled by the idea of me being a real witch. It had nothing to do with me as a person. In my imagination, I had always pictured him falling madly in love with my quirky sense of humor and making me his girlfriend. Then the whole school would be in awe of me, even like me, and would stop looking down on me as a pathetic outcast. Instead, he saw me as his own personal ghost hunter.

With a sigh, I texted back that I had plans and I would see him at school on Monday.

"What's wrong with me?" I wondered aloud. I was utterly depressed by Ian's desire to hang out with me. A part of me wanted to just pretend he was totally into my average looks and snarky persona and ignore his excitement over my powers so I could soak in his charming presence. Maybe if I was a little shallower I could do it, but I wanted to be appreciated for who I am, not for what I am.

Flopping over on my bed, I curled up and stared at my phone. I considered texting Adam, but he was probably telling Mark all about our adventure. Instead I reached out and turned off the lamp.

The image of the noose rose in my mind again. Shivering, I tugged the comforter over my body and pressed my hand against my eyes. I didn't want to think about the lovesick ghost and his terrible demise. I didn't want to think about Ian either. I tried to switch the channel in my head, but it refused to obey.

Instead I fell asleep thinking of Ian's face as he stared at the ghostly noose swaying in a silent wind.

Callie's low growl woke me from a hazy nightmare. Teeth chattering, I shivered under my comforter as I checked the time. It was a little after three a.m. Rolling over I saw that Callie was at the end of the bed. Her back was arched, her ears lay flat against her head, and she alternated between hissing and growling.

"Callie?" I whispered, unnerved.

The cat gave me one sharp look, her yellow eyes glowing in the darkness. I got the distinct feeling she was warning me to stay still. Clutching my covers to my chin, I stared into the murky darkness of my room. The only light was

151

the dark blue illumination of my alarm clock and it barely pierced the blackness. My cat had a preternatural glow about her, light rippling along her calico coat.

As my mind woke completely, so did my witch senses. I gradually realized there was a presence in the room. It wasn't just the latest cold front that was making my room feel like the Arctic Circle. There was something in the room drawing the energy from the air and plunging my room's temperature into North Pole iciness.

"Who's there?" I called out, my voice breaking.

My eyes slowly adjusted to the dark the longer I peered into it. I could feel my eyes dilating, attempting to drink in what little light was in the room. Out of the gloom, my vanity took shape. The clutter sprawled across its surface were dark lumps beneath the mirror. I quickly averted my eyes, afraid to peer into a mirror in the dark, especially on All Hallow's Eve.

Again Callie let out a low, warning growl. She edged toward the middle of the bed, her gaze firmly set on the vanity. Nervously, I reached out to turn on the lamp. I opened my mouth to call out for my parents, but my voice refused to obey. With trembling fingers, I turned on the lamp. For a brief moment my room was filled with warm, yellow light. In that split second, I saw that my mirror was completely frosted over and the words "Marek is the Devil!" was etched in the icy surface. Then the light bulb popped, thin shards of glass tinkling to the floor, and the room was filled with the night.

This time the darkness was absolute. I could see nothing, not even my alarm clock. Again I opened my mouth to scream, but the only sound that issued out of my tight throat was a thin, weedy whistle.

Callie yowled right beside my head and sent me tumbling out of the bed in fright. I landed hard on my right hip, gasping at the pain. Seconds later, the window next to my bed exploded, glass raining over my bed. Something landed with a distinct thump on my bed and I heard an angry grunt.

"Where are you?" a low, terrifying voice rumbled.

Callie slipped into my arms, her body tense and ready to fight. Too afraid to move or make a sound, I lay on the floor beneath my comforter, staring at the dark shape dimly illuminated by the moonlight creeping through the broken window. It was crouched on my bed, red eyes glowing, turning slowly as it sought me out.

Even though I was terrified, I realized that either I had hidden myself, or Callie had. Several times I saw the red eyes stare right at me, but it did not acknowledge my presence. I was torn between trying to scream for my parents again and risking the creature detecting me, or cowering in silence hoping it would leave.

"Where are you?" It hissed the words out, reptilian and cruel. "Witch, you can't hide from me."

I'm doing a pretty good job, I thought snarkily, but refrained from speaking aloud. Terror had me frozen in place. Whatever this creature was, it wanted me and very badly. I had a feeling it didn't want to be my friend.

It slowly stepped off my bed. In stealthy movements I watched the shadow creeping in front of my windows. Callie shot me a quick warning look and slid off my lap. She positioned herself between me and the creature slinking through the gloom. Again her fur shimmered with light as she sank into a predatory stance, ready to attack.

"Witch," the inhuman voice whispered. "Witch, I can smell your flesh. Smell your fear. Smell your blood."

Instinctively, I knew it was trying to frighten me into revealing myself. I fervently hoped my wildly beating heart wouldn't alert it to my location. It sounded so loud in my ears and its hard thumps in my chest actually hurt. Eyes riveted to the hunched form stalking through my room, red eyes blazing, I pressed my clenched hands to my mouth, trying to hide the sound of my heavy breathing.

Again, Callie gave me a stern look before returning her attention to the intruder. Shifting on her haunches, Callie's tail whipped back and forth.

"I'm going to rip your head off your shoulders and bathe in your blood, witch," the coarse voice whispered. The creature sounded pleased with itself. It obviously believed it had the upper hand. "Come out and fight, witch."

Curling up against my bed stand, I tried to draw my legs in as tightly as I could against my torso. I cursed my rounded belly and thicker thighs. It made it hard to be small when I was so tall and curvy. I had to do something soon. I knew that much, but what? Either it was the cold or my fear, but my teeth started to chatter.

"There you are," the being breathed with delight, rounding my bed with frightening swiftness and agility. Its dark shape sluiced through the murk, heading straight for me.

Callie launched herself at the creature with a wild growl. Her glowing form struck the attacker's chest and her claws dug in, eliciting a pained cry.

Scrambling to my feet, I cried out in pain as the sharp shards of the light bulb bit into the curve of my left foot. That one cry unclogged my voice and I screamed loud and long. Snatching up the lamp, I yanked the cord free of the wall and limped forward to help Callie fight off the monster.

Both Callie and the creature hissed and growled. Red eyes flashing, sharp teeth glinting in the pale moonlight, the intruder grappled with my wildly clawing and biting cat. I struck the being with the base of the lamp, aiming for the head. I managed to side-swipe its ear before it slapped the lamp out of my hand, bending back my fingers and drawing a pained cry from my lips.

The closet door burst open with a thud. The air crackled with purple energy as the stupid broom hurled out of the depths of my closet and whacked into the attacker's torso, just below Callie's writhing body. The force knocked the creature off its feet and tossed it against the far wall near the broken window. In the moonlight I caught a flash of white skin, dark hair, and burning red eyes. Callie slashed its face one last time, then leaped onto my bed to resume yowling.

The broom rushed the creature again, this time aiming for it like a spear. The creature screeched, evading the broom by mere inches. The broom handle punched into the wall, shimmying with the force of its strike.

Light exploded into my room from the hallway as the door banged open. Tawny hair flying, eyes blazing bright, my mom soared into my bedroom with her nightgown flapping around her bare feet like wings.

The words spilling from her mouth were in the tongue of the witch race and they burned in the air like incense. I literally saw the energy of the words billowing from her lips like smoke and twisting together in the air to form a mighty spell.

Everything was happening so fast I barely saw the dark-garbed intruder hurl itself through the broken window, arms raised to cover its face.

My mother's spell followed, but shimmered to a stop over the window. Golden vines of power wove over the window frame then spread along the walls.

The floor shook beneath my feet and the walls shuddered as a massive man with wild red hair and a big shaggy beard burst into my room, silver sword in hand, gold armor shining in the radiance of my mother's magic.

The spell my mother had cast rapidly spread through the house, making it tremble.

"Wow," I gasped.

"Is it over?" the big man asked, sword raised, blade cruelly glinting.

"It's gone. I banished it and put an even stronger ward on the house," my mother answered. She descended to the floor, careful to land away from the glass.

I stared at her in amazement, then looked to where the broom was trying to dislodge itself from the wall.

When I l returned my attention to my mom, she was switching on the lamp on my vanity and my dad was yawning. There was no sign of the giant red-haired man. I felt my eyes widen as I stared at my dad. He just gave me a big goofy grin.

"Was that a glamour?" I asked suspiciously.

My dad shrugged and tugged at the white t-shirt he had worn to bed. His pajama bottoms had penguins on them.

My mom avoided all the glass on the floor and helped pull the broom out of the wall. "Christy, are you okay?"

I nodded, mutely staring at the broken window and all the glass covering everything in my room. The broom started to sweep it up and if a broom could be smug I would have sworn it was. Callie gingerly avoided the debris from the window and jumped onto the vanity.

"Good job, broom," my dad said, patting the handle.

"The broom was hiding in my closet again. Again!" I complained. My hands were shaking so violently I had to press them to my sides to still them.

"Eh, it was just doing its job," my dad answered.

Mom peered out the busted window then slowly turned toward me. "What happened, Christy?"

Still scared, but relieved now, I told my parents everything that had happened that night. By the time I had finished the glass was all cleaned up, the window was magically restored, and the broom was making a big show of swishing back and forth in front of my bedroom windows like it was a guard before Buckingham Palace.

"Your spell may have stirred up something, or drawn a roaming beast toward you. It is Halloween. Well technically it's the Day of the Dead, but it is a day when the veil between the human world and the supernatural is very,

very thin," my mom said. She sat on the end of my bed looking thoughtful. "The spell was an invitation and that's why it was able to get into your room."

My dad snorted. "I'll invite my fist to its face the next time it tries anything."

With a thoughtful look in her eyes, my mom studied me, then the room. "I wonder if this is the power I have been sensing."

"It had red eyes. And lots of sharp teeth," I said.

"That could describe quite a few monsters," my dad said with frown. "None of them nice."

"Werewolf, ghoul, demon, poltergeist... " my mom rattled off.

"Vampire?" I offered.

My parents exchanged a look that I didn't care for. It was the one that said they knew something I didn't. Finally my dad said, "Christy, vampires are extinct. The witches killed them when we first entered this world. They were dangerous to our kind."

"Also, they were wreaking havoc on this world," my mom added. "They were on one big killing spree and out of control. The Dark Ages weren't called that for nothing. It was a very dark time in human history because they were on their way out at the hands of the vampires when we arrived."

"So what attacked me?" I asked.

"My guess is that it was a wandering spirit that managed to manifest by drawing on the energy from the group at the bridge tonight," my mother answered. "I think it may have honed in on you because of your power. It threatened you because it wanted to feed on your fear and your power."

"What power?" I rolled my eyes. "I didn't do anything when it was stalking me."

"You hid," my father pointed out. "You made yourself invisible again, which was the right thing to do. Callie and the broom did their jobs as your helpers and protectors." He flashed a wide grin at me. "It turned out okay, kiddo. Superwitch here had your back."

Rolling her eyes, my mother slid off the bed. "You don't need to worry about that spirit anymore. The new ward will keep it out and I banished it from this house. It can't enter again."

Sliding under the covers, I stared at my parents thoughtfully. "Are you sure?"

"Oh, I'm sure." My mom winked.

"So the big sword guy... "

My dad chortled and did a little jig. He looked like a drunk Santa. "I got tricks up my sleeve, kiddo."

My mother shoved him out the bedroom door and turned back one more time. "Christy, you didn't do anything wrong. We all struggle when we first get our powers. Sometimes things may be drawn to you that may want to do harm. That's why Callie and the broom watch out for you. They'll help you. And you need to remember that you have the power within you to defend yourself. It will just take time to learn how to work it properly."

She shut the door on my pouty face and I flopped back on my pillows. I felt safe with my mom's magic crackling along the walls like flashes of lightning. I knew the ward would soon settle into the house completely, but in the meantime I did feel safer being able to see the spell in action.

The broom continued its imitation of a guard on sentry duty in front of my windows. I left the restored lamp on as I snuggled down to sleep. I still felt shaken inside at the thought of those glowing red eyes and the flash of sharp teeth and decided to sleep with the light on.

Callie leaped onto the bed and stared at me intently. It took me a second to realize she had something dangling from her mouth. I was about to gross out thinking she was clutching a mouse by the tail, when I saw it was actually a leather cord clenched between her teeth. Dangling from it was a strange cross with three beams, one of which was crooked.

I started to reach for it, but Callie hissed a warning. Carefully, she maneuvered onto my bed stand and dropped it next to my cellphone. The cross looked scorched and maybe very old. The sight of it gave me the shivers.

"Did the intruder drop this?" I asked Callie.

A slight inclination of the head was my answer.

"It's evil, isn't it?"

Another short nod.

"But you didn't show Mom for a reason, did you?" I stared at the cat, trying to figure her out. I know she's not an ordinary cat and is hundreds of years old, but sometimes she's just so cat-like I forget that she's my mom's familiar.

Callie stepped onto my mattress and rubbed her chin once against mine before curling up against me. I wasn't too sure how to read this, but it felt like a confirmation.

"Is this Marek's?" I asked her, rubbing my lips lightly against her ear.

She twisted about to stare into my eyes and blinked very slowly.

"Marek is Mark, isn't he?" The trembling inside of me grew stronger because I had been in denial ever since Adam had asked to know who was deceiving him and now I had to accept the truth.

Callie bumped my forehead with her head then settled down on my pillow to stare at me.

"Crap."

Chapter 12

Warnings and Trouble

Christy

How do you tell your best friend that his boyfriend is probably some weird monster with red eyes and lots of sharp teeth? How do you confess that your stupid spell to bring him true love instead brought him a true psycho? I had screwed up royally and guilt ate at me like a hungry hippo.

I wished I could go back in time to when Adam and I used to play that game all the time. I always lost. Which made perfectly weird sense to me now that I had managed to screw up Adam's life. I was the big loser in the game of life.

I usually walk to Adam's house when we hang out, but today I felt afraid of traipsing down the three blocks to his house. What if Mark, aka Marek, was lurking in the trees or bushes waiting for me? He was pissed at me, that was for sure. Why else would he have busted through my bedroom window and hunted me down?

The drive over to Adam's house was quick and in silence. I left the radio off and concentrated on not being distracted by my constant scanning of my surroundings. It was hard to pay attention on the road when a scary thing with red eyes and sharp teeth and a big dislike for witches might possibly leap out at any moment.

After all the insanity of the night before, it was strange to see Adam's house looking so peaceful and normal. When I walked up to the front door, I could hear voices chatting. Adam's mom was the easiest to hear and whatever she was saying was interrupted by Amelia's annoying whine.

Taking a deep breath, I knocked on the door and it was barely a few seconds before Adam's mom, Ashley, opened the door. Even though it was in the low forties and misty, she was wearing a pink and aqua tank top that read "Shoe Whore" in sequins, tight blue jeans, and glittery wedge heels.

"Christy!" She grinned and gave me a tight hug. The scent of pancakes and syrup filled my nostrils. "Come in! We're eating breakfast! I made blueberry pancakes!"

"I wanted chocolate chip," Amelia complained.

"Well, you're getting blueberries. Deal, Am!" Rolling her eyes, she slammed the door shut. "Am is pissy over missing out on the ghost last night. Adam told us about it when he got home, and he said it was creepy and cool."

"It was... weird," I answered. Shoving my trembling hands into the pockets of my gray hoodie, I trudged into the kitchen.

A massive stack of pancakes sat in the center of the table along with a pile of crunchy bacon. Amelia was begrudgingly eating her pancakes. Adam was nowhere to be seen.

"Ghosts are weird. All moody and cranky about dying." Ashley shivered and took her place at the table. Her tablet was at her elbow and I could see Twitter was running on it. "I think it's cool that your witchy powers drew it out. Shows you're growing up and all that."

"I'm not a... witch," I said nervously.

Rolling her eyes, Ashley said, "Whatever."

Amelia stared at me, her eyes slightly narrowed.

"Did Adam say—"

"C'mon, Christy. I may be an airhead, but I'm not stupid. Remember the time I thought marijuana had fallen out of your pocket and it was sage? Total witch stuff." She winked at me and I wasn't sure if she was serious or pulling my chain.

"Witches are dumb. Wizards are better," Amelia informed me.

"Am, behave, or you're not spending the night over at Brandy's."

"Mom!"

"Am!"

The two females of Adam's family glowered at each other. Finally, Amelia shoved more pancakes into her mouth and looked defeated. Ashley smiled triumphantly.

"So is Adam up yet?" I glanced toward the doorway.

"Adam!" Ashley screamed at the top of her lungs. "Get your ass down here!"

"Can I go up?" I asked cautiously. "I have to talk to him about something. It's, uh, personal." I eyed Amelia who was watching me like a hawk. Sometimes she looks like a creepy, but cute leprechaun.

After studying me for a second, Ashley said, "Sure, go on up. Are you okay? Anything wrong?"

"Yeah," I answered truthfully.

"If I can help, let me know. Okay?" Ashley tilted her head, her hair falling gently against her cheek. It made her look very young and sweet, but there was cold steel in her gaze. Adam often says people underestimate his mother, which is a total mistake.

"I will."

I hastily escaped the kitchen as Amelia said in a furious voice, "No one ever tells me what is going on!"

"Eat your pancakes, Am. You don't need to know everything," Ashley answered.

I darted up the stairs and pounded on Adam's door when I reached his room.

"Mom, I'm up. Lay off," he grumbled on the other side.

"Adam, it's me."

A second later the door swung open and he stared at me with a sleepy expression. "Christy, what's up?"

"We need to talk. It's urgent."

Rubbing his eyes with the heels of his hands, he stepped back to let me in. He was still dressed in pajama bottoms and a t-shirt. His red hair was sticking up in jagged spikes and he had pillow creases on his cheek. My heart felt so full of love for him, tears sprung into my eyes.

Adam flopped onto his bed and rubbed his stomach. "I ate way too much candy. Ugh! My stomach is killing me."

Sitting at the end of the bed, cross-legged, I stared at him in silence, not even sure where to start. How do you confess to your best friend in the whole world that you have totally screwed up his life?

Rolling onto his side, he rested his head on his hand and regarded me with a slight frown. "This isn't a good look for you. You look like you just saw a ghost."

I blinked fiercely, trying to fight the tears welling in my eyes.

"Wait! *Did* you see a ghost?" Adam sat up, suddenly concerned and looking wide awake.

I nodded mutely.

"When?"

My lips quivering, I tried to speak, but my stupid throat felt tight and painful.

"Christy? When did you see the ghost?" Adam took my hand gently.

Clutching it, I looked him in the eye and told him what happened. As I spoke in a soft, halting voice, I could see the fear, then the disbelief in his eyes.

"This thing that got into your room, was it the ghost?" Adam rubbed my arm gently, trying to comfort me.

"My parents don't know what it is. They're trying to figure it out. It was really freaking scary Adam. I think the ghost tried to warn me that the monster was about to attack. It warned me about Marek."

I could literally see the fear and disbelief in Adam's eyes. It was if I could see the gears in his brain working as he pieced things together. "You think it's Mark."

The defensiveness in his voice made me wince. I gave one short nod.

"It can't be, Christy. I know you're scared. I know that whatever it was it terrified you. I can see it in your eyes. But I know him, Christy. Mark is sweet, gentle, and so alone in this world. He's had it so rough. He loves me and I love him." Adam ran his fingers through his hair, mussing it up even more. Despite his words, I detected a slight trace of panic in his tone. "He couldn't do that, Christy. He's so sweet. When we're together, he makes me feel so safe. So loved. And I want to be there for him. Protect him from all the bad things he's gone through. It's not him. It can't be. It just can't be."

Sniffling, I whispered, "Adam, the name Marek is just like Mark."

"That spell was wrong!" Adam shook his head adamantly. "Or maybe you wanted it to say Mark, so you confused it."

I didn't want to hurt Adam. I didn't want to show him how much I had screwed up, but I knew I couldn't keep the truth from him. The creature in my room had been cruel and evil. It had wanted to kill me. I knew that. I also knew it had been Mark.

"It was him," I said at last.

"You said you only saw red glowing eyes and sharp teeth," Adam said defiantly. "You didn't see Mark's face."

Reluctantly, I reached into the hoodie of my pocket and withdrew a clean white washcloth I had taken from my bathroom. I laid it on the bed and slowly unfolded it. Adam watched me, eyes wide, his breath coming fast.

"But he left this."

The weird cross came into view.

Adam drew in his breath sharply. Covering his face with his hands, he wagged his head. "No, no."

"Callie gave it to me after the attack. She fought the monster that broke into my room. I think she might have torn it off him. It's Mark's, isn't it?"

Tears in his eyes, Adam nodded in silence, stretching his hand out to touch the cross, but I stopped him.

"Callie wouldn't let me touch it. I don't think you should either. I think only the cord is safe."

Adam dropped his hand and raised his eyes toward the ceiling. Tears glittered in his red lashes. "I saw him wearing it."

"Mark *is* Marek," I continued. "And he attacked me last night."

Adam laughed bitterly. "Do you realize what you're saying?"

"Yeah. Mark is a monster."

"And he's my boyfriend."

"You believe me?" I huddled on the bed, ready to take the brunt of Adam's despair.

There was a long stretch of silence, then Adam said in a defeated tone, "Yeah. I believe you."

"I'm so sorry, Adam!"

"Don't be," Adam said firmly. "It's not your fault."

"I did the spell," I countered.

"We did a spell the day before Mark went to school. So what? Do you really think your spell just made him materialize in our town?" My best friend ran his hands over his hair, ignoring his tears. "Mark knows about our town. He's either been here before, or was here all along."

"But... but... "

Adam again took my hands. The ugly necklace rested between us. "Christy, I felt something at the bridge. A presence. It touched me several times and called my name. I think the ghost was trying to warn me, too."

"I did the spell," I repeated, my voice cracking.

"But you said your powers were weak," Adam pointed out. He finally brushed his tears away with his forearm. His face was devastating with its heartbreak, but his gaze was full of strength and understanding. "You couldn't have brought him here. You didn't cause this. Mark did this. He came after me. He played me. If he's this monster you described, this Marek, then all of us are his victims." With a sad, wry smile, Adam again shook his head. "It makes perfect sense now. He was trying to create doubts in me about you.

Dropping hints that you were trying to come between us when he was the one trying to come between *us*."

"So I'm still your bestie?"

Adam snorted. "Well, duh. I've known you almost my whole life. You're more than my bestie. You're family, Christy."

"Do you think he came after me because I'm your best friend?"

Adam stared toward the window, but I could tell he was pondering something. "No. No. That's not it. If Mark is Marek and the ghost is warning us about Marek, then I think Mark came after you because you summoned the ghost at the bridge. Or maybe because you could summon the ghost." Nodding, Adam looked back at me. "Yeah, I think that's it. It feels right. He came after you because you're a witch."

"Do you really believe I'm a witch?" I arched an eyebrow at him.

Shrugging, Adam said, "Uh, yeah, I think I do. After the ghost last night... "

"I can do more than that now."

"You mean going invisible like you described?"

"Yeah."

"Could be helpful if you have to hide again."

The reason why I may need to hide again made us both lapse into silence. I folded up the washcloth, hiding away the disturbing cross and tucking it into my pocket.

"So what do we do now?"

Adam sighed. "Well, I think I'm going to cry for a little bit. Then I'm going to break up with my monster boyfriend."

"He'll probably try to talk you out of it."

"I know he will," Adam said, lifted one shoulder. "but I'm not stupid. It's all fitting together. I don't think we have a clear picture yet, but... " The emotional storm Adam had been fighting back finally erupted. Violent sobs wracked his body and he fell over on his side, his hands over his face.

My own tears fell as I lay down behind him, my arm over his waist. I held him, listening to him weep, offering my presence as a comfort.

Despite his words absolving me, I felt like an utter failure. Maybe my spell hadn't brought Mark to Trinity Springs, but I had pushed Adam toward him. Guilt ate at me, but it was fear that completely filled my heart.

If Mark/Marek was a monster of some sort, what would he do when Adam told him to go away?

Adam

Torture couldn't describe the way I felt.

After Christy left, I lay in bed for what seemed like hours, though each and every time I checked only a few minutes had passed. The reality of the situation kept deepening with every passing minute. My hopes, my dreams, my future with Mark...it was all fading away. It's easy for straight people to think that moving on is simple. I suppose that when you're certain there are more fish in the sea, as Mom would say, it's not as devastating to lose the person you love. But when you're gay like me, the future doesn't seem so bright. When one flame flickers out, the rest look too distant to ever reach.

I'm fairly certain someone could have ripped my arm right off and I wouldn't have felt a thing.

In the final hours of the morning, I realized that postponing the inevitable was just adding fuel to the fire.

I rolled over and reached for my phone.

The one face I didn't want to see stared back at me when I turned it on.

Mark.

It was awfully convenient that his contact pane would appear on my phone right when I needed it.

Mark, I typed. *Call me. We need to talk.*

Clicking 'Send' seemed like the hardest thing I've ever done.

I leaned back against my headrest and waited.

One minute passed, then two. Five went by and I began to panic, but I knew I was just being paranoid. He'd left his phone in his bedroom and couldn't find it, or was listening to music and hadn't heard my message come in. It was nothing more than that.

The phone beeped.

I threw myself toward it.

Heard from him yet? Christy asked.

No, I replied, then grumbled and tossed the phone onto the mattress.

When fifteen minutes went by, I sent another message.

Call me, I said.

A reply came in. It wasn't from Mark. It was my annoyingly faithful best friend.

Now? Christy asked.

No, I'll let you know.

Thus my perpetual cycle of misery continued.

After the third message to Mark within the span of forty minutes, I started to pace the room. Nerves eventually got the best of me and I started to clean my room. Clothes went into the hamper, books got put back on the shelf, papers were tossed and my closet rearranged. I even took the time to tidy my desk, a task never accomplished due to the fact that I was always moving everything.

I was so lost in time that I hadn't realized an hour had passed. I'd been judging time by the number of texts I'd been getting from Christy.

When I went back to check my phone, I was expecting *something.*

I brought my screen up to check my messages.

If Hell existed, this had to be it.

Defeated, I brought Mark's chat session up, clicked the text bubble, then typed, *Call me when you can,* then left it at that.

There was nothing more I could do.

My suffering would continue.

It was only a matter of time before I lost my mind.

The knock that came at the door nearly scared me out of my skin. "Adam?" my mother called out.

162

"Come in," I said.

The door opened to reveal Mom carrying a plate of still-steaming food. "I brought you breakfast because so far you've been the invisible man today," she said, looking down at the pancakes and bacon on the plate. "I figured you might be hungry."

"Thanks," I mumbled, glancing at my phone.

Mom set the plate on the desk. "Talking to Christy?"

I shook my head. "Not texting her," I said. "Mark."

"Ah, I see," Mom said coyly. "You look frustrated." She studied me, suspicion in her eyes.

"He's not answering."

"He'll answer eventually."

"I think that's what scares me the most," I confessed. "Not knowing what he's going to say."

"About what?"

"About me breaking up with him?"

Mom's brow furrowed in confusion. "Breaking up with him?" she asked. "What's going on, Adam? What aren't you telling me?"

"I wasn't sure what was going on at first either," I said. "I thought him being concerned about me and Christy being so close was just him being jealous, but then I started putting some things together and I realized... " I closed my eyes and took a deep breath.

"Realized *what*, Adam?"

"That he was deliberately doing things to push me and Christy apart," I said. "Mom... I think he set up that fight with Jayden so he could be my hero. So I would be with him."

Mom didn't respond immediately. At first I thought it was because she hadn't heard or couldn't believe me, but when I looked at her face, I realized what was really going on.

When Mom gets angry, I mean *really* angry, she undergoes this metamorphosis that changes her entire demeanor. First she gets quiet, which is scary because she's usually always so bubbly, then she starts to turn red. I guess the best way to describe it would be like those old cartoons where the toon changes color and then steam comes out of its ears, except in Mom's case, it's not steam that comes out of her, it's the flurry of curses that make even my oil-rig father blush in embarrassment.

"What, the... FUCK?"

Thankfully Amelia was downstairs watching TV with the sound turned up loud. This cursefest was doomed to be epic.

"THIS IS RIDICULOUS!" she cried, throwing her hands in the air. *"He set up the attack with Jayden?* Oh my God! It makes *total* sense now! Him wooing you, him being so nice, him being weird around Christy, he—oh God! Do you think he made Christy sick at the party? Did he put something in her drink?"

"I don't know, Mom. All I know for sure is that Christy heard Mark talking to Jayden the day he attacked me and he's been acting jealous about me and Christy being so close."

"This is unacceptable!" she cried. "Completely una-fucking-cept-a-fucking-ble!"

"I know, Mom. Don't worry. I'm going to handle it."

"I'm glad you're breaking up with him! That *asshole!*"

"I don't plan on keeping him around. That's why I was texting him."

Her metamorphosis ended just like that. Regular Mom appeared in but an instant. "I'm sorry I lost my temper," she said, idly picking up a piece of my bacon and taking a bite out of it. "It's just that I get so worked up and it has to come out *somehow.*"

"It's okay, Mom. I know how you feel. I mean, past the temper part."

"You always were your father's son. You got that stoic German thing from him. But you got your sexy red hair and freckles and good looks from my Irish roots." Mom finished eating the piece of bacon and pulled me into a hug. "Let me know if you need anything, Adam. I'm here for you."

"Thanks, Mom," I whispered.

The day passed by in slow motion. No texts came in other than the million from Christy, no knocks came at the door, Mom's phone didn't ring, which had to have been an act of God, considering it was usually always going off. Even Amelia was surprisingly good despite her usually-bratty self, and when Brandy's mom came by to pick up my little sister for her slumber party, I barely even noticed. I mostly moped around my room and waited for some kind of sign, though if Christy's incessant texts were a sign of anything, something was bound to happen eventually.

I mean, this Hell couldn't go on forever, could it?

By the time night fell, I realized I was wrong.

Forced from the secure depths of my room by my mother when she called out that she would soon be making dinner, I trudged down the stairs and into the kitchen to grab myself a soda.

I reached out to open the fridge.

My phone buzzed.

I looked down.

"Ugh, Christy," I growled, reaching for the pull-down tab to see what I inevitably knew was her message. "You know you'd be the first to know if I heard anything from—"

A knock came at the front door just a few feet from where I stood.

"Mark?" I whispered.

Dad had replaced the door glass insets the last time he was here after Mom thought she saw someone peeping through the front door. The person on the doorstep was nowhere near the windows that flanked either sides of the door, so there was no way I could know who it was. That didn't matter though. It was like I *knew* he was out there, like there was some kind of magnetic energy pulling me forward to beckon the stranger in.

I uncurled my hand from the fridge's handle and stepped forward.

The phone buzzed in my hand, and I ignored it.

The knocks came again, this time more urgently.

Why wasn't the person using the doorbell? They probably hadn't seen it, or maybe it'd been covered up with one of the Methodist Ladies League's flyers they left on the door. That had to have been it. I was just being paranoid because of the whole situation with Mark. Nothing more than that.

A knock came at the door again.

It's me, a voice said. *Open up.*

"Mark?" I asked, narrowing my eyes to fight off my lightheadedness as I reached forward. "Is that you?"

Open the door.

"I am," I said, unlocking and turning the doorknob. His face coming into view sent a wave of relief over me. "You scared me. Why didn't you use the doorbell?"

Mark pushed his way into the house without bothering to say hi.

"Mark?" I asked, trying as hard as I could to remain calm despite his unusual behavior. "What are you doing here?"

"I lost my cross," he said, eyes sweeping the house as he started into the kitchen.

"What're you—"

"I lost my fucking cross!" he growled, pushing papers and other objects across the island.

"We need to talk," I said, taking a step forward.

"Do you know how important that thing is to me?" he asked, eyes burning with panic and a rage I hadn't seen since the night I'd been attacked by Jayden. "It's a family *heirloom,* Adam. It's been in my family for *two-hundred fucking years."*

"What makes you think it's here?" I asked. "Are you sure you didn't lose it somewhere—"

Mark's hand lashed out across the counter in his anger.

The China teacup that Mom kept as an island focal piece fell to the floor.

Even a gunshot wouldn't have been any louder in that moment.

Frozen, I stood there, staring at the last glimmering memories of one of grandma's most treasured possessions.

"Adam?" Mom asked from the living room. "Did something fall? Are you okay?"

Mark's eyes shot up.

"You need to get out of here," I said. "Now."

"My cross," Mark said. "I have to find—"

The sound of my mother's footsteps and then the sight of her stepping through the threshold stopped Mark in his place.

Though I've never seen a predator just before it strikes its prey, I imagined it would look something like my mom.

"What the fuck are you doing here?" Mom asked, eyes darting from Mark, then to the China cup broken on the floor. "Did you do this?"

"I'm looking for my cross," Mark said. "I lost it."

"And that gives you reason to... *what?* Break into *my* house? Break my things?"

"It was an accident."

"Just like setting Jayden Croft against Adam was?"

Mark's silence was a far greater answer than anything he could have said.

"Don't think I don't know," Mom said, stepping into the kitchen and narrowing her eyes not only at Mark, but at me as she jerked her head to the side to gesture me behind the island away from Mark. "I've had a bad feeling about you since you stepped into this house, Mark. You seemed... *wrong*... like you weren't supposed to be here. But I gave you the benefit of the doubt, because I thought I was maybe just being overprotective of Adam. In the back of my mind, I *knew* you had something to do with Adam getting attacked. Now I know I'm right."

The first inclination I had when Mom stepped forward was to get around the island and between the two of them. She didn't know what had happened to Christy. Mark was insane, a monster. He'd broken into my best friend's bedroom in the middle of the night and attacked her. What would he do to my five-foot-tall mother? When Mom took a few steps toward him and stared directly into his eyes, the pendulum of tension dangling in the air seemed to loom ever so close, its sharp edge swaying not toward Mark, but my Mother.

"You don't belong here," she continued. "You're *never* to come here again. You will *never* touch Adam. You will never so much as even *look* at or *talk* to him, because if you do, I swear I will shoot you dead. And if you try anything at the school, I swear I will bring holy hell down upon you, because when you fuck with the cub, you mess with the fucking mama bear. Now get out. *Now.*" As if Mom's words were the command of God resting on high, Mark retreated toward the door. There was no struggle, no retaliation, no attempt to step back into the kitchen. It was as if an invisible hand kept pushing him away until he passed over the threshold and onto the front porch.

"I lost my cross," he growled, pressing his hands against the doorjamb. "I want it."

"Your cross isn't here," she replied. "Get out of here. I'll call the cops if I see you again."

She slammed the door, bolted the lock and strung the chain.

"Mom?" I asked, taking my first real breath of the last ten minutes as she kneeled to clean up the pieces of China. "Are you okay?"

"I'm fine. It's you I'm worried about."

"I'm okay. Really."

"This didn't hurt you?" she asked, lifting the pieces up to the light. "*He* didn't hurt you?"

"No, Mom. I'm fine. I mean... a bit freaked out by what happened, but other than that I'm okay."

"I'm so glad your sister wasn't here to see that," she sighed. She grudgingly dropped Grandma's broken China into the trash and let out a long exhale.

"You shouldn't have done that, Mom. I mean, put yourself between me and him."

"I'll protect you for as long as I live," Mom said. "I know I can't do it forever, but while I can... I will."

Stepping forward, I wrapped her in a hug. "I love you," I whispered.

"I love you too," she said, pressing a kiss to my brow. "Will you be okay?"

"Yeah. I think I'm just going to go to bed and try to forget about the day."

"I don't blame you," she said. "Fuck! I need a cigarette! I'm going to go out for a smoke. I'll be in soon."

"Goodnight, Mom."

"Goodnight, Adam."

Mom swiped her cigarettes from the counter, parted the sliding glass doors that led into the back yard from the living room, and made her way out onto the back patio.

I started for the stairs.

Each step up was a test of resolve.

I was trying hard not to cry.

Halfway up the stairs, I reached into my pocket for my phone, ready to tell Christy what had happened.

What sounded like an explosion shook the back half of the house.

Mom screamed.

What sounded like a train slammed into the house.

Then all was silent.

It took but a moment to realize what had happened.

In one great leap, I bounded off the stairs, onto the ground floor, then ran as fast as I could toward the sliding glass doors.

My heart stopped beating the moment I hit the living room.

There, just beyond the glass, was the very branch that used to scrape against my bedroom window.

I've been telling your father that thing's going to hurt somebody, Mom used to say.

Mom was wrong.

It hadn't just hurt someone... it had killed someone.

It had killed *her.*

My whole life, I was always told death was peaceful. But when I looked at my mother's face—when I saw in her beautiful eyes a horror I couldn't begin to describe—I realized I'd been lied to.

It didn't take me long to realize what I had to do.

Our whole lives, we'd been told the adults were our helpers. In times of need, they were the ones to turn to, that would help us when things went wrong and people got hurt. What they hadn't considered was the idea that there might be things beyond our control—that one day, when everyone least expected it, evil would come to the small town of Trinity Springs.

I speed-dialed Christy.

"Christy," I said the moment the phone picked up. "My Mom... she's dead... you have to help me. I don't know what to do."

"Adam?" Christy asked. "What do you mean your mom is dead?"

"Christy, I think Mark killed my Mom."

Chapter 13

Dark Magic

Christy

Adam's cries of despair made it hard to understand him on the phone, but I had understood enough. Mark had killed Ashley and it was my fault.

"I'm coming," I said, my voice raspy with emotion. "Don't call anyone else. I'll bring her back." The words were out of my mouth before my brain could even start to piece together a plan. What was I saying?

"Bring her back?" Adam's voice was edged with hope. "Christy, can you do that?"

An image flashed in my head. It was of one of the books my mother had stored in the spell room. One day a few years back I had been browsing through the book when I had a seen a spell to return someone to life. At the time my mother had explained that the spell was only to be used when someone was unjustly killed by a dark entity. At the time I hadn't really understood what she meant, but now I did. Mark was a dark entity and he had unjustly killed Ashley. The spell would have to work.

"Yes," I answered, confidence filling my voice. "I can. I'll be right there! Don't move her!" I hung up and immediately dialed Drifter's number.

"Hello?" he answered, sounding wide awake. He was probably playing Guild Wars 2. He's completely addicted. "What's up?"

"Drifter, I need you to get to Adam's house immediately. Don't ask questions just go! It's an emergency!"

"Sure. Okay." He sounded uneasy, but I trusted he would do as I asked. "I'll be there in a few minutes."

"Good." I clicked off and called Olivia. She answered, but her voice was muffled. "Olivia?"

"Uh huh." I could hear the sounds of a scary movie in the background and realized she was chewing on chips. "What's up?"

"I need you to get to Adam's house right away! Like right now! Something bad has happened. Don't ask questions. Just go!"

"I would protest your interruption of my yearly ritual of watching *Hellraiser* on the Day of the Dead, but this sounds serious."

"It is. Trust me. You need to go now!" As I spoke I pulled on my jeans and grabbed a hoodie off a hanger.

"I'll throw some clothes on and be there," Olivia answered. She hung up on me.

Shoving my phone into my pocket, I tugged on the hoodie and snatched up a striped wool scarf with silver skulls on it. My mother had bought it for me the year before and it's my favorite. Shoving my feet into my Doc Martens, I considered calling Ian, but thought better of it. Drifter, Olivia and Adam would be enough to assist me.

Snatching one of my backpacks from the closet floor, I shoved my cauldron into it and headed toward the door. Callie hopped off my bed and followed. I had forgotten all about her after I had answered Adam's call. The cat's bright yellow eyes regarded me coolly as I started down the stairs. Hesitating, I looked up at her and whispered, "I need to do this. Please don't tell Mom and Dad. I screwed up and Adam's mom shouldn't have died."

Callie slowly blinked, tilted her head to one side, made a soft *burrrring* noise, and the broom hopped out from behind a curtain. I was too upset to even accuse it of spying on me. It zipped over to the familiar and Callie jumped onto the bristles. Together, the broom and cat floated downward through the stairwell.

Nervously, I followed, hoping that they wouldn't stop on the floor where my parents were sleeping to tell on me. To my relief, the cat on the broom continued to the main floor and waited for me. I didn't pound down the stairs like I usually do, but tiptoed as quietly as possible. When I reached the foyer, I kept on my toes and scurried toward the hallway that led to the spell room.

I had never been able to open it before, but tonight I knew I could. The second Adam had told me his mother was dead by Mark's hands, I had again felt the sensation of something deep inside of me popping. I knew adrenaline was coursing through me, but I felt something else too. It was as if warm water was rushing through my body, churning just below my skin, ready to erupt at my beckoning.

Reaching the concealed door, I found Callie and the broom waiting for me. Languorously licking her back, Callie barely acknowledged my presence. I understood instantly that she was not going to open the door for me. I would have to open it myself and prove I was witch enough to enter the sacred room.

Lifting my hand, I felt the warm power enveloping my hand, waiting my command.

"Open," I said softly. For an instant I thought I was being overconfident, imagining that I was now in control of my abilities. The secret door swung open, revealing the room beyond.

Sunlight filtered through the leaves of the birch tree and somewhere far above birds chirped. Stepping inside, I slid my gaze over the many volumes and items filling the shelves.

Callie sauntered past me and jumped onto the table where my mother mixed her spells. Her keen yellow eyes watched me with great interest. The broom skipped past me to lean against the trunk of the tree.

The name of the book came to me just as I began to panic that I couldn't find it in time. Raising my hand, I again felt the power within me swishing about, waiting.

For the first time in my life, I spoke the language of the witches.

High above my head, a book shot off a shelf and floated downward as though it were as light as a feather. It settled on the table before me, its pages flipping open to exactly the spell I was seeking.

"I'm doing this, right?" I asked Callie. "Not you. Me. I have my powers now, right?"

She yawned and cleaned the pink pads of her front foot.

Nervously, I scanned the spell. It was if a new part of my brain had unlocked and knowledge poured into me. I wish I could have enjoyed the moment, but I was too freaked out over Ashley's death. My mind was buzzing with a new language, the history of my people, and the knowledge of how to do so much magic, yet all I could think of was Adam weeping on the phone.

The spell was simple in ingredients, but very specific about the situation. The person could not be dead longer than an hour, the soul had to still be lingering by the body, and the death had to be an unjust one at the hands of a dark power. I had a feeling that the word unjust may mean more than I was willing to admit, but I dismissed any misgivings I had. I couldn't let Adam down.

It took less than five minutes to gather all the items and ingredients needed for the spell. I crammed them all into my bag and pulled out my phone. I took a picture of the page with the spell on it and was relieved when it actually photographed. I had feared it wouldn't.

"Broom," I said, annoyed at what I was about to say.

It scooted away from where it was leaning against the tree and stood upright before me.

"Broom, I need your help. I need to get to Adam's house superfast. Can you take me?"

It scooted right to me and nudged my hand. With a grin, I clutched it and headed out of the spell room. I heard a thud behind me as Callie jumped off the table to follow.

Sneaking through the kitchen, I hurried outside, the broom positively vibrating in my hand. I had the strangest feeling it was dying for a midnight flight. The back door had barely shut behind me when the broom shot upward. I gasped, dangling dangerously from it by one hand. Luckily, my backpack was already on my back, so I was able to clutch the handle with my other hand and held on for dear life.

We were just above the treetops when I felt the familiar nuzzle of Callie's nose against my check. Turning my head, I saw she was clinging to my backpack with her claws. She meowed softly then turned her face into the rushing wind.

The world spun around me as the broom skimmed along the top of the trees. It didn't fly horizontally, but at an angle. It took several kicks, but I finally managed to get my foot hooked over the broomstick.

"Could you not kill me on the way there?" I groused.

The cold wind blasted my face and threw the hood off my head. A part of me wanted to look down to see the trees and houses beneath my feet, but I was terrified that if I stopped looking at my fingers gripping the broom I would lose my tenuous hold and fall.

It felt as if my journey across the sky dangling awkwardly from an old broom was over in a matter of seconds. If I hadn't been so distraught over Ashley's death, I may have lamented the awkwardness of my landing. The stupid broom seemed determined to have every tree branch smack me on the way down. I finally dared to look below to see Adam crouched beside his fallen mother staring up at me. Drifter and Olivia were just rounding the side of the house and they too lifted their faces to gawk as I descended.

The broom was kind enough to lower me all the way to the ground before twisting about in my hands and skimming along the edge of the yard. Callie leaped off my backpack and landed at my feet. She immediately began to prowl around, ears back, yellow eyes blazing.

"You're... you're... you're... ." Drifter stammered.

"Awkward landing," Olivia said at last from around her lollipop.

"You can do this!" Adam exclaimed, his gaze full of hope. "You can do this because it's true! You're a witch!"

"Keep it down. Neighbors and all that," I said gruffly. I was trying hard not to stare at Ashley's crushed form. Her head was twisted at a weird angle and I could see blood on her face. Adam had obviously dragged her from under the fallen tree branch.

"Oh, shit!" Olivia exclaimed, seeing Adam's mother.

"Oh, man! I'll call 911!" Drifter immediately fished his phone out of his pocket.

"No!" Adam and I chorused.

"We have to get help!" Drifter protested.

Olivia kneeled next to Ashley and gingerly pressed her fingers to her broken neck. "There's no pulse."

"She's dead," Adam sobbed. Tears streamed down his cheeks. His face was so red I could barely see his freckles in the light cast from the fixture next to the sliding glass doors. "The branch... fell."

I fell to my knees and immediately unzipped my backpack. "We're not calling 911 because I'm bringing her back."

"Can you do that?" Olivia pulled the lollipop out of her mouth and studied me thoughtfully.

"Yes. I can." I could feel the magic inside of me swelling, preparing to do my bidding. "I can do it. But I need your help."

"Is this black magic?" Drifter asked warily.

"Does it matter?" Adam nearly shouted, clutching his mother's hand.

"I don't do black magic. It's pure magic." I lifted my head to give Drifter a sharp look. "I'm doing the spell. I'll suffer whatever blowback that might happen. I just need you to help me maintain the circle. Okay?

Nodding nervously, Drifter said, "Okay. What do you want me to do?"

Gesturing to the patio table and chair, then the ruined barbecue pit that had been taken out by the tree branch falling, I said, "Move those off the patio. I need the space to lay the circle."

172

"I'll help," Olivia said, scrambling to her feet.

Withdrawing a crystal, I whispered the spell my mother had taught me after the ghost had appeared in my room. It was very simple and would reveal any spirit that was in the area. I couldn't even start the resurrection spell until I was certain Ashley hadn't moved on. I hoped I had arrived soon enough that she hadn't entered the white light to the next realm. Callie joined me, sitting at my side, watching the crystal intently. After a few heart wrenching seconds listening to Adam weeping, I saw a luminescent form taking shape over his shoulder.

"She's here!" I gasped, relieved.

Adam looked up, his grief an ugly mask. "She is?"

"Standing over you," I said pointing.

Behind me, I could hear Olivia and Drifter grunting and struggling to move the heavy patio furniture.

Adam shot a quick look over his shoulder, though I knew he wouldn't be able to see her. "Mom, we're bringing you back."

"Yeah, do not go into the light," I ordered the ghostly form of Adam's mom. Callie meowed in agreement.

With the furniture out of the way, it would be easier for me to draw the circle. As Drifter and Olivia dragged away the battered barbecue pit, I stood and studied my surroundings. It was a flagstone patio, so I couldn't draw a circle evenly. I would have to use salt.

"Okay, we're going to have to move your mom just a little bit to the right," I said to Adam.

"Her neck," he whispered.

"I'll hold her head," Olivia offered.

Adam and Drifter stood on either side of Ashley and tucked their hands under her sides. I picked up her feet, briefly noting her pretty shoes, and Olivia gently raised her head. I averted my eyes to avoid seeing the weird disconnected way Ashley's head moved. We all carefully lifted her and moved her a few feet before laying her down in the direct center of the patio.

Pulling out a bag of salt, I began to make the circle. Callie walked at my side, gently nudging me if I started to make it more oval shaped. "I'm going to leave a part of the circle open. All three of you need to enter at the opening. Adam, you sit on her right. Olivia, you sit on her left. Drifter, you sit at her feet."

My friends silently obeyed. Adam still wept, but very quietly. I saw the ghost of his mother follow him into the circle and felt a delicate squeeze on my arm as Ashley passed. Callie entered last and took position above Ashley's head. Taking a deep breath, I poured the final bit of salt to close the circle.

There was a loud whoosh as a shimmering curtain of white light sprung up, forming a barrier around us.

"Wow!" Drifter said in amazement.

"Cool," Olivia said with approval.

"Your circles have improved," Adam said, sniffling. His sad smile made me want to hug him, but I had to finish, and fast.

Sitting next to Callie I drew out the items for the spell. I handed Adam a red candle, and white ones to Olivia and Drifter. "Place those in front of you and make sure the flames don't go out."

"What flame?" Olivia asked.

"They'll ignite when the spell starts." Setting my cellphone on my lap, I pulled up the picture of the spell. The base of the spell was a basic healing spell that my mom already had made. It would fix Ashley's broken neck and internal injuries. I poured the contents of the soft cotton bag into the cauldron. Next, from a small blue bottle I added a little bit of water from a freshwater spring from the world of the witches. The concoction swirled with blue and green magic.

"Adam, I need three drops of your blood. Since she's related to you, your blood can draw her back." I handed him the long silver needle I had taken from my mother's things.

Without hesitation, Adam took the needle and held it over his hand. "Is there a specific place?"

I shook my head.

Drifter was breathing so rapidly, it sounded like he was hyperventilating. I didn't notice when Olivia ditched her lollipop, but her lips were now pressed into a somber line as she watched Adam.

"Do the thumb," she suggested.

Adam took a breath, then stabbed his digit. Wincing, he held out his hand and the needle. I took his thumb between my fingers and carefully squeezed out three bright red drops into the cauldron, then quickly jerked his hand away before any more could fall.

A plume of bright white magic floated into the air. I grinned, happy to see the spell was doing exactly what it was supposed to do. I checked my phone again, making sure of the next step.

"You're reading a spell off your phone?" Drifter asked.

"I took a picture of the spell book," I answered.

"You're a weird witch," Drifter decided.

Biting my lower lip, I pulled out the washcloth that contained Mark's necklace in its folds. "Adam, are you sure Mark did this?"

"What?" Drifter and Olivia exclaimed.

"Absolutely. Yeah. Without a doubt. He was so angry with her. I know that branch was dangerous, but it's too coincidental," Adam answered, his voice steady. "I saw the way he looked at her. He looked totally crazed."

"Okay. The first part of the spell is to heal. The second is to reconnect the spirit with the loved one to anchor it. The next step is to steal a bit of the life force of the person who killed them." I unfolded the washcloth and stared at the hideous necklace. Taking out a small dagger, I took a hold of the cord and sliced off a piece.

"Is that his?" Drifter asked. "Mark's?"

Adam nodded. "He dropped it when he attacked Christy."

"He attacked you!" Olivia's eyes widened. "What the hell?"

"Long story. We'll talk after this is done." I flicked the tiny bit of leather cord into the cauldron.

The candles clutched in the hands of my friends burst to life, eliciting startled gasps from them. The magic in the cauldron swirled in a myriad of colors: red, blue, green, and white. Callie's eyes glowed bright in the light. She tilted her head toward me and I sensed approval.

"The spell is active," I whispered.

"This is really happening," Drifter said in awe.

"Ashley, I summon you to return to your body. I call to you in the names of your children and by the power of their blood," I said aloud. Picking up the white crystal I had used earlier to find Ashley's spirit, I dipped one end of it into the spell, then rested it over Ashley's heart. "Find your way home to your body, home, and family."

For years I have been complaining about the lack of fireworks during my spells. I can't complain anymore.

A bright, brilliant white light burst out of the crystal, filling the circle and rising up above us like a pillar. The air sang with the melodic music of the spell and a funnel of air swirled around us.

"Protect the flames!" I cried out, but I saw my friends were already shielding the candles with their hands.

Despite the direness of the situation, I laughed aloud, overwhelmed by the beauty of the magic. Another blast of magic filled the circle, this time erupting out of me. I felt the dam within me burst, letting loose the power that had been slowly building within me since I was born. The magic was green and flecked with speckles of white and smelled of spearmint. I held out my hands over Ashley's body, barely able to see her through all the swirling, glittering magic.

"Return!"

Like water rushing over a waterfall, the magic poured into Ashley's body. As quickly as it had filled the circle, it was gone, leaving us blinking the spots out of our eyes and a little breathless.

Ashley moaned, then slowly raised her hand to her head.

"Mom?" Adam cried out, disbelief and joy mingling in his eyes.

Sitting up, Adam's mom looked around at us, the circle, the candles, and the cauldron. Running her fingers through her hair, she drew in a deep breath, then slowly exhaled. Drifter stared at her with his mouth hanging open while Olivia slowly unwrapped a lollipop and popped it in her mouth, her eyes as big as saucers.

"Mom?" Adam asked again, nervously.

"That asshole!" she exclaimed. "He broke my neck!"

Exhaustion hit me like an avalanche and I barely registered Adam hugging his mom as I passed out.

Adam

Olivia and Drifter carried Christy into the house while I helped my Mom to her feet. Though disoriented, she seemed like her normal self, regardless of the fact that the branch had broken her neck.

"Mom," I asked as she swayed on her feet. "Are you okay?"

"I'm fine," she said. "Well, as fine as anyone could be after being brought back from the dead."

"Are you in pain?"

"Nope. Not at all."

I smiled when I looked into her eyes. Regardless of the fact that they seemed full of life, I'd expected something else, like for them to be glazed like they say they are after you die. Then again, maybe it was because she hadn't been dead for too long. Or maybe it was because Christy had used magic to bring her back to life.

"We shouldn't stay out here," Mom said, breaking my trance. "He might come back."

I agreed and led her toward the house.

Inside, Christy was just beginning to come to. Trembling, she accepted a glass of water and a lollipop from Olivia while Drifter began to check the doors and windows. I was just about to slide the glass doors shut when Callie scurried in, promptly followed by the broom.

I gazed at Mom, mystified by what I had seen. No more than a few minutes ago, she'd been dead, yet here she was standing right beside me alive as ever. I could barely wrap my mind around the absurdity of it all. My mom had been dead and now she was alive because my best friend was actually a real witch.

"So let me get this straight," Drifter said, his eyes darting from Christy, the broom, then back to my Mom. "Either I'm crazy and this is just a dream, or Mark killed Adam's mom, Christy rode over here on a flying broom, then used magic to bring her back to life."

"Pretty much," I said.

"Yup," Olivia agreed.

"That asshole totally killed me!" Mom cried out angrily.

"So you saw him? Definitely?" I gasped, my greatest fear confirmed. I had lied to Christy during the spell. I hadn't been one hundred percent sure Mark had killed my mom. I guess a piece of me had hoped that he hadn't, but now I knew the truth and it was a bitter blade in my heart.

"Oh, yeah. Up on the roof right before he kicked the branch, broke it off and it landed on my damn head. Which reminds me... " My mom winced. "Ow."

"I'm just a good Baptist kid," Drifter said, obviously struggling with everything he had seen and what we were telling him. "I'm not sure I believe in all this stuff."

With the roll of her eyes, Olivia said, "Uh, hello. Jesus came back from the dead. Walked on water. Turned water into wine. *And* he parted the sea."

"That was Moses," Drifter corrected her.

"Pffft, whatever. I wasn't paying attention that day."

"The important thing is," I said, "Christy did it. She brought my mom back to life after Mark *killed* her."

I tried my hardest not to ball my hands into fists, but I couldn't help it. I didn't want to scare my friends. I wasn't the type to get visibly angry. When it all came down to it, I was mad—so mad, in fact, that I just wanted to throw my head back and scream, but I couldn't do that right now. Mom said I'd always had Dad's passive temper—that unless I was really pissed, I wouldn't react badly to anything. But at that moment it was all coming down like a solar eclipse. The moon had just aligned with the sun stealing my light and thrusting me into darkness. A ring of hope glimmered in the sky, yet I couldn't seek it out because to look would be to blind myself. I had to see clearly in the darkness to defeat the monster that had killed my mother.

Christy raised her head, her face pale. "Ashley?" she asked. "Are you okay?"

"You did it honey," Mom said. "You showed the world what *Hocus Pocus* is really about."

"Without the horrible songs," Olivia snarked.

"Hmm. Anyone else concerned that I don't have a pulse?" my mom asked, frowning as she pushed her fingers into her wrist.

"What?" Christy asked, rising, steadying herself on Olivia as she stumbled forward. "You don't have a *pulse?*"

"No. Check me, Adam." She stuck her arm out for my approval. "I'm not that big of an airhead. I'm pretty sure I can read my own pulse, and I don't think I have one."

I took my Mom's wrist and pressed my fingers against it. I waited, dreadfully, for what seemed like minutes to feel pulse. None came. "She doesn't have one," I said, turning my head up to look at Christy. "I thought you said—"

"I've never done something like this before, Adam. I knew I could do it, but... I just didn't know how it would turn out."

"Either way," Ashley said, starting for the kitchen, "we need to call the police."

"No!" Christy and I shouted. Mom stopped dead in her tracks.

"Uh, guys. He tried to kill me."

"He *did* kill you," I said. "He dropped a branch on your head and broke your neck."

"I'll have to see a chiropractor about that," my mother groused, rubbing it.

"We can't call the police," Christy said. "What're we going to tell them? That you died, then were brought back to life with magic? I'm not Sabrina the Teenage Witch. I can't magically get away with everything. Look... you can't tell anyone about this. None of you can. Not even my parents. They'd flip."

"Christy?" I asked. "Your mom and dad don't know?"

"No. And they don't need to know, at least not until after we deal with the jerkface who killed your mom." I didn't want to explain that my parents didn't trust me. Their lack of confidence in me still stung.

"Deal with Mark?" I laughed, hysteria gripping me. "How are *we* supposed to deal with Mark? He *killed* my Mom by breaking a *tree branch* and *dropping it on her head*. I can't *deal*. Guys... you don't understand."

"Don't understand what?" Drifter frowned.

"I thought everything was perfect. I had a great life, a great Mom, a great sister, great friends. Then to top it off, I had a boyfriend—an *actual* boyfriend. And then what happens? I get attacked by the jocks, confronted by a ghost at Halloween, and my Mom is *murdered* by my boyfriend! I... " I paused. The sight of everyone staring at me seemed to bring this all to a peak. "If he's not... . *human*... then I don't even know if my feelings for him were real."

"Wait a minute," Drifter said. "We're being serious here. You don't think Mark is human?"

"He isn't," Christy said. "Whatever attacked me in my room was wearing Mark's cross, and I know for a fact that wasn't human."

"I think it's time to call in my stepbrother," Olivia announced.

"Huh?" everyone asked.

"He's a vampire hunter."

"How do you know Mark's a vampire?" Drifter asked.

"Vampire, zombie, werewolf, doesn't matter—he hunts them all."

"Then what was all this 'vampires pfft, witches pfft' thing about?" Christy asked.

"Well, it does sound crazy that there are zombies and vampires and werewolves and witches, right? You brought Adam's mom back to life. Pffft. How crazy does *that* sound?"

"So let me get this straight," Drifter said. "You're going to call in your stepbrother, some badass *vampire hunter*. How's he going to help? Is he going to *hurt* Mark?"

"No," Olivia said sarcastically. "He's going to kill him."

Drifter gaped at her in disbelief.

"You ever wonder why Houston's so miserable to live in? And I'm not talking about the horrible traffic that makes you want to die. I'm talking about all the crazy violence. It's because of the monsters. My stepbrother hunts them. Think of him as the resident Buffy, except taller... and grungier... and a lot smellier than she could've ever been."

"He's in Houston?" I asked, a flicker of hope lighting in my chest.

"Yeah. And seeing that Mark's tried to kill one of us already, I know he'll try again." Olivia pulled out her massive touch-screen, Betty Boop-decaled smartphone from her Betsey Johnson purse. "Give me a few minutes and I'll get this taken care of."

"Wait!" Drifter exclaimed. "Do we actually believe there are monsters in Houston?"

"Well, d'oh." Olivia gave him a scornful look. "The pale people robbing the blood banks? Vampires. All those missing cats? Werewolves."

Callie angrily hissed from where she sat listening to us. Christy picked her up, giving her soothing kisses, but Callie still looked none too happy.

"But this can't be real!" Drifter protested.

178

"Hello! Broken neck! You helped bring me back to life! Christy on a broomstick." My Mom pointed at the broom swaying gently back and forth a few feet away. "Drifter, c'mon. Get with the program. Sheesh."

Drifter fell silent, dropping his head in thought.

"Gawd. I'm hungry. Anyone else hungry? Let's get a snack while Olivia does her thing." Mom gestured the remainder of our troop into the kitchen and immediately set about gathering a snack for me, Christy and Drifter. "So fill me in on why I got my neck broken by your ex-boyfriend, Adam."

While Olivia talked in the other room, detailing to her stepbrother the night's happenings, Christy and I filled Mom and Drifter in about all the weird things that had been happening since Mark had arrived.

"Ugh," Drifter moaned. "This just keeps getting better and better."

"I *knew* there was something wrong with him! A mother is always right when she has a weird feeling," Mom said. The sight of Callie appearing in the kitchen, followed by the broom as they patrolled the house, gave her pause. "About the broom...can I borrow it, Christy? You think it's better than a Roomba?"

"It'd be more inclined to hide in your curtains than do any housework," Christy grumbled. The broom promptly began to do a sweeping motion in midair, shimmering dust descending in its wake.

My mom, who had been dead just a few minutes before, broke out laughing while Drifter chuckled and Christy slightly smiled.

The humor of the situation was lost on me. While they were seeing a playful magical broom, I was seeing my reality crumbling. Mark wasn't human. Mom had been murdered. After riding three blocks on her magical flying broom, Christy had brought Mom back to life with magic. And to top it all off, Olivia was calling in her stepbrother, some kind of monster hunter. The world wasn't safe anymore. Life wasn't normal. *My* life wasn't normal. And it was all on account of a guy named Mark, who had claimed to love me.

"Well," Olivia said with a sigh as she stepped into the kitchen. "I talked to him."

"And?" I asked.

"He just has to pack a few things and he'll be on his way."

"But we're not safe," Christy said. "Not by a long shot."

"I've got a gun," Ashley nodded, turning to face the fridge. "I'm a Texas mama. I'll shoot him to kingdom come if he tries to come in here."

"But that's the problem," I said. "We can't just stay locked up in the house. We have to go to school. The store. What if he tries to get Am? Or you, Drifter? Or Olivia? He's already tried to kill Christy, and he already did kill you, Mom. None of us are safe—not anymore."

"I can make protection spells," Christy said. "Give me until tomorrow."

"To quote Buffy, we need to go into research mode," Olivia said a little more somberly than we were used to. "Nathan says we need to see what we can find out about Marek, the bridge, and that ghost. It's all connected."

"We can meet at the library when it opens tomorrow at noon. It's only open in the afternoon on Sundays," Christy suggested.

"I'm in," I said tersely. "I want to know what's up with Mark and how to deal with him."

"Uh, guys," Drifter said. "I hate to rain on the Buffy brigade, but I think we have a problem."

We all turned to face my mother.

"What?" Mom asked, shoving pieces of raw ground chuck into her mouth. "I was hungry."

"Yeah," Olivia said. "We have a problem."

Chapter 14

Truths Revealed

Christy

I was a groggy mess when I stumbled through the heavy oak doors into the library the next day. Clutching a steaming hot latte with an extra shot of espresso, I said a silent prayer to the coffee gods that they would grant me lucidity.

My sneakers squeaked on the marble floor as I trod toward the staircase that led up to the second floor where the Reference/Local History section was located. The librarian behind the heavy walnut information desk gave me a searing look when I passed her. I forced a smile, but I knew she saw me as a punk kid based on my attire of a black hoodie, faded jeans, a vintage Blondie t-shirt and dirty pink Converse sneakers. Of course, I could peg her as a shrew based on her face-stretching tight bun, cat-eyed frame glasses, and tweed dress. When she looked away I stuck out my tongue at her.

Clomping up the stairs, I felt my backpack shift on my back. I hesitated in midstep, tilted my head, and tried to see if my backpack was actually wiggling or if I was hallucinating. A very soft meow came from inside the bag.

"Callie?"

A small white paw lashed out of the slight gap under the flap and smacked my arm as if to tell me to shut up.

"Great," I mumbled. Just what I needed. A meowing stowaway familiar.

I continued my ascent to the scary dark inner sanctum of the local library. Another shrew—or maybe she was a harpy—stood watch behind yet another desk made of dark varnished wood. This one had a bowl haircut, oversized glasses, and was wearing a denim dress and loafers.

"You need to be quiet," she said tartly the second she saw me. "And no drinks in the library."

"What drink?" I asked. I willed my coffee to vanish from her sight. Her befuddled look said I had achieved my goal. After raising Adam's mother from the dead, I was pretty confident in my abilities.

"Oh, I, uh... .well, for future reference, no drinks in the library." Embarrassed, she swiveled about and started looking over her work.

I stuck my tongue out at her, too.

To my surprise, when I reached the study area in the very back of the second floor, I found Drifter and Olivia already stacking books on the table. Drifter was in his usual uniform of jeans, a t-shirt under a button down, and a hoodie. Olivia took the librarian trope and twisted it. She had her blond-pink hair pulled back into a fancy bun with lots of curls and braids and was wearing cute pink cat-eyed glasses with rhinestones edging the top. Wearing a white blouse tucked into a black skirt cinched at the waist by a big pink vinyl belt with a rhinestone buckle, she looked as adorable as ever.

"Hey," I said grumpily.

"Hey, Glinda. What's up?" Drifter asked.

"And where did you get the coffee? The warden claimed ours," Olivia said.

"Magic," I answered.

"Lucky." Olivia pouted.

I slung my backpack onto a chair, remembering at the last moment that my cat was inside. It landed with a thump, but I didn't hear any kitty protest. Opening it up, I found it empty except for the protection spells I had spent most of the night making, my notebook, my personal spellbook, and a bag of chips. Either I was going crazy or Callie had made a magical escape. Slumping into a chair, I nabbed a book from the pile Drifter was organizing. It was some sort of census.

"This looks boring," I declared. "On *Buffy* it was so much more exciting."

"Tax rolls, census, voter registration," Olivia read off to me. "From the start of the town to the turn of the last century. It's our best way to find Marek."

"I'm about to snag the copies of the journals and diaries from the local townsfolk that were donated to the museum." Drifter checked his phone, studying a photo he had taken of his earlier book search on the library computers. "Be right back. If you could magic up a coffee and a breakfast taco, I will love you forever."

"I made it invisible. I can't conjure out of thin air." I pondered for a second. "At least I don't think I can."

Olivia settled into the chair next to me and grimaced. "You're right. This looks so much more exciting on TV shows."

Warming my hands on my coffee cup, I flipped the book open and tried to figure out how to actually glean information from it. Gradually I realized it was a ledger of all the immigrants, carefully recorded ship manifests, land grants, and other tidbits. The book was typewritten, but a lot of information was handwritten in the margins. Just as our museum trip had taught us, most of the immigrants were from Bohemia, which accounted for the heavy Czech influence in the town architecture and culture.

"Here are the diaries and journals," Drifter said, setting down several black binders with typewritten labels. "I'm off to find the copies of the photo albums."

Olivia shoved aside the voter registration documents she was looking at and grabbed a journal. Flipping it open, she wrinkled her nose at the photocopies tucked into clear plastic sheaths. "Ugh. I thought my handwriting was bad. And where is Adam? He's supposed to be suffering this torture with us."

182

My heart did a little stutter at the thought of something bad happening to him and my expression must have reflected my panic.

"I'm sure he's okay! He's probably just running late. You know... with his mom being all zombie and stuff."

"She's not a zombie," I said defensively.

"Right. No heartbeat and likes raw meat. Totally not a zombie. Not that she's not a totally nice zombie and kinda cute and nowhere near rotting and gross... " Olivia bit her lip. "I'll shut up now."

Adam skidded into the table, his hands full with a bag from the local bakery and a carton full of coffee. "Sorry I'm late. Mom insisted I bring food and then I had to avoid the harpies."

I grinned at him. We're so in sync with each other sometimes it's scary.

"What?" He eyeballed me suspiciously.

"I totally pegged them as harpies, too."

A slight smile quirked his lips. Flopping into a chair, he looked at the books. He looked as tired as the rest of us, but his eyes were swollen and red from crying, too. I knew he was relieved that his mom was alive—well, in a weird new way—but he was devastated over Mark. I couldn't blame him for being heartbroken and angry at the same time.

"So is your mom still on her raw food diet?" Olivia dared to ask.

"She was slurping down raw bacon this morning," Adam said, sighing. He hooked his hands together on his chest and shrugged. "But she's still here. She's still my mom."

Drifter returned with more binders and a gleeful grin erupted on his face at the sight of the food and coffee. "You're the best, Adam."

"Mom's idea. I take no credit." Adam took a coffee for himself as a mild frenzy erupted, the bag rustling while coffee steam filled my nostrils.

Olivia shoved a book across the table to Adam. "Research."

"Tax Records 1888. Sounds awesome." Adam winced and flipped the book open.

Callie landed on the table, the loud thump making all of us start. Licking one paw, she surveyed us calmly.

"Uh, Christy, I'm pretty sure there's a no pet rule." Adam flicked his attention back and forth between me and Callie.

Callie narrowed her golden eyes at him.

"She's not a pet. She's a familiar," Olivia said and offered the cat a piece of her kolache.

Sniffing the bit of pastry and sausage with interest, Callie kept one reproachful eye firmly on Adam.

"Sorry, Callie," Adam muttered.

"Is the broom here, too?" Drifter twisted around in his chair searching for the spying fiend among the bookshelves.

"Not that I know of. But then again I didn't know she was along for the ride either." I sipped my coffee and glared at Callie. "She stowed away."

Lightly nibbling on Olivia's offering, the familiar ignored us while she ate.

"So we're looking for Marek and anything about the bridge?" Adam stared at the book, his eyes already starting to glaze over.

"Yeah! Cool, huh? Kinda like we're in a mystery," Drifter said around a mouthful of food.

"Where people die and we have monsters hunting us," Olivia reminded him, giving him a dark look.

"Oh, yeah." Looking shamefaced, Drifter grabbed a photo album off the stack. "Sorry, Adam."

Adam gave out the nervous little laugh he gets when really emotional. "It's okay. It sort of doesn't feel real to me, either."

"Oh, yeah. Before I forget... " I pulled out four small beige bags. They smelled pungent and spicy. "The protection spells. Put them in your pocket or somewhere on your body. I don't know exactly what Mark is, so it's kind of basic." I honestly had no idea if they were even going to work, but I had to try.

Olivia tucked hers inside of her bra while the guys pocketed theirs. I pushed my own into my hoodie pocket.

"Smells kinda nice," Olivia decided.

We lapsed into silence while we ate, sipped coffee, and flipped pages. Callie finished her bit of food and stalked to the center of the table where Drifter had stacked all the books and binders. Sniffing each one, she looked like a little busybody. I ignored her until she slapped the first book off the table with one swift smack of her paw.

"Callie," I hissed.

She smacked another one, sending it sailing toward the edge of the table. Drifter grabbed it just in time. Olivia hopped up to look for the nosy librarians as Callie sent another book skittering across the table. This time it stopped right in front of Adam. Again she whacked another book, sending it off the table. I barely caught it.

"Callie, stop," I ordered in a low voice.

The cat gave me one sharp look, then sent another book toward Drifter. It stopped right before it reached it him.

"She's sorting them," Drifter said in awe. "That's what she's doing!"

"Well, she needs to do it quietly," Olivia said under her breath. "The librarian is looking in our direction."

We were hidden in the stacks, and we didn't need company. Now that we knew what she was doing, Callie was much quieter. She quickly worked her way through the books until we each had a new book to look at and the rest were piled on a chair out of the way.

"Your cat is kind of a bitch," Olivia decided.

Satisfied, Callie lay down on the table and flicked her tail.

Resuming our search for the mysterious Marek, we lapsed into silence. The only sound was the distant hushed voices of other visitors and the turning of pages.

"Found him," Adam said about ten minutes later. "I found him."

We all scrambled to gather around Adam to see what he had discovered. At first the photocopy just looked like a group of young men posing by the old bridge, but after a few seconds I saw Mark's face peering over the heads of the people in front of him. Tucked into the back row, he was taller and more striking than the others. Underneath the picture were the names of the men in the picture. Marek Černý was listed as Mark's name.

184

"It's him," Adam breathed.

"When was that taken?" Olivia asked excitedly.

"The late 1800's," Adam answered. His hands were visibly shaking.

"I'm reading the diary of that guy right now," Olivia said, pointing to another name. It was for a shortish young man in the front row with a big smile and jaunty cowlick. "Dušan Barta. He was an apprentice tailor."

"He likes us petite," Adam observed. He looked shell shocked and I hugged him gently from behind. He gripped my forearms tightly and leaned into me.

"This is creepy," Drifter said in awe. "I was just reading about the suicide at the bridge. It was that guy. Dušan. It was a real big scandal because he was supposed to get married to the daughter of one of the founders of the town, and she went missing and was never found. I was just reading where they did an inquest and people testified that he seemed afraid and uneasy right before she disappeared. His best friend, Marek, testified that Dušan had grave misgivings about getting married before she vanished. They fought the night Dušan died. Marek claimed he was trying to calm his friend, but Dušan stormed out of Marek's home. He knocked over an oil lamp on his way out and set Marek's house on fire. Marek barely escaped with his life."

I swallowed hard, my grip tightening on my best friend.

"What does it mean?" Adam asked breathlessly. "Christy, what is he?"

"The cross must mean something," Olivia decided. "I think I can kinda see it in this picture of Marek."

"It's a St. Andrew's cross."

"Dušan sketched it in his diary. He was talking about his love wearing it and how it unnerved him whenever he saw it," Olivia said, biting her lip thoughtfully.

"So he's really old, right? Mark is Marek, right?" Drifter's brown eyes scrutinized us all. "That's what we're all thinking, right?"

We all nodded.

"So he's a vampire?" Incredulity and fear fought for dominance in Drifter's eyes.

I almost blurted out that vampires were extinct, but Olivia said, "But if Mark is a vampire, why would he wear a cross of St. Andrew?"

"Because," a voice said from behind us, "St. Andrew is the patron saint of vampires."

Turning as one, our little group stared at the good-looking guy standing a few feet behind us. Vivid blue eyes peered out of a handsome face graced with good cheekbones, a noble nose, and thin, but shapely lips. Clad in jeans, a navy thermal shirt, and heavy boots, he looked like just a regular guy in his late teens.

"Nathan!" Olivia smiled and scurried over to hug him.

"Hey, sis," Nathan leaned down and embraced her before returning his attention to us. He was clearly all business and it was strangely reassuring. "So I'm Nathan. I'm a monster hunter and here to help you."

"I expected someone older," I confessed.

"Everyone does," Nathan admitted, smiling. Carrying his messenger bag over to the table, Nathan studied us each thoughtfully before finally looking at Adam. Slowly, he extended his hand to my best friend. "I'm sorry to hear what you're going through. Olivia told me all about it and explained to me who you all are."

Adam shook his hand, but didn't speak. His gaze returned to the picture of Marek.

Callie walked over to stare at Nathan and he held out his hand, palm up, allowing her to sniff him. Callie gave him a quick inspection, then hopped off the table and disappeared into the bookshelves.

"So, let's get started," Nathan said, rubbing his hands together. "Let's find out what kind of monster we're hunting."

Adam

I was in hell. It was hard to concentrate on the newcomer or anything going on around me. When Drifter had talked about Dušan burning down Marek's house, I had entered a twilight state where the world was gray and foreboding.

The image of Mark's cross lingered in my mind. It had looked burned.

It's an heirloom, he'd once told me. *It's been in my family for generations.*

"So you think it's a vampire?" I asked Nathan.

Shrugging his shoulders, Nathan set his laptop on the table and started booting it up. "Well, the cross might indicate a vampire, but lots of things come out to play on St. Andrew's Day."

"You said that the cross is about vampires, right?" Christy slowly took out the folded washcloth that contained the cross.

"It can be. But vampires are rare. Very rare," Nathan answered.

Christy placed the cloth-wrapped cross on the table. "Don't touch it," she said. "I don't know what it'll do."

Nathan unfolded the cloth and immediately recoiled. "How did you get this?" he asked.

"It came off whatever attacked me Halloween night," Christy said, chewing her bottom lip nervously.

"It's Mark's cross. I saw it on him," I said in a somber tone.

Nathan continued to study the cross, his brow furrowed. "The thing that attacked you... what'd it look like?" "I was too busy hiding to see anything other than its glowing red eyes and mouth full of razor-sharp teeth."

"It's a good thing you hid," Nathan said. "It obviously wanted you dead because Adam loves you."

Christy and I exchanged looks.

"We're totally not like that—" Christy stammered.

"Just best friends—" I cut in.

Nathan gave us a wry smile. "I meant that Adam loves you like family. That's why Mark killed Adam's mom."

"I think he did it because she threw him out." I wished he would put away the cross. It made me feel sick looking at it.

"Maybe. Or maybe a bit of both." Nathan shrugged. "This cross is very unsettling."

"Mark was upset that he lost it." I shifted uncomfortably in my seat. "Really upset. Do you know why the cross is important?"

"No. I don't."

"But I thought you've dealt with these things before?"

"I have, but I can't say for sure what Mark is yet. We just need to figure out what kind of monster he is," Nathan answered. "If we all work together we can figure it out."

I sat there for several seconds trying to gain my bearings before I rose and said, "I need some air."

"Away from the books?" Drifter asked.

"Yeah. Away from the books." I needed a moment to process before the feeling inside me became the match to kerosene. It was becoming too much.

Somehow, I was able to keep from crying.

At the series of windows spread out along the far wall, I looked out at the old downtown area of Trinity Springs and tried to imagine just how long this creature had been hiding, waiting, *preying* on the inhabitants of Trinity Springs and waiting for just the right moment to strike. He could've been anywhere at any given time and I wouldn't have known anything about it. I was exactly what he wanted me to be.

Prey.

Shivering, I crossed my arms and pressed my hands against my ribcage.

The wind that ruffled the trees should have been peaceful. Yet here I was, wondering whether or not Mark was waiting for me. Correction. I *knew* he was waiting for me.

"Care if I join you?" Nathan asked.

I looked over at him and gave a slight nod. He took up position beside me and leaned against the windowsill, eyes scrutinizing the town before us.

"Just between the two of us," he said, turning his attention to me, "I know what it feels like to find out the person you love is a monster."

"Somehow I doubt it," I said darkly. "This isn't like a regular breakup. Whatever a regular breakup is."

"Actually, I really do. I was seeing someone who I discovered was a monster."

I gave him a look of surprise, then said, "So you do know how much it sucks."

"Yeah," Nathan agreed, "especially when you build up trust only to have it ripped away."

"What happened to you?"

"My first boyfriend turned out to be a werewolf. We hit it off right away... kinda like you and this guy Mark did, according to my sister. I thought a lot of his weird behavior was just because he was eccentric. Really artsy type. Preparing to go to college for linguistics. He was going to graduate at seventeen. I thought his sudden disappearances when we planned things together was nerves. Turned out it was because he was eating the neighbor's pets and the occasional human being."

"So how did you find out what he was?"

Nathan exhaled, long and slow. "Well, he showed me what he was. He wanted to make me into a werewolf. And he wouldn't take no for answer."

"What'd you do?"

"I did what I had to. I pulled a gun with a silver bullet on him the next time he came around. He'd fully changed. He wasn't coming back. No 'light of the full moon' bullshit. He wasn't human anymore. So... I put him out of his misery. Saved a lot of lives by doing that. And prevented him from making any more of what he was."

I sighed.

Nathan did too and returned his gaze to the window. "I'm here because Olivia knows I can help you get rid of him," he said.

"I don't want you to get rid of him," I said.

"What?" Nathan asked, surprised.

"I said I don't want you to get rid of him," I repeated, turning my head to look at my friends sitting at the library table. "This isn't your fight. It's not theirs either. It's mine. Whatever he is, *I* have to get rid of him. I'm the one who has to kill Mark."

The closer the clock edged to six, closing time at the library and sunset, the more dread filled my heart.

Hell wasn't the word to describe what I felt.

Over the next few hours the four of us pored over books—Christy over newspaper clippings, Drifter diaries, and Olivia crime reports, while Nathan consulted a group he called The Society online. I had the luxury of scouring yearbooks to try and find the one face I never wanted to see again.

"Anyone finding anything?" Nathan asked, lifting his head from his laptop.

We all begrudgingly answered no.

"Well," he frowned, "I'm sure we'll find something soon."

I flipped the page in a nineteen-eighty-one yearbook.

Mark's face looked back at me.

The blood in my veins chilled to ice.

Mark Black.

"Guys," I said. "I found something."

We leaned forward to view my findings.

"How far back does he appear?" Nathan asked, narrowing his eyes at the books before us.

Given that Trinity Springs had only started printing single pictures in yearbooks in the nineteen-fifties, it wasn't hard to find out.

Mark could be visibly seen in each decade's yearbook starting from 1952 all the way up until 2002. In each picture he looked his same dashing self, from his magnetic eyes to his charming smile. The only thing that changed was his name and his appearance. Even then his hair only changed in style, not length.

"Twinkles, can you check and see if any crimes fit the dates Adam wrote down?" Nathan asked.

"Twinkles?" Drifter lifted an eyebrow.

"Shut up, *Drifter*." Popping a fresh lollipop into her mouth, Olivia immediately began cross-referencing crimes committed at the same time.

188

Half an hour later, Olivia looked up ashen-faced.

"I have matches to those years and it's not good," she said somberly. "Listen to this: Starting in 1882, a young man has gone missing and then been found dead and brutally mutilated every twenty-five years up until nineteen-thirty-two. But that's not the weird thing. What *is* weird is that after thirty-two, it turned to every ten years until nineteen-ninety-two."

"Ugh! That was the year of that weird murder!" Christy shivered.

I swallowed a lump in my throat. It was the one murder that had terrified my mother so much that when I had come out she had turned into a Valkyrie to defend me at the slightest hint of danger. "The Werewolf Murder."

"What happened?" Nathan asked.

"A gay guy back in the nineties was found mauled to death on the outskirts of town near the park," I explained. "They called it The Werewolf Murder because some people claimed to have seen the victim with another guy."

"He was pretty munched on," Christy added.

"It freaked out everyone. It was after Halloween so people were saying it was Satanists, vampires, werewolves," I continued. "But it was ruled an animal mauling."

Olivia pointed at another article. "But this one says it happened again."

I nodded grimly. "A few years later another suspected gay guy was found mauled. His family said it had to be a serial killer, but the police said it was another animal attack."

Olivia kept up her search, her eyes widening with horror. "It kept happening every few years. Some young guy getting mauled."

I nodded somberly. "Every time the police dismissed it as an animal attack. A few people said it had to be a serial killer. I remember my mom telling my dad that one of the victims was a friend of theirs that they suspected was gay." Anger tore at the edges of my mind. "Of course, since they were possibly gay men, the police just swept it away under the rug."

"Stupid homophobes," Christy groused.

"They all happened in late November, because the bodies weren't found until early December." Olivia rubbed her furrowed brow and glanced at her stepbrother. "Help! What does it mean?"

Nathan hastily typed some notes into his computer before looking up. "Mark has a St. Andrew's Cross. November 29th is Saint Andrew's Eve."

"So he's a vampire," Drifter said. "Right?"

"But the bodies were mauled," Olivia reminded him. "Torn up to the point where the cops said a coyote got them."

"He... *ate*... them?" I swallowed a lump in my throat.

"So he's a werewolf?" Drifter's confusion reflected all of ours. We were all lost, trying to fit pieces together, trying to figure out what Mark was and what he wanted with *me*.

Christy narrowed her eyes at a series of clippings she'd pulled out and sighed. "This is too creepy to be coincidence."

"What?" I frowned.

"There are reports of animals digging up the old graves on the far side of town *between* the murders... and only got worse after 2004." Christy cradled her head in her hands. "Ugh! What does it mean?"

"He's a werewolf-vampire that digs up dead bodies?" Drifter frowned. "I don't get it. What does he need dead bodies for?"

Christy widened her eyes. Fingers trembling, she said, "If it was Mark, y'all he was eating *bones,* Drifter. Not *chewing* on them; *eating* them." Christy lifted one of the pictures in plain view.

My stomach flipped.

The splintered femur displayed appeared to have been gnawed on by a piranha with three-inch-long teeth.

"Okay, what kind of monster eats bones?" Drifter threw up his hands. "This doesn't make sense."

Nathan's attention was still squarely on his laptop, but he answered in a tense tone, "Ghouls."

"Ghouls?" we chorused.

"They're like a cross between a zombie and a vampire. They eat the dead, and sometimes the living. They hang out in cemeteries and munch on the dead bodies," Nathan answered.

"So totally gross," Olivia exclaimed, waving her blue lollipop around.

"Everyone give me their notes real quick. I'm talking to some of the other members of The Society and I think we might be onto something." Nathan gestured at us and we all scooted the notes to him.

"What is that? The Society?" Christy asked suspiciously. "Is it like the Watchers Council on *Buffy?* Because those guys sucked."

"No, no," Nathan said with a slight smile. "It's a group of people who communicate via a secret online forum. All of us have had encounters with the supernatural and we share stories, compare notes, and when something really bad starts up—like this situation—we form a task force."

"Do you actually kill the monsters?" Drifter asked, leaning forward eagerly. "Like go in guns a'blazing?"

Nathan shrugged. "When we have to. Kill the monster, exorcise the demon, put a ghost to rest... "

It was obvious that Nathan was used to this sort of thing. He was utterly calm while he perused the notes and typed them into his computer. It was easy to imagine the little gears in his head whirling about, clicking as things came into focus. I envied him. I couldn't focus on anything other than the darkness that had enveloped me. I was relieved that my phone was silent all day except for a few quick text messages from my mom. Mark hadn't contacted me and it was a relief.

"Okay, we think we've got something," Nathan said twenty minutes later. "Marek said Dušan accidentally burned down his house after they quarreled. Which explains the burned cross and why Dušan ended up hanging himself and not being mauled like the other victims."

I sighed, sadness filling me. "Can you imagine how hard it must have been to be gay back then?"

Christy squirmed around on her chair, her hands plunged into her hoodie pockets. "Dušan must have killed himself to escape Marek." She flicked her gaze toward me worriedly.

"I'm not killing myself," I told her pointedly. "He messed me up emotionally, but I'm not going to let him win."

190

Christy gave me a sweet, yet sad smile. "I love you, dorkface."

"I love you, too, pain in my ass," I answered, reaching over to squeeze her hand.

Nathan rubbed his chin, staring at the screen thoughtfully. "I think we have an answer as to why Adam hasn't heard from Mark during the day anymore. The St. Andrew's cross is associated with vampires, but one of my contacts says there is a little known myth that the cross can allow vampires to be awake during the day and walk in sunlight."

Christy rolled her eyes. "Oh, God. So cliché."

Olivia smirked. "Ha! Stupid high school attending vampire!"

Nathan shushed his stepsister, who promptly stuck out her blue tongue at him. "One of the people I'm talking to right now is an expert in tracing genealogy. She just told me that there is a vampire legend attached to the town in Bohemia that the immigrants who settled Trinity Springs came from. Another contact in Romania is confirming this right now." Nathan watched his screen anxiously. "Okay, according to my sources the very vain son of a rich landowner near the town was a seducer of young men. His father found out and disinherited him. The son vanished for a year before returning and taking up residence with his father. His father and mother both died soon after he reappeared and he reclaimed his inheritance. He quarreled with the local priests over his seduction of young men and the church was mysteriously burned to the ground. Soon it was rumored he was a vampire and things got really uncomfortable for him."

"And his name was Marek, wasn't it?" I said, my stomach in knots.

Nathan nodded. "The townspeople who came here emigrated to get away from him, but right after they left, Marek was no longer seen at his estate in Bohemia."

"So he came with them and he is a vampire!" Drifter looked pleased. "So we stake him and he turns to dust and we're done!"

Nathan wagged his head in the negative. "I think Mark started out a vampire, but he's not anymore. The maulings, the graves being broken into and the bones being eaten are not the signs of a vampire."

"You think he's a ghoul?" Christy sunk deeper into her chair.

Callie let out a soft cry and jumped onto Christy's lap. We hadn't seen her all day, so we all gasped.

Nathan eyed Callie thoughtfully while saying, "I think he is now. See, it all goes back to that first guy. Dušan. He killed himself rather than be with Marek. I think Mark was doing the same thing he did with Adam. He was seducing Dušan to be with him, but Dušan turned him down. Maybe he really was in love with the fiancé. Maybe he was bisexual. Whatever the case, Dušan killed himself rather than be enslaved to Marek as a vampire. I think someone cursed Marek in the aftermath. Maybe a family member of Dušan's."

"This is starting to kinda make sense," Christy said.

Callie set her paws on the table and gave out a small meow in agreement.

"I don't get it," Drifter said, shrugging.

"A curse warps the person it's cast on," Christy explained. "It makes them do terrible things that will bring them pain. Make them be in their own personal hell."

Olivia sat up straight and waved her hands with excitement. "Like every so often Mark has to eat someone! Or eat bones!"

"Twinkles, you're so smart!" Nathan grinned at her. "I think you nailed it. The ritual pattern. Kill a young gay man on St. Andrew's Night by eating his flesh. Eat the bones of the dead."

"Rinse. Repeat!" Olivia nodded with satisfaction.

I was nauseated with how much it made sense. I closed my eyes, trying to somehow reconcile the theory being suggested by my friends with the sweet guy I had dated. It was difficult to do. Mark's calm gray eyes called to me. I wished I could go to him, comfort him and be comforted by him.

"Adam? What are you doing?" There was alarm in Christy's voice.

Opening my eyes, I saw my friends staring at me in fear. "Huh?"

"Look." Olivia pointed.

I saw movement out of the corner of my eye and looked down to find my hand scribbling across the notepad in front of me. Shocked, I watched words form in handwriting completely different from my own. "I don't know," I said, dumbstruck. "It's just doing that!"

Callie hissed low in her throat while Christy shoved back her chair and rushed to my side. Leaning over my hand, she was careful not to touch me. "It's a little hard to read, but I think it says 'He killed the one I loved, now he must kill the one he loves.' And this is much fancier and nicer writing than Adam's!"

"Automatic writing," Nathan breathed. "It's the ghost. It has to be."

Now that Christy had read what had been scrawled out on the pad, my hand stilled. It felt strange. Cold, disconnected, and far away from me, like a weight had been lifted from my shoulder. It was like it wasn't a part of me anymore.

"Dušan?" Christy whispered.

My hand jerked. A word appeared.

Yes.

"It's him!" Christy exclaimed.

No one moved. We were all afraid. The air around us was growing colder, more ominous. When Nathan spoke, his breath was misty. "Dušan, what did you do to Marek?"

Marek is the devil.

Christy read the response aloud.

"Did you curse him?" Olivia asked. "Were you angry with him?"

He killed the one I loved. Now he must kill those he loves or suffer.

My teeth started to chatter. Again, the feeling of being prey had returned, yet at the same time I felt as though I were the predator who had long since grown tired with watching its prey. I wasn't only scared—I was angry, and not only because of what Mark had done to me.

"It feels," I said, trembling, the rage within me rising like a dormant volcano becoming active, "like he's in me."

"You're gonna be okay," Nathan said. "Just stay calm."

"Calm?" I asked. "How can I be calm! My hand's been hijacked!"

My hand jerked so violently that I cried out in surprise.

192

He lured her away, the beginning of the script said, *and took her somewhere where she could never be found.*

"Who?" I asked.

The one I loved.

Christy read the responses aloud. "So he did love his fiancé and Marek killed her."

He hid her bones, now he must consume them. He stole her flesh, now he must eat it. He killed the one I love and now he must kill those he loves. He will not have peace. He will suffer. I took his beauty, his life, his loves, and I will have him SUFFER.

The throes of despair wracking my body were not my own, and were instead inflicted upon me by a force whose anger transcended death. I fought to maintain control of my body but I wanted to scream, to hurl the pencil away from me, to rip the notepad into a billion tiny pieces and throw myself from my chair, yet I couldn't. I was trapped in this cruel and twisted game and I had no control over it. He was the king and I his simple pawn, the gladiator in the ring, and the one I had to fight was not only the first person I had fallen in love with, but a monster cursed to do his bidding.

This is pain, the ghost continued to write. *This is torment. This is torture.*

The lights above flickered.

Everyone at the table looked up.

My hand stilled.

Christy looked over at me. "Is it gone?"

My hand began to move again.

His suffering will be endless, the ghost wrote.

The jolt of something leaving my body struck with such force that I went flying back in my seat.

I lost my breath.

Then the lights went out.

Christy

We all rushed out of the library and out into the courtyard. Dusk was falling and the world was gray and cold. I shivered, cradling Callie in my arms. When the power had gone out, she had immediately scrambled into my hoodie. Now her head poked out as she somberly surveyed our surroundings.

There were a few people out and about this late on Sunday afternoon. Cars glided by and pedestrians hurried to the few shops open downtown. The world seemed abnormally quiet.

We stood in a ring, all of us still in shock over what had happened. Adam stood close to me, his arm just barely touching mine. Nathan looked the calmest of all of us, but even he was a little pale.

"So... .he seduces young gay men. Makes them love him. Then he kills them because Dušan's curse makes him destroy what he loves," Olivia said, breaking the silence. "Talk about a bad breakup."

"But the bones!" Drifter said, obviously trying to wrap his mind around it all.

"Vampires drink blood. Ghouls eat bones and flesh," Christy said, ticking them off on her fingers. "Dušan cursed Marek aka Mark into being a ghoul every X amount of years to get revenge."

"All the kids with mono... " Drifter exclaimed. "He's drinking blood from them!"

"When I saw him with Jennifer!" Adam shook his head in disbelief. "They weren't making out. He was drinking from her!"

"So he's a vampire who wears a St. Andrew's Cross to go out in sunlight. So we stake him." Drifter folded his arms over his chest. "Makes perfect sense."

"He *was* a vampire. But he was cursed," Nathan amended.

"So now he's a ghoul," I said, shivering. "They can't go out in sunlight either, right?"

Callie meowed in agreement.

We all warily looked at the setting sun.

Nathan nodded slowly. "Yes. I think the curse has altered Marek/Mark into a hybrid. He's a vampire until the cycle starts again, then he starts becoming a ghoul. The ritual killings, the time schedule, all that, I think it's what Mark must do to keep the curse from completely taking him over. Dušan makes Mark kill the ones he loves to stave off tuning completely into a ghoul. It's a punishment. It's a cruel curse. Kill the ones you love to remain mostly human or become a monster. Plus, the cycle is happening more often. The ghost is very vengeful."

"I can almost feel bad for him," Olivia said, her hands on her hips. "You know, if he wasn't a stalking murderous creep."

"So can we stake him?" Drifter looked as antsy as I felt.

"Won't work. It doesn't work on vampires either. Just immobilizes them. To kill a vampire you have to chop off its head." Swinging his bag over one shoulder, Nathan glanced toward the setting sun. "But that's not going to work either. We're going to have to do a vanquish spell."

Chills swept down my spine and Callie laid her ears back. "That's some serious mojo, Nathan."

"What will that do?" Drifter asked.

"It destroys the monster in this realm and banishes them to the netherworld," Nathan answered. "It's serious stuff. But if we try to kill Mark and fail, he could come back stronger."

"So we're going to kill him," Adam said in a small voice. His head was down and his shoulders tensed.

"Do we have a choice? He killed your mom," Olivia pointed out.

"He's going to be coming for you at some point," Drifter agreed.

"How long do you think we have?" I asked Nathan.

Nathan let out a long, drawn out breath. "Well, I have a feeling Mark may expect Adam to turn to him for solace in the aftermath of Adam's mother's death. He's going to wake up tonight and find out that's not the case."

"So tonight?" Drifter looked at the sun lowering on the horizon. "That's not that far off."

"If your resident witch can help me get the ingredients for the vanquishing spell, we should be able to deal with him tonight. Adam, I suggest you stay home, and do not go out. Make sure your mom and sister stay indoors, too." Nathan pulled out his phone. "Christy, I'll text the ingredients to you."

I yanked out my phone and we exchanged numbers. "Okay. I think I can get what we need. Where do we meet? I can't do at my place."

"Do it at mine," Adam said. "Mom knows what's up."

"I can distract Amelia with a makeover," Olivia offered.

"Meet up at your place in two hours then?" Nathan suggested.

Nathan's gaze was so warm and caring when he looked at Adam, it touched me. The second I saw Olivia's handsome stepbrother he had pinged on my gaydar, but my matchmaking days were over. I was just glad that Adam had someone in his corner that understood what he was going through.

With a sigh, Adam nodded. "Sounds good. I'll let Mom know what's up."

Nervously, I fingered my cellphone. Guilt weighed me down like a heavy wet blanket, smothering me. I couldn't help but feel that all the terrible events surrounding Adam were my fault. Logically, I knew that it wasn't the case, but that didn't stop me from feeling like the worst friend in the world.

As if he sensed my remorse and fears, Adam slung his arm around me. I shifted into his warmth, grateful for his friendship.

"It'll be okay, Christy," Adam assured me. "Nathan has a lot of resources and you're a badass witch. Plus, we got Olivia and Drifter backing us up."

Though Drifter's usually calm demeanor was edged with anxiety, he nodded. "I've got your back. No bad guy is going to hurt you."

"The vanquishing spell will be tailored just for Mark. All any of us will have to do is hit him with it," Nathan explained.

Everyone nodded.

"Piece of cake," Olivia said confidently.

Again, an uneasy silence loomed among us. Callie brushed her head under my chin as though trying to comfort me.

"Tall, golden and hunky is staring at us," Olivia said after a beat.

I rotated on my heel, surprised to see Ian across the street. A plastic shopping bag was clutched in one hand and he had his car keys in the other. He stood awkwardly next to his truck staring at us. On impulse, I gave him a little wave. A smile broke out on his handsome face and he returned the gesture.

"Great. Now he's going to come over," Drifter said.

To my dismay, Ian did exactly that. He jogged across the street and right over to us. "Hey!"

"Hey," Adam said in a solemn voice. "What's up?"

"My mom sent me out for some pepper spray. They only carry it at the old hardware store so I made the trip over. She's really freaked out about Courtney."

"What about Courtney?" I asked, dreading the answer.

"She went missing Halloween. Didn't you hear? It's all over the news." Ian shook his blond head. "Man, it's so bad. Everyone is freaking out over it. My mom thinks it's a serial killer."

Our little group exchanged frightened looks. We all knew what had surely happened to Courtney. She had upset Mark in some way and now no one would ever see her again. Ian reached out to stroke Callie's head. He smelled so good and I was briefly distracted from the terrors enveloping our lives by his closeness. Looking up into his handsome face, I realized there was no way we could include him in our little group. He was so nice and innocent.

Slowly, Ian realized we weren't reacting to this news like he expected. "I know she wasn't nice to you guys, but she wasn't that bad. I mean, she didn't deserve to get kidnapped." His tone was a tad defensive.

"That's not it," I said miserably. "We just had some bad stuff happen to us, too." I realized too late my mouth was moving and my filter wasn't working. "Adam's mom almost got killed when a branch fell off the big tree outside of Adam's house."

"Oh, wow. That's bad. She okay now?" Ian seemed sincerely concerned for Adam.

"Yeah," Adam nodded. "She's fine now."

Olivia was warning me with her eyes, but I was completely thrown off balance by everything, plus I was just so tired.

"I never thought of Halloween being really evil, but this year is just whacked out. Really weird stuff going on." Ian glanced at Nathan. "Oh, dude, sorry to be rude. I'm Ian."

Nathan shook the proffered hand. "Nathan. Olivia's older brother."

"Good to meet you. Anyway, I better head home and give this to my mom. She's already loading all the guns in the house. I don't know why she needs pepper spray." Ian shrugged slightly. "I just hope they find Courtney."

"Me too," Drifter said somberly. "Me too."

To my utter shock, Ian gave me a quick side hug and headed back across the street.

Olivia slowly unwrapped a new lollipop and narrowed her eyes slightly. "So, Mark offed Courtney. Why?"

"It doesn't matter. We need to deal with him and now, before it gets worse," Nathan declared. "Two hours. Adam's house. Make sure you get something to eat. Tell your parents you're studying at Adam's tonight. Wear a cross or any other holy relic you might have. Christy's protection spells might work against Mark, but he's not a normal monster, so we can't be sure."

"This looked so much more fun on *Buffy*," Olivia groused. "But right now I feel like throwing up."

"I was about to say the same thing," Drifter agreed.

"If you're talking about the stark terrifying fear that we're all going to die, I'm right there with you," Adam confessed.

"Except we're not going to," Nathan assured us. "There is only one of him."

Reluctantly, the group broke apart and Adam and I walked to my car in silence.

Chapter 15

Things Fall Apart

Christy

"So how was studying?" My mom's question hung in the air almost like an accusation. There was nothing in her tone to indicate that she was suspicious, but I felt so guilty about not including her in what was happening that the simple question sent me on edge.

"Fine," I said.

Callie walked into the kitchen behind me and leapt onto the table. Licking one paw, she regarded me thoughtfully.

"So that's where you were all day!" My mom frowned at the cat while finishing making her cup of tea. "Callie, I needed you for a spell earlier."

Callie remained intensely catlike as she twisted her head about to wash her back, completely ignoring my mother.

My mother sighed.

"She just cruised around the library and kept us company." I set my backpack on one of the kitchen chairs. "It was a long day. I still have more stuff to do later at Adam's. I'm basically on a break."

"Well, I'm glad you're working on your history. That B last semester was a little bit of a shocker," Mom said, winking. "Oh, and did Ian find you okay? He came by earlier looking for you."

"He did?" I blinked.

"He did find you, right? I told him you were at the library studying."

"Yeah, he found me," I said, unsettled. Ian had actually come to my house to see *me*. What did that mean? He couldn't actually like me, could he? No, it had to be because he knew I was a witch.

My mom dropped a lemon slice into her tea and leaned against the kitchen island. Cradling the tea cup in her hands, she said, "I think that boy has a sweet spot for you."

"Uh, no."

"Uh, yes."

"I'm fat and ugly," I blurted out.

"Christy!" My mom looked horrified.

"I'm nowhere as pretty as Courtney and—" I stopped in mid-sentence. Courtney was dead. She was rotting somewhere, hidden away from everyone who had loved her, and it was my fault. Tears brimmed in my eyes.

My mother's look softened. "You heard about her."

I nodded my head.

"Hopefully they will find her."

I just stared at my mom in silence.

With a remorseful look, my mother set her tea down. "Though I doubt it. I tried to do a location spell. It didn't work. Which means she's probably... "

"Dead."

My mother nodded.

"I don't feel like eating. I think I'll just grab some stuff for a protection spell out in the garden."

"I could make you one," my mother offered.

Shaking my head, I headed toward the back door. "I need to start learning, right?"

Casting a worried look at the window, my mom said, "I'd like you to be back inside by sundown."

"I have to go over to Adam's soon," I reminded her.

"Humor me," my mother answered.

"Fine." I grabbed one of the fresh cotton bags my mom kept in a drawer near the back door and headed outside.

Callie followed.

The backyard was full of shadows beneath a sky that was full of vibrant colors slowly fading to black. I snagged a pair of pruning shears from the garden shed and set about gathering the herbs needed for the vanquishing spell. Callie prowled through the plants beside me as I gently snipped off the bits I needed from mom's assortment of plants. Yawning, I carefully laid out my cuttings, tying them with twine that was tucked into the bag I had taken. Mom is terribly organized.

The outside lights automatically flipped on as the sun reached the top of the tree line surrounding the house. Warily, I studied the growing shadows. Callie yanked a few bits of leaves off a plant and dropped it next to me.

"Yeah, yeah, Callie. I'm hurrying." I double checked my list and the stuff I had gathered.

"Christy?"

"Yeah?" I carefully placed the herbs inside of the cotton bag.

"Christy?"

The voice was not my mother's. A wave of icy energy flowed over me. Slowly, I raised my head. Standing under the trees was Courtney. Her skin was gray and her body was a mangled mess. Her Snow White costume was smeared with blood and her neck was nothing more than ripped flesh.

"Courtney!" I gasped.

"He killed me," she stated. "Mark killed me."

"I know," I whispered.

"He called me out of my own party, then told me that I was nothing to him. That I had hurt Adam and he wouldn't allow it." Her black lips remained still, but I could hear her voice. Her sorrow was palatable. "I wasn't supposed to die young."

"I'm sorry, Courtney," I answered and meant it. No one deserved to die so cruelly.

"I was so mean to Adam." The edges of her body began started to appear hazy and her voice was fainter, her ghostly powers waning. "I never dreamed…"

"What do you need me to do, Courtney? Why did you come to me?" I stood up, clutching my bag. Callie sat at my feet watching the ghost with narrowed eyes.

The ghost's form blurred and suddenly she was standing directly in front of me, her face inches away from mine. Awash in freezing air, I gasped, ice crystals forming on my lips. Courtney's eyes were black as night.

"He will kill Adam. Mark is on his way right now."

Gasping, I staggered away from the apparition, my body shivering violently.

The ghost vanished as swiftly as it had appeared.

With trembling fingers, I yanked my phone out of my pocket. The battery was completely drained. Courtney had drained it in order to manifest. Terrified, I ran into the house to use the landline phone. I had to warn Adam.

To my relief the kitchen was empty. I grabbed the phone, and dialed the number I had memorized in kindergarten. It rang multiple times, then I heard someone pick up.

"Adam?"

"No. It's Amelia."

"Amelia, I need to talk to Adam!"

"Are you a witch?"

"Amelia, this is urgent! Give the phone to Adam!"

"Why don't you talk to me anymore? You used to." The ten year old's voice was both accusing and edged with hurt.

"Amelia!"

"Aren't we friends anymore, Christy? Because friends don't keep secrets like if they're *witches*."

"Amelia, please give Adam the phone!"

"Are. You. A. Witch?"

I wanted to reach through the phone and strangle the little munchkin. Taking a deep breath, I finally said, "Yes. I am. And if you don't give Adam the phone I will turn you into a toad."

"No way."

"Yes way! Am, give Adam the phone!"

"I can't. He has company."

"What do you mean he has company? Who's over there?" Panic started to fill me.

"It's not Mark," Amelia said snottily. "Adam has a new boyfriend. He has blond hair and lots of muscles. His name is Ian."

My brain sputtered for a few seconds. "Ian?"

Suddenly, it all made sense. Ian's interest in me, the kids being sick at school, Ian looking for me. Mark was still part vampire and Ian was in his thrall.

"Am, give Adam the phone!"

"Like I said, he has company."

I slammed the phone down, not wanting to deal with the brat another second. Running to the back door, I clutched my spell bag in one hand. Callie met me at the threshold, her tail swishing.

"I have to go!" I told her, desperation tearing at me.

Her yellow eyes glowing eerily, Callie yowled sharply. Seconds later, the broom rose out of the garden and zipped over to me.

"You little spy!" I hissed at it.

It twirled around, smacked the back of my knees and pushed its gnarled handle under my hand as it tripped me off balance. Falling, I gripped the broomstick as it hurtled into the sky. Callie landed in front of me and together we zoomed toward Adam's house.

Adam

"I really didn't expect you to come over here," I said, leading Ian through the house and up to my room. "What's going on? What's so urgent?"

"I think Mark had something to do with Courtney disappearing. I went over and talked to Christy about it and she filled me in," he said.

I paused at my bedroom door and turned to face him. "What?" I asked.

"I was concerned about what happened to Courtney, so after I dropped the stuff off with my mom, I stopped by Christy's place. No one has said anything to the police yet, but a few people saw Mark with Courtney at the party. There was some drinking going on and some pot, so people are nervous about getting busted. The weirdest thing is that Jennifer said Mark's eyes were glowing red. I told all this to Christy and she told me the details about Mark, Adam. I know what's going on and I want to help."

The unease hinged within my chest was matched only by Amelia shouting downstairs about she didn't want raw hamburger tacos. "Let's talk inside my room," I said. "My sister is on a rant." I did not want Ian to wonder about my mom's new penchant for raw meat.

Ian obliged.

Inside, I closed the door and watched as Ian unslung the knapsack from his shoulder. He pulled from it a string of garlic, a vial of water with a cross decal placed on its surface, and a spoon.

"A spoon?" I laughed despite the seriousness of the moment. "You're going to use a spoon on Mark?"

"Yeah," Ian replied. "It's silver. Because, you know, he's a vampire."

The humor of the situation dissipated almost instantaneously, like a flame being forcefully extinguished. As Ian turned his head toward me, offering a tight, fake smile that seemed completely unlike his normal self, an ominous chill began to set into my bones.

Ian was lying. He hadn't visited Christy. She'd never told him Mark was a vampire. Something was up and my mind was racing.

With panic strumming my heart, I looked around the room, desperate to find something to protect myself. It'd figure that I'd lead Ian away from my family where it would be easy for him to subdue me. There was no way I could take him. He was eight inches taller than me, if not more. He was too damn charming for his own good. I'd fallen perfectly into Mark's trap, because it had to be Mark's trap. Ian was in Mark's thrall.

"You need to leave," I said, taking a few steps back.

"What's wrong?" Ian asked, matching my retreat. "Why're you so jumpy?"

"You know why."

"Adam, I'm here to help."

"Help who?" I asked, the words out of my mouth before I could catch them.

Ian stopped. His concerned expression was instantly washed away, then slowly replaced by a grin that took over his face. "He's awake Adam," Ian said, his eyes glazing over like mist over a crystal ball, "and he's coming for you."

I lunged for the ceramic tea light holder sitting on my bookshelf.

Ian immediately moved to intercept.

His arm caught me under my chin, hitting my throat, causing me to choke, and sent me stumbling back against him.

"Don't scream," he said as I coughed and struggled to breathe. Ian's eyes glowed a faint red and retained a misty, faraway expression. It was as if he were listening to a voice and repeating all it said. "Don't scream, Adam. Don't scream. Want to see your mother die again? Want to see me *eat your little sister's bones?*" It was Mark's voice coming out of Ian's mouth.

I threw my fist at Ian, trying to knock him away and escape.

He caught my arm and twirled me around, pinning my arm around my neck. "You're not going to escape, Adam."

I still couldn't speak. Ian's blow to my throat had successfully muted me, but I wasn't even sure I wanted to call out and risk my mother and sister. Ian was possessed by Mark's power and, therefore, very dangerous.

Directly outside my bedroom window, right where the fork in the tree began, a figure hid in the shadows. Red glowing eyes sent arrows of terror into my heart.

"Say hello, loverboy," Ian whispered. He violently kicked out the window, glass raining down on both of us.

"Adam," a voice hissed through the night. "Come to me."

Before I could protest, Ian hurled me out the window and into the monster's arms.

Christy

The broom zoomed around several large oak trees and into Adam's backyard just as his bedroom window splintered into a thousand glittering shards. Adam's small frame hurtled out seconds later and into the boughs of the pecan tree. A dark shape unfurled from the shadows, clinging to the tree trunk, and snatched up Adam's falling form.

"Adam!"

Leaping onto the roof of Adam's house, the ominous shape revealed itself to be a creature with glowing red eyes and many sharp teeth. In the moonlight the face barely resembled Mark's, but I could tell it was him.

"Witch!" The familiar, terrifying voice slithered through the air.

Callie hissed, hunkering down on the broomstick hovering a few feet from the house just outside of the broken window.

I wasn't prepared. I had no spells ready. I had no idea what to do. Adam dangled over the Mark/Marek monster's broad shoulder like a broken rag doll, bits of glass stuck in his red hair.

"You can't take him!" I shouted. I raised my hand, but I had no idea what I was doing. All I knew was that I had to stop Mark from taking Adam. I was shocked when an orb of green-blue energy formed in my palm.

With a low growl, Mark ran along the roof toward the front of the house.

I flung out my hand, and the ball of energy arced toward him.

Mark leaped off the roof and into the front yard a split second before the orb slammed into the spot where he had just stepped.

"No!"

Another shape flew out of Adam's bedroom window, crashing into the broom, me, and Callie. I barely held onto the broomstick with one hand and my legs. I toppled over and dangled above the ground. Callie yowled and clawed at the person clutching the broom and prying at my hands. All of us crashed to the grass, momentum sending us rolling.

I came up to find Ian lunging for me. His normally pretty eyes were glazed over and faintly glowing red. Flinging out my hand defensively, I was relieved when a bolt of energy struck his chest and knocked him back into the tool shed. He collapsed to the ground and was still.

The back door to Adam's house slid open with a bang and his mom stumbled out. "What's happening? Where the hell is Adam?"

"Mark got him," I sobbed. "Mark got him."

Adam

Stunned breathless from having the wind knocked out of me, I could barely concentrate on the world around me. The only thing I could discern was that we were moving so fast that the world was nothing more than a blur.

It seemed like our flight through the darkness would never end.

Then we stopped.

I struggled to maintain control of my breathing, and reached up to grab at my throat. I blinked, trying to adjust my eyes to my surroundings. The whispering wind stirred the trees, rustling leaves. The soothing sound of water echoed in my ears. The ground, hard and textured, lay beneath my body, so cold it as if I were turning into ice.

"Do you know where we are?" Mark's voice asked.

Though he remained hidden in the shadows, I could make out his red eyes glowing in the darkness.

"Mark, why?" I gasped, taking in a deep breath.

"Do you know where we are?"

I blinked furiously, trying to adjust my eyes to the dark.

Gradually, the world began to fill in around me.

The trees, the distantly running river, the roundabout path that surrounded the fountain in the center of the park—it took but a moment for me to realize where we were.

"We're in the park," I whispered.

"Or, more specifically, the house Dušan nearly burned me alive in."

A vision of the past flashed before my eyes. The flames, the screams, the sound of breaking glass as windows shattered and stonework crumbled. Then there was nothing, save the image of a shadowed person standing in a building where ash fell like fresh snow.

"This was my home once. Did you know that? With all your searching and spying on my past in the library today, did you find that out? Did you?" Mark's voice was dripping with sarcasm and hurt. "Ian saw you at the library with your group of little friends. With your *little* witch."

"You attacked Christy and killed my mom," I retorted. "What did you expect me to do? Forgive you? Take you back?"

There was a fearsome laugh from the darkness. "Yes, because you love me."

"I know what you are!"

"Oh?"

"You're a monster!"

"I was not always this way!" Mark's voice was surprisingly soft and hurt. "I was a beautiful god once. Then... then... "

"You were cursed," I said triumphantly. "I know more than you think. I know about Dušan."

"Dušan! *Dušan!*" Now his voice was monstrous again.

"I know you killed the woman he loved and he burned you alive before killing himself rather than be with you." I wanted to hurt Mark in that moment.

"Is that what you think?" Mark's voice was low and very dangerous.

"It's what I know," I said confidently. I had to buy time until my friends arrived to save me. I knew they would. Christy would never allow Mark to hurt me if she could help it.

"Did your little books tell you that? Is that what you pieced together from all the *lies* kept by the historians in this town?"

"No, it's what Dušan *told* us when he *possessed* me, Mark."

The silence that followed my revelation was terrifying.

Struggling to sit up, I shivered in the cold wind. Fear ate at me, but I knew Christy would come. I just had to hold on.

"Are those the lies he's still telling after all these years?" Mark's voice was a hiss of anger. "You see, Adam... *baby*... Dušan and I were lovers. I loved him and he loved me! We should have been together forever, but he wouldn't have it. He claimed he didn't want to lose his soul by becoming a vampire. That he didn't love me like he loved his pathetic, simpering fiancé Brynn. He was too stuck in *society's* definition of what a man should be to realize that we *belonged* together. I thought getting rid of Brynn would solve the problem, but he still refused me! He wouldn't admit that he loved me as much as I loved him."

"Because he loved Brynn! Maybe he wasn't gay like us, Mark. Maybe he was bisexual and you just lost out to his love for Brynn! Did you think of that? Or are you just too crazy, Mark?"

"He loved me!"

"He loved her more! Why else would he curse you like this? You're not a vampire anymore, Mark! You're something... *worse*."

The anger seething in the darkness was terrifying, but I was not going to relent.

"Dušan and I were meant to be!"

"You're fucking crazy, Mark."

"You would be too if you were cursed to live like I do," Mark said. "If you were cursed to look like *this*."

He stepped into the moonlight for the first time that night.

It was hard to make out more distinctive features. His beauty was long gone. A semblance still remained, but it was shattered by the morbid aspect of death. His flesh had a sallow pallor and holes pocked the hollows of his cheeks, revealing yellowed teeth. His frame had thinned, his clothes hung loose, and chunks of his hair were missing, exposing his scalp. Most gruesomely, his skin had begun to stretch over his bones. He was a few steps away from looking like a complete skeleton.

"All I ever wanted," Mark said, "was for him to love me. For *someone* to love me. And then he made it my curse. Love. *Love.* How can such a beautiful thing be so painful? That's what I don't understand."

I, too, couldn't understand how love had become so painful, so terrifying, so deadly.

"You killed what he loved."

204

"Now, I kill what I love. I *have* to! I have to eat the flesh of the one I love so I will not be this... this... monster! Dušan cursed me to destroy those whom I love!"

"I know," I said. "I know. And it's getting worse, isn't it?"

"He isn't satisfied with my despair! He's never satisfied! He turns the screw and tightens the lock and makes me want to scream!"

It made sense why the timeline was so screwed up. Dušan's need for vengeance was growing over time, not diminishing. He needed to see Mark suffer more and more to assuage his own endless thirst.

"Why don't you love me?" Mark's voice was a plaintive cry.

"You tried to destroy my life," I said, fingering the ground for any remnant I could use as a weapon. "You tried to kill Christy! You *did* kill my Mom!"

"You let them get between us! You let them separate us!" His voice was now a terrifying howl. "I was *everything* you could have *ever wanted*! I was tall, handsome, athletic, smart, kind, charming, *loving*. I was *perfect*. Why did you need anyone but me?"

"Because life isn't just about one person, Mark." My anger now matched his. I could see so clearly now how he had tried to separate me from the ones I loved and who loved me.

He screamed and it echoed across the park.

"Do you love me?" he asked, leaning close enough to reveal the disintegrated depths of his nose, which now appeared to be nothing more than two holes on his face. "Tell me you love me, Adam. I need it. I need you."

I felt something trying to wrestle with my mind. Something cold and dark, but it could not push its way into me. I thought of Christy's protection spell in my pocket and was glad for it. Mark demanded love, but he was going to get the truth.

"You were my first love." My voice trembled as I spoke. "You gave me so many things, Mark. I loved you once, but now I realize it was all a lie. Now I can't feel anything but sorry for you, because you're nothing more than a monster who lives off other people's emotions and flesh to keep yourself alive. I don't love you. Not anymore."

Mark reared his head back.

His scream rent the night.

His jaw opened as wide as it possibly could to reveal a mouthful of teeth so sharp they could compare to nothing I had ever seen.

"You're lying," he said as he brought his head back down. "You have to love me! I know what I felt. You can't deny what was between us. You're lying because you think it will save you."

My hand circled around what felt like a broken branch.

Mark leaned so close I could feel his decaying breath on my face. "I love you and you love me. I will never forget you, Adam. Your love, your betrayal, the sweetness of your flesh."

"Adam!" Christy screamed. *"Adam!"*

Mark turned his head. "The *witch*!"

I slammed the branch against his head.

I scrambled to get away, but he grabbed me from behind and wrapped a grisly claw around my neck.

Chapter 16

Battle Royale

Christy

The kitchen was crowded and it was difficult to move. Everyone was trying to help, so that meant that everyone was tripping over each other. Nathan and the others had arrived just a few minutes after Adam's abduction. They had found me and Ashley in near hysterics while Amelia screamed at us to tell her what was going on.

Ten minutes later, our little group was in a frenzy to figure out where Mark could have taken Adam so we could launch our rescue. Drifter, Olivia, and Ashley were crowded around Ashley's computer, Nathan and I tried to get our spell ingredients ready, and Amelia was underfoot.

"Do you have a cast iron skillet?" Nathan called out to Ashley. "We don't have a cauldron."

"Duh. I'm a Texan. That's the only way to make decent refried beans. It's on the left hand side of the oven," Ashley answered.

"I got it!" Amelia cried out, nearly tripping me as she dove for the cabinet.

The cat was literally out of the bag where Amelia was concerned. We couldn't keep the truth from her anymore. She had taken the news about Mark a lot better than we had expected. In fact, she had informed us that she had never liked him because he looked "stupid." I guess the kid gets points for being perceptive about monsters.

Callie sat on the island watching us with her keen golden eyes.

"Sorry I forgot my cauldron and stuff," I mumbled to Nathan.

"No worries. You were freaking out and I don't blame you," Nathan answered.

Amelia dragged the heavy cast iron skillet out of the cabinet and slammed it down on the stove.

"Hey! Watch it, Am!" Ashley looked up briefly, then returned to her internet search with Drifter and Olivia. "Your friends on this forum are awesome, Nathan. We should know where Adam is soon."

I opened up the spellbag and dumped out the ingredients. Nathan winced.

"What?"

"You shouldn't have put them in the same bag. They need to be freshly mixed in the spell," he answered.

"Great, just great," I grumbled. "Will it work now?"

Nathan shrugged. "We have to give it a try. Let's do this."

"This vanquishing spell is going to get rid of that asshole forever, right?" Ashley called out. "No coming back. No sequel. He's gone. Finito! Right?"

Nodding, Nathan started to mix the ingredients in the skillet. "Absolutely. I'm a little nervous using it, though. It's a pretty dangerous spell. It only works on supernatural beings."

I blanched. "Ugh! What about me?"

"No worries. Your blood has to be drawn to actually make the spell work," Nathan assured me.

"So we have to hurt Mark then throw the spell at him?" Olivia rolled her eyes. "Well, that sounds easy enough!"

Drifter patted the weapon he had set on the counter when he arrived earlier. It was a crossbow. "I can get him. Blue Ribbon four years in a row at camp with this baby. If we're lucky, he'll turn to dust."

"I don't like Mark," Amelia said loudly. She dragged a stool over to watch me and Nathan mixing the spell. "He's stupid."

"We agree, Am. Totally stupid." Ashley lightly touched her neck as she kept reading.

Nathan was using bottled spring water for the base, which made me nervous, but I couldn't go home and grab ingredients at this point. Time was of the essence and I couldn't risk my parents stopping me. I considered telling them what was going on, but that explanation would take too long and I was far too deep into the hell of my own making. I angrily brushed a tear away.

"Don't do that!" Nathan grabbed my hand before I could wipe my other cheek. "We need that. One tear of remorse."

"How do you know I'm remorseful?" I asked while Nathan carefully scooped up my tear with the end of a mixing spoon.

"Cause you look guilty as hell," Ashley answered.

"Totally," Olivia agreed.

"Well, I'm the one who cast the midnight spell!" I sniffled loudly, rubbing my nose. "You don't need my remorseful snot for the spell, do you?"

Nathan smirked despite the tension in the room. "I'll pass."

"C'mon, Christy. You had nothing to do with it. Mark's done this before." Drifter walked over to give me a pat on the shoulder. "Don't feel bad."

"I'll not feel bad after we have Adam," I responded, but I was grateful for his kindness. I gave him a brief hug, then went back to helping Nathan.

"Got it!" Ashley flung her hands up. "We got it! Mark's old house is in the park! He has to be there!"

"And the bridge nearby is where Dušan killed himself," Olivia pointed out. "Makes total sense. Let's roll!"

"We have enough here for three spells," Nathan decided. "Ashley, do you have three empty glass jars?"

"Gimme a sec!" Ashley bounced off her seat and rushed to the pantry. When she turned around, she had two jars of marinara sauce and a jar of jelly in her arms. Hurrying to the sink, she dumped the contents out and started scrubbing out the jars. Amelia joined her, managing to be helpful and in the way at the same time.

"So what's our plan, big bro?" Olivia asked. Dressed in black jeans, a black turtleneck, and a leather jacket with her hair up in a high ponytail, she looked ready for a fight.

"We take the Jeep to the park, hope they're there, vanquish Mark, and live happily ever after," Nathan answered. "But in more detail, we arm ourselves. Drifter has a crossbow, I have a sword in the car, and Christy's got her magic. And you can do that thing you're so good at," he added with a wink.

"You mean kick your ass?" Olivia arched an eyebrow.

"Except direct the ass-kicking at Mark," Nathan answered.

Ashley scooted the freshly washed jars our way. "There you go!"

Nathan carefully measured the spell into the three jars and twisted the caps on. "Okay, Christy. You need to recite this spell to activate them."

I took Nathan's phone from him and arched my eyebrow. "You wrote it out phonetically? Nice. I don't know Latin."

"It's Aramaic." Nathan grinned.

"Oh."

"Am, get back," Ashley ordered.

Nathan and the others took several steps back as I read over the spell in my mind, preparing myself. Already I felt the warm watery feel of my magic building inside of me. Callie moved to sit beside the jars, her ears tilted forward.

"Here it goes," I breathed. I probably sounded like an idiot trying to get the words out correctly, but somehow I managed to get through the spell. Nothing happened. I was about to freak out, when I saw that I was supposed to recite it three times.

"Nothing happened. She sucks as a witch," Amelia grunted.

"Am, go to the living room!"

"Mom!"

"Go!"

"Start over, Christy. It's okay. Just read it through three times without pausing," Nathan instructed.

Taking a deep breath, I felt my magic stirring inside of me. "Should I cast a circle?"

"No time," Nathan replied.

"Stop stalling and do it," Olivia ordered.

I heard the refrigerator door open and close. Glancing to my right, I saw Ashley eating a handful of raw beef chunks. I wrinkled my nose.

"What? I eat when I'm nervous! Hurry up, Christy! My baby is out there!"

"Right." I was losing focus. Exhaustion, fear, guilt, and doubt were eating at me. I had to save Adam. I had to be strong. I had to make this spell work. In a forceful voice, I repeated the spell, this time not tripping over the words at all, not pausing, and repeating it thrice.

As the last word left my lips, a tendril of misty, sparkly blue-green magic slipped out of my mouth, forming the words of the spell for a split second before streaking into the bottles to illuminate the water flecked with herbs.

The magic infused the water, churning it violently within the glass containers, then they began to glow a pale greenish blue.

"You did it!" Nathan surged forward to grab the jars

"Uh, Mom?" Amelia said from the doorway into the living room.

"Not right now, Am," Ashley answered.

"MOM!" Amelia persisted.

"Not right now, Am! We're busy trying to save your brother!"

"But what about the zombies outside?"

In a panic, we all ran to the large windows that looked over the front lawn. Ashley drew back one of the curtains and gasped. The yard was filled with kids from school. They stood motionless, staring at the house, their eyes glazed and shimmering red.

"He sent them to stop us!" Nathan exclaimed.

"Ian," I gasped. I ran to the back of the house and peered out into the backyard where we had left him. He was on his feet, eyes glowing red, staring at the house. At his side were Jayden and his crew of jock thugs. "We're surrounded!"

"They can't get in. Mark isn't allowed in the house, so they're not either," Nathan said swiftly.

"Ian got in earlier!" Ashley protested.

"Because Adam invited him in," Nathan answered. "But I think you effectively disinvited him when you tried to put your heels through his head while screaming 'Stay out of my house' earlier."

Ashley smiled. "True."

"If we go out there, they're going to attack us, aren't they?" Uneasy, Drifter stood near the front window, his crossbow in his hand. "We can't hurt them. It's not their fault Mark has control of them."

"I'll hurt them if they're keeping you away from saving my baby! I'll get my gun and that will scare them off!" Ashley headed toward the gun safe secured under the stairs.

"No, it won't! They'll just do what Mark told them to do," Olivia protested. "We can't fight all of them. They *will* hurt us. We can't hurt them."

"We need to get to my car," Nathan said somberly. "We can try charging them."

"There are at least fifty out there and how many in the back?" Drifter adamantly shook his head. "We need to think of something else."

Time was ticking away and we all knew it. Yet, we stood frozen in the living room, unable to make a move. Then it hit me.

"The broom!"

The handle popped out from around the corner. The little sneak had been listening in on us.

"C'mere, you!" I pointed at it with an accusing finger. "You little spy!"

It scooted around the corner and sashayed over to me. Callie yowled at it and I could swear it came to attention.

"How is that going to help us?" Olivia arched an eyebrow.

"We all hold on and fly over the crowd. Nathan's car is parked on the street, so we just need to move fast to get inside once we land." I took hold of the broom and felt it vibrating with excitement.

"What's the weight limit on that?" Drifter asked obviously wary.

"Does it matter? It's magic," Nathan answered. "We'll have to launch out of an upstairs window to get out over their heads."

"I'm *so* not feeling this idea," Olivia protested.

Nathan grabbed his laptop bag and shoved the jars inside, using several paper towels to cushion them. "We don't have a choice. Time is running out for Adam."

"I'm going," I said. "You can stay if you want to."

I ran toward the stairs with Nathan on my heels. Callie darted up the staircase in front of us.

"Take off from my room!" Ashley called out after us.

"I want to watch!" Amelia exclaimed.

"We'll watch from the living room window, Am. Good luck, Christy!"

Nathan and I reached the second floor. I ran down the hallway to Ashley's room, my heart thudding in my chest. I was scared out of my mind, but positive the broom could carry us. The broom sent flurries of magic into the air, obviously revving up.

Once inside Ashley's room, Nathan slid the window open and glanced out. "This will have to do. I see the Jeep."

I leaned out next to him and was disturbed by all the red eyes turning up to regard us.

"That's scary," Drifter breathed beside me. I hadn't realized he had followed us.

"Ready?" Nathan asked.

I nodded, letting go of the broom. "You're going toward that red Jeep, okay?"

The broom twirled in the air and dropped into a horizontal stance. Callie leaped onto the bristles and then it rose over our heads.

"So we just hold on, huh?" Drifter asked. "We don't ride it?"

Gripping the handle with both hands, I nodded. I had yet to ride the damn broom like a proper witch, but I wasn't about to say that.

Nathan took the front spot, holding onto the floating broom tightly. Drifter got behind me. Olivia was nowhere to be seen, but I couldn't let myself feel hurt.

"Lift up your legs," Nathan instructed.

Taking a deep breath, I curled my legs upward, letting the broom carry my full weight. It dipped slightly, then caught itself. Rising in the air, it angled us toward the window.

"You better hold on everyone, this broom tends to take off like a bat out of—"

My words cut off as the broom raced through the window, our bodies barely clearing the opening. We swung out over the front yard, the wind whistling in our ears. Callie hissed at the possessed teenagers below us. As one, the kids with the glowing red eyes reached up for us. The broom lost a little altitude, making us all gasp, but it recovered and hoisted us upward just enough to avoid the clutching hands from below.

"Go higher, go higher!" Drifter chanted at the broom.

My sweaty fingers were losing their grip. The broom had to dodge lower to avoid some low hanging branches and for a brief instant I felt fingers on my rear.

"Hey!" I shouted, not sure if I was screaming at the broom, or whoever had felt me up.

We reached the street, our altitude dropping fast. Mark's minions raced after us in silence, determined to stop us from our rescue. Dropping to the ground, I ran toward the Jeep in terror. Callie and the broom zipped past me, not stopping but arcing upward into the night sky. Nathan ran just ahead of me with Drifter close behind. Our footfalls were drowned out by the loud thunder of the people pursuing us.

We were almost to the Jeep when Olivia popped out from around the front of it, her fingers clicking the remote in her hand. The car unlocked loudly before she whipped open a door and slid into the driver's seat. I dove for the handle of the passenger door while the guys climbed into the back. I slammed my door shut just as the wave of Mark's minions hit the vehicle. I caught sight of Jennifer and Maribel's glowing eyes seconds before Olivia peeled out from the curb, narrowly missing a few students trying to throw themselves in front of the car.

"Floor it," Nathan ordered.

"You don't have to tell me twice," Olivia answered.

"Oh, and nice play to finally drive my car," her brother added irritably. "When did you lift my keys?"

"When you weren't looking, dumbass." Olivia swung us around a corner and we all screamed as she narrowly missed another car.

"Don't kill us!" Drifter shouted at her.

"How did you get to the car?" I asked.

Olivia grinned. "I have my ways."

Holding on for dear life, we endured Olivia's chaotic driving all the way to the park. Somehow we managed not to get into an accident, or draw the attention of the local police. When we hit the park, Olivia didn't even bother with the neat little road that led to the parking lot. She just drove across the park, bouncing us around inside the vehicle.

"Christy, use your magic to get Mark away from Adam. Drifter, shoot at Mark. Try to wound him. I'll take the three spells and the sword and finish him off. Olivia, you know what to do," Nathan said in an authoritative tone.

The old ruined house that had been revitalized into a picnic spot came into view, its façade illuminated by the moon above. All that remained of the house was the two foot high stone exterior wall and the chimney. But tonight the shadows had reformed the old house, the inky walls and ceiling hiding the interior from our view. Yet, I knew that Adam was inside, trapped by Mark. The hair on the back of my neck rose as I felt intense evil flowing out of the ruin.

"They're here!" I exclaimed.

Olivia slammed on the brakes just before we hit the picnic area. We all gasped, our seat belts snagging us. There was a mad scramble to get out. I shoved my door open, leaping out. The cold, icy air blasted my face, but I paid it no heed. Running toward the remains of Marek's home, I screamed Adam's name.

A ghastly creature appeared out of the darkness. Its red glowing eyes and sharp teeth were all too familiar. I didn't hesitate. I lifted my hand, willing my magic to explode outward in a ball of powerful energy. The glittering ball of green-blue magic slammed into Mark, tossing him back into the ruins.

"Great shot!" Drifter shouted.

We all ran toward the house, determination etched on our faces. Nathan's sword glinted dangerously in the moonlight. Together, we closed in on where Adam was being held prisoner.

Adam scrambled out of the walls made of darkness. The terrible creature followed, grabbing Adam's ankle. Twisting about, Adam fought with Mark, flailing against the terrible creature.

"We need to get them apart!" Nathan cried out.

The two figures struggled on the ground, rolling over each other. Mark was bigger and stronger, but Adam was small, agile, and fast. It was difficult for the gruesome creature to wrestle my best friend into submission. Adam managed to get his knees up between their bodies and with a mighty push, knocked Mark away.

I heard the sharp bark of Drifter's crossbow beside me, then Mark's body jerked as the bolt smacked into him. In the darkness it was difficult to see and I hoped Drifter knew what he was doing. I didn't want him hitting Adam. In a moment of inspiration, I tossed an energy ball into the air willing it to illuminate the area. It hovered over our heads, exposing the disgusting creature Mark was devolving into.

Adam raced in our direction. Nathan sprinted toward him, sword in one hand. Mark howled like an animal in pain, thrashing on the ground as Drifter unloaded another bolt into him.

"Keep him pinned!" I yelled. I summoned another bolt of energy, ready to unleash on Mark.

Drifter scurried to one side, trying to get a clear bead on Mark, while I darted to the other, Olivia hot on my heels. Adam and Nathan closed in on each other.

"You can do it, Adam!" Nathan cried out.

The hideous creature that was Mark screamed in agony, then launched himself through the air at Adam. I shouted wordlessly, tossing my energy bolt, but I missed the flying being. Mark crashed into Adam, pinning him briefly to the ground, before tossing him over his shoulder and launching into the air again.

Gasping, our breath billowing in the cold air, the four of us ran at top speed, tracking the descent of Mark's jump.

"He's heading toward the lake!" Nathan plowed through some bushes, his sister close behind. "Olivia, you may need to follow."

"I'm on it!" Olivia answered.

There was no way Drifter or I could hit Mark without risking Adam. We were helpless, but we both kept running. Ignoring the stitch in my side, I shoved my way through the bushes lining the walk that wound along the shore. Seconds later, Mark and Adam plunged into the center of the lake.

"He'll drown him!" I cried out. "He'll drown him and kill him!"

"Don't worry!" Olivia shouted over her shoulder running down the wood pier that's used for fishing and diving. "I'll get him!"

"He's dangerous!" Drifter yelled after her.

"No worries! So am I!" Olivia pounded toward the end of the pier. "Form of bull shark!" she yelled, then took a swan dive into the dark water.

"Nathan, Mark will kill her!" I exclaimed, grabbing Nathan's arm.

"No, he won't," Nathan said confidently.

"Look!" Drifter pointed, eyes wide.

A dorsal fin broke through the moonlight dappled dark waters and swam toward the center of the lake.

"Uh... .uh... uh... " Drifter and I stammered.

With a proud look, Nathan said, "Olivia's a shapeshifter."

Our night could not get any weirder.

Adam

I only barely managed to take in a breath before Mark plunged us into the water.

The cold was absolute. Wrapping around my body, twisting within my hair, filling each and every pore on my skin with ice—the initial shock left me momentarily frozen, but it took little for me to realize that I had less than five minutes to get out of the water.

Mark grappled with me. Hands snared within my shirt, he lashed out to reveal glowing red eyes and a mouthful of razor-sharp teeth.

I twisted within his grasp.

A grisly claw reached for me.

I slammed my elbow into his sternum and almost cried out in relief when I felt his grip loosen.

I started to swim.

You're mine, a voice said within my head, its humanity replaced with something primal. *You're mine, Adam. I will never let you leave me.*

I fought through the fog of his desire and scrambled to swim as fast as I could. Weighed down by my wet clothing, I struggled. My heart beat so hard in my chest that I thought it would explode and the icy chill of the Trinity Springs lake water threatened to seize my body. My only solace in finding escape was from the full moon, which pierced into the water like an angel's great dagger of redemption.

Mark's voice continued to whisper in my head.

Somehow, I was able to block it out.

I dared not look back. I dared not falter. I dared not try to swim toward my friends on the shore behind me. If I did, I knew Mark would catch me.

A dark apparition appeared out of the corner of my eye.

I panicked, thinking it was Mark.

When I saw a much larger mouthful of teeth and pitch-black eyes, my fear of Mark instantly faded.

The legend was true! There *was* a bull shark in Trinity Springs.

I kicked my legs out and propelled my body to the side just in time to see the shark dive toward Mark. Its jaws opened and clamped around one leg before Mark could dart away.

Blood billowed in the water encompassing me. My lungs begging for air, I swam toward the wavering moon that was slowly tainted red. Breaching the surface of the lake, I dragged a deep, painful draught of air into my ravaged lungs. To my relief the other side of the lake loomed close. I had to escape the water and the monsters that swam beneath its surface.

Still gasping for air, my teeth chattering, my limbs numbed by the icy water, I swam.

A massive form breached the water to my left.

I turned, gasping.

The gargantuan bull shark reared its head out of the murky water and flung Mark through the air. He landed on the shoreline, twitching, one leg missing and his body badly battered.

A few quick, terrified kicks later, I felt the mud of the shoreline beneath me. I crawled forward on my hands and knees away from Mark. I retched a bit of water from my lungs in my scramble to escape.

Mark's screams ripped through the chaos of my raging mind, and I could not make sense of his unintelligible rantings. I pushed myself to my feet despite the weight of water upon my body. I tried to call for help, but my voice was caught in my throat.

The whisper of Christy's flying broom drew my eyes to the sky, where Nathan dangled from its handle by one hand. The laptop bag swung wildly at his side and he clasped a massive sword. "Adam!" he shouted. "Watch out!"

Mark's grisly form hurled itself at me.

I dodged, barely missing a claw.

A roar knocked my attention away from Mark just in time to see a massive giant panda pin him to the ground, mouth bared in a snarl.

Starting forward the moment the broom deposited him on the ground, Nathan said, "I've got the vanquishing spell."

Finding my voice at last, I croaked, "Give it to me!"

Nathan dug into his bag and handed me a glowing jar. "He's bleeding," he said. "All you have to do is pour it on him."

"What about... *that?*" I asked, looking toward the panda.

"That's Olivia," Nathan answered.

"*Olivia?*"

"Adam, you're mine!" Mark screamed. "You're *mine!*"

The white and black creature thrust its head forward and tore Mark's neck out, silencing him.

"I've been wanting to do that for a while now," Olivia's voice said from the panda's mouth.

"Oh-*kay.*" Teeth chattering, my body violently shaking, I uncapped the jar and stepped forward. Mark's convulsing form stilled when I neared.

He tried to say something. I could only imagine it was my name.

"It's time for you to go," I said. "You don't belong here anymore."

The red eyes faded to gray. Once more the winter sky of his gaze touched my heart, but I knew I couldn't hesitate.

"Goodbye, Mark."

As Olivia in panda form darted away, I poured the contents of the vanquishing spell onto Mark's body. It spread across his skin like a ravenous plague, enveloping his body, making it glow blue and green, forcing tendrils of spidery veins across Mark's arms, face and the visible portions of his filleted chest. An agonizing scream ripped from his chest and a gust of air began to whirlwind about him. Dirt flew, leaves soared, twigs and rocks began to twist about Mark's body. A horrible screech tore through the night like a crane falling in a big city just before his body turned completely white.

A moment later, he burst into a cloud of dust that instantaneously caught fire the moment it hit the air.

The rocks, leaves and twigs fell.

The wind came up.

All that was left was ash.

"He's gone," I said, reaching up to finger a gash across my cheek I hadn't realized I had.

"Yeah," Nathan said. "He is."

Christy

Callie, Drifter, and I raced across the old bridge, our feet sending dirt and splinters into the water below. I was terrified we were going to fall through the rotting boards at any second, but I had to get to Adam's side.

Right after Olivia had vanished into the lake and turned into a bull shark, Callie arrived with the broom. We had watched Adam struggling toward shore while we ran for the bridge. It was Nathan who volunteered to go across the river riding the broom, and I had agreed. I wanted to go, too, but the damn broom had taken off before I could make a grab for the handle.

Exhausted, I leaped over a hole in the bridge and took the last few steps to the old dirt road. Darting around the "Do Not Enter" sign, I ran along the soggy shore. The pine trees rose above my head like sentinels. Fast moving clouds briefly obscured the moon, plunging the world into darkness. Only the orb of my magic hovering over my head lit the way.

Shouting, growls, and screams filled the night air and I feared the worst.

"We need to hurry!" Drifter shouted, passing me.

Pressing my hand to my aching side, I kept running. My lungs burned in the cold air, my muscles screamed, and my vision swam. Callie darted through the underbrush just ahead of us, yowling encouragement.

Then we arrived on the oddest scene. A panda sat on Mark's ruined body, blood pouring out of a stub of one of its legs and staining its pelt. Nathan and Adam stood over them, the glowing vanquishing spell in Adam's hand.

216

Drifter grabbed my arm, stopping me. I wanted to run to Adam and hug him, but then I realized why Drifter had stilled me. Adam needed to do this himself without any of us helping him.

Together, Drifter and I stood and watched Adam vanquish Mark from our plane of existence. It was beautiful and terrifying. When the last embers faded into the cold air, Adam fell forward on his knees. Nathan instantly grabbed him, holding him close. The panda shimmered into the form of Olivia, fully clothed (much to my relief), and she gripped Adam's other arm, hoisting him up.

"Adam!" I screamed.

Drifter and I ran the last few feet to our friends. I lifted my hands and summoned the ball of magic over our heads. I willed it to be warm and comforting and unfurled it like a blanket. Wrapping it around Adam, it seeped into his pale, icy skin and vanished. Instantly, Adam's clothes, hair, and flesh were dry and his shivering stopped.

A slow smile spread on my best friend's lips. "You're the best," he said.

"No, you are," I answered.

Folding me in his arms, Adam clung to me while our friends formed a circle around us.

Then out of the darkness came a sight that sent chills to the core of my being.

My parents.

"Good riddance to bad rubbish," my dad said, his hands tucked into his heavy sweater jacket. His white hair was slightly disheveled and he was clad in his pajamas and bunny slippers.

My mother was in a caftan with a heavy cloak thrown over it. She waved her hands, her hair stirred by her magic as it sparkled around her. The tiny bits of light zoomed all around us, swirling through the air like little searchlights. After a few seconds, they darted back to my mother, dissipating around her head.

"Ah, he's completely gone." Giving Nathan an approving smile, my mother said, "Good job on that spell."

"What... what... .what... ?"

"Christy, do you really think we wouldn't know what was going on?" My mother arched her eyebrows.

"But... but... "

"Kiddo, we might be your parents, but we're a badass warrior and a high witch. We've been watching from afar as you kids dealt with this thing. This was your battle to fight, not ours." My dad held out his hand to Nathan. "Nathan, it's good to meet you."

"So you knew? All along?" Olivia asked, eyes wide.

My mother chuckled in amusement. "Yes, we did. The broom and Callie have been keeping tabs for us."

"I knew it! You *spy!*" I hissed at the broom.

It skipped around my mother, dripping flurries of magic in its wake.

"Why didn't you do something earlier?" Adam asked, his voice holding traces of hurt.

"Every witch has her trial when she obtains her power. This was Christy's, Adam. This was your battle and Christy's to fight."

"But... my mom... " Adam's voice caught, his emotions high.

"Oh, we won't tell her!" my mother said swiftly. "It's best we keep her in the dark. She doesn't need to know about all this."

Adam and I exchanged quick looks, understanding quickly passing between us. My parents didn't know *everything*.

"I think we should all get you somewhere warm," my mother continued. "I can make hot chocolate."

"With marshmallows?" Drifter asked hopefully.

"With marshmallows," Mom assured him.

Callie leaped onto the broom and they floated together along the shoreline, my parents following. The rest of us trailed behind them, sharing warning looks, and coming to a silent understanding.

The death and resurrection of Adam's mother was not to be revealed to my parents. Callie had kept it a secret for a reason and so would we.

Chapter 17

Letting Go and Moving On

Christy

Like Texas weather is prone to do, the freezing cold night had given way to a beautiful warm day. Though it was Monday, I wasn't in school. My mother had called the high school and reported that I wasn't feeling well. She wasn't surprised to hear that most of the school was out sick. Everyone was suffering the aftereffects of Mark's power being broken. I was sure all his minions had massive magical hangovers to recover from, along with anemia.

Spread out on a blanket near my mother's garden, I stared up through the branches of the pecan tree my mother had been treating. It looked healthier, despite the change in the seasons. Callie dozed next to me, a bundle of warm kitty fur and love. She's a mysterious creature, and I love her to bits. Mom says that Callie is now my familiar, too, and also a teacher. The cat is also one of my dearest friends. I don't know why she's hiding the death and resurrection of Adam's mom, but I'm grateful. Nathan has sworn he will do some research and hopefully help me bring Ashley completely back to life. So far the only really noticeable side effect of her resurrection is her taste for raw meat, which is pretty gross.

To my surprise and pleasure, Adam sprawled out beside me. His red hair glinted in the afternoon sunlight and his blue eyes sparkled at me. The warmth of his fingers when he took my hand was soothing.

"Hey," he said.

"Hey," I answered.

"Are we moping?"

"Are we?"

Adam turned his head to gaze up through the branches of the tree. A few leaves floated down toward us.

"Nope," he said after a beat. "Mark's not worth it."

"But it has to hurt."

"It does," Adam admitted. "But it won't forever."

"How's your mom?"

"She was trying to figure out how to make pancakes with chunks of raw meat in it this morning. Am was not happy."

"I'll find a way to fix her. I swear!"

"I know you will. I'm just glad I still have her. Even if her eating habits are screwed up, her fetish for stilettos remains the same."

Scooting closer to him, I rested my head against his shoulder. "I'm grounded."

"I kind of figured that. For how long?"

"A month. I have to report in for magic lessons every day after school, I'm forbidden from doing magic on my own, and I have to help Dad clean out the garage."

"I thought you passed the witch trial of puberty, or whatever it is."

"Oh, I did. But I failed the all-important including of the parental units in the dire situations test."

"Ah," Adam said. "That sucks."

"Friends can visit, but I'm restricted on social stuff. At least they only grounded me for a month. I'll be free and clear in December for the holidays."

We fell silent again. The wind rustled the trees and the birds sang softly. Callie lightly snored beside me.

"I love you, Christy."

"I love you, Adam."

"I love you enough to tell you that you're being dumb about Ian."

I hit his arm. "Shut up! You know he was one of Mark's minions!"

"Not until the end of it. Mark targeted Ian after he realized you were a witch. Mark went after Ian on Halloween night to make him a minion."

I bit my bottom lip, processing this. "How do you know?"

"Ian told me. Just now. When I arrived. He's parked in front of your house hoping you'll go out and talk to him."

"No way!"

Moving his head to gaze at me, Adam gently smoothed my hair back from my face. "Christy, Ian likes you. Go talk to him."

"I'm fat. I'm ugly and—"

"Christy!" Adam shoved me off the blanket. "Go talk to him!"

Rolling onto my knees, I glared at my best friend. "You suck."

Tucking his hands behind his neck, Adam winked at me. "Go. Talk to him. I'll be right here waiting for a full report."

Callie yawned, stretched, and moved to rest against Adam's side. Through narrowed eyes, she watched me grumpily. I had a feeling she wanted me to go talk to Ian too.

Defeated and outnumbered, I stood and trudged around the side of the house. Sure enough, Ian was leaning against his truck waiting for me. He looked far neater than I did. He was clad in jeans, cowboy boots, and a dark blue sweater. My ragged brown hoodie, Pikachu t-shirt, and beat-up brown corduroys had seen much better days.

I gave him a slight wave as I approached.

"Hey, Christy!" he said, his blue eyes lighting up in a way that terrified me.

"Uh, hi," I mumbled.

"Hey, about all that stuff that went down last night, I have to tell you that I couldn't control myself and—"

I waved my arms, cutting him off. "No worries. I get it. Honestly."

"Everyone at school is freaked out. We all remember what happened now that Mark's gone and his power is broken. And a few of us remember you and the broomstick thing. That was epic," Ian continued, his eyes sparkling with adoration that made me uneasy.

I lowered my head and stared at the tips of his cowboy boots, thrusting my hands into my hoodie pockets. "Uh huh."

"I'm not sure how much of the school was affected, but they all kind of know now that you're... a witch."

Tilting my head upward, I shrugged. "I can't help what I am."

Ian nodded, still smiling. "I think it's cool, you know. I always knew you were a little different, a little special, but it all makes sense now."

"But it's not all I am," I said defensively. "There is a lot more to me."

The smile on his handsome face slightly faded. "I didn't mean—"

"All my life," I said, knowing I was about to run off at the mouth in an epic way, "I was in love with you. Did you know that? Since kindergarten!"

"Is that why you hit me all the time?" Ian asked. "Cause you hit hard!"

I rolled my eyes. "Yes, that's why. But that's not my point! I was so in love with you. I had all these stupid fantasies in my head about you wanting me to be your girlfriend and being popular and—"

"Really?" His goofy grin almost got him punched.

"Shut up! Talking!" I wagged my finger at him. "And now you're paying attention to me because I'm a witch! The thing everyone used to call me to hurt my feelings is the only reason you think I'm cool now!"

The grin vanished from his face. Standing up straight, Ian glared down at me. "Hey, that's not fair!"

"What do you know about me, Ian? What do you like about me other than I'm a witch?" I returned his glare.

"I think you're cute," he answered. "And funny. I like the way you talk. How you just say all sorts of weird, but funny stuff."

"Oh," I said.

"And you wear cute t-shirts with stuff I like on it. I really love Blondie and I used to play Pokémon when I was a kid. I have a huge collection of cards. I also like science fiction movies and books."

"Oh."

"And I like how you're a really good friend to Adam. You're loyal and you love him a lot." Ian folded his arms across his chest. "I don't know a lot more, but I'd like to."

"Oh."

I was floored, unable to think straight.

"And we both know you like me, so we're ahead of the curve, right?"

I sighed. "But that's the thing, Ian. I just found out a bunch of stuff I never knew about you! I had a crush on Fantasy Ian. This perfect imaginary Ian in my head. I used to pretend I was talking to you and those conversations are nothing like our real ones. I was so totally in love with Fantasy Ian that I'm scared out of my mind of the real Ian... you."

Frowning slightly, Ian squinted his eyes, then nodded. "I can see that."

"I just wanted you to be my boyfriend so you could save me from being the uber-dork." I couldn't believe I was telling him this, but I couldn't stop talking. "You were like this get out of jail free card. In my stupid imagination, Fantasy Ian would make everything... perfect."

"I hate to clean my room, my socks have holes in them, and I tend to belch after eating Mexican food. I'm not perfect," Ian assured me. "I also fall asleep at boring movies and snore really loudly."

I unsuccessfully tried not to giggle.

"So you're a witch and I'm not prince charming."

"I need to lose weight and I'm ugly," I blurted out.

"You're cute and frankly, I like your curves. I think if I hugged you, it would feel nice," he said, blushing.

And with those words, he rendered me speechless.

"Look, Christy, I know you're grounded. Your dad told me. But maybe when you're ungrounded we can go on a date. And at school, maybe we could talk?" He held up his cellphone. "Maybe text? You say you don't know me and I don't know you, well, let's hang out and get to know each other."

Heart racing in my chest, my mind a flurry of fearful excuses, I managed to nod.

"So that's good? Right? The nod?" Ian tilted his head, slightly smiling.

"Yeah."

Very carefully, like I would break or fly away, Ian hugged me. His body was all hard muscle and strength, but strangely comforting. Slowly, he drew away. "Yep, I was right. That was real nice."

I playfully hit him.

He grinned. "See you tomorrow at school?"

"Sure."

"I'll text you later, okay?"

"Sure!" I sounded like an idiot.

Still smiling, he walked around to the driver's door, popped it open, and climbed inside. Like a dork, I stood on the curb and waved as he drove away.

Spinning around, I squealed in delight, flailing my arms like an idiot. Then I realized I was being watched.

The broom vanished from an upstairs window. Adam and Callie peeked around the corner of the house, and I glimpsed my mom and dad quickly closing the curtains in the living room.

I rolled my eyes.

I was totally spied on.

But I didn't care.

Ian liked me enough to try to get to know me better.

Life was grand.

With a wide grin, I ran toward Adam anxious to tell him everything.

Adam

We stood at the edge of the Trinity Springs River looking down where it emptied out into fast-moving white water that disappeared into the wilds of East Texas where, eventually, it led to Louisiana. I'd asked Nathan to bring me here so I could get rid of the final piece of Mark's hellish existence.

I stared at the birthday gift Mark had given me swaying from its chain. I couldn't seem to get my fingers to release it into the foaming waters below. "I don't know why this is taking so long," I said, then laughed to try to take the edge of.

"It's okay," Nathan said. "Take your time."

Truth of the matter was, I *did* know why it was taking so long. It wasn't every day you killed your boyfriend, and it wasn't every day you relinquished the last good memory of him either.

"You know," Nathan continued, "you don't have to throw it away. Me and Christy never did try and see if he'd put an enchantment on it."

"It doesn't matter if he did or not," I sighed, watching the swaying, wire-wrapped heart before me. "It's not about that. It's about letting go. Moving on. *Forgetting.*"

"Sometimes it's best not to forget what happened, Adam."

I didn't respond.

Instead, I stepped to the edge of the water and extended my arm as far as I could.

The pendant's chain began to slip from my grasp.

I watched in the midafternoon light as the golden wirework reflected the sun across my face.

Forevermore, I heard Mark's voice say.

"No," I whispered.

The chain slipped from my grasp.

The water swallowed it into its depths.

And just like that, I watched it fade away, its progress marked only by the light glimmering off the chain.

I waited. Even when it disappeared there didn't seem to be any consolation. Getting rid of Mark hadn't fixed anything. It hadn't saved Courtney, it hadn't kept my mom from dying and then being brought back to life, it hadn't prevented kids at school from being possessed by Mark's power. This place was filled with history, and while destroying its monster would prevent it from wreaking any further havoc, the damage had already been done.

"Ready to go?" Nathan asked, setting a hand on my shoulder.

"I guess," I said as we turned and headed back to his Jeep.

"You did a hard thing, Adam. But you know what? You're stronger for it now." Nathan paused. At his Jeep, he glanced toward the river, then smiled as his eyes trailed upstream to where Trinity Springs loomed in the distance.

"What do you plan on doing now that Mark's gone?" I asked, hopping up into the Jeep. "It's not like there's anything worth staying for here."

"I'm sure I could find something," Nathan laughed. "Besides, small towns are nice when there aren't any monsters."

"I hear ya."

"What about you? Any plans?"

"Get through the rest of my junior year." I laughed nervously. "Try to figure out how to turn my mom back into a human."

"We'll find something, Adam. Don't worry."

Nathan pushed his key into the ignition and started the Jeep.

On the way back to Trinity Springs, we passed through an old wooded road that held remnants of the past. Old houses snarled in vines, steer skulls hanging on old posts, paths that led into the woods to places that no longer existed—looking at the relics of the old world, I couldn't help but wonder just how many people had died as a result of a lover's quarrel.

For over one-hundred years Mark had rampaged through our small town, using the guises of ignorance and homophobia to get away with his crimes, and in one second I had used a spell to banish him forever.

The monster of Trinity Springs was gone.

His reign was over.

Epilogue

Christy

Did the midnight spell bring Mark to Trinity Springs? No, I don't think so. His evil had always been here, waiting to spring again. But did the midnight spell work? I have to wonder.

Nothing has really been the same since the midnight spell. Adam and I have expanded our circle of friends. I'm a pretty powerful witch now. We have a friend who is a shapeshifter, and another one who is now officially obsessed with monsters. Ian and I are going to go on that coffee date when I'm finally ungrounded and we've been texting back and forth almost as often as I do with Adam.

A few times I've called over to Adam's house to find Nathan hanging out. I haven't teased Adam about their growing friendship. I know the wounds Mark inflicted on him are too fresh, but Olivia and I are lying in wait.

Nathan is definitely sticking around town. He doesn't trust that Dušan is at peace. Though I understand why Dušan was so vengeful, his hatred twisted not only Mark, but himself. I'm not sure a ghost with that much anger and hatred will ever rest in peace.

Maybe this is the new normal for us. Monsters, magic, good friends, and dating.

Oh, yeah... and Adam's zombie mom with a penchant for high heels and raw meat.

Yep, things will never be the same.

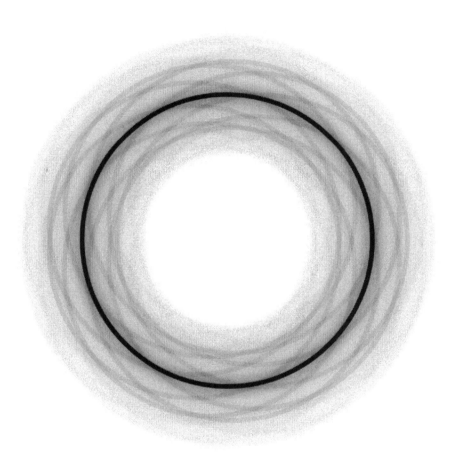

About the Authors

Kody Boye was born and raised in southeastern Idaho. He has been published dozens of times in various anthologies, magazines and webzines. His first novel, *Sunrise,* debuted in 2009 and was recently rereleased in 2013. He is the author of *The Brotherhood* fantasy saga and several other works of fantastical fiction. You can visit him online at KodyBoye.com.

Rhiannon Frater is the award-winning author of over a dozen books, including the *As the World Dies* zombie trilogy (Tor,) the *Pretty When She* trilogy and the *Vampire Bride* saga, as well as independent works such as *The Last Bastion of the Living* and *The Living Dead Boy and the Zombie Hunters.* She currently lives in Texas and is represented by the Foundry Literary Agency. You can visit her online at RhiannonFrater.com.

Made in the USA
Charleston, SC
02 June 2013